Praise for Donna Grant

The Dark King series

"Loaded with subtle emotions, sizzling chemistry, and some provocative thoughts on the real choices [Grant's] characters are forced to make as they choose their loves for eternity." —*RT Book Reviews* (4 stars)

"Vivid images, intense details, and enchanting characters grab the reader's attention and [don't] let go."
—*Night Owl Reviews* (Top Pick)

The Dark Warrior series

"The world of the Immortal Warriors is a thoroughly engaging one, blending powerful ancient gods, fiery desire, and touchingly human love, which readers will surely want to revisit." —*RT Book Reviews*

"[Grant] blends ancient gods, love, desire, and evil-doers into a world you will want to revisit over and over again."
—*Night Owl Reviews*

"Sizzling love scenes and engaging characters."
—*Publishers Weekly*

"Ms. Grant mixes adventure, magic and sweet love to create the perfect romance[s]." —*Single Title Reviews*

The Dark Sword series

FROM ST. MARTIN'S PAPERBACKS
HeroesandHeartbreakers.com
Original Stories, Sneak Peeks,
Exclusive Content, and
Much More!

WITHDRAWN
FLAME

DONNA GRANT

St. Martin's Paperbacks

This is a work of fiction. All of the characters, organizations, and events portrayed in this novel are either products of the author's imagination or are used fictitiously.

FLAME

Copyright © 2020 by Donna Grant.

For information address St. Martin's Publishing Group, 120 Broadway, New York, NY 10271.

ISBN: 978-1-250-18293-7

Our books may be purchased in bulk for promotional, educational, or business use. Please contact the Macmillan Corporate and Premium Sales Department at 1-800-221-7945, ext. 5442, or by email at MacmillanSpecialMarkets@macmillan.com.

Printed in the United States of America

St. Martin's Paperbacks edition / 2020

10 9 8 7 6 5 4 3 2 1

To Monique

There is a special kind of relationship between an author and editor. After fifty-one books together, I can honestly say that I've loved every minute of it. Thank you!

CHAPTER ONE

June
Scotland

This was suicide. Noreen knew it.

But there wasn't another way. Which left her no other choice. No matter what happened, she would pay for the consequences of her actions.

It was the least she could do.

She swallowed hard and stared at the laptop screen sitting before her. On her left was a cup of tea with tendrils of heat rising from it. She looked up and let her gaze slowly wander the café.

The glamour and magic she used prevented humans from seeing her true coloring—or feeling the attraction they always experienced when a Fae was near. It was necessary to keep a low profile.

Though it wouldn't keep her hidden from everyone.

Noreen glanced out the windows of the internet café to the passersby. The world looked normal. But then again, it usually did right before everything went to shite.

She didn't like being so exposed. It was only a matter of time before she was found. There wasn't a single person she trusted. Already, they scrutinized her every word. She was a good liar, but when so many were double-checking the things she told them, it didn't matter how thorough she was. They *would* find out.

Of all the options she had, this was the best one. There was no way she could walk up to a Dragon King. They would likely kill her before she got the first word out. She opted not to ring them either since she would prefer to keep her identity a secret.

Noreen quickly crafted her message using a buffer email account and a VPN. The virtual private network would allow her to make anyone who read the email think she was halfway around the world. With a throwaway email as well as using Proton Mail as the host, she was as anonymous as she could get.

As soon as she hit send, she signed out of everything and rose from her seat. No one around paid any attention to her. She tugged her baseball hat low over her face and strode from the café.

As soon as she walked outside, it felt as if every eye in Scotland was focused on her. The nearest Fae doorway was over thirty miles away. She could teleport there, but there were those who could follow the trail of her power. Was this how humans felt? Always having to do everything on their own without the use of magic? She hated it.

However, if she wanted to live, she would do it.

And she very much wanted to live. Now more than ever.

Noreen stopped dead in her tracks when she spotted the Light Fae walking with a human female. The two were laughing and talking. She gazed at the Fae with the thick strip of silver in her black hair and realized that she was looking at none other than Shara.

The Fae had once been Dark but turned Light and mated with a Dragon King. Noreen hadn't believed the story the first time she'd heard it, but it was soon revealed to be the truth. Seeing Shara with her own eyes was much different than hearing a story, though.

Noreen took a step toward the Fae. Maybe Shara would listen to her. No sooner had the thought gone through her head than Noreen realized it was a terrible idea. She ducked out of sight and went the opposite way so as not to run into Shara.

"Suicide," Noreen whispered to herself. "If the Dragon Kings don't get me, then the Others will."

She'd known the reality of her situation when she decided to take action, but that didn't mean she wasn't terrified. How many more times would she stand before the Others and lie? How long before they realized what she was about and executed her?

One of her skills was the ability to deceive others convincingly. She did it with little effort, actually. It came naturally. Then again, she'd never had so much on the line before. She worried that she would try too hard, and others would start to see through her lies—and she'd be caught.

The constant worry was exhausting. It was bad enough that she had the Others watching her. Now, because she just had to go and do the right thing, she was about to have the Dragon Kings on her arse, too.

Because no matter the steps she'd taken to be anonymous, they were smart enough—and powerful enough—to figure out who she was.

That was fine. She was prepared for that. She just wanted to make sure that she was long gone from this realm when it happened. All she had to do was get one King to listen to her—and believe what she was saying. Then, they could take it from there, and she could hightail it to safety somewhere else.

At least, that was the plan. A part of her thought about

sticking around and fighting with the Kings against the Others, but she didn't particularly like the sight of blood or death. Strange for sure for a Dark Fae, but everyone had their quirks.

Noreen's mind went through options of what might happen with her email. She hoped the words she'd used would alert the Kings that it wasn't a hoax. Surely, they would take such information seriously.

How long should she give them before she sent another message? The only option she'd left them was to reply to her, but they didn't have to do that to believe her. For all she knew, they could have already read it, taken her words to heart, and were in the process of getting things ready for war.

She rolled her eyes at her hopefulness. That wasn't going to happen, and she knew it. But it would be nice if it did. It would solve all her problems.

Well, not all of them, but a majority of them. Yet, she wouldn't be able to leave until she knew for certain the Kings had listened to her.

"Shite," she mumbled.

That meant she would have to check the new email account she'd set up in case the Kings contacted her. More than likely, she'd have to send several more messages. All the while keeping her actions secret from the Others.

Maybe it would've been better to take her chances by just going straight to Dreagan and knocking on the door. She nearly laughed out loud at the thought. She—like all Fae—knew of the barrier around the sixty thousand acres owned by the Dragon Kings. The moment she stepped through it, they would know of her arrival and be on her in seconds.

It was one way to get their attention, but with the way

things were going, the Dragon Kings were more the strike-now-and-ask-questions-later kind of guys, and that didn't really work for her.

She rubbed her thumb over the pads of her fingers as she itched to use magic to make a laptop appear so she didn't have to visit another internet café, but it was a chance she couldn't take at the moment.

"Things really go to shite when you try to do the right thing," she said as she walked into the abandoned house that she'd come across.

But was this the right thing? For so long, she'd believed the Others were in the right. Noreen wasn't sure when she'd changed her mind. It wasn't one thing she could pinpoint, but she suspected several instances had happened over the thousands of years. And now here she was, her loyalties changing sides. She'd debated on this course of action for the past fifty years, but it was the most recent turn of events that had finally swayed her.

For one, she had really liked Balladyn. She hadn't wanted to. She had actively hated him at first. Then, she'd seen what he'd done for the Dark when he became king. He wasn't just after power. He wanted to unify the Dark and make them great again.

Then, Usaeil had killed him. Noreen fisted her hand as she recalled seeing the Queen of the Light sink her sword into Balladyn's back and take his life.

And she hadn't been the only Dark outraged by the murder.

Then, the infamous Rhi had killed Usaeil. Or so they'd thought. Leave it to a power-hungry bitch like Usaeil to ensure that she couldn't die. But that was something few knew about.

It would be a cold day in Hell before Noreen bowed

before Usaeil and accepted her as queen. It didn't matter if Usaeil was really Dark or not. She had crossed too many lines, even for a Dark.

It was an oxymoron, Noreen knew. The Dark were the epitome of wicked to the Light, but the truth was, there were varying degrees of evil within the Dark. It's why it was so difficult for the Dark to band together on anything.

Noreen swiped at a long strip of black hair that had fallen into her face as she plopped down on the torn cushion of the hideous floral chair. She dropped her head back and looked at the ceiling.

She had lived for six thousand years. During that time, she had done a great many things, seen every inch of the planet, and thoroughly enjoyed life.

Without a doubt, she knew these were the last days of her life. Instead of doing what she wanted and using her magic, she was hiding.

All because she felt she had to help the Dragon Kings.

CHAPTER TWO

Dreagan

"You won't miss one donut, Ryder," Cain stated as he reached for one of the last two remaining pastries in the box.

Ryder didn't take his eyes from the row of monitors before him as he moved the box to his other side. "Get your own."

"Let me take one, and I'll buy you two more boxes."

Ryder snorted loudly. "You owe me six already."

Cain winced. Fuck. He did owe him six. "Then I'll bring you eight boxes. Today."

"No."

Kinsey, Ryder's mate, who sat on the other side of him, let out a loud sigh. "For goodness sakes, you two. You're worse than kids. Ryder, let him have one. And Cain, bring him the eight boxes within an hour, or I'll make sure you never get another donut again."

Cain met Kinsey's violet gaze and nodded. "You have my word."

Ryder rolled his eyes but held out a jelly donut for Cain. Before he could walk away to enjoy the delicious pastry, Ryder called his name.

"While you're here, you can go through the emails Dreagan has gotten in the last twenty-four hours," Ryder said with a small smile on his face.

Cain glanced at the donut and sank his teeth into it, the strawberry jelly filling his mouth. He didn't care that it had cost him several boxes or time at the computer going through monotonous emails. It was worth it.

After he stuffed the last bite into his mouth, he moved his hands over the table to await the keyboard to appear through the glass.

"Wipe your hands first," Kinsey cautioned.

Cain glanced in her direction and saw the murderous expression on Ryder's face. "Right," he said and hastily licked his fingers clean before wiping them on his jeans.

Ryder shook his head in agitation, but he returned his attention to whatever it was he was working on. Cain had learned long ago not to ask. Ryder's skills were something that Cain had no interest in. He was grateful that Ryder was able to do the things he did, but Cain was doubly thankful that he didn't have to do them himself. Answering emails was bad enough.

One by one, Cain went through the various messages from satisfied customers, to those asking questions, as well as some who wrote in to complain about one thing or another.

It didn't matter how many he read, he was always shocked at the manner in which humans felt they could say such horrid things, simply because it was through an email. Face-to-face, those same people wouldn't speak in such a way, but a screen had a way of making people more daring than usual.

Cain was just about finished when five new emails came through. At this rate, he'd be answering the messages for eternity. As soon as he finished one, two more came in.

He didn't know who normally answered them, but he suspected it was Ryder and Kinsey, and it gave him a whole new respect for them.

He didn't read the subject line of the next email as he opened it. It wasn't until the first few words registered that he stopped reading and glanced at the subject. IMPORTANT! READ IMMEDIATELY DRAGON KINGS.

The fact that someone was calling them by their name wasn't common. Cain slowly read the email, his gut twisting into a knot as he did. When he finished, he sat for a moment and let it sink in. Then he reread it.

Was it a joke? Or could it be for real?

"Ryder," Cain said. "There's something you should read."

Ryder kept typing as he said, "I'm sure you can handle it."

"It's important."

There was a sigh before Ryder said, "Read it to me."

Cain swiveled in his chair so he faced Ryder. Then he began to read. "To whom it may concern. I know whoever is reading this is a Dragon King. I know because I'm a Dark Fae. I took this route in contacting you because I didn't believe you would listen to me if I showed up at Dreagan. However, what I have to say is important, so I hope you take this seriously since I'm putting my life on the line."

By this time, Ryder had stopped typing and was staring at him, as was Kinsey.

"For most of my life, I've been a part of the Others," Cain continued. "I truly believed it was better for everyone if your kind was gone. It no longer matters what justification I had for my thoughts and actions before now. No species has the right to be annihilated by another. I've seen the truth of what the Others truly are, and I want no part in it. It's why I've come to you. I can help you take them down.

"Now, some might believe this is a trap. Honestly, I would as well, but it isn't. This is one Fae who wants to stop the Others. I can tell you where they will be so you can attack and end all of this once and for all."

There was a deep frown on Ryder's face. "How was it signed?"

Cain glanced at the signature. "Just with an N."

"We can discover who it is," Kinsey said. "The IP address is easy enough to find."

Cain glanced at the top of the email and shrugged before he scooted the chair away. "Have at it."

Ryder rolled his chair to the keyboard and monitor Cain had just been using. Though Cain could've taken the opportunity to leave, he found that he wanted to stay and find out if this was real or not.

He watched as Ryder entered some code, though he was too fast for Cain to see exactly what it was.

"They're hiding their location," Ryder said. "Whoever this is wanted to stay anonymous. They've used Proton Mail, which makes it difficult for most people to track."

"But not you," Kinsey said with a grin.

Ryder looked at his mate and winked. "Damn straight, sweetheart."

Cain grinned at the two of them. They were something together. With so many Kings finding their mates, he couldn't help but wonder if he'd get as lucky. Not that he was going to hold his breath for such a thing.

"Got it," Ryder said and sat back with a smile. "The email originated in Scotland, about twenty-five miles from here."

"That's close," Cain said.

Ryder glanced his way and nodded. "Yes, it is."

"Give me the IP," Kinsey urged.

Ryder did something on the keyboard, and then Kinsey was furiously pounding away at hers. A short time later, she let out a little whoop. Cain watched the two rows of monitors act as one huge screen as Kinsey hacked into the CCTV of where the email had come from.

"It's an internet café," Ryder said.

Cain's gaze roamed around the screen to the various computers and people sitting at them. "We'll never be able to figure out who it is."

"Oh, ye of little faith," Kinsey said with a smile.

Ryder chuckled, and all Cain could do was watch in awe.

"Here we go," Kinsey announced as she hit the enter button with a flourish.

The monitors blinked, and Cain found himself staring at a woman's face. The silver in her hair and her red eyes may be absent, but there was no doubt she was using glamour to hide herself. She kept her baseball cap pulled low, and her gaze scanned the café frequently as if she were worried about being followed.

"She looks scared," Cain said.

Ryder blew out a breath and laced his hands behind his head. "If her email is legit, then she has every reason to be."

"Or," Kinsey said, letting the word linger for a moment, "she knew that we'd hack in and find her, so this is all a show."

Cain shrugged. "Is it a chance we can take?"

"I doona believe it is, and I think once we tell Con, he'll agree," Ryder pointed out.

Kinsey's lips twisted in a frown. "All I can think of is a trap. We've suffered enough."

"But the Others need to be dealt with." Cain got to his feet. "I'll find Con and tell him the news."

Ryder gave a nod. "I'm forwarding the email to his computer so he'll be able to read it for himself."

Cain left the computer room and made his way to Constantine's office. The King of Dragon Kings was rarely far from Dreagan, but it wasn't just their businesses of sheep and cattle as well as distilling whisky which kept him there. Con was the glue that held everyone together.

He was the one who had forged a way of life for them on Dreagan when they sent their dragons away after the war with the humans. He was the one who found a way for them to live among the humans thousands of years later while still hiding. It was the whisky that made them the most money, and no mortal who came to Dreagan even realized immortals lived there.

And that's just how they wanted it kept.

However, the Dark Fae, and now the Others, were making that difficult. The Dark Fae had been after the weapon Con had kept hidden in his mountain. That weapon was now gone, though Con still wouldn't tell any of them what it was.

While the Dark wanted the world to know about the Dragon Kings, the Others just wanted their death. The Kings had already been through so much as they encountered trap after trap from the Others, set millennia before in anticipation of their plan falling into place.

Cain didn't believe that their paths were set before them. Or, at least, he hadn't. The Others were proving his theory of free will false, because how else could a group of Dark and Light Fae and good and evil Druids know exactly what the Kings would do and when?

Cain stopped outside of Con's office. The door was slightly ajar. He gave a quick knock.

"Enter," Con said from inside.

Cain pushed open the door and walked into the office. Con sat behind his desk dressed in his usual dark suit and dress shirt, looking through a file that contained several papers as well as photos. He closed it and looked up at Cain with his fathomless black eyes.

"You have some jelly on the side of your mouth," Con stated.

Cain reached up and wiped it off with the pad of his finger before sticking the digit into his mouth and savoring the last bit of sweetness.

"That tells me where you've been," Con said. He sat back in his chair. "And I'm guessing the ding of my email is from Ryder?"

"There's something you need to read," Cain explained.

Con didn't need to be told twice. He turned to the open laptop. It didn't take him long to read the message in his inbox.

"Ryder and Kinsey determined that the note originated twenty-five miles away. They also pulled up the CCTV footage. The email is from a woman. She used glamour as well as a hat to help hide her face."

Con's gaze slid to him. He smoothed a lock of wavy blond hair from his forehead. "You doona think this is a trap?"

"I can no' say for sure, but I think it's something we should check out."

"By the email, the Dark intends to tell us where the Others are meeting. Reply to her, and then go to the café and see if she returns."

Cain raised a brow. "You want me to confront her?"

"She'll tell you more one-on-one."

"Or she'll run."

A quick smile pulled at Con's lips. "She willna get far with you chasing her."

CHAPTER THREE

Minimal magic. That's all she could do without being caught, and even that was pushing things. Noreen rubbed her chest. It felt as if an elephant sat on her.

She had trouble breathing, and that didn't even factor into the knot in her stomach that had kept her up all night. Maybe she was making a mistake. Were the Dragon Kings worth all of this? Were they worth her life?

No, they weren't. Because they wouldn't give their lives for her. She was a Dark, after all.

Noreen wrapped her hands around the cup of coffee to help warm them. She was ice-cold, and it had nothing to do with the weather. She dropped her head forward, letting her hair hide her face. But she felt even more exposed.

It had taken all her will not to return to the café until this morning. She wished she had some kind of device of her own so she could check her email as often as she liked. Instead, she was back at the shop this morning and waiting for as long as she could to check her email.

If she checked and there was no response, she wouldn't allow herself to remain. It kept her in one spot too long, and that was something she couldn't chance. She knew for a fact that the Others kept tabs on those within the group. Her time was running out in Scotland.

Noreen closed her eyes. If she was smart, she'd leave now. She could sign onto her email somewhere else. She didn't need to be here. So, why had she stayed?

She knew why. She had thought to work up the nerve to go to Dreagan herself. Even when she had realized that she didn't have it in her, she still hadn't left. At this rate, she'd be dead within days.

She was supposed to be great at lying, moving about without being seen, and getting others to do what she wanted. Now, she was making rookie mistakes that only an idiot would make.

Noreen rose from her chair and made her way out of the café. She glanced to her right as she turned left on the sidewalk, and her heart jumped into her throat because she recognized one of the Others.

"Shite. Shiteshiteshiteshite," she mumbled and ducked around the nearest corner.

Every instinct screamed at her to teleport away, but that's what someone who had done something wrong would do. Noreen drew in a deep breath and steadied herself as she put her back against the building and bent her right knee, pressing her booted heel to the wall.

Seconds later, the Fae casually turned the corner, his silver eyes blazing with happiness as if he had caught her. And he had. But she wasn't going to let him know that.

"Brian," she said in way of greeting.

His lips turned up in a smile. "Noreen. What are you doing here?"

"I could ask the same of you," she retorted.

Brian laughed and smoothed a palm along his perfectly coiffured short, black hair. He was dressed in a pale gray suit with a large grid pattern, a silver shirt, and a solid dark gray tie. His shoes likely cost a small fortune, but then again, the bastard had always loved to dress like a dandy.

Unlike her, Brian didn't bother to dampen his effect on the mortals. Women and men alike stared at him as they passed, their desire and need rolling off them in waves that made her want to vomit simply because it had to do with Brian.

"Trying to turn this on me?" he asked with a smirk. "That isn't going to work."

She cocked her head while holding his gaze. "You've been working on your pronunciation. It's only taken you a few thousand years to lose the rough edges of your Irish accent so you no longer speak like you came from the gutter."

Noreen knew the dig would hit just as she wanted. Brian had always hated that he was low-born and had done everything he could to claw his way up the ranks of the Light. In fact, she was surprised that he hadn't turned Dark. He had it in him. Maybe it was just a matter of time.

As she expected, his face went tight, his grin no longer cocky as his nostrils flared in anger.

This time, she was the one who grinned. She'd hit her mark, and it had left a whopper of an imprint. It was a good thing Brian was the one who had found her. It was easy to turn his attention with little digs against his upbringing. But that would only work for so long.

"Why are you here?" she demanded.

He swallowed and folded his arms over his chest. "Checking on you."

"Well," she said with a long pause, "we always check on each other."

She let the insinuation fill the air. A heartbeat later, his eyes narrowed on her. His arms fell to his sides, and he took a step back.

If he asked, she'd have to tell him that she wasn't there to check up on him, but Brian didn't always think things through. He let his emotions rule him, which worked in her favor. Because as long as he didn't ask questions, she wouldn't have to think up more lies.

"I'm only here for you," he said.

She shrugged. "I don't care what you do. I, personally, like Scotland. There's nothing wrong with admitting that."

Brian's lips peeled back in a sneer. "Ireland is far superior to this place."

"I'm not saying it isn't. I'm simply stating that Scotland is pretty."

The Light snorted and shook his head. "I know why you're here."

"Do you?" she asked nonchalantly.

"You want to stay close to the Dragon Kings to get the first shot at them."

Why hadn't she thought of that? It was brilliant! Noreen simply smiled in response since it was better than words.

Brian rolled his eyes. "You're such a kiss-ass. If you think this will get you higher in the order, you're wrong."

She shrugged. "Maybe so."

He turned to the side and walked away, mumbling, "bitch," as he did.

"Be sure to file your report," she called after him.

That stopped him in his tracks. Brian turned to her, his confident smile back in place. "By the way, did I tell you I wasn't the only one here. It seems that two of us were sent to look in on you. Think about that, Noreen."

She waited until he was gone before she swallowed.

Slowly, she lowered her foot back to the ground, but she didn't pull her hands from the wall. They shook too badly.

"Sounds like you're in a wee bit of a jam," came a deep voice from her other side.

Noreen's head whipped around to find a man leaning one shoulder against the building. He had black hair cut short on the sides but left longer on top. His deep green eyes were framed by thick lashes and locked on her.

He filled out his deep gray shirt well, showcasing broad shoulders and hard sinew. Denim hung low on his hips, the jeans just tight enough to give a hint of the muscles they encased. But it was his face she couldn't stop staring at.

With a strong jaw and chin, his face appeared cut from granite. He had a shadow of a beard that she'd always been partial to. His lips were wide and thin and didn't hold a shred of mockery. Good thing since he was a Dragon King.

If only she knew which one. She'd love to have a name to put to such a gorgeous specimen.

"I'm fine," she replied when she finally found her voice.

He pushed away from the wall and took a step toward her. "I beg to differ. And the fact you sent an email to us says you have much to say."

Noreen glanced at the sky. So much for taking precautions. She'd done everything she knew of to keep her identity from the Kings. How had they found her?

"I made a mistake," she said as she shifted and backed up slowly. "Forget I said anything."

"Your words were convincing. I believe you meant them. Someone who would go to such extremes doesna seem like the kind to scare easily."

She busted out laughing. "You'd be wrong about that."

He didn't smile in return. Nor did he look away. "Tell me what you know, and I'll help you get away."

"They're here," she said, her eyes wide in the hopes that

she could get the point across. "Not one, but two of them. That means they know I'm up to something. They've killed for less."

"Then you need to make a decision. Whatever happened that led you to email us hasna gone away. It's still there, and it'll rise again."

She wished she'd never sent that email. She wished she'd never grown a conscience. And she really wished she'd never had doubts about the Others. It had sent her down a treacherous path she didn't know how to navigate.

"Look at me," she said and let her glamour fall so he could see her red eyes and the silver in her hair. "Take a good, hard look. I'm a Dark. You don't believe us."

"You have no idea what I believe."

She nodded and closed her eyes, bringing her glamour back up. "I made a mistake. Forget you ever got anything from me. Forget you spoke with me. I choose life."

Noreen turned on her heel and stalked away. But not before she heard him say, "So do we."

She didn't stop walking. The farther away she got from the Dragon King, the better. She hadn't even gotten his name, but that didn't matter. No, she needed to concentrate on doing all the right things to get the Others off her back before they executed her without giving her a chance to tell her side.

Out of the corner of her eye, she spotted Brian standing at the corner of an intersection. She glanced in his direction but didn't give him any more time than that. He might be lying about there being another of them in the city, but he could also be telling the truth.

"Fek," she whispered.

What was she going to do? Running wasn't an option. She had to remain. And she had to come up with a believable lie. Brian's suggestion that she wanted to get a first strike at the Kings was a good one. She'd definitely use that.

She was halfway to the cottage she was squatting in when a figure walked out onto the sidewalk in front of her. She came to a halt when she recognized Moreann, the Empress of Druids. It was a rare thing for her to venture to this realm.

Then again, Moreann had been coveting this realm for quite some time. Long enough to put the humans here to see what the Dragon Kings would do with them. Then using Druids and Fae together to create the Others.

"This is a surprise," Noreen said.

Moreann smiled. "Is it?"

"You don't normally come here."

"And you don't usually visit Scotland."

Noreen smiled as she lifted a shoulder. "I like keeping an eye on my enemy."

"Hmm. Is that so?"

"Keep your friends close and your enemies closer."

Moreann's green eyes were intense as they pinned Noreen. "There has been some speculation that you aren't acting yourself."

"Times are changing," Noreen replied. "I'm trying to keep up. I've put in a lot of time to take out the Kings. You know I want them gone for what they did to my family."

"Remind me again what they did."

Noreen wasn't a fool. Moreann knew exactly what the Kings had done, because she was there and had been the one to tell Noreen. But Noreen would do as she was bidden because there was no other choice.

"They killed my family during the Fae Wars. You saved me before they could finish me off."

Moreann grabbed Noreen by the chin. "Remember who your friends are, child."

"I've never forgotten."

"Good. You're one of my best. I'd hate for you to lose your way."

The threat hung in the air as Moreann dropped her hand and walked around her. Noreen didn't turn and watch her go. She squared her shoulders and headed toward the cottage.

CHAPTER FOUR

"Well now," Cain said as he watched the beautiful Fae walk away, his gaze lingering on the sway of her hips and her pert derrière.

It looked nearly as good as her oval face and incredible mouth. When she'd dropped her glamour, and he'd seen her crimson eyes, he'd been unable to look away. Not because he was repulsed.

But because he wasn't.

Noreen was gorgeous. All Fae were beautiful, but there was something unique about her that he couldn't quite put his finger on. She had a body made for sex, and despite knowing she was supposed to be his enemy, he felt desire quicken his blood.

He'd imagined she would have some spunk. After all, it took a great amount of courage to do what she had—if it wasn't all some kind of trap. He still wasn't sure of that or not.

Cain was leaning toward believing her, especially after witnessing the interaction between her and the Light. At first, Cain had thought it was all a setup in case someone had been watching. But the emotions that crossed both Noreen's and the Light's face hadn't been faked.

Neither had Noreen's shaking hands when she thought she was alone.

It was that fear that prodded her to retract everything she'd written the day before. Cain could understand and appreciate the trepidation that consumed her. It was in her eyes, in her voice, and in her very bearing.

When he added all that up, he accepted that she was being honest. But he held back full judgment until he could speak with her some more.

Cain opened the mental link the Dragon Kings shared. *"Con."*

"I'm here," the King of Dragon Kings replied.

Cain was glad that they had managed to stop the Others from listening in on their communications. Otherwise, things would be more difficult for them. *"I found the Dark."*

"And?"

"Just as I was about to approach her, someone else beat me to it. A Light, and by their conversation, he was sent by the Others to check up on the Dark."

Con was silent for a heartbeat. *"It could all be done for the benefit of any of us watching."*

"That was my original thought as well, but Brian, the Light, was too intent on trying to catch Noreen in the act of something."

"Noreen is the Dark, I presume?"

Cain walked from the alley to the sidewalk and turned his head in the direction Noreen had gone. *"Aye. She's terrified, Con. So much so that she told me she takes back everything she sent yesterday."*

"If the Others are on to her, then they'll want to stop her before she can give us anything."

"*Exactly.*" Cain spotted Brian and decided to trail the Light for a bit. "*I doona think they know what she's done, but they're suspicious. Brian told her that there were two of them here to check on her.*"

"*Find her, Cain. If there's any information she can give us, get it. Do whatever it takes, because we need an advantage.*"

"*Even if it means sheltering her?*"

Con blew out a breath. "*The safest place for her is Dreagan.*"

"*I doona think that would be a good idea. The Others have already attacked us once and did significant damage.*"

"*You have something else in mind?*

He started walking toward the Light Fae. "*Actually, I do. The Fae Realm.*"

"*That's risky.*"

"*We have to take some risks. The Others have been two steps ahead of us at all times. We need to even the score.*"

Con made an indiscernible sound. "*Usaeil told me she met Moreann on the Fae Realm. You'd be bringing the Dark straight to them.*"

"*That's just it, they'll never think we would do such a thing. The Others will be looking for her on Earth. If Noreen is safe, then she'll give us what she needs. She's no' using magic, and that in itself tells me she's going to great lengths to make sure they can no' track her.*"

"*You're going to need help getting to a Fae doorway. I'll have Ulrik bring you his bracelet.*"

Cain's pace slowed as he reached the corner of the block and looked around it. As soon as he spotted Brian, he lengthened his stride. "*That will make things easier.*"

"*Check in daily.*"

"*This is the right move. You know it. Doona worry*

about me. I can handle this. I'll get us what we need, and then we can take down the Others once and for all."

Con said, *"Doona forget that she's been a part of them for a long time. She might turn on you."*

"I'll watch my back."

Cain disconnected from the link when he saw Brian head into a pub. He walked to the door and went inside. He found the Light Fae at the bar, talking to two women, both of whom couldn't keep their hands off him.

The Fae was too intent on his conquests to take any notice of him. Cain sat close enough that he could hear what the Light was saying, but far enough away so as not to draw attention to himself.

Cain ordered a whisky and pretended to look through his mobile as he took pictures of Brian and sent them to Ryder. It was another face they could put to the Others, and that was a good thing.

As he listened to Brian talk to the women, Cain's thoughts turned to Noreen. He doubted the Dark even realized that he'd been there long enough to hear her and Brian's entire conversation. She hadn't been interested in learning his name. In fact, she couldn't get away from him fast enough.

He'd give her some space. He'd find her soon enough and make his offer. She was intelligent. She'd realize that what he could give her was more than she could get while out on her own.

A thread of worry still dangled, however. Brian had told Noreen that two Others were looking for her. If Brian was one of them, that meant there was someone else nearby. Cain really wanted to find out if there was and get a picture of them, as well.

"Cain? Where are you?" Ulrik's voice filled his head.

Cain gave his friend the location. A heartbeat later, the

King of Silvers and his mate, the Druid, Eilish, walked into the pub. While everyone else took notice of the handsome couple, Brian didn't even look their way.

Ulrik pulled out a chair for Eilish and waited until she sat before he lowered himself into his seat. He glanced at Brian. "Interesting choice."

Cain nodded to Eilish before he looked into Ulrik's gold eyes. "You could say that. He's too into the women to notice us."

Eilish rolled her green and gold eyes before flicking her long, dark hair over her shoulders. "What an idiot," she said in her mix of American and Irish accents.

"That's what makes them so special, love," Ulrik told her. Then he swung his attention to Cain. "I hear you're going on a wee trip."

"I figured some space is needed."

"Good idea," Eilish said with a nod.

Ulrik leaned back in his chair. "It's going to be dangerous."

"When are things no'?" Cain asked with a chuckle.

Ulrik didn't crack a smile. "You shouldna be on your own. Another should be with you."

"Everyone needs to stay at Dreagan. If anything happens to me, it's just me and no' two of us."

"I doona like it," Ulrik stated.

Eilish leaned forward and put her hand on his arm. She gave it a squeeze and looked at Cain. Eilish lowered her voice to a whisper. "We all know firsthand how dangerous they are. We don't know what could happen."

"I'm verra aware of the stakes." Cain looked from Eilish to Ulrik. "But we need this."

"I can no' dispute that," Ulrik said with a resigned sigh. "I just wish you were no' going alone."

Cain flashed a smile. "I'm no'."

"Spoken just like a single man," Eilish said with a chuckle.

That had all of them laughing for a brief moment.

Ulrik jerked his chin to Brian. "What about him?"

Cain leaned forward and told them the story of how he'd come upon Brian and Noreen.

Ulrik raked a hand through his long, black hair and grinned. "Oh, I believe my darling wife would love to put him in his place."

"You're damn straight, I would," she stated, anger shooting from her eyes.

"Find her," Ulrik said as he held out his hand. "And be safe."

Cain clasped his hand and felt the silver cuff in his palm. He gave a nod to Ulrik. "I willna let any of you down."

"I know Con would agree with me, so I'll say that we'd rather you come home and live to fight another day if it comes to it."

Eilish tapped Ulrik's arm. Just as she was about to follow Brian and the women out, Brian teleported away with them.

"Damn," Cain murmured.

Eilish gave a loud snort. "It's too bad he got away. But there will be a next time."

"Go," Ulrik said. "Find the Dark and get us answers."

Cain nodded to the couple before they left. He put the silver cuff on his wrist and waited five minutes before he rose and walked outside. He stood silently for a moment, thinking of where a Dark might go if she were trying to hide.

She wasn't using magic, which meant she also wasn't using money to pay for anything. Instead of flashing her smile and getting her way with her looks, Noreen was keeping her Fae allure dampened. It was as if she didn't want anyone to notice her.

Cain turned right. He walked back to the intersection where he'd seen Brian earlier. Then he crossed the street and kept walking. There was no sign of Noreen, but he hadn't expected there to be. The village was rather small. There weren't a lot of homes around, but he guessed that Noreen wouldn't be too close to town. Nor would she be too far away.

It took just a few minutes talking with Ryder for Cain to pinpoint exactly where she was. It took him twenty minutes to walk there, and when he arrived and spotted the derelict cottage, he knew it was exactly the place the Dark had chosen.

There was a stream running along the back of the dwelling. It was a quaint, beautiful setting. Cain couldn't believe no one lived there now.

He walked to the door and rapped on the wood. "I know you're in there, lass."

Only silence met his words.

Cain sighed. "I can stay here the rest of the day and all night if need be. It willna hurt for you to listen to what I have to say. You're just listening. Surely, that can no' get you into any sort of trouble."

"You're going to make things worse by being here," she said, her Irish lilt muffled.

He held back his grin. At least she was talking to him now. "I can help you."

The door flew open, and she stood there looking irritated and angry, sparks flying from her red eyes. The fire that ran through Cain's blood didn't surprise him at all. He'd always been partial to women with spirit, and Noreen certainly had that.

The attraction he felt only made him want this mission to succeed even more. Though he wasn't going to give in to the desire. He had enough control not to let that happen.

"Leave," she demanded.

"I can make sure they doona find or hurt you."

She rolled her eyes before tucking a strand of her long, black and silver hair behind her ear. "Right. Because that's worked out so well for your people."

"I can make sure you are no' found."

All the anger went right out of her. "Is this some trick?"

"I doona trick people." He held out his hand, waiting for her to take it.

CHAPTER FIVE

The Dragon King was her only hope.

And he knew it.

Noreen slowly extended her hand and slid it against his palm. His long fingers softly closed around hers as he smiled.

It wasn't an arrogant grin. It was a pleased expression, and somehow that made her happy. Noreen didn't delve into that too much because she didn't want to think about liking his smile—or the fact that it was directed at her.

But she did give herself a moment to take in how it felt for him to touch her. It was . . . nice. Actually, it was much more than nice, but if she thought about it too much, she wasn't sure she would like the road it took her down. Besides, she needed to keep her focus on staying alive, not worrying about getting the hot Dragon King out of his clothes so she could have her way with him.

Hmm. That wasn't a bad thought, actually. She swallowed, thinking about removing his clothes with a snap of her fingers and getting a real good look at that fine body of his. Although, at the moment, her gaze was on his mouth. No doubt he was a master kisser. And she loved a man who knew how to kiss.

Noreen gave herself a mental kick and dragged her mind out of the sex gutter. It was time for business. There might be time later for fun, but not now.

Before she stepped out of the house, she pulled back on her arm just enough to halt him. "I don't know your name."

"It's Cain," he said in his smooth Scottish brogue.

"Mine is—" she began.

"Noreen," he finished for her. "I overheard your . . . exchange . . . with Brian, remember?"

She nodded. "Right."

"You're making the right decision," Cain told her.

She blinked, thinking how warm his hand was around hers. It wasn't sweaty or clammy, proving that he was calm and not nervous.

"For years, I thought I was doing the right thing. Now, I've switched." She didn't know why she was telling him this, but the words kept tumbling out. "They're onto me. I know it. And they're waiting for me to make a mistake. You standing out here is that mistake."

One side of his lips lifted higher as his deep green eyes twinkled. "I would've thought it was me holding your hand."

Despite the severity of the situation, Noreen chuckled as she briefly lowered her eyes. When she returned her gaze to Cain, he gave her a wink and a nod.

"It really is going to be all right. I willna let anything happen to you. I give you my word."

"You can't promise such a thing," she stated, though his vow made her heart skip a beat.

He stepped closer, his fingers tightening slightly on her hand. The smile was gone, and his eyes blazed with intensity. "I never give a promise I can no' keep. Perhaps it's difficult for a Dark to understand that."

Noreen took a deep breath and released it. "It's not that I don't trust you. I know firsthand how powerful the Others are. I'm trying to tell you that I won't hold you to that promise."

"You doona have to hold me to anything. We Scots hold ourselves accountable."

She lifted her chin, ready to defend her fellow Irishmen, but she thought better of it.

"If we're going to do this thing, then we should get moving," Cain told her. "You doona want them seeing us, do you?"

Her gaze lifted, scanning the area around the cottage. "No."

"Well, lass. What is your decision?"

Noreen glanced at their interlocked fingers. With Cain holding her hand, she didn't feel as alone or frightened as she had for the last several weeks. If there was even a remote chance that she might live after betraying the Others, she knew that likelihood increased in the company of a Dragon King.

She stepped out of the cottage, closing the door behind her. Cain gave her a quick grin of encouragement. "You should know that the first place the Others will look is Dreagan."

"Then it's good we willna be going there."

She blinked, taken aback by his words. "There is nowhere else on this planet the Others can't find me."

"I know," he said as he turned them to start walking—all while keeping a hold of her hand.

Noreen wasn't sure if he just liked touching her or if it was because he thought she might bolt. Frankly, she was debating that very thing. "I planned on standing with you to battle them. But . . . well, I thought we might have some time to plan things."

"We will."

When he didn't say more, she rolled her eyes. "We can't just go strolling through the village. Do you want them to see us?"

Finally, he halted and faced her. "If they suspect you've switched sides, they're going to head straight to Dreagan. I doona want that. At least no' yet," he added.

"Oh," she said as it dawned on her. "You want them to see us leave together."

"Aye. They'll come after us."

"For a while, maybe. Eventually, they'll turn to Dreagan."

"By that time, lass, we'll have everything we need to bring them down."

Noreen couldn't believe that this was actually happening. All her fears and worries had been for naught, because she knew in her heart that the Dragon Kings were stronger. Even Moreann knew that. It's why she'd gathered together so many to build the Others' power. But all it took was one crack.

And Noreen was that chink in the armor.

"Ready?" Cain asked.

She shook her head but whispered, "Yes."

He laughed softly. "I've got you. Remember that."

They began walking again. The closer they got to the village, the more nervous Noreen became. "They can follow my magic."

"But no' mine," he answered. "We'll be going to several different locations."

"You're going to throw them off?"

"That's the plan. I figure they'll eventually trace where

we've gone. At the verra least, they'll figure out the first spot, but I doona want to take any chances."

They walked for several minutes in silence before she said, "I didn't realize the Kings could teleport."

"We can no'."

There was no more after that little quip. Noreen tried to let it go, telling herself that not everyone explained things like she needed. But the irritation became too much. "Please elaborate. I need more than that."

Dark green eyes briefly slid her way. "Do you now?"

"Yes."

He was silent, and she began to think that he wouldn't tell her more when he lifted their joined hands and pointed at the silver cuff on his wrist with his free hand. "This. It was given to one of us by a powerful Dark Fae."

"For a group who has been in nearly constant battle with the Dark, you seem to have friends there."

Cain lifted one shoulder. "I suppose we do."

The village came into view, and Noreen's stomach knotted so hard that she grew nauseous. Would it be Brian or Moreann who saw her? Sweat broke out on Noreen's brow, and it became difficult to breathe.

"Easy," Cain whispered. "I've got you."

"So much could go wrong."

"Think about it going right," he told her. "Doona let doubt creep into your mind. Keep your thoughts focused on our goal, on you gaining the upper hand with those against you."

Noreen turned her head to look at his profile. His *handsome* profile. "You make it sound so simple."

"It is. Our minds are incredibly powerful. They can overcome fear and doubt, but you have to let it happen."

She straightened her shoulders, doing exactly as he

suggested. It took a few minutes, but by the time they reached the edge of the village, she was once more in control of herself.

"Verra good," Cain said. "Now, get ready, because it's about to begin."

Her gaze scanned the people, and in an instant, she spotted Brian. She jerked, the fear once more trying to take over her. Cain kept walking and squeezed her hand. She put one foot in front of the other and tamped down the terror that threatened.

Brian's mouth fell open in shock. He forgot all about the woman he was charming as he stared. Noreen and Cain came to a halt together.

"Ready?" Cain asked.

She smiled at Brian and told Cain, "You bet."

And just like that, they jumped to the next location. No sooner had they arrived, then they were gone again. Noreen stopped counting when she reached the thirty-third spot. She might be a Fae who could teleport, but even she was getting dizzy.

Finally, they stopped. She bent over, her hands on her knees as she drew in deep breaths while trying not to vomit. A breeze rushed around her, and the cool air felt good against her heated skin. Cain was near but no longer touching her. He didn't say anything as she slowly regrouped from their journey.

Only when her legs no longer felt like jelly did she lift her head. She spotted the vast expanse of sea before her, reaching far into the horizon. The wind buffeted them, the gusts so great that she had to take a step back.

"The Shetland Islands," Cain told her. "Remote, but immensely beautiful."

"I was here long ago. It's as desolate now as it was then."

"It is." He turned to her then. "How do you feel?"

"Like I once more have my feet beneath me."

His lips curved into a small smile. "Aye. I wasna feeling so great myself, but it had to be done. We didna use your magic, and they can no' follow us, but just in case they have a way to track you, I wanted to make it difficult for them."

"You've done that, I believe."

"We've crisscrossed the globe several times, and we've visited the same places multiple times."

Noreen laughed. "That should confuse them for sure."

"That's the hope. Now, if you're up for it, we have one more jump to make."

"And where is that?"

"To a Fae doorway."

Noreen frowned, her brows drawing together. "The Fae that are part of the Others will probably have them watched."

"Hmm. That's a good point. Can you make one yourself?"

"Absolutely. It'll take significant magic that will be like a beacon pointing straight at us, though. They know what my magic looks like. Just as I know theirs."

Cain looked out over the sea as the waves tossed about. "Then we have no choice. We have to get to a doorway."

"And where exactly are we going?"

"The Fae Realm."

The wind howled around her, so she wasn't sure she'd heard right. "I'm sorry. Can you repeat that?"

Cain looked at her, their eyes locking. "The Fae Realm."

"Have you lost your mind?" she asked as shock rippled through her.

"No' at all," he answered calmly.

She threw up her hands before letting them fall against her thighs. "We can't go there. I know for a fact that Usaeil and Moreann used to meet there. Moreann is the—"

"Leader of the Others."

Noreen's mouth fell open. "H-how do you know that?"

"Usaeil wanted Con. So much so that when he wouldna willingly go to her, she kidnapped him."

"Bloody hell. That's where Usaeil disappeared to, then. We were searching for her."

Cain nodded. "Aye. She also captured her nephew, but we've no' found him yet."

"You probably won't," Noreen said with a shrug.

"While Usaeil had Con, he convinced her that he was with her in all things. She told him about Moreann and their meetings on the Fae Realm."

Noreen gave him a flat look. "Then why do you want to go there?"

"Because it's the last place Moreann will think to look for you. Or at least that was my hope when I thought we could get through the doorway without being seen."

It was a good plan. A very good one, she had to admit. "There are two doorways that lead to the Fae Realm. I'm sure there are more, but those are the only ones I know of. They aren't used anymore, obviously, but one of them is pretty hidden. So much so that I doubt anyone remembers it."

"Then that's where we're going. Take my hand and think of the location. Then touch my bracelet," he bade her.

The moment her fingers interlocked with his, Noreen felt a rush of excitement. She shouldn't like touching him so much, but there was no denying it. She glanced at his face, thankful that he was the Dragon King who'd found her. Then she touched the cuff.

CHAPTER SIX

"What the hell do you mean she's gone?"

Brian couldn't hide his cringe at Moreann's indignant, piercing tone directed at him in the middle of the clearing. "I saw her with a Dragon King. Th-th-they were holding hands."

Moreann's nostrils flared, her eyes narrowing as her voice lowered to a dangerously calm tone. "Holding hands?"

"Yes," Brian hastily replied, nodding his head as he did. He was a fekking Fae. Why was he so intimidated by a Druid? He hated that he couldn't stand up to Moreann. So what if she was empress to her people? She was still only a Druid.

She wasn't any better than him. In fact, if he had to guess, he had more power than she did. But he didn't want to put it to a test.

Moreann drew in a deep breath and clasped her hands before her. She wore a burgundy shirt with gold thread on the hem of the billowy sleeves, scooped neck, and hem. She was in a pair of black pants Brian had seen many executive businesswomen wear.

The empress might have used magic to live for thousands of years, but she couldn't stop the signs of aging completely. She looked like a woman in her fifties, who had taken great care of herself. She was on the thinner side, however her stomach was rounded, and her waist thicker. Despite what Brian saw as flaws her magic couldn't fix, she was still a very beautiful woman. Her long, brunette locks—without a single gray hair—freely hung down her back and over one shoulder.

"They were holding hands," she said, more to herself than to him.

Brian was thankful. He didn't like it when Moreann's attention was on him. However, he enjoyed being a part of the Others. He, along with everyone else in the group, wanted the Dragon Kings removed forever. He hadn't been happy about waiting so many years to see it done, but he hadn't been part of the original group. Maybe if he had, he would've voiced his thoughts.

But he knew that for the lie it was.

He glanced around, wishing he could leave. No doubt, whatever Moreann was concocting would put him in the line of fire with the Dragon Kings, and he didn't want to face them on his own. He fully acknowledged the coward that he was. That's why he was with the Others.

"No one said anything about her having a relationship with anyone," Moreann stated into the silence.

Brian slid his gaze to her and found the Druid staring at him. She claimed to be a *mie*, a good Druid, but he had his doubts. Even if she were, that didn't mean she wouldn't make him scream in pain if he angered her.

"I didn't hear anything about it," he said.

Moreann cocked her head to the side. "How did you know she was in this village?"

"One of my old friends mentioned seeing a Fae near

Dreagan. The Fae tend to stay away from this area because of the Kings. Well, except for Rhi."

Moreann slashed her hand through the air. "We're not discussing her right now."

"My friend knew it wasn't Rhi, but he didn't recognize the female either."

"Curious," Moreann said. "If Fae stay away, what was your friend doing in the village?"

Brian's mind went blank for a second as he struggled to recall the information. "He moves stuff around for those who don't wish to leave Ireland or the Light Castle."

"And it brought him here?" she asked skeptically. "To this remote village in Scotland near the Dragon Kings?"

"Apparently. He was here long enough to get what was needed and leave."

"In that little bit of time, he managed to catch sight of Noreen? Really?"

"Well, he is a Fae. He thought she was Light."

Moreann's doubt was evident. "Then, out of the blue, you decided to come and look for yourself?"

He swallowed, the sound loud even to his own ears. "Yes."

"Why?"

"I thought it would be prudent to know if any Fae were helping the Kings."

"Why?"

"The more we know of who our enemies are, the better."

Moreann took two steps forward, halting inches from him. "We have one enemy—the Dragon Kings. I could care less how many Druids, Fae, or mortals help them. It won't matter, because we're stronger."

"Usaeil always liked to know if any Fae were partial to the Kings."

"In case you haven't noticed, Usaeil isn't running things. She never was."

Brian didn't dare say anything to contradict that. When it came to Moreann and Usaeil, he used to let them pretend that each of them was running things. Truth be told, if he had to choose a side, it would be with his queen. Usaeil had been his sovereign for as long as he could remember, and he didn't care if she was Light, Dark, or something else. She was Fae, and he would always bend the knee to her.

But she wasn't the one standing before him now.

"I know," he told Moreann, hoping that was what she wanted to hear.

She rolled her eyes. "So, you came here to get information for Usaeil. Am I correct?"

Fek. He couldn't take it back now. "You are."

"Even though she can't help you, much less herself?"

His mouth filled with saliva again, and he had to swallow. "Y-yes."

"I see."

"But I brought the information to you, not Usaeil," he hastily added.

Moreann dropped her arms. "That's a good thing."

"If I hadn't come, then you wouldn't have known that Noreen was up to something."

"No, I can't refute that." She sighed loudly and shook her head. "Of all the ones I thought would turn, it was never Noreen."

Brian had known for a long time that Noreen was Moreann's favorite. It shouldn't bother him, but it did. It didn't matter what Noreen did, it was never wrong in the empress's eyes. Yet, if he did the littlest thing, he was reprimanded and berated in front of everyone. It left a mark.

It was obvious that Moreann didn't care for him. Though

if that were the case, then why had she come to him, asking for him to join the Others? Their group wasn't large. They were with each other more often now, which meant they all had to get along. Well, all of them but Moreann. She always went off and did her own thing.

"What do we do now?" Brian asked.

Moreann jerked her head to him and pinned him with a steely look. "You don't do anything. I'll take care of Noreen."

He wanted to ask if she would kill the Fae, but Brian didn't have the courage. Just as he could never ask what it was about Rhi that made Moreann go to such extremes to try and recruit the Light.

"I see you don't agree with my decision," she said icily.

Brian held up his hands before him and shook his head. "I'm just thinking, is all. You're very close to Noreen. It'll be painful for you to have to punish her." He didn't say *kill* on purpose because he wanted to see how the empress would respond.

"You don't think I have it in me?"

"I know you do. However, what Noreen has done wasn't just against you. It was against every one of us. Let us bring her to justice."

Moreann hesitated before she gave a single nod. "You have a point, Brian. I'll allow you to go after her first since you were the one who told me of her involvement with a Dragon King. Don't fail."

"I won't," he said as he bowed his head then turned on his heel and left.

He only went two steps before he gathered his magic and teleported away. He had no idea where Noreen went, but he knew someone who could track her—Usaeil. Unfortunately, that meant he would have to go against Moreann in order to succeed.

Brian arrived in the top of the tower of the derelict castle in Ireland. Half the roof was gone as rain pelted the stones, turning them a deep gray as moss grew on them.

"My queen," he said as he got down on one knee and lowered his head.

"I'm not so queenly now."

He looked up at the sound of clinking. His gaze landed on the thick, heavy chains that bound Usaeil's wrists, ankles, and waist. "You are forever my queen."

Red eyes turned to him. "Even though I'm Dark."

"You're my queen. You led us justly for eons, and you wanted to join the Dark and Light together as we once were long, long ago."

A hint of a smile played upon Usaeil's face. Her hair was matted and dirty. Her sweater frayed at the neck and cuffs, the pants threadbare, and her boots had a hole in the toe. Moreann had dressed Usaeil in such a fashion to prove a point, but it infuriated Brian.

"You're royalty. You shouldn't be treated this way," he said through gritted teeth.

Usaeil turned her head back to the small window. She was confined to a little corner to keep away from the rain. The moment the water spread across the floor and touched her boots, she sat on the stool and drew her knees to her chest. "Oh, I won't be here forever."

"No, you won't. I plan to free you."

"Sweet, Brian," Usaeil said without looking in his direction. "I appreciate your words, but we both know you can't open this lock." She lifted her hands, showing him the chains. "And Moreann has made sure I can't either."

Brian got to his feet, uncaring that the knee of his pants was now damp. "I need you freed. The Fae need you free."

"So I can go against Moreann?" Usaeil asked with a chuckle.

"To join us once more and prove that you still want to take down the Dragon Kings."

Usaeil lowered her eyes before she turned her head to him. "Does it matter to you at all that I fell in love with Constantine?"

"Should it? Like the rest of us, you vowed to do whatever was needed to make sure we ended the Kings once and for all. Look what Con did to you. And it isn't just him. Rhi betrayed you, and yet Moreann would have her join us."

"And you don't understand why."

"No, I don't." Brian raked a hand down his face. "I hate Rhi and everything she stands for. She tried to kill you, but more than that, she sided with the Kings. She needs to die along with them."

Usaeil smiled. "I won't disagree with that."

"We need you, my queen. Desperately."

"Then you better talk to Moreann, because she doesn't want to hear anything I have to say."

"That's why I'm here, actually," he said. "Noreen has switched sides."

With those four words, Usaeil's entire attitude changed. She straightened on the stool and put her feet on the floor. "What do you mean?"

"I saw her less than thirty minutes ago, holding hands with a Dragon King before they disappeared."

"Which King? Describe him to me," Usaeil demanded as she rose to her feet.

"Black hair, green eyes. He had a shadow of a beard."

Usaeil nodded. "Cain. I saw Con talking to him once before I could no longer go to Dreagan. And you're sure he and Noreen were holding hands?"

"Positive. She actually smiled at me before she teleported."

"Are you sure it was her?"

Brian shot her a confused look. "Of course. The Kings can't jump like us."

"With help, they can. If it was Noreen, you should be able to track her magic. Did you?"

He really hated when he did stupid stuff, and he always seemed to be doing exactly that. "I was in such a hurry to tell Moreann that I didn't think to check."

"Then you should." When he didn't immediately move, Usaeil bellowed, "Now!"

Brian returned to the village where he'd seen Noreen and checked for any sign of her magic. It was one thing about being in the Others that he didn't like. He knew why Moreann had used magic to make it so any of them could find other members by their magic, but he didn't like the idea of anyone being able to follow *him*.

Apparently, neither did Noreen, because he found no trace of her magic anywhere in the village. He'd known she'd been acting weird, but it appeared that she had nearly gone to ground by halting any use of magic. If his friend hadn't seen her, and Brian hadn't come to investigate, there was no telling what Noreen could've done. But that was over now.

Brian returned to the castle and Usaeil. "Nothing," he reported.

"Just as I figured. Cain is the one teleporting."

"I vowed to find her," Brian said. "I want you to help me. If we bring Noreen in together before she can give the Kings any information, then you'll be back in Moreann's good graces."

Usaeil smiled. "What a fabulous plan. There's just one hitch." She lifted her arms, jangling the chains.

Brian returned her smile. "I've been thinking about that.

Moreann might have made it so none of us can teleport into the room with you, but that's not going to stop me."

"You aren't even supposed to know where I am. No one is."

His grin widened. "I'm resourceful. As soon as I learned Moreann had taken you, I made it my mission to discover where you were."

"I'm thankful you did."

"Now, I need you to get as close to me as you can."

"The chain around my waist won't allow that."

He nodded patiently. "I know. Just come as close as you're able."

She did as he asked. Brian then leaned his hand through, pushing against the metal bars that separated them until he couldn't move any more. He used his other hand to grasp the bars as leverage, and then managed to touch the chain near her wrist with his fingertips. He pushed magic through his fingers.

Sweat broke out on his brow and slid down his face into his eyes, but he didn't wipe it away. He could feel the metal breaking until, finally, it fell with a loud clank to the floor.

"I'll be damned," Usaeil said.

CHAPTER SEVEN

Cain hadn't interacted with many Dark Fae, but even he knew there was something different about Noreen. He couldn't quite put his finger on it, however. And that bugged him.

She was beautiful, yes. It didn't matter if she used glamour to hide her coloring or if her red eyes were flashing at him in anger. She was breathtaking. From her oval face to her pouty lips that turned his thoughts carnal.

Then there was her body.

His mouth watered each time he glanced at her shirt that molded to her full breasts before hugging her trim abdomen. No matter how Cain looked at it, there was no denying his body's response. He was attracted to Noreen.

And he didn't even care.

So what if she was Dark? Everyone had one affair they weren't exactly proud of. And it wasn't as if Noreen was an enemy. She was helping them. Which could put her in the friend column.

His thoughts were so intent on the need flooding his body that didn't immediately notice that she had already jumped them to the doorway until a bird screeched in outrage and flew so close to Cain's face that the feathers brushed his cheek.

He glanced at the bird before looking around at the ruins of the keep. By the tall grass, weeds, and trees growing up in the abandoned rooms, no one was taking care of the castle. It was a shame, really. They had been grand structures during their day. And by the way the tourists flocked to see them—even those barely standing—this one shouldn't be left to rot, forgotten.

Cain jerked his gaze to Noreen to find her staring at him. Her expression was thoughtful, but he didn't ask her what she was thinking.

Their eyes held for a heartbeat before she released his hand. "The doorway is this way," she said as she headed to the stairs.

He watched her, his gaze going to her hips as she ascended the steps. He wondered if she knew how sexy she was. Or that she was making him think of nothing but her with every sway of her backside.

Noreen glanced over her shoulder at him. Their gazes briefly met, and that's all it took for him to see that she knew exactly what she was doing to him. Once she turned away, he smiled. If that's how she wanted to play things, he was game.

Cain followed her up the stairs to the second floor. They went down a short hallway, and then she entered a room. No one but a Fae could see their doorways. When Cain walked into the chamber, all he saw were leaves that had blown in from the bare window.

"You trust me?" she asked.

"Aye."

A frown flashed across her face. "Why?"

"You trusted me."

"I had no choice."

"Neither do I."

Noreen gave a small shake of her head. "If I were in your shoes, I wouldn't trust me."

"Why no'?" he asked.

"Really?" She gaped at him. "Not only am I a Dark, but I'm also part of the Others. You walked up to me less than an hour ago and believed everything I said."

Cain shrugged, curious as to where she was going with this.

"I could be taking you through a doorway straight to the Others."

"You could," he replied.

Her eyes widened in disbelief. "Doesn't that make you angry?"

"If you betray me, you betray me. Trust me, lass, I can defend myself."

Noreen sighed loudly. "You're missing the point."

"Actually, I'm no'. The truth of the matter is, I *do* believe you. I went to the village to talk to you and discern if you were setting a trap for us. Then I saw you with Brian. Now, there's a possibility that you and he set all that up in case someone at Dreagan was watching, but I doubt it. Your expression—and his—was too genuine for it to have been planned. After we spoke, and you tried to tell me that you took it all back, I knew for certain that fear for your life drove you to make such a statement."

"You could be wrong."

"I could be," Cain admitted. "It wouldna be the first time, and I doubt it'll be the last. But if I can obtain even a shred of information to help my brethren, then it'll be worth it."

Noreen briefly closed her eyes before she walked to the window and looked out it. "They want all of you dead."

"We know."

"No, you don't." She paused, her hands resting against the stone surrounding the window. Her voice shook when she continued. "Moreann plans to find the rest of the dragons once all of the Kings are dead. Then she'll wipe them out, as well. There will be no more dragons. Anywhere."

Cain took that bit of news and quickly relayed it to every Dragon King through their mental link. Then he disconnected before any of them could ask him questions. Noreen's words didn't really surprise him, but the thought of the Others wiping out all dragons left him cold inside.

"You shouldn't trust me," Noreen continued.

Cain walked up behind her but didn't touch her. "But I do."

"I don't understand that."

"Because you doona trust anyone."

Her silence was her answer. Cain had no idea what it was like to live as a Dark. He'd heard stories from Shara, as well as from some of the Kings who had interacted with Balladyn and other Dark Fae.

"You took a stand," Cain told her. "Stop worrying about me. You should be focused on other things."

Noreen turned to face him. "I don't understand you. That's why I ask these questions."

"I need you, and you need me. The fact we need each other means that we have to trust one another. I'm willing to do it. Are you?"

Red eyes bored into his. Finally, she said, "Yes."

"Good. Is the doorway here?"

Her chin jerked to the left. "It's right there."

"Shall we go through?"

"Anything could await us on the other side."

Cain shrugged, grinning. "That could be said for anything. Personally, I like adventure."

"I usually do, too. But I've never been in fear for my life."

"I've got you," he told her.

She shot him a fierce look. "Keep telling me that, and I just might believe you."

He didn't bother to reply. Cain didn't want to wait around the castle. The longer they were on Earth, the greater the chance of someone finding them. But he didn't rush Noreen. He gave her the time she needed to get her fear under control.

They had covered their tracks pretty well, but Cain wasn't going to underestimate the Others. The group had shown how resilient and persistent they could be in their desire to be rid of the Dragon Kings.

But they couldn't have predicted Noreen's move. No doubt Moreann and everyone else in the group was reeling over Noreen flipping sides. Cain would love to see their faces, but it was enough to know that, for once, the Kings had delivered a blow to the Others.

It was just the beginning, however. If Noreen was true to her word and gave him the information the Kings needed, then the Others' days were numbered.

Too many had suffered already. And not just dragons. Humans, as well—though they didn't know the extent of things and likely never would. Even if they were told the truth, they wouldn't believe it. Mortals were an untrusting lot. Not that he could blame them.

He thought of his dragons. It had been so long since he'd seen his clan that he almost forgot what it felt like to have them. Maybe that's what the Others wanted all along. Cain thought of his twin nephews. They had only been a few months old when the Kings sent the dragons away.

Watching his family leave was one of the hardest things Cain had ever done. But he'd stood tall until every last one of his Navies was over the bridge. It wasn't until he got to his mountain on Dreagan that he had broken down as the full impact of what had occurred that long-ago day hit him.

The Dragon Kings weren't killers, and it was easy to second guess decisions made eons ago. But he did. There wasn't a day that went by that he didn't think about how different things would be if the Kings hadn't allowed the humans to remain when they arrived. Ulrik wouldn't have been betrayed and begun the war with the mortals. Con wouldn't have banished Ulrik and stripped him of his magic. And the dragons wouldn't have been sent away.

Life without his clan was a struggle for Cain. He put on a good show, all the Kings did, but every day was a battle.

The Fae's realm might have been destroyed because of their civil war, but at least they still had each other. The Kings couldn't say that. Cain had thought once V regained his sword that he could locate the dragons and see how they were, but that hadn't happened.

Cain understood. While V hadn't exactly told anyone the details, Cain could well imagine what it would be like to be the one who learned if their dragons were alive and thriving—or dead. He wouldn't want that responsibility. So, he didn't begrudge V for not being able to do it.

With an inward shake of his head, Cain threw off such thoughts. He couldn't let himself be pulled down by his emotions. Not now. He blinked and focused on Noreen to find the Dark staring at him.

She had tucked her shoulder-length hair behind one ear. The silver added an element of dimension to her black locks that he actually found appealing. And, for the first time, he noticed the garnet stud earrings she wore.

"Pretty," he said.

She touched her earring and smiled. "They're my birthstone. At least, per the mortals. I like the stone. It's my favorite. What were you thinking about a moment ago? You looked . . . sad."

It was on the tip of his tongue to tell her that it was nothing, but before those words could fall from his lips, he said, "I was thinking about my dragons."

"This may seem like an insensitive question, but do you miss them?"

"Verra much. Imagine if you didna have your family."

"I don't," she replied.

Cain was taken aback by the news. "I'm sorry."

There was a flash of something in her eyes that was gone as quickly as it had appeared. "It was a long time ago."

"So was my clan leaving. It doesna diminish the pain."

"I've heard mortals say that time heals all wounds, but I'm not sure it does."

Cain lowered his gaze to the ground. "I think it helps us deal with the pain so it isna so raw, but that's all I can say it does."

"I'm sorry your dragons are gone."

He lifted his eyes to her and forced a smile. "Thank you."

Noreen held out her hand. "Ready?"

He knew he didn't need to hold her hand to go through the doorway, but he liked that she offered it. He slipped his palm against hers, his fingers folding over her hand. "Ready."

CHAPTER EIGHT

Noreen had made a point of not returning to the Fae Realm after it had been destroyed. Some of her friends had gone back, but she hadn't understood why. There was nothing there for anyone. It was why Moreann had chosen it as the meeting place for her and Usaeil.

The moment Noreen walked through the doorway from Earth to the Fae Realm, she was hit with the epic destruction that hundreds of years of constant war between the Light and Dark had done to the planet. She was glad she had Cain's hand because it was difficult to see with her own eyes what they had done to their home.

"Are you all right, lass?" he asked in a soft tone.

Noreen blinked back tears as she recalled how happy she'd been there. She had been very young, and her memories were colored by that fact, but she could still recall her mother in the kitchen baking, and her father telling one of his many corny jokes to get them to laugh. It was a good memory, which was probably why she'd held onto it.

"It's . . . hard," she finally said.

"Aye."

She sniffed and looked around, trying to get her bearings. "I was young when we had to leave. I don't even remember where our home was. But I did see a map of the Fae Realm once while in the Dark Palace."

"I doona think it matters where we go," Cain said. "We just need to find some shelter. We'll want to remain close to the doorway in case we need to leave quickly."

Noreen glanced at him, her lips twisting. "I'd vote for getting far away from it in case someone comes through. We don't want them to find us."

"I doona expect we'll be out so they can find it. However, seeing who comes through, if anyone does, would be a boon for sure. Remember, we'll only be here long enough for you to give me the information you have. Once I relay it to the other Kings, we'll begin preparations for battle."

She inwardly winced at the sight of the dead trees and plants all around her. There was nothing alive on the planet, except for them. "I'll be here a lot longer since Moreann won't stop looking for me until no more breath fills her lungs."

"Sorry, lass. I did forget about that. I willna leave you alone. I'll remain with you."

Once more, the Dragon King surprised her. "Why would you do that? You could be captured. Besides, you should be with your brethren, strategizing."

"I've given you my word."

"You should think of yourself at times. Maybe that's why your kind is in this predicament in the first place."

The moment the words were out of her mouth, she wanted to take them back. Yet, the apology wouldn't come.

Cain didn't look away from her. He drew in a deep breath and shrugged. "Perhaps you're right. If we had been selfish, if we had slaughtered defenseless mortals, I wouldna be standing here willing to put myself between you and whoever shows up to kill you."

"I shouldn't have said that," Noreen said, ashamed of herself. She looked away, wishing Cain had gotten angry. It would've been easier to bear if he had.

"You said what you felt." He walked past her as if it were the end of the discussion.

There was more Noreen wanted to say, but maybe it was better to let it drop. Especially since she didn't know how to fix things. All Cain had done was help her, and all she'd done was question and insult him at every turn. It was any wonder why he remained. Then again, she had the key to helping the Kings become victorious over the Others.

Or did she?

Noreen hurried to catch up with him. "Now that Moreann knows what I've done, any plans they've made will change."

"I've already thought of that."

"Oh." She hadn't. She'd been too intent on staying alive to think that far ahead. Obviously, she wasn't very good at whatever it was she was trying to be at the moment.

Cain suddenly stopped and faced her. "Knowledge is power, lass. We need everything you can tell us about the Others. There will be something in there we can use to our advantage. The Others have come at us sideways for too long. It's time we leveled the playing field."

"I can do that."

"You give me the information, and I'll keep you safe. That's the deal we've made. Right?"

She nodded because she knew he was irritated at her. When he'd been patient and kind, she had thrown that back in his face. Now, she deserved whatever it was he gave her.

"I have a bad habit of lashing out at people when my emotions are all jumbled. It was wrong, and I want you to know that I'm sorry."

Cain gave a nod of his head and faced forward to continue walking.

Noreen wanted him to say something like he had earlier. To smile at her and call her *lass* and tell her that everything was going to be okay. But she had ruined that all on her own. With a sigh, she trailed slightly behind him.

There wasn't much near the doorway. Only fragments of buildings remained. Even after so many thousands of years, the planet hadn't recovered enough for new plant growth. That's how much damage had been done.

Noreen might not have taken part in the war because she'd been young, but she still held a wealth of regret for it all. She believed that every Fae should come and see their old realm so perhaps they would never do such a thing again.

Her feet crunched on glass and other debris as they continued their journey. She didn't know where they were going, and it didn't matter because Cain was going where he wanted to go. And if she wanted to stay alive, she would go with him.

"It was a beautiful place once," she told him as they walked through the remnants of a city. "Ireland reminds us of what this place once was. That's why Usaeil and the old King of the Dark chose it as our home."

"Chose it without bothering to ask the occupants of the realm," Cain stated.

"Yet the Kings allowed us to stay, and gave us Ireland."

"More mistakes we made, I presume."

She shook her head and came even with him. "If you had refused us, we wouldn't have had anywhere to go."

"You would've found a place. Just as you found our realm."

Noreen swallowed at the hard edge to his voice.

He glanced at her and said, "And we wouldna been involved in the Fae Wars or had to constantly battle the Dark, who kill mortals."

At the mention of the Fae Wars, Noreen looked straight ahead. She tried not to think of that time since it was when she'd lost her parents. They had been the only two people in the entire universe who had loved her. They had encouraged her to be whoever she wanted to be, even if it wasn't a Dark.

Since she hadn't wanted to follow that path, she was glad to hear their thoughts. But everything had changed the day they were murdered.

"You can dish it out, but you can no' take it, huh?" Cain retorted coldly.

"I don't like talking about the Fae Wars."

"Why is that?" he demanded.

She jerked her head to him and looked into his deep green eyes. "Because it was the day a Dragon King killed my parents."

She lengthened her strides after delivering her declaration. If she thought he would apologize or say something, she was wrong. He remained silent—and behind her. Which suited Noreen just fine.

They walked for another thirty minutes before she felt a vibration beneath her feet.

"Did you feel that?" she asked Cain as she came to a stop.

He gave a nod as he came up beside her. "It came from up ahead."

"I heard about the magic used at the end of our civil

war. It was ten times that of a mortal's nuclear bomb. Look around us, Cain. There's proof that whatever made that vibration isn't good."

"We willna know unless we look."

She crossed her arms over her chest. "Well, you go on ahead and do that. I'll stay here."

"Where's your sense of adventure?"

"Flew out the window the moment I sent that email to you."

He shrugged and looked forward. "Stay here, then. I'll be back."

"Sure you will," she said as he walked away. If he heard her, he didn't respond. Then again, he had a habit of doing that.

It wasn't a bad trait to have. She might want to think about doing that, as well. It would prevent her from saying things she later regretted.

"That will cut back on a lot of apologizing for sure. Then again, I might end up never talking again," she said to herself.

That made her chuckle.

She sobered as she realized that Cain might never come back. If he didn't, she would only have herself to speak to for the rest of eternity.

Her head turned back in the direction from which they'd come. It would be easy to leave and look for another door that would take her to another realm. The problem was, she didn't know how many doorways had survived—or where they led.

She frowned then as she let her eyes move from one side to the other, taking in the rampant destruction and lack of renewal. How was it that a doorway had survived such annihilation? It didn't make sense.

The tremor she'd felt earlier rumbled beneath her feet

again. Her head snapped in the direction where Cain had gone. Something didn't make sense. The planet should've had some kind of regrowth after so many eons.

She took a tentative step after Cain. Then another. Then she began jogging after him. She was about to shout his name, ask him to wait for her, but just as she opened her mouth, he disappeared.

Noreen slid to a halt, her heart hammering in her chest. Cain hadn't touched the cuff on his wrist, so she knew he hadn't teleported away. But where had he gone?

She slowly began walking to where she'd last seen him. As she reached the spot, a disembodied arm suddenly appeared, and the hand clamped around her wrist. Noreen fought to get away, but it held onto her tightly before yanking her forward.

In the next moment, she found herself pulled through some kind of shield. She immediately had to raise her hand to block out the bright light of the sun. She blinked repeatedly and tried to get her bearings.

"I've got you," Cain said from beside her.

She realized then that he was the one who had grabbed her and pulled her through the barrier. Noreen looked behind her and saw a thin shield, allowing her to see the desolation on the other side, but it blocked anyone from seeing *inside*.

"Take a look around," Cain urged her.

She looked at him through squinted eyes that were adjusting to the light. As she scanned the area, her mouth fell open in shock at the vivid greens of the trees and plants. The sky was the brightest blue she had ever seen with huge, puffy clouds floating past. Birds sang so loudly and clearly that it felt as if she were surrounded.

"What is this place?" she asked.

"Something someone wanted to hide is my guess."

Noreen took a step back. "Do you think someone else is here?"

"Only one way to find out," Cain said as he started forward.

She rolled her eyes in exasperation. "Stop doing that."

CHAPTER NINE

Dreagan

She didn't want to return. She'd put it off, but in the end, she was back.

Melisse stood behind a large tree and stared into the distance where Dreagan was. She knew the instant she'd helped Bernadette against the Others that she had crossed a line she couldn't stand behind any longer. What other option did she have? In a short time, she had seen the utter chaos of the world for herself. Something had to be done before the mortals were pulled into it.

For a brief moment, she'd thought the TruthSeeker and JusticeBringer might be able to take action, then she realized that the siblings were still learning their roles. Though, she had to admit that the JusticeBringer was acquiring his knowledge quicker than expected. With the right nudge, he would gain everything he needed to fully utilize his potential.

At the thought of Henry, Melisse's mind drifted to their all-too-brief meeting in Madrid. The worst thing she could've done was talk to him, and yet, that's exactly what she'd done. She hadn't been able to help it. It was like something had pushed her right to him.

Just as it brought her to Dreagan now.

She knew that's where Henry was. He might not be a Dragon King, but he was special in his own right. The Kings had recognized that long before anyone knew the link Henry and his sister, Esther, had with the ancient Druids.

Melisse needed to leave. She couldn't let Con or any of the other Kings get a glimpse of her. That would undermine everything she'd done up to this point. If only she could have one look at Henry, then she would be okay. But he rarely left the mansion.

"Henry," she whispered.

She was jeopardizing everything by her arrival in the village. It wasn't just the Kings she wanted to stay away from, but the Others, as well.

The simple fact was that she should be as far from Dreagan as she could get. Why then was she still here? She knew the answer. She might not like it, but she accepted the truth.

Melisse turned and put her back against the bark of the tree. She closed her eyes. No matter how she looked at it, she was on her own. If anyone found out who she really was, then it was all over.

She didn't want to be pulled into a war, but there was no choice for her. And if that was the case, then she was going to choose—and she chose herself.

It wouldn't be long before the Others began actively looking for her—if they weren't already. Moreann kept such things to herself, but Melisse was no fool. She was the ace in the hole of the Others. Which meant, Moreann was no doubt looking for her even now.

Just as the Empress of Druids had her sights set on Rhi.

Now that had come as a shock to Melisse. Though, perhaps it shouldn't have. The Light Fae was more special than anyone—even the Dragon Kings—realized. Everyone had their thoughts about what Rhi should do, including Death.

Melisse wondered why the goddess hadn't paid her a visit yet. She wasn't naive enough to believe that Death didn't know of her. But that begged the question as to why she had been left to her own devices.

There were too many sides to this impending war. Everyone thought they were in the right, but were any of them? Was she?

For so many years, Melisse had watched as enemy after enemy piled up against the Dragon Kings. She'd hated the Kings for so very long—and with good reason. But even she had to set that aside and look at the big picture.

No matter their faults, the Kings protected this realm and all who lived in it. They had sacrificed greatly to ensure that.

And while she hated to admit it, the one who had sacrificed the most was Constantine.

Melisse didn't want to think about the King of Dragon Kings—or any of the Kings, for that matter. She would rather focus on Henry, but she couldn't. She needed to get a glimpse of all the players in this looming war and figure out the best strategy. She couldn't wait for Henry to come into his powers, or for his sister to realize just where they fit amidst all of this.

More than that, Melisse needed to find Usaeil. The Queen of the Light had fooled everyone, even her. And Melisse didn't like being duped. It was only the second time in her life, and there wouldn't be a third.

Usaeil was key to it all. The queen had deceived the Light for so many millennia, but they hadn't been the only ones Usaeil had lied to. There were the Kings, Druids, and most importantly, Moreann and the Others.

Anyone who went to that kind of trouble to hide who they really were from absolutely everyone meant that Usaeil had a plan. Much like Melisse was devising now. But no one knew where Usaeil was. Few Fae even realized that she was alive as the Light and Dark quibbled among each other over who was going to lead each division.

Melisse rolled her eyes. There was so much more at stake than who had power, but that was all the Fae ever thought about. And while they concentrated on that, someone would rise up and rule them—and the fools wouldn't even see it coming.

It was on the tip of Melisse's tongue to call for Death and fill the goddess in on what she knew, but she didn't want the attention of Death or the Reapers. And so what if the Fae were wiped away? They had done enough damage to this realm.

No one belonged here but the dragons. That was fact. Everyone else had made Earth their home. The result was the end of an era with the dragons and the Kings hiding their true power. But she didn't think it could be hidden for much longer. Whether any of the Kings wanted to admit it or not, the time was coming for the world to know of them.

Melisse wasn't sure what would happen to the mortals once that happened. There couldn't be another war with the Kings, because this time, the Kings wouldn't stand aside. They had already lost everything. They were backed against a wall, and a group as lethal and fierce and strong as the Dragon Kings would retaliate in the only way they knew how.

Death.

Destruction.

Annihilation.

And, honestly, she wouldn't blame a single one of

the Kings for such an action. They had been pushed and pushed and pushed until they couldn't be pushed any more.

She blew out a breath in exasperation at the idea that she was defending the Kings, even to herself. After what they had done to her . . . well, that wasn't easily forgiven. If she could forgive them at all.

The easiest thing to do would be to just leave the realm. Thanks to watching other Fae, she knew the doorways, and Melisse had made sure to mark them for herself. There was another way for her to leave, as well, but that was only as a last course of action. If she did that, she would announce herself to everyone on the planet.

With so few options available, she didn't know why it was difficult for her to choose one. All she had to do was make a decision and then stay the course.

The problem was that she didn't like her choices. In fact, she hated all of them. She kept trying to find alternatives, but there weren't any.

The sudden quiet of the birds told her that she wasn't alone. Bloody hell. That wasn't what she wanted. All she could do now was pray that it wasn't a Dragon King, because if it were, she would have to fight them—and damn the consequences.

Out of the corner of her eye, she saw movement. Her head turned to the side, and her gaze landed on none other than Henry. She drank in his brown hair, hazel eyes, and incredible body. He hadn't shaven in a few days, but she didn't mind the beard. It accentuated his strong jawline.

"Melisse?" he asked in his refined British accent, a frown furrowing his brow. Before she could say anything, he took a step toward her. "I heard your voice. In here," he said as he tapped his temple. "I heard you call my name."

"That's not possible." She shook her head, not wanting to believe what she'd just heard.

"Did you call for me?" he pressed.

She parted her lips to deny it when she remembered whispering his name.

A grin split his wide lips. "You did."

"You should return to Dreagan."

"Come with me."

"No."

His frown returned. "Why? They're good people, and they can help if you're in trouble."

"I'm not the one in trouble. All of *you* are."

"What are you talking about?"

Melisse wished she'd kept her mouth shut. She licked her lips and pushed away from the tree to face him. "You have a lot of power within you. You need to unlock it. Quickly. You and Esther can do a lot together."

Instead of being glad at her words, he became wary and took a step back. "How do you know about Esther and me?"

"I know a lot."

"Apparently."

He was pulling away from her, she could feel it. And while she knew it was for the best, she couldn't seem to let the connection fail. "I'm your friend."

"Are you?" He shook his head. "I'm not so sure. If you were, you'd tell me what you know."

She briefly closed her eyes. "I can't."

"Can't? Or won't?" he demanded.

"Both."

He nodded and glanced away. "Then why did you come?"

Lie. You have *to lie. Say anything but what you really want to tell him.* "I don't know."

"You don't know. Right." He turned on his heel and started to walk away.

Melisse watched him. She even bit her tongue when she wanted to call out his name. He got fifty feet away before she could no longer contain herself. "Henry. Please, stop."

To her shock, he came to a halt. But he didn't turn to face her.

She drew in a deep breath and started toward him. Melisse came to a stop a few feet from him. She reached out her hand, wanting to touch him, but she held back. No one had touched her. Not in . . . so very, very long. She'd forgotten what it felt like.

The fact that she yearned to put her hands on him, to feel his warmth and the hard muscles beneath his skin frightened her. That . . . longing . . . could spell trouble for her.

Could? she asked herself with a snort. *Look where I am. It's already causing me problems.*

"What do you want?" Henry demanded.

She swallowed, trying to find the words. *"You"* was on the tip of her tongue, but she managed to keep that to herself. "No matter what else you believe, I'm your friend."

"You aren't exactly acting like it."

Her gaze lowered to the grass at her feet. "There are things I can't explain now. I might never be able to. I shouldn't even be here, but I came because I wanted to see you."

At that, he slowly turned to face her. "I'm glad you did. I've been thinking about you."

Her heart leapt for joy. It was the worst thing he could've possibly said because it made her want to stay with him forever—even as she knew she couldn't.

"Stay safe, Henry. And stay vigilant. Your powers are just beneath the surface. Trust yourself, and you'll be able to use them."

He reached out for her but dropped his hand before he made contact. "Don't go. Please."

"I'll see you soon," she promised and hurriedly walked away.

CHAPTER TEN

There had to be someone else on the Fae Realm. Cain was sure of it. How else could the shield exist?

"We're supposed to be hiding, remember?" Noreen said as she caught up with him. "Going looking for whoever did this might not be a good idea."

He glanced at her to see her gaze moving around nervously. "It's better to know what might be here than no'."

"It could be Moreann."

Cain gave a half-hearted shrug. "It could be. But do you no' think it's to our advantage to discover if that's the truth? It could be someone else entirely, someone who might be a friend."

"I suppose you're right."

He bit back his smile at her begrudging admittance. They walked onward steadily, if cautiously. It would be better if he could take to the skies and fly over the area to see how large it was. It would certainly take less time than walking, but he wasn't sure Noreen would be up for that yet. She needed more time.

"Why you?" she asked him.

He held back a branch of a shrub for her, then walked through himself. "Why me, what?"

"Why did you come find me, and not another King?"

"I got lucky, I guess," he said with a chuckle. Then he twisted his lips. "I was the one who found your email. Ryder and his mate, Kinsey, hacked the CCTV in the café and found you."

"The cameras," she said to herself with a roll of her eyes.

"It wouldna have mattered. Ryder is a master at hacking all things. You did a good job of concealing your identity, and it would've worked with most anyone else."

"Just not Ryder," Noreen said with regret. "I wish I'd known that."

"Would it have stopped you from sending it to us?"

Her red gaze met his briefly. "I'd been debating telling the Kings something for months. When I finally realized that I needed to do it, I'd planned to go to Dreagan, but I knew that wouldn't work well."

"Why?"

"It's not like the Dark and the Kings have a great relationship," she replied sarcastically.

He grinned. "Point taken."

"Besides, I wanted to keep my identity a secret. I figured all you needed was information, not me."

"So, you came up with the idea of the email."

She sighed heavily. "I thought I'd done enough research on what the humans use, but apparently, I didn't."

"Doona blame yourself. Ryder is just that good."

Noreen shrugged. "It doesn't matter now. And, honestly, I think it would've worked out this way regardless of what I did. I was a fool to think I could keep this away from Moreann and the Others."

"You were no' a fool," he told her. "You were trying

to find a way to do the right thing while keeping yourself safe. Most anyone would've done the same."

She flashed him a grateful smile. "Thank you for saying that. That still doesn't tell me why you came to see me. You found my email, but any of the Kings could've been sent."

"That's true, but since I found the message, I wanted to be the one to see this through."

She nodded but didn't say anything else.

They walked in silence for a few more minutes while his thoughts turned to what she'd told him about the Kings killing her parents. He wasn't sure how to bring it up because he was certain it was a touchy subject. But he needed to know more.

"I'm sorry about your parents."

She didn't look his way as she said, "Thank you."

"I know you probably doona want to talk about it, but I was hoping you'd answer a couple of questions."

Noreen paused to look at some animal that'd disappeared in the foliage, but she still wouldn't look his way. "What do you want to know?"

"The Fae Wars were chaotic, as all wars are. Are you sure it was a King who took your parents' lives and no' another Fae?"

"Positive."

"Who gave you that information?"

"I was there."

His brows snapped together. "You could've only been a child then. Did you really go to the battlefield?"

She halted and drew in a deep breath before turning her head to him. "My parents weren't involved with the war. We were at home when the Dragon King came and scorched our house with his fire."

"But you were no' harmed?"

"I was spared."

Cain shook his head. "I doona see how that's possible. Dragon fire is the hottest thing on our realm. Anything that gets near it is incinerated."

"That's right. There was nothing left of my parents," she stated angrily.

"Were you in the cottage?"

"Of course."

Cain pressed his lips together as he tried to sort out what was missing from the story. "Then you shouldna be alive. The dragon fire should've taken you, as well."

"It didn't, but I was there. I watched as my father looked back at me with terror in his eyes. I will forever remember my mother running toward me, her arms outstretched as I reached for her. She never made it. The flames swallowed her up before she could grab hold of my hand."

"Did you see the dragon?"

"I heard it."

Cain wasn't sure what to make of the story. There was no possible way that Noreen should be alive if a King had breathed dragon fire on the home. None.

Yet, here she stood.

"You don't believe me," she said with a hard look.

Cain lifted one shoulder. "Something doesna make sense. If you were in the home, and everything was destroyed, then you should be dead."

"But I'm not."

"Nay, lass, you are no'."

Her eyes narrowed as she crossed her arms over her chest. "What are you saying? That it wasn't a Dragon King who killed my parents and destroyed my life?"

"All I'm pointing out is that there's no way you would've survived if it had been dragon fire."

"I know what I heard."

"But you didna *see* a dragon?"

She gaped at him. "You think I don't know what you sound like? I do. It didn't matter that we weren't part of the war. The sound of your roars could be heard for miles away from the battle."

"I realize that."

"You still don't believe me." She snorted loudly. "I don't need you to. I know what I heard. I felt the heat of that fire all around me. And I watched my parents turn to dust before my eyes."

"No one should have to endure such a thing," he said softly.

Fury burned in her gaze. "No. They shouldn't."

It made him realize that her coming to the Kings had been a huge step. "You hate us."

Noreen shrugged and turned away, dropping her arms to her sides. "Does it matter?"

He wasn't sure how to respond. Everything that came to mind sounded . . . lame and lacking. Cain stared at her profile. If he were her, he wasn't sure he would've done what she had. She blamed the Kings for her parents' deaths, and she had carried that hatred and loathing around for thousands of years. To put something like that aside took a great deal of effort.

Cain couldn't help but wonder if she had fooled him, if this was all some kind of setup to trap him. But if it was, why would she have told him about her parents? That was something she would've kept to herself so he wouldn't doubt her.

Or maybe it was part of her plan.

Cain ground his teeth together. The questions went around and around in his head. He'd been positive back on Earth that Noreen was telling the truth. Now, even after this new information, what little doubt he had wasn't enough for him to reconsider the mission.

That didn't mean that he wouldn't keep an eye out, though. In all his long years, he'd seen every kind of deception there was. If Noreen thought to fool him, she had another thing coming.

She blew out a loud breath and started walking, letting him know she was tired of waiting. Cain let her get a few steps ahead of him before he followed her. He kept coming back to how she had survived. Either she had massive amounts of magic that could keep dragon fire from burning her—and only a Dragon King had that ability—or it hadn't been a Dragon King who killed her family at all. He was betting on the latter, but until he had proof, there was no use telling that to Noreen.

For the next several hours, they walked in silence. They encountered several animals but didn't see anything that would indicate another being was around. It was a mystery, but Cain knew they'd solve this one sooner rather than later.

It was dusk when they came upon a lake. The blue water sparkled with shades of gold from the setting sun, making the ripples look like diamonds blinking from the waves. It was a particularly stunning sight.

"We'll stay here for the night," Cain said. "There is cover in the trees. I think it's safe for you to use magic to build a fire and whatever else you need."

Her red eyes slid to him. "And what will you be doing?"

His gaze lifted to the darkening sky. "I'm going to figure out how big of an area this is."

"You're going to fly?" she asked in surprise.

"It's the fastest way to see the area and to scout the terrain. No' to mention, if there is someone here, I'll be able to spot them."

"I don't think that's a good idea. You could be seen."

"It's a chance I'm willing to take."

A black brow cocked. "Before I give you the information you want?"

He knew her sarcasm stemmed from earlier. He'd hoped she would get past it, but that kind of pain didn't fade easily, so he didn't hold it against her.

"If you doona want to be alone, then come with me," he offered.

She gave a half-snort/half-laugh. "Right. Because I can fly."

"You can ride on my back."

Her sneer died as she stared at him with a frown. "Are you serious?"

"I wouldna offer if I wasna."

She didn't hide her hesitation.

Cain then said, "You'd be able to get the lay of the land, as well. You might see something that could be important, an observation I might otherwise dismiss. No' to mention, another set of eyes is always good."

"I wouldn't be able to see as far as you."

"You're Fae. You have magic."

She licked her lips, considering his offer. After a moment, she turned away. Cain sighed. He'd thought she might be interested in riding, but perhaps her hatred for the Dragon Kings was too great. He walked to the water and looked at the sun slowly sinking into the horizon.

"All right," she said from behind him. "I'll do it."

He turned and smiled at her. "Good."

CHAPTER ELEVEN

Was she doing the right thing? Noreen's anger was misdirected, she knew that, but she couldn't seem to stop taking it out on Cain. And still, he asked her to go for a ride.

But not just any ride—one atop him while he was in dragon form.

She had immediately wanted to agree, but she paused to think things through. Then she realized there was nothing to think about. She—a Dark Fae—was going to get to ride atop a Dragon King.

And it had nothing to do with sex.

Although, the moment she thought about sitting astride Cain, all she could imagine was seeing him naked and having him fill her. Noreen tried to shut off her thoughts, but her body had already reacted to the mental images, which meant there was no stopping her mind or body now.

She wanted to fan herself as her blood heated, but she fisted her hands instead. After lashing out at Cain, it wouldn't make any sense to him if she suddenly let her desire show. He would think she had lost what little sense she had.

Or . . . perhaps that's exactly what had occurred. After all, she could hardly tell up from down at the moment. Her emotions were all over the place, making her feel as if she had no control—which only made things worse.

The smile he bestowed on her when she agreed to the ride was mesmerizing. Something intense and all too male flashed in his eyes when he looked at her. It left her breathless and . . . needy.

"I take it you've seen us in our true forms, aye?"

Why did that damn Scots brogue sound so fekking sexy on him? Noreen had to think about what he just asked before she nodded. "Yes."

Black brows shot up on his forehead. "Oh? When, if I may ask?"

Was he always so damn polite? Or was that only for her? Really, it didn't matter. Noreen was just trying to find something to anger her so she might stop thinking such lustful thoughts about him. Unfortunately—or maybe fortunately—nothing was working.

He gave her a pointed look, making her realize that she hadn't answered his second question.

She swallowed, finding her mouth dry as a desert. "The Others have been watching the Kings for centuries. I've witnessed a few things, like the fight with the Dark Fae at Dreagan that was recorded. I was also near the Light Castle when the Kings faced off against Usaeil."

At the mention of the former Light Queen, Cain's lips twisted in disgust. "Do you know what happened to her body?"

Noreen gave a nod. "Moreann took it."

Cain's eyes widened. "Is that so? Interesting. Since you've seen us before, you willna be surprised by my size."

Without meaning to, her gaze drifted down his body, pausing between his legs, which caused her nipples to harden. She hastily looked away when she comprehended what she'd done. "I'm ready."

He turned away, and she could've sworn that she heard him chuckle. With the way she was acting, she wouldn't be surprised. She took the opportunity to press against her aching breasts in an effort to get her nipples to return to normal.

But it seemed that wasn't possible with a Dragon King so near, one who also had the ability to make her knees weak with only the sound of his voice and her own thoughts.

"Once you're on, hold tight," he warned her as he looked over his shoulder at her.

"Right."

Their gazes met, and in the next instant, a dragon stood where Cain had been. Noreen took an involuntary step backward at the up close and personal view she had of him. Cain was . . . gigantic.

Shiny scales in a blue so deep they looked almost black met her gaze. She knew the moment her eyes landed on them that she had never seen him before. With a color like Cain's, she never would have forgotten him.

Her heart raced as she took a closer look at him. The deep blue lightened slightly on his underbelly. His talons were razor-sharp. His long tail had a stinger on the end of it, reminding her of a scorpion.

Cain stood as still as a statue, giving her time to take him in. She could feel his eyes on her, but she wasn't ready to look at his face yet. Instead, she lingered on his wings tucked against him. They were the same blue as his scales but appeared leathery.

She looked at the top of his back where she would be sitting and noticed the double row of spines that trailed all the way down to the base of his tail. At least she would have something to hold onto.

Finally, she looked at his face and into the huge pale yellow eyes staring at her. His nostrils flared as he drew in a deep breath. As he blew out, the force of the air lifted her hair.

Cain moved so he was lying down. She knew it was now or never. Either she grabbed hold of the adventure he offered, or she forever remained on the ground, wondering what it was like to be taken for a ride on a Dragon King.

Her life could end tomorrow. She was going to take whatever was offered to her and experience it to its fullest. She gave Cain a smile and walked to his side. She used his front leg to climb up.

It was awkward, and she nearly fell off twice, but she finally managed to get settled. It wasn't until she looked down that she saw how far she was from the ground. And Cain hadn't even spread his wings.

He got to his feet, and she could tell he was being cautious. She held onto the spikes before her, using the ones behind her to lean against.

Cain spread his wings, and an excited thrill went through her. He gave her no warning before he launched himself into the air. The force of it took her breath away. Her hands slipped on the spikes, but thankfully, the ones at her back held her in place. She squeezed her legs as hard as she could to help keep herself steady, but it did little good.

It wasn't long before he leveled out, allowing her a little breathing room so she didn't feel as if she were going to plunge to her death in the next heartbeat. The wind whipped about her, and the sound of his wings beating was a loud whoosh each time. Only then did she draw in a steadying breath and look around.

"Oh, wow," she murmured.

The sight before her was so beautiful, she was at a loss

for words. It was as if this part of the Fae Realm hadn't been touched by war. She knew that wasn't possible, however. Yet, there was no denying that something or someone had gone to a great deal of effort to return this section of the realm to the beauty that had once been here.

Cain remained high in the sky, but anyone who looked up would see him. Noreen felt like they had a target painted on them. Yet she couldn't deny that their vantage point gave them a view they wouldn't otherwise get.

The area within the shield was larger than she had thought possible. No matter how many passes they made, she didn't see any signs of Fae or any other beings besides the animals.

She liked being on top of Cain. It was exhilarating and empowering. The idea that there might be an end to the dragons forever was like a knife to her heart. If she'd had any doubts about her decision to help the Kings before, they were well and truly gone now.

To her regret, she felt Cain begin his descent. She knew their time was up when she saw the lake coming into view. The sun was gone, and the sky was darkening, the stars becoming visible. She wanted to ask him to stay out a little longer. Instead, she held onto him and lifted her face upward to let the wind brush against her.

Before she knew it, Cain had landed. She gingerly dismounted and looked into his eyes. He remained in his true form for a heartbeat longer before he shifted.

Noreen's stomach fluttered at the sight of him nude. Cain was utter perfection. Hard sinew covered every inch of him from his broad shoulders, to his thick arms, washboard stomach, and toned legs.

Her gaze caught on the dragon tattoo on his chest. The red and black ink formed an intricate design of him as a dragon, standing with his head turned to the side and his mouth open, his wings half-spread. The tail ended just below his navel, and she couldn't stop her gaze as it lowered to his cock.

He was semi-hard, but the moment she looked at him, it jutted upward as if straining to get to her.

She didn't even attempt to deny the desire that swelled within her at the sight of him. It had already been there, swirling and tightening. Now, it demanded release.

It demanded *him*.

She raised her gaze to his face. Their eyes clashed. Desire burned in his, leaving her no doubt that he wanted her, too. She was the first to take a tentative step toward him. Once she had, he began to walk. They met halfway, but still didn't touch.

He was right before her, and yet she was afraid to touch him, scared that this was all a dream. But if it were, she never wanted to wake up.

Her heart skipped a beat when his gaze dropped to her mouth. She wanted his kiss, needed it. To taste him, to feel his tongue against hers. She thought about flying through the sky upon his back and knew that being in his arms, having him fill her with his gorgeous cock was going to be just as thrilling, just as breathtaking.

His hands slid to either side of her face as he searched her eyes. His thumbs moved gently across her cheeks. Then his head lowered.

Her eyes shut as his mouth drew near. She waited, her breath locked in her lungs, awaiting the feel of his lips against hers. The moment they touched, she sighed in contentment. His mouth was soft yet insistent. His lips moved over hers with practiced ease.

The instant his tongue slid into her mouth, his arms

went around her, bringing her close. She melted against him, her hands lifting to hold onto him as their tongues danced, heightening the desire in her already heated body.

He deepened the kiss and moaned, making chills race over her skin. She held nothing back, giving as much as he did. One of his hands fisted a handful of her hair while the other pressed against her lower back, bringing her against his arousal. She dug her nails into his skin as she groaned in response.

Then, suddenly, he stepped back, ending the kiss. She tried to get her bearings, but the world was spinning, and the only one who could anchor her was Cain.

"You doona have to," he said in a voice roughed by need. "This isna part of my deal to protect you."

She reached for him, blinking to focus. "Shut up and kiss me."

He didn't need to be told again. The next instant, she was plastered against his body. And this time, the kiss was molten-hot. It scorched her, leaving her body quivering for more. The more he kissed her, the more she wanted his kisses.

Actually, she wanted *all* of him.

This time, she was the one who ended the kiss. When she stepped out of the circle of his arms, she used her magic to remove her clothes, leaving her as naked as he.

"Och, lass," he murmured as his hot gaze raked over her. "You're the most beautiful thing I've ever seen."

There was a smile on her face when she reached for him for another kiss.

CHAPTER TWELVE

The desire was inescapable. It consumed Cain, enveloping him in a cocoon of lust that drowned out everything else. There was only Noreen.

The hunger, the yearning within him was dark and ominous. He knew if he gave in, there would be no turning back. But he didn't care. He had to have her, needed to taste her, hold her.

Claim her.

Cain rested his hands on her hips as she kissed him. Then he slid his hands upward, over the indent of her waist until his thumbs touched the undersides of her breasts. His balls tightened when he felt her hard-tipped nipples against his chest.

Unable to hold off another moment, he cupped her full breasts, one in each hand, and ran his thumbs over her turgid peaks. She gasped and ended the kiss. Her moan, low and throaty as she leaned her head back, made him want to sink into her in that very instant.

Somehow, he managed to stay in control. But it was fast slipping away. He'd never felt such longing, such craving before. He wanted to experience pleasure with her because he knew it would be something spectacular and special.

He drank in her exquisiteness. From her pale skin that felt as soft as silk to the way the moon shone upon her like a spotlight. The silver in her hair glowed in the moonlight like a platinum flame.

She was ice to his fire. Like yin to yang. They shouldn't complement each other, but they did. And he felt it all the way to his soul.

He rolled her nipples between his fingers, his breathing coming faster as her nails sank deeper into his arms. Her mouth was parted, the pulse at her throat rapid and erratic. He ground his aching rod against her and heard her answering moan.

As much as he loved her breasts, he wanted more. He bent his legs and moved his hands below her shapely behind before he lifted her. Her legs came around him at the same time her eyelids rose, and she looked at him. Her eyes had darkened to a deep crimson, the desire so flagrant that her gaze burned with it. It made his heart race knowing that she wanted him as much as he wanted her.

No matter who they were, no matter what sides of the war they were on, passion didn't know or care. They were proof of that.

"Cain," she whispered as her hands caressed his shoulders.

He knelt on one knee and gently laid her on the ground. Right before her back touched the grass, a blanket appeared beneath her. She smiled up at him, letting him know that she had done it.

After shifting to his side while propping himself up on an elbow, his eyes drifted down her amazing body. There was a small patch of black curls on her pubis, but to his delight, her sex was devoid of any hair.

She spread her legs, letting her knees fall open so he could get a good look at her. His cock jumped at the sight before him. But Cain wasn't quite ready.

He ran a hand down her side to her hip and then lower to her thigh, moving all the way down to her calf. She had long, lean legs that he couldn't wait to have wrapped around him as he plunged deep inside her.

His fingers glided slowly up her inner thigh. When he neared her sex, he paused and looked at her face. She was staring at him expectantly. When he didn't move, she lifted her hips, causing her body to touch his hand.

He groaned when he felt her wetness. His hand moved to her sex, cupping it lightly before his fingers found her swollen clit. The moment he began teasing the tiny bud, her body stiffened, and her fingers fisted the blanket.

Knowing she was already on the verge of an orgasm made him smile. He held her on the brink, keeping her teetering on the edge. Her low moans turned to cries of pleasure. She was beautiful. So much so that he could watch her for eternity.

Cain bent and drew a nipple into his mouth. As he suckled, he slid a finger inside her. Her back arched, and she groaned in response. Her wet heat called to him, but he managed to hold himself in check for a little longer.

With his finger still moving inside her, he positioned himself between her legs and put his mouth on her. His tongue swirled around her clit, alternating suckling and swirling the bud.

He knew the moment her climax claimed her. Her body went taut, her mouth open on a silent scream. He watched the ecstasy overtake her as he continued teasing her body, giving her more and more pleasure until she went limp.

Noreen thought she knew what pleasure was. The truth was that she'd had no idea until she was in Cain's arms. He pushed her past boundaries she hadn't known she had, crushing them as he urged her to give more of herself.

And she did it without hesitation.

Her body still pulsed with utter bliss. It felt so good, she wanted another orgasm. But not before she got her fill of his body.

He rose up, smiling at her. When he crawled over her, Noreen pushed him onto his back and straddled him. But she didn't take him into her body. Not yet. First, she wanted to run her hands over that fine form of his.

She flattened her hands on his chest and smoothed them over the wide expanse, feeling the bulge of sinew as she did. The way his gaze watched her with such craving made her grind herself against his cock. It would take nothing to move him inside her, and she wanted that desperately.

But since he had teased her, she was going to do the same to him.

Noreen leaned forward and gave him a long, slow kiss. Then she placed small licks along his neck, over his chest, and down his abdomen. She shimmied lower until she kneeled between his legs. Her gaze lifted to his as she wrapped her fingers around his arousal. His nostrils flared, and his hands clenched into fists, but, otherwise, he didn't move.

She held his gaze as she bent toward his cock and slowly let her lips wrap around the head of him. He hissed in a breath, his hips rising slightly as she took him deeper.

Her hand moved up and down his length as he filled her

mouth. He called her name in a low whisper full of such
desire that it made her stomach flutter.

She intended to make him climax, but her body had
other demands. Noreen released him and moved to strad-
dle him again. He grabbed her around the waist and
flipped her onto her back. In one move, he was inside her.

The feel of him was so intense that she gasped. He filled
her, stretching her as he thrust deep. Then he held still as
if to give them both a moment to relish the feeling of being together.

Then he began to move. He set a steady rhythm that she
matched. She looked down to see him sliding in and out
of her. It was so erotic that it nearly made her climax right
then. She glanced up at him to find him staring at her. Her
gaze became trapped, just as her body was.

She knew in that instant that she would be Cain's for
as long as he wanted her. Without knowing how or why,
she recognized the feel of him. His hands, his mouth, his
tongue. His cock.

And even his soul.

If she believed in destiny, she would think they had
been meant for each other. But she didn't believe.

Did she?

She forgot all about that as his pace increased, sending
her spiraling into pleasure. Desire tightened low in her
belly as he brought her closer to release. She both wanted
it and wanted to hold off to enjoy the moment longer.

Before she could tell him, he thrust harder, deeper, and
she was flung once more into the bliss of orgasm. She
grabbed hold of him, wanting him to feel what she experienced.

She heard her name as if from a great distance. As her
body drummed with the aftershocks of the intense climax,
she realized that he was nearing his own. Noreen forced

her eyes open and saw his neck muscles strain as he thrust faster until his seed poured into her womb.

When his chin dropped to his chest, she pulled him down atop her and held him, wrapping her legs around him the same as her arms. They remained like that for several minutes.

She couldn't believe what she had felt. Nothing before had ever come close to such . . . ecstasy. Sex had always felt good, but nothing like this. This had been mind-blowing, heart-stopping.

Eye-opening.

It had been utterly sublime.

"Wow," she murmured as she caressed her fingers over his back.

"Aye," he whispered. "It certainly was that."

She wanted to stay just as they were, their bodies locked together. They could remain in this place they'd discovered on the Fae Realm, and no one would ever find them. It would be just the two of them. It would be the closest thing to Heaven they could get.

And while it sounded dreamy and perfect, the reality was that it couldn't happen. Cain had obligations to his brethren. And she had an organization to keep running from.

Cain rose up on his hands to look down at her. His smile was gentle and full of an emotion she couldn't name. It would be so easy to let herself have feelings for him, but that would be the stupidest thing she could do.

Or would it?

He'd promised to protect her, but she knew better than anyone that if the Others wanted someone dead, they died. It was simply a matter of time for her. She had told herself she was going to seize the opportunities given to her in the time she had left. Was falling for a Dragon King one of them?

"Damn, lass," he said as he pulled out of her and fell onto his back. To her shock, he rolled her toward him, nestling her against his side with her cheek on his chest. "Something verra special just happened."

"It was, wasn't it?"

"You felt it, too, then?"

She nodded, smiling dreamily. "Did I ever."

"Hmm," he said and blew out a breath. "You should rest. We're not going to be doing much more of that tonight."

Noreen lifted her head to look at him as she laughed. "I should rest? I think you're the one who needs to rest to keep up with me. I had two to your one orgasm."

"That's a fine point. We should even the score," he said with a wicked grin.

She liked this side of him. "Since I seem to climax so easily when you touch me, that might be difficult."

"Is that right?" His grin widened. "I like that. Perhaps I should make sure you have five to my one. Nay. Ten."

Noreen laughed louder as she shook her head. "I don't think that's possible."

"Ah. A challenge, then? I'm up for it."

Her laughter halted as she stared at him wide-eyed. She was about to tell him he didn't need to do that for her when she realized how stupid that would sound.

"I see you like the idea," he said with a satisfied smile. "So do I, lass. So do I."

She laid her head back on his chest and looked at the night sky. "It's too bad we can't stay here forever."

"It's tempting for sure. As tempting as you."

She pressed a kiss to his chest and was surprised when he bussed the top of her head.

"Trust me, Noreen. I've got you."

With a smile on her face, she closed her eyes.

CHAPTER THIRTEEN

Cain stared at the stars above him as he held Noreen in his arms. He thought of her words about them remaining on the realm. A part of him wished they could. Away from war, from hiding who he really was. The temptation was great.

Then there was the Dark herself. Cain wasn't sure what was going on between them, but he knew it felt good. Really, really good. So great that he didn't want it to end—no matter the consequences.

But they couldn't remain on the Fae Realm. He had a duty to his brethren, and he wouldn't leave them to fight the Others alone. They had all endured so much. They would triumph over another enemy together, as well.

Cain turned his head and breathed in the smell of wind and mint from Noreen's hair. She fit against him perfectly, as if her body had been specifically molded to match him as they lay thus.

If only he could focus on them and forget everything else, but he couldn't. It wasn't how he was wired. He had an obligation to fulfill, and he had given the Dark his word that he would protect her. He couldn't do that unless he knew all the facts. And right now, he knew very little.

That's what bothered him the most. His view of the territory within the shield was surprising. He thought there might be a few hundred acres that had somehow been preserved. Yet there were thousands and thousands of acres. He had flown across more land than what Dreagan owned, which meant someone had done this.

But who? Usaeil?

He inwardly snorted at the thought. Usaeil wanted Earth. She had given up on the Fae Realm. She wanted the Fae united and for her to be mated to Constantine—none of which was going to happen. And he was very happy about her not being with Con.

Cain suppressed a shudder at the thought. He wasn't opposed to a King with a Fae. Rhi had been the first. Then there was Shara. His thoughts immediately went to Noreen. Without meaning to, he wondered if she could be his mate. A Dark Fae.

While Shara had been Dark, she'd turned Light. Rhi was Light. Cain couldn't be sure how the other Kings would react to a Dark Fae as his mate. Not that it would matter. If Noreen were his, he wouldn't care what she was.

He held her tighter, images of them making love filling his head. She had been his match in every way. And while he wished his thoughts could stop there, they couldn't.

Noreen was in danger because she wanted to help the Kings. The Others would be coming for her. Everyone at Dreagan was on high-alert because the Others could be near and watching. Still, Cain didn't want the Others targeting Dreagan yet. That's why he had let them see him and Noreen leave. Hopefully, the plan had worked.

The Fae Realm was the perfect place to hide. He'd

believed that before arriving, but now, within the shield, he knew for sure. If they hadn't gone exploring the realm, he would never have felt the barrier or investigated it.

He'd never come to the Fae Realm before. There had never been a need, but that didn't mean he hadn't heard about the complete and utter destruction of it. There wasn't a Fae alive who would've missed this slice of paradise and fought to remain in it.

There were parts within the shield that looked as if the plants and trees had been around for some time, while other sections looked newer. As if the barrier was expanding—or someone was increasing it so that more things could grow.

Moreann's intent seemed to be focused on Earth, but Cain wasn't going to assume that. Still, he couldn't figure out why anyone would want the Fae Realm, other than a Fae. Especially when everything was supposed to be dead and destroyed beyond repair.

The water of the lake gently lapped against the pebble-lined shore. It was soothing. The entire place was calming and peaceful. It reminded him of what Earth had once looked like before the mortals arrived.

No. He wouldn't let his thoughts turn in that direction. That led only to anger and violence. He was well past that now, mainly because he had accepted his fate, even if he might not have forgiven the humans.

For hours, Cain's mind went over and over who could've created such a nirvana. He kept coming back to one person, but it didn't make sense. He kept it to himself as he thought on it some more.

A few hours before dawn, he finally closed his eyes and tried to shut off his mind. He couldn't quite complete the latter task, but he was enjoying his time too much to let it consume him.

Noreen hadn't moved other than to shift her leg higher on his thigh. She slept like the dead, not even twitching when an animal made a loud sound near them. Either she trusted him, or she'd sunk so deeply into slumber that nothing disturbed her. He wanted to believe it was the former, especially since he knew how scared she was of the Others coming for her.

He put his free hand behind his head. If he didn't, he would begin rubbing on her in a way that would lead to him taking her body again. While he desperately wanted that, he also wanted her to sleep. She needed the rest.

Cain hadn't thought about how hard it would be for her to return to the realm. Like she'd said, she had been young, but she also had memories of her time here. It couldn't be easy to see her once beautiful realm in such ruins, but she hadn't complained once. Her need to live outweighed everything else.

That was the smart move. Had she resisted, he would've thought twice about her sincerity. But he did wonder how someone who had been involved with the Others for so long came to realize that they were on the wrong side. Maybe she would tell him. Then again, it didn't really matter. He was just grateful that she'd had the courage to come to them.

A lock of her hair blew across his face. He moved his hand from behind his head and lifted the strands. They were mainly silver with a few black hairs throughout. It was odd how he'd always believed the Dark Fae to be an image of evil because of their red eyes and silver hair. He didn't see Noreen as evil. Perhaps it was because she was willing to help them against the Others. Maybe it was because he was attracted to her. What was obvious was that he saw her differently than he did other Dark.

And since he'd fought enough Dark since they'd

appeared on Earth so long ago, he could say that with certainty. Was there a chance that Noreen could become Light as Shara had? And why was he even thinking about that? He'd had sex with her, that was it.

It had been glorious, hedonistic sex, but it had just been sex.

Liar.

He ignored his subconscious and shifted his mind to other matters as he released her hair because he didn't like the feelings that arose within him when he thought about Noreen. Yet it never entered his mind to turn her over so she wasn't lying on him. He *wanted* her against him.

Period.

Cain blew out a breath and opened his eyes to see the first streaks of red crossing the sky, signaling that the sun was rising. The stillness of the realm was something he had missed on Earth long before the dragons were sent away.

It made him wonder why the Kings hadn't left Earth to go with their dragons. Sure, the realm had been theirs before the mortals came, but it hadn't been the Dragon Kings' since.

This place that he and Noreen had discovered on the Fae Realm made him consider what life might be like if the Kings wiped their hands of Earth, the humans, the Fae, and the Others and walked away to find someplace new to start over. V would be able to call the dragons home, and they could have the world they'd once had.

If their dragons were alive.

Cain loved Earth. It was his home, and he'd never considered leaving before. But he'd also never found a place that came as close to being the paradise Earth had been when it was just the dragons. In a new realm, the Kings would no longer have to be in human form. They could take to the skies as often as they wanted without needing to hide.

He smiled, thinking about it. He shifted his head, wanting to tell Noreen. His gaze landed on her shapely leg, and he realized that many of the Kings were now mated—to humans, and a Fae. No dragon left his mate behind. Ever.

His smile faltered as his grand plan began to fall apart. The mated Kings wouldn't leave their mates, and their mates wouldn't want to leave Earth. And even if the mates did, how would the humans and Fae fit in this new world of dragons that the Kings would create?

They wouldn't. The mates would be isolated and alone.

Cain's mood dampened. The answer had been so simple. If only none of the Kings had taken mates.

Noreen stirred then, her hand moving over his chest as she drew in a deep breath and arched her back. She was the sexiest thing he'd ever held in his arms. His cock hardened just watching her, need thrumming through him fast and fiery.

Her head shifted toward him, and her eyes fluttered open. Crimson irises met his, and then she smiled. He grinned back at her, thinking how beautiful she looked in the morning light.

"Mmmm," she murmured and wrapped her arm across his chest to hold him tight as she buried her face against him. "I like waking up next to you."

"I think you should do it every morning."

Her eyes snapped to his, searching his face to see if he was jesting. "You'd like that?"

"I doona say things I doona mean. What about you? Would you want that?"

She swallowed and nodded. "I think I'd like it very much."

He wasn't sure what had just transpired or why he'd told her what he had, but it felt good. All of it.

"Did you sleep at all?" she asked.

Cain shook his head. "It was nice to see that you did."

"I haven't slept that good in weeks."

He'd thought just that, and his chest puffed out in pride that she felt safe with him. "You didna move all night."

"I think it's this place."

And . . . his inflated ego was busted just like that.

"Although," she said as she once more shifted her head to look at him, "I think it really had to do with you."

His arm tightened around her. "Rest as much and for as long as you need."

"I'm surprised you aren't asking me for the information on the Others."

In fact, he had forgotten that little tidbit until she mentioned it. "I figure you'll tell me when you're ready."

She placed a kiss on his pec and sat up, drawing her legs up to her chest and wrapping her arms around them as she did. He put his hand on her back while she looked out over the lake. Noreen was silent for several minutes before she pulled in a deep breath.

"The Others consists of six individuals. A Dark and Light Fae, a *mie* and *drough* from Earth, and a *mie* and *drough* from the Druid Realm. Moreann is the Empress of the Druids. She is the one who saw Earth and wanted it. She is the one who found Usaeil and first convinced the Fae to join her."

Cain frowned as several questions entered his mind all at once. "Is Moreann immortal? She has to be in order to live that long. But how can that be if she's simply a Druid?"

"The Druids you know from Earth aren't like the Druids from where Moreann comes from." Noreen looked over her shoulder at him. "But as powerful as Moreann and the Druids on that realm are, the magic there is fading rapidly. She was the first to realize why so many were born without magic on their realm."

"The magic of the realm couldna continue to give," he guessed.

Noreen looked away as she nodded. "That's when Moreann began looking for another place. She found Earth and set her sights on it when she realized how powerful the dragons were."

Cain sat up as he let that sink in. "It all makes sense now. She took her people without magic and brought them to Earth. She knew that if there was enough magic on our realm, that it would eventually make its way to the humans. And it did. They became Druids."

"That's when she tried to find a way to take your world from you, but she couldn't because she wasn't strong enough."

"So, she went looking for someone who could join her."

Noreen met his gaze. "She didn't have to look far to find our realm and see our war. We also needed a place to go, and she knew that. She seized the opportunity and created a bond with Usaeil that began it all."

CHAPTER FOURTEEN

"Why Usaeil first?"

Noreen shrugged at Cain's question. "Because Moreann recognized her power. Usaeil had just taken over as Queen of the Light."

"Did Moreann know that Usaeil had her family killed?" he asked.

"She might have. I didn't find that out until just recently, though it explains a lot about Usaeil."

Cain's deep green eyes slid from her to the blue waters of the lake. "I doubt Usaeil would've given up that kind of information, no matter who she aligned with. Usaeil and Moreann would've seen the possibilities each brought to the table. I can see why they teamed up. So, Usaeil was the original Light Fae."

"Actually, Usaeil was the Dark."

Cain's head swung back to her. "Aye, I suppose she would've been. Do you know who the Light was?"

Noreen swallowed, unable to meet his gaze. "I do."

"Are they still alive?"

"No."

"I get the feeling you doona want to tell me who it was."

She sighed and shook her head. "I really don't."

"Why?"

"Because it isn't my part to tell." She saw him frown from the corner of her eye.

Cain made a sound in the back of his throat. "What is that supposed to mean? The person is dead, so it shouldna matter if you give me their name."

"But it does."

"Why?"

There was no getting around it. If she didn't tell him something, he would keep pressing. "Because they're related to someone you know."

Cain's brow furrowed deeper. Then, suddenly, his face went slack. "Shite. It's someone connected to Rhi."

Noreen briefly closed her eyes. Then she met his gaze and nodded.

"Fuck me," he murmured. "That explains why she acted so weird in Iceland and after. There was a huge wall of rock that had Light and Dark Fae writing on it, as well as Druid text. Our magic allows us to understand and read different languages. Still, neither V nor Roman got around to the Fae side where Rhi was. There was something there about this person, right?"

"There was. A name."

Cain ran a hand down his face. "I doona know what to say. Rhi never told us she knew someone who was a part of the Others."

"I think it's because she didn't know until Iceland."

"I'd like to think so, but I would've thought she would tell us."

Noreen rolled her eyes. "Seriously? Did you just say that? Knowing how everyone feels about the Others, why would Rhi give you a name that connects them to her?"

"We know her. We would've believed her."

Noreen shot him a flat look. "At first, perhaps. Then you would've thought about it. After that, when something came up, you would've wondered if she was part of it, or if the Others had gotten to her and turned her."

Cain's lips twisted in regret. "You're probably right."

"Usaeil was the first to join Moreann. I don't know how they got the Light Fae to be a part of it."

"I gather this person was high-ranking?"

"Very. They held a lot of influence. When I first realized who it was, I was surprised. They weren't someone I would've thought would join the group. But for some reason, they did."

Cain leaned back on his hands. "And kept it from Rhi."

"Once the Fae were on board, Moreann brought on her *drough*."

"On Earth, the *mie* and *drough* doona associate with each other."

Noreen lifted a shoulder in a shrug. "The Light and Dark Fae don't really either, but there are a few instances where it happens."

"Have you been to Moreann's planet?"

"She won't even tell us where it is."

Cain made a face. "Why does that no' surprise me?"

Noreen raised her brows and pressed her lips together. "Those four combined their magic and used it against your kind, but it did nothing."

"Nothing?" Cain repeated in surprise.

"Moreann says it's because the group needed six, but I believe it's because the Druids from Earth brought magic from your realm. Without that, I don't think the Others would've been able to harm you."

Cain climbed to his feet and walked to the edge of the lake. He stood with his arms folded over his chest for a long while. Finally, he said, "One more reason why we never should've allowed the mortals to remain."

She rose and walked to stand beside him. They had yet to put any clothes on, and she liked that. "We lost our home because of our stupidity. You lost yours because you did something right. You gave those who needed a home a place to put down roots. And despite what happened, you did it again for us."

"I lay there last night with you in my arms, thinking how much the quiet and stillness of this realm reminded me of Earth before the mortals arrived. I kept thinking we should just leave our realm and find somewhere else to go."

"What of the mates?" Noreen asked.

He briefly looked at her. "I didna think of them at first. I was only thinking of being free once more to be who I am."

That wasn't something she understood, because the Fae didn't hide themselves unless they wished to. The Dragon Kings didn't have a choice.

"I'm sorry," she said and put her hand on his arm. "Some might say your kind have been dealt this hand because you deserved it. I think it happened because only the Dragon Kings are strong enough to come out of it on top."

"I used to think that, as well," he admitted as he dropped his arms to his sides. He blew out a frustrated breath and shook his head. "We doona know where our dragons are. We doona even know if they're still alive. And now, we can no' leave Earth because of the mates. How can we move forward? We will forever be hiding because we can no' call the dragons home. And we can no' go to them."

"There has to be a compromise."

"It's a nice thought, but the reality is what it is." He turned his head to her and forced a smile. "I've come to accept that."

She made a disbelieving sound. "No, you haven't. I see it in your eyes. You need to be free as you were yesterday. So, go be a dragon. Spend the day flying in the sun."

His lips turned up in a rueful smile. "It's a nice thought, but I can no'."

"Sure you can. I won't tell you anything else unless you spend at least two hours in the sky," she stated, her chin raised.

This time, he chuckled and reached for her, pulling her against him. "Nice try. Will you finish your story?"

"There isn't much left to say. The Others had to wait for the mortals to gain enough magic to become Druids on Earth. Then, Moreann recruited one from each sect."

"Good and bad Druids and Fae," Cain murmured. "A mix of magic few would think to try. And it worked."

Noreen shrugged and looked up at him. "Yes."

"And each time a member died, they were replaced?"

"There are always six."

He was silent for a full minute before he asked, "And how did the Others know what traps to set or actions to take for things that would happen millions of years in the future?"

"That, I don't know. It isn't something anyone talks about, and the one time I asked Moreann about it, she cut me off before I could finish. Some Druids can see the future, as you well know."

Cain rubbed his hand down her back. "Aye, that is a possibility, but I think it's something more. The fact that none of you know how Moreann and the original Others set everything up has me concerned. Moreann is hiding something, and people only do that when whatever they want hidden can be used against them."

Noreen suddenly had a thought. She moved out of his arms to stand before him, grinning. "You forget, there is one other person from the original group who is still alive."

"Usaeil."

"Exactly," Noreen said. "We need to find her."

Cain wrinkled his nose. "I doona think she'll willingly tell us anything."

"Moreann took her body," Noreen pointed out. "Usaeil might have found a way to stay alive, but before she could wake, Moreann swooped in. I know Moreann has been furious with Usaeil for a while for her actions regarding Con and the Dragon Kings."

Cain's green eyes narrowed on her. "If Usaeil was the original Dark Fae, then how did you come to the group since there's only supposed to be six?"

Noreen bit her lip and glanced at the ground. "My involvement did not come about in the usual way. Moreann found me after my parents were killed. She took me in and gave me a home."

"Bloody hell. I thought you said you didna go to her planet?"

"We didn't. She kept me on Earth. She told me everything because she said I would be joining the group eventually. She wanted me to take Usaeil's place, but she couldn't get rid of Usaeil. It has something to do with a magical pact they made. Really, I'm part of the Others, but like an . . . alternate."

"Are there others like you?"

She shook her head. "It's just me and those who want to join. When Usaeil went and did her own thing, I stepped into her role and became a full-fledged member. Usaeil was so preoccupied that she didn't know or care, which is exactly what Moreann hoped for."

Cain ran a hand over his mouth and jaw. "I knew the Others wouldna let you go easily, but I didna know this other bit. You've betrayed Moreann twice. No' just as someone part of the Others, but as someone she raised as her own child."

"Now do you understand why this decision was so difficult?"

"Aye, lass, I do." He leaned forward and placed a kiss on her forehead. "So, the group has seven members now?"

"Technically, Usaeil is still a part of the group, so yes. But Moreann has cut her out. If Usaeil wants back in, Moreann has to allow it."

Cain's eyes brightened. "That's interesting news. Perhaps the two of them can go at it and save us all some trouble."

"That would be nice. But Moreann clearly put Usaeil somewhere and hasn't told anyone."

"Oh, Usaeil is nothing if no' determined. She'll find a way to get free. And perhaps that's just what we need. If Usaeil is angry enough, we willna even have to get her to attack Moreann. She'll do it on her own."

Noreen winced at the thought. "Moreann is powerful. More so than most realize. She keeps her magic contained so others don't realize it. They underestimate her."

"Something we willna do, but she's making a mistake regarding the Dragon Kings. And you."

He took her hands in his and pulled her against him. Noreen liked how affectionate Cain was. She pressed her cheek against his chest as he held her. "You make it all sound so easy."

"Because it will be."

"There's still much I have to tell you." She leaned back and met his gaze. "And we should start now."

CHAPTER FIFTEEN

Con wasn't quite right. Ulrik had sensed it from the moment his friend had returned from his prolonged stay with Usaeil. Though each time Ulrik asked him about it, Con replied that everything was fine.

The one thing Ulrik knew was that Constantine was anything *but* fine.

"You look concerned," Dmitri said as he walked up.

Ulrik glanced into azure eyes and shrugged. "It might be nothing."

"It's something all right. You've been watching Con for weeks now. I think it's time you told me what's going through your mind."

Ulrik's gaze was pulled from Con, who was on his way up the stairs to the side door of the manor. A moment later, Henry stalked through it, looking angry and irritated, before disappearing into the conservatory and through the door that led into the mountain.

"Seems Con isna the only one with something going on," Dmitri stated.

Ulrik stared at Henry long after the mortal was gone. He knew Con had spoken to Henry several times, trying to nudge the human in the right direction of the weapon without telling Henry anything specific.

The only reason Ulrik knew what the weapon happened to be was because he'd gotten into Con's mountain and saw it. It was a secret Ulrik didn't like to keep, but he understood why he had to. Just as he knew why Con had refused to tell any of them about it before—and even after—the other Kings learned there was even such a weapon on the property.

"Your silence isna easing my worry."

Ulrik had forgotten that Dmitri was beside him. He faced the King of Whites. "What have you noticed about Con?"

"That he's quieter than usual. That doesna seem possible since he's always kept to himself, but now it feels as if he's distancing himself more than ever."

Ulrik drew in a breath, Dmitri's words adding to the worry and disquiet he already felt. "Aye. I've seen it, as well."

"He's no' talking to you?" Dmitri asked in surprise.

"Whatever is going on, he's keeping to himself."

"Damn," Dmitri mumbled and ran a hand down his face. "This isna good. No' good at all. We need to find out what's going on."

Ulrik had a good idea exactly what it could be, but the moment he brought it up, he feared Con might very well explode. Then again, maybe that's exactly what his friend needed.

"How is Faith?" Ulrik asked to change the subject.

Dmitri's face said he knew exactly what Ulrik had done. "She's fine, though she's worried about Claire. All the mates are."

As if they didn't have enough on their plate, Usaeil—the raging bitch—had to make sure that Claire became pregnant with V's child. It was a blessing, but also a curse since no human/Dragon King coupling had led to a live birth.

Each day the babe lived was one that Claire and V celebrated, all while holding their breaths for the inevitable.

"And you? How are you?"

Ulrik started at the question. He frowned while shrugging. "I'm fine."

"Right," Dmitri said with a snort. "Just as Con and Henry are fine. Do you even know what that means?"

Ulrik rolled his eyes. "You do realize that I've watched the *Italian Job*, too? It means freaked out, insecure, neurotic, and emotional."

"Exactly. You know it's horse shite when Con tells you he's fine, so doona give me the same line."

"Fair enough." Ulrik blew out a breath. "Con is the glue that holds us all together. If he falls apart, then so do we."

"Then we make sure he doesna fall apart."

"There's only one person who can fix him now."

Dmitri grimaced. "I admit that you're probably right, but you can no' go there with Con. None of us has been able to, not since he let her go."

"For us." Ulrik couldn't imagine the pain Con had experienced. The mere thought of letting Eilish go was enough to bring Ulrik to his knees. If he lost her for whatever reason, it would be like ripping his heart out of his chest.

And Con had let his mate go freely. After their dragons left, Con had been the first of them to fall in love. Ulrik had been banished from Dreagan then, but he'd known about the affair all the same.

He'd been insanely jealous at the time. Ulrik might also have rejoiced when the affair was over. At least, he had back then. Now that Ulrik had a mate of his own, he understood the depths to which Con had plummeted after it was over.

Ulrik didn't know how Con had survived. Actually, he did. Con had turned his attention to Dreagan and the Dragon Kings. It was the only reason Con hadn't sunk into a despair so great that he couldn't come back from it.

Yet, that's the exact road Con was on now, though the King of Kings probably didn't even realize it.

"None of us would've begrudged him love," Dmitri said into the silence.

"Aye, we would have. It would've happened over time, and he realized that."

"But look what it's done to him."

Ulrik looked to the stairs leading up to Con's office. "I think he suffers more than any of us know."

"He can fix it."

"Can he?"

Dmitri sighed loudly. "Maybe no'."

"I doona want to say that Con is a lost cause, but he verra well may be. Though, whatever is wrong, he needs to get it sorted quickly before we go to war with the Others."

"Unless Cain and this Dark he's with can help us."

Ulrik thought about what Con had recently informed them of as he returned his gaze to Dmitri. "If Cain trusts Noreen, then there is a chance. The problem is that now that the Others know the two of them are together, they'll change whatever plans they made."

"Perhaps no' all of them," Dmitri pointed out. "There are some things that might have been put in place years before, like my White on Fair Isle."

"And what occurred in Iceland."

"Precisely."

Ulrik considered that for a moment. "Although, if Noreen knows all those secrets, Moreann might think it more prudent to halt whatever might be happening next to no' only prove Noreen untrustworthy, but also make us doubt anything she tells us."

"I could see that, but I also think that Moreann wants us gone too badly to stop something that has the opportunity to truly set us back on our heels."

"Good point."

Dmitri jerked his chin to the conservatory. "Do you want me to talk to Henry?"

"He's got his own issues with being the JusticeBringer, as well as being determined to find the weapon."

"Do you think he will find it before it lands in the hands of one of our enemies?"

Based on what little Ulrik had gleaned from Con, that was a distinct possibility. "Aye, I think he has a chance."

"You've no' spoken about Rhi."

Ulrik shrugged and crossed his arms over his chest. "What is there to say? She's gone, and likely forever. If Phelan couldna find her, and she considers him a brother, I'm no' sure anyone can. Usaeil killing Balladyn was the last straw for her, I believe."

"She doesna even know yet that Usaeil is alive."

"That might be a good thing. You know how volatile her temper is on a good day. With her emotions all over the place as they are now, she could well destroy this planet."

Dmitri shook his head. "Rhi wouldna do that."

"Think of everything Usaeil has done to her. In an effort to wipe out Usaeil for good, Rhi just might."

"I still doona think she has it in her. We're her friends. Has Rhys tried calling for her?"

Ulrik knew there was one who might get her attention, but he wouldn't do it. Ulrik knew that for sure. "Aye. We all have."

"No' all of us," Dmitri replied angrily.

"If he wanted to bring her here, then he'd call for her. He hasna. That should tell us something."

Dmitri's lips twisted in a sneer. "That he's an imbecile."

"I can no' argue with that." Ulrik dropped his arms and blew out a ragged breath. "I'm going to try and talk to Con again."

"Good luck," Dmitri called as Ulrik walked away.

The entire trek up the stairs, Ulrik thought about what he would say to his old friend, but even when he knocked on the door, he still hadn't come up with anything.

"Enter," came Con's deep voice through the door.

Ulrik walked inside and shut the door behind him. He found Con staring out his office window with his hands in the pockets of his dress slacks, which was becoming the norm of late. On the large desk sat a small stack of files that Con usually dealt with immediately instead of letting them pile up.

"I know what you've come to say," Con stated without turning around.

Ulrik's brows rose. "Do you?"

"You think something's wrong with me."

"There is."

A beat of silence passed before Con said, "Aye. There is."

Ulrik couldn't believe he'd admitted it. Instead of pressuring Con about it, Ulrik let the silence lengthen to give his friend additional time to say more. It didn't matter that Ulrik couldn't see Con's face because Con had the innate ability to hide whatever he was thinking and feeling.

"I thought I could handle Usaeil on my own," Con finally said. "I knew beginning an affair with her was dangerous, but I was confident in my ability to control her. I underestimated her power and her strength. I put all of you in danger to get information from Usaeil, and even in that, I got verra little. Cain is going to get what I couldna."

"We survived the short time without you," Ulrik said. "We all knew thàt Usaeil couldna hold you unless you wanted to stay."

"I put Claire and the other mates in jeopardy. They could've died. All because I thought I knew it all."

Ulrik narrowed his gaze at his old friend. "Is this what's wrong with you? Is this why you're acting so weird? Because your plan didna come to fruition as you wished?"

"Of course, no'." Con slowly turned around. "But it highlighted a bigger realization that I've no' wanted to admit."

"And what's that?"

"That perhaps I shouldna be King of Dragon Kings any longer. That I've been the leader for too long."

Ulrik snorted derisively. "Oh, please. We've all been Kings for too long. It's only been made worse by the fact that we doona have our dragons with us."

"Maybe you were right when you were fighting us. My time has passed."

Ulrik took two steps closer to him and sliced his hand through the air furiously. "Stop this nonsense right now. You've held everything together for millennia, and you'll continue to do so because you were chosen as the King of Kings. Look at everything you've done for us."

"And look what I did *to* us."

"If you're referring to the mortals, we all agreed to protect them when they first came."

Con glanced at the ground. "I knew you were right in wanting to rid our realm of them, but I stood against you."

"Which was the right thing to do. My anger clouded my judgment."

"Maybe," Con said and turned back to look out the window once more.

Ulrik started to walk around the desk when he saw the red journal beneath the stack of files. Con had tried to hide it, but Ulrik knew what it was. Con only brought them out when he wrote about his mate and the love he still held for her.

No matter what idiocy came out of Con's mouth, Ulrik now understood the root of it. His friend was lonely—and hurting. He needed his mate.

If only there was a way to bring her back.

CHAPTER SIXTEEN

Fae Realm

Cain couldn't remember the last time he'd spent the day naked. Neither he nor Noreen bothered to put their clothes back on as they walked along the lake and even swam in the waters while she went into detail about the Others.

"Moreann's counterpart is the most powerful *drough* on their realm. In fact, he and Moreann clashed several times when he believed he had what it took to become emperor."

Cain took her hand as they exited the water so the sun could dry them as they lay on the blanket. "She rules the entire planet?"

"Yep. She has something akin to sheriffs who oversee portions of land and report to her, but she is the one everyone answers to," Noreen explained.

"Tell me about Brian."

Her lips twisted in distaste. "He's a nincompoop. I honestly don't know why Moreann chose him."

"She alone decides who comes onto the Others? There isna a vote?"

Noreen laughed at his question. "She's used to making

decisions for an entire planet, she's not about to let a group of six dictate anything."

"Hmm. What do you think led her to accept Brian? And when did he come on?"

"He's been with the Others for about two hundred years longer than I have. He's a follower, which she likes. But Brian is also a true believer. He detests the Dragon Kings and wants Earth for the Fae."

Cain gave her a flat look. "He does realize that Moreann isna going to share the realm with the Fae, right?"

"One of the promises she made to Usaeil was that the Druids and Fae would share the realm. It was said during the magic that bound them, so Moreann can't get out of it."

"Oh, I bet she's found a way."

Noreen's red eyes grew troubled as her brow furrowed. "There's no way to get out of such a bond."

"Someone like her doesna remain empress for so long without knowing her way around things such as that. She went to a lot of trouble to have Earth, and she doesna seem like the kind who shares anything."

"I have to admit, you have a point there." Noreen lay on her back and linked her hands beneath her wet hair as she looked at the sky.

His body heated for her, but he didn't act on it, not while they were still talking. There was much he had yet to learn about the Others. The tiniest detail could be the thing that gave the Kings an advantage that led to a win over the group.

Cain turned on his side and rested on his forearm while staring at Noreen's gorgeous body. "And the Druids from Earth?"

"Both women. They have a decent amount of magic,

but nothing I'd consider powerful. Compared to the Druids who have already served in the group, these females have just a smidgen of power."

"Who are they?"

"One is from some island near South America. Another is a *mie* from Turkey. She's very self-righteous in wanting her people to have the realm."

He made a sound in the back of his throat. "That was my next question. How does Moreann convince the Druids from Earth to join her?"

"She shows them what happened between the Kings and the humans."

Cain stilled, ire coiling through him. "Does she now? And does she show the *entire* truth?"

Noreen's head turned to him as her brows drew together. "What does that mean? I, myself, have seen what happened, but you make it sound as if she left something out."

Instead of telling the story, Cain said, "Tell me what you saw."

"Well," the Dark said as she rolled onto her side and propped her head up with her hand, "Moreann was there. She paid regular visits to your realm once she put the mortals there to see how things progressed."

"Like she was waiting for something to happen?"

Noreen's face lined with remorse. "Now that you say it like that, that's probably exactly what she did."

"Go on," he urged.

"As best as I can explain it, the way Moreann shows it is very much like a movie. It shows the mortals arrival, and the Kings shifting into human form."

"Which, by the way, was the first time we ever did that. It was a way to communicate with the humans."

"Oh," she murmured. "I didn't know that."

There was probably a lot more she didn't know, but Cain once more bit his tongue to remain quiet.

"The imagery moved quickly to show the Kings accepting the humans and giving them land. It seemed as if you did so willingly. Did you?"

"Aye. We all agreed as one that because the humans didna have magic, we would allow them to remain and protect them. Each King gave up land from their clan and gave it to the mortals so they could have a place to stay. Did you also see us helping them build their shelters?"

"Actually, I did," she said with a smile. "I was surprised by that. The images once more moved fast through several years."

"Decades, actually," he corrected.

She gave a nod, her red eyes holding his. "Some Kings took mortals as lovers."

"Many did."

"Did you?"

He didn't hesitate to tell her the truth. "Aye."

Noreen's gaze darted away as she plucked at the blanket. "Then, the images focused on one Dragon King—Ulrik. He also took a human as his lover, but when she wanted to end it, he wouldn't let her. Ulrik's uncle then stepped in and helped her."

Cain sat up. Hearing the lies was almost too much. He wanted to interrupt Noreen and tell her the truth, but he remained quiet.

Noreen paused as her gaze returned to him. She slowly sat up and crossed her legs as she faced him. "The next set of images were of the Dragon Kings hunting down the female and killing her. Then Ulrik began attacking the mortals and killing them, starting the war between your species. The only part I didn't believe was where it showed the humans beating the Kings and the dragons being sent away."

"Is that all? Did she show you any more?"

"Only how the mortals prospered once the dragons were gone and the Kings went into hiding. By the tightness of your face, I take it you don't like that she showed others that?"

He shrugged, trying to control the anger in his voice. "She can show the entire universe for all I care, but she should show the truth."

"What did she get wrong?"

"Just about all of it. I could tell you, but would it do any good? You have no reason to believe my words. Besides, you could say my side of it is colored because I was part of it. No doubt Moreann has told others since she was a third-party bystander, she has no sides to take."

Noreen swallowed and wrinkled her nose. "Actually, she said something very similar to that."

"You know it's a lie, right? She has a verra big stake in things. Surely, others have seen that, as well? She brought the mortals to our realm and placed them there to see what we would do."

"I realize that. I'm not sure others have come to that conclusion, however."

Cain got to his feet and walked a few paces away. It had been eons since he'd been this irate. He knew the Kings had made some bad decisions and mistakes along the way, but if someone was going to show their story, then they'd damn well better get it right.

He didn't appreciate being put in such a bad light. Then again, wasn't that what villains did to their enemies? Moreann made sure that anyone she brought to the Others would think the Kings the worst of the worst. Hell, if he'd been in that situation, he might have, as well.

Though he'd like to think he was smart enough to ask questions instead of taking anyone at their word, regardless of what was shown to him. Anything could be manipulated, and whatever it was that Moreann had shown Noreen and the others was most definitely engineered to paint the Kings as the enemy.

"I'm sorry."

He closed his eyes at the sound of Noreen's voice behind him. He turned to her and forced his lips to relax enough to give her a small smile. "It isna your fault."

"I didn't stop to think that what I was telling you might hurt you. And I want to hear your side."

Cain shook his head. "It doesna matter. It's in the past. I doona need to convince you to help us. You came to us on your own."

"True, but that doesn't mean I don't want to know the truth."

"I've tried no' to hold onto the past. Your words shouldna have upset me so."

She cut him a dark look. "Cain, stop being an arse. What happened changed your world forever. Regardless of specifics, the dragons were sent away. You lost your people. That leaves a massive scar. And I don't care how many times you tell yourself to let it go, that wound will always be there."

He couldn't deny her words.

"I want to know the story from your perspective," she said in a soft voice.

"It will be my word against Moreann's."

"Not necessarily." The Fae licked her lips and shifted nervously. "I have . . . well, the thing is, if a person allows me, I can link with their mind and see whatever memory they want to show me."

Cain's brows shot up. "That's one hell of a power. Do you use it often?"

"Rarely. It takes a lot out of me, but this is one time where I think it's important. It won't be your words I hear. I will get to see everything as you lived it."

"A person can alter their memories if they try hard enough."

She laughed softly. "I might think that of others, but not of you."

The idea of telling her had been hard enough. But now Noreen was asking him to open his mind and replay the entire horrible experience.

Noreen took his hands in hers and pleaded, "Please."

He searched her eyes, wondering why he was so willing to do whatever she asked. It didn't matter what she believed, and yet, he wanted her to know that Moreann had lied. It was important, though he wasn't exactly sure *why*.

"I will only be able to see what you show me," she told him. "I can't go searching through your mind for anything else."

He would make sure she couldn't, but he didn't tell her that. Cain looked down at their hands. The fact that she wanted to know his side was something. She could've simply accepted the fact that he'd said Moreann got things wrong.

But he was coming to learn that wasn't Noreen.

He lifted his gaze to her face and nodded. "All right."

CHAPTER SEVENTEEN

She couldn't believe Cain had agreed. Noreen swallowed and pushed down a moment of panic at the thought of entering his memories. She hadn't lied. She would only be able to witness what he allowed her to see.

Noreen briefly lowered her eyes to their clasped hands. His was so very large that they dwarfed hers. She thought about him in his true form and shivered at the power she knew he possessed. If any Fae—Light or Dark—had ever had anything resembling such mastery, they wouldn't have hesitated to use it to dominate one and all.

Yet the Dragon Kings had done the opposite. They had given up their realm because of a promise. They had lost nearly everything simply because they were honorable beings.

And now, they were being threatened again. This time by a force that had the potential to wipe the Kings out for good.

"Lass?"

She forced her lips to relax and curve upward in a grin. "I'm just thinking about seeing you as a dragon."

Cain's green eyes darkened as he gave her a seductive grin. "Like it, did you?"

"Oh, yeah. Very much."

His fingers tightened on her hands. "What are you worried about?"

"What do you mean?"

He lifted a black brow and shot her a dry look. "Your hesitation says it all."

Noreen took a deep breath and gave a little shake of her head as she glanced away. "It's just that I've never done this with a Dragon King."

"Good. I'll be your first. And, hopefully, your last."

"I don't think any other King would even contemplate allowing me into their memories."

"They doona know you like I do."

Another shiver went down her spine, and this one had nothing to do with his magic and everything to do with the way he'd brought her such ecstasy.

"Stop looking at me like that, or my story will have to wait," he warned her.

"Right." She cleared her throat and emptied her mind of the carnal thoughts about Cain. Noreen closed her eyes. Her magic was specialized, but she wasn't powerful enough to enter someone's memories without touching them. She needed that connection to ground herself and the other person.

Her magic ran down her arms and through her palms, then wrapped around Cain's arms before moving to his entire body. She heard his small gasp of surprise the instant her magic touched him, and it made her smile inwardly. It had been a sound of pleasure, not one of disapproval.

"I trust you."

His words warmed her heart. Never in all her years had she ever imagined that a Dragon King would say such a thing to her. Noreen moved a step closer to Cain while keeping her eyes closed. She feared that if she looked at him, she would forget about her magic and give in to the desires of her body.

Noreen concentrated on her gift. Many Fae had to use spells to even attempt what she was doing, but it came naturally to her. She didn't know why or how, and no one other than Cain knew she could even attempt such a feat. She hadn't even told Moreann.

Since Cain was expecting her, she didn't need to sneak around to try and get into his mind. It was like he'd left a door open for her. The moment she stepped through, her breath lodged in her chest at the beauty she gazed upon.

The Earth was alive with magic. There was so much of it that even Noreen could sense it easily. There was much she wanted to look at, like the thick foliage of the jungle that surrounded her, but she wasn't in control. Cain was. This was his memory.

She might be looking through his eyes in a way, but she was merely a passenger, witnessing and hearing everything that had taken place. A smile pulled at her lips when Cain jumped into the air and began to fly. She was able to see through his eyes to the ground below. Moreann had cautioned her that dragon senses were heightened, but truly getting a glimpse of Cain's vivid eyesight was something altogether different.

The sheer distance he could see—and so clearly— boggled her mind. He took a deep breath, and she was able to smell the coming rain and feel the electrical currents of the lightning that flashed behind him.

Noreen had never wished to be anything other than a Fae, but that was changing quickly with this exercise. A dragon had a perspective that altered everything.

As Cain's memory continued, she found herself gathering with other Dragon Kings before they landed behind a gold dragon that, thanks to Cain, she knew was Constantine. Before Con stood a group of humans, huddled together in fear.

The moment all the Kings were together, they shifted for the first time. Noreen gasped at the pain that ripped through Cain's body and hers. Cain ignored it, his gaze on the mortals. Noreen's stomach rebelled at the agony of the shift, but she fought against it to listen to what was being said.

The humans were the first to speak. A man in his early sixties hesitantly stepped away from the others. Cain didn't understand the words at first, but within a few seconds, his magic translated it for him.

It was just something else that impressed Noreen. When Cain glanced at the other Kings, she saw all of them holding swords. It took her a moment to realize that Cain also held one. But the swords weren't the only things the Kings now had. There were tattoos on each, as well. Each one was as different as the King who wore it, but all were done in a red and black mix of ink that wasn't natural.

Before she knew it, the Kings all vowed to protect the mortals. In a flurry of images, she found herself once more back in the jungle with Cain, informing his navy dragons what was going on and relaying the information about the land that was being given to the humans. His clan wasn't thrilled, but none disobeyed him. The one thing Noreen felt was Cain's uncertainty about what the arrival of the new species meant for not only the dragons but also the realm.

For the next few minutes, she was able to see how adaptive the dragons were with their new neighbors. The humans had more trouble. Upon their arrival, they knew their names, but nothing else. Not where they came from, nor how they had gotten there.

The Kings had to teach them how to hunt and prepare food. The Kings showed them how to build structures to keep themselves warm and dry. They even showed them how to get fire and make weapons.

Noreen was flabbergasted at the extreme measures the Kings went to in order to give the humans a chance at survival. Weeks turned to months, and months to years. With each cycle that passed, the humans bore more children and asked for more land—and the Kings gave it to them.

Cain never hesitated to protect the mortals on his land, but he never stopped being suspicious of them either. While he had told her that he'd taken a human to his bed, she found herself wanting to look away when one caught his interest. Thankfully, Cain didn't finish that memory. He skipped ahead to a meeting of the Dragon Kings.

She stood in awe as they spoke through the link in their minds, each voice different. Her amazement faded as she began to focus on the words and comprehended that they had been called by Con because the mortals were hunting the smaller dragons for food.

Cain didn't voice his opinion on how to handle the situation, but Noreen still saw and felt how his apprehension grew.

After much discussion, the Kings came to a consensus, and Con, along with Ulrik and Hal, went to find the leaders of the tribe of mortals who had been caught in the act. A part of Noreen wished that Cain had gone with them, but if he had, she wouldn't have seen just how split the Kings were on what to do about the humans going forward.

Some didn't hesitate to voice their frustration regarding how greedy the mortals continued to be, while others cautioned patience, reminding the rest of them that the humans didn't have any magic.

Through it all, Cain remained silent, listening to each opinion offered. All the while, his mind turned over scenario after scenario. He was hopeful that it would all work out, but he also expected the worst.

Noreen's heart hurt for him because she knew what was coming even if he hadn't at this moment in time. Or perhaps he had, but he hadn't wanted to think about it.

It wasn't long before Con and the other two returned to say that the mortals responsible had been punished and all now knew that there would be no more hunting of any dragons allowed. Cain stared hard at Con as he spoke. She felt his frustration, yet Cain did nothing.

His memories fast-forwarded to yet another gathering. This time, it was a dragon who had killed a human. While the Kings had been content with the punishment of the mortal for slaying a dragon, the humans wanted the death of the dragon who had killed a mortal. This time, the negotiating took three times as long.

And when Con, Ulrik, and Hal returned to the others, the tension had increased. Every one of them knew that this was just the beginning.

Noreen next found herself flying over the jungle that was Cain's domain. The thick canopy was now greatly diminished as the mortals kept chopping down trees for more land and homes.

Cain's heart ached for the beautiful land that was being torn up for whatever the humans wanted to change or build. His clan was becoming restless and angry, and he had to remind them daily of his vow, and who the mortals were.

That memory turned into one where the Kings gathered once more. It took her a moment to realize that several years had passed with the truce between the dragons and the mortals becoming shakier and shakier. Yet, all of that was about to change with the marriage of Ulrik, King of Silvers, to a human.

Noreen saw the couple through Cain's eyes. It was obvious that Ulrik was smitten with the beautiful mortal female. The woman, Nala, gave Ulrik a beaming smile as they held hands and announced their intentions to marry.

Every King clapped, but one didn't seem at all thrilled with what was going on—Constantine. At first, Cain thought it was jealousy, but he soon realized that wasn't the case. Con watched the woman's interactions with Ulrik, analyzing every word, every gesture.

"Everything all right?" Cain asked Con as he walked up to the King of Dragon Kings.

Con shrugged. "As fine as they can be."

"You have no' stopped looking at Nala yet. Some might think you want her for yourself."

Con's black eyes pinned Cain to the spot. "They would be wrong."

"Then tell me what's going on."

"Nothing, I hope."

"But you think it's something."

Con gave an agitated shake of his head. "I doona know. All Ulrik has ever wanted was a mate and offspring. He says he doesna care that Nala willna be able to bear his children, but I can no' believe that."

"Though no mortal yet has carried a bairn to term, maybe Nala will be the first."

Con's lips twisted. "And how many times will she have to lose a babe before she turns bitter, and it rips them apart?"

Cain didn't have an answer.

"Aye," Con said with a sigh. "If she is Ulrik's mate, then I will be the happiest one of us for them."

"But if she isna?"

Con's head swiveled to him. "Then she will pay."

Noreen's mouth fell open at Con's words. But she could understand why he would say such a thing. The Kings were a close bunch, and none were closer than Ulrik and Con. Con was merely watching out for Ulrik as a friend did.

Cain didn't reply to Con's comment. Nor did he follow Con when he walked away. Instead, Cain's gaze slid to Nala and Ulrik, taking up the watch that Con had abandoned. The feelings churning through Cain were unsettling. The easy alliance between the dragons and the humans was crumbling quicker than anyone could rebuild it. So much hinged on this marriage, but Cain didn't think that was the answer.

Nor did he believe that was the reason Ulrik was doing it.

No, Ulrik was marrying Nala because he loved her and believed her to be his mate. Since no King had found a mate that wasn't a dragon, Cain wasn't sure how the marriage would work.

Noreen wanted to learn more, but Cain's memories shifted once again. He was with the Kings once more, this time at Dreagan. There was no manor or buildings yet, but there was no mistaking the place. Con stood in human form. As each King landed, they also shifted.

Con's face, usually devoid of emotion, burned with a fury that shone in his black eyes. "My brothers, I've gathered you here because one of us has been betrayed," Con said, his voice carrying across the glen.

"Who?" Vaughn asked.

There was a beat of silence before Con said, "Ulrik."

Cain clenched his hands, his lips flattening.

A chorus of voices rose up, each demanding to know what had happened.

Con held up a hand, quietening them instantly. "A couple of you know I had my doubts about Nala. I'd hoped I would be proven wrong so I could ask Ulrik for forgiveness, but, unfortunately, that isna the case. I'd been keeping my eye on Nala for some time, but only when I was with the two of them. A few months back, I was having dinner with Ulrik, Nala, and her family when I saw her revulsion when Ulrik kissed her. She turned away, but I saw it nonetheless."

"That can no' be," someone said from behind Cain.

Nikolai, King of Ivories, gave a nod of his head. "It's true."

Con swallowed. "After that, I began following her, knowing that if Ulrik caught me, it could well end our friendship. My gut kept telling me that something was off. Earlier today, she snuck out of the home Ulrik had built for them and went to the village."

Cain didn't want to hear any more. He knew whatever Con had to say would divide the Kings, but more than that, he knew that what he'd been dreading all these years was about to come to fruition.

Noreen regretted wanting to see Cain's memories because his feelings were so overwhelming that she felt as if it were all happening to her.

"Nala went into a home while I stood outside near a window," Con continued. "A man spoke to her about the evil of dragons and how we needed to be stopped, and how it all started with her. He went into detail about how she should kill Ulrik on their wedding night and begin the destruction of the Dragon Kings."

The shock of the Kings reverberated all around Cain.

Noreen was so surprised that her knees threatened to give way, but she managed to stay on her feet.

She listened numbly as Con went into detail regarding his plan to get Ulrik away as the rest of them tracked Nala down and killed her before she could carry out her plans to murder Ulrik—despite the fact that she couldn't kill a Dragon King. No one talked about that, or how it didn't take all of them to track her down. No, this was about a tight-knit group who was protecting one of their own.

Tears burned Noreen's eyes. She didn't want to see any more, but she also didn't want to walk away. She watched, tears rolling down her face as the Kings waited for Ulrik to be sent on a mission before they gathered together and went off to hunt for Nala.

The mortal knew the moment she saw the Kings that they were on to her plan. Terror filled her eyes as her face drained of color. She ran, but it did little good. Soon enough, they cornered her atop a waterfall.

To Noreen's shock, Cain didn't hesitate to plunge his sword into her.

After Nala lay dead, the Kings said nothing as they each shifted and returned to their land. But Cain knew that no matter what actions had been taken that night, war was on the horizon.

As soon as he returned to his clan, he began preparations. He told no one his reasoning. He made sure that he put more distance between his dragons and the mortals on his land as an extra precaution.

He stayed awake all night, never resting, never stopping. Just before dawn, he took to the skies and watched the sun crest the horizon. His heart was heavy, his emotions running high. He didn't regret what he'd done to Nala, but he knew the consequences might be steeper than he'd ever imagined.

Noreen's tears rolled thick and rapidly down her face. She wanted to wrap her arms around Cain and hold him close, but she kept their hands laced together and bided her time, fortifying herself for whatever was coming next.

She didn't have to wait long. Cain's head whipped to the north toward Dreagan as Con's voice rang through his head, calling all the Kings to Scotland.

Cain flew fast and furiously. By the time he arrived, it was to see a division between the Kings. Con was on one side, Ulrik on the other. To Cain's surprise, there were more of them on Ulrik's side.

Cain landed between the groups, his gaze shifting from one to the other as the two friends stared at each other. Ulrik listed the crimes of the mortals throughout the years, ending with what his bride had wanted to do to him.

Con had no rebuttal. There was nothing he could say against the humans because everything Ulrik stated was true. One by one, the Kings moved to side with Ulrik until only Cain was left.

"Cain?" Con said in his head. *"What is your decision?"*

Cain blew out a breath. *"I've known for a while that this is where we would end up, but I hoped we wouldna be divided when it happened."*

"Say what you really want to say, Cain," Ulrik demanded.

Cain's tail slammed against the ground as he growled at Ulrik. Then he looked at Con. *"No matter what we did or could have done, it would've led us to this moment. We can no' live alongside the mortals."*

"You think we should've killed them that first day?" Con asked.

"There is no right answer," Cain admitted. *"But we have to make a stand now, or we'll lose everything."*

"If we go to war, then we really will lose," Con stated.

Cain shook his head. *"We've already lost."*

Noreen's mouth dropped open when Cain walked to stand with the other Kings. As one, the group took to the air, calling their clans as they began attacking the human settlements.

The screams of the mortals could be heard over the roar of the dragons. The carnage was swift and complete.

But Con didn't stand by and do nothing. He began talking to each King repeatedly through their mental link. Because Con was King of Kings, they couldn't block him. Instead, they had to listen to him.

For Cain, this was especially difficult because he wanted to agree with Con, but he knew that something had to be done. Yet, as he and his clan attacked more villages, he became less sure about his choice. Finally, Cain pulled his clan back and returned them to their land. The mortals there had either been killed or fled, so it was quiet. But Cain knew that could change quickly enough.

He set up sentries to make sure no mortals came across their boundary. He laid out plans of action for what needed to be done to protect his dragons. Then, he went to Dreagan to see Con.

Cain wasn't the only one who'd had a change of heart. Many other Kings were there, as well. Cain walked straight up to Con and bowed.

The King of Dragon Kings merely gave a nod of his head. There was no need for Cain to explain his actions. Con let him know that he understood why Cain had chosen as he had. It was enough that Cain was with him now.

Those at Dreagan split into smaller groups and began protecting villages from the onslaught of dragons. Just the sight of them standing with the humans was enough to stop most of the dragons, but not all.

It didn't take long for more Kings to return to Con's side until only one stood against him—Ulrik.

"Ulrik, please," Cain begged his friend to listen.

But Ulrik refused to hear any of them. He didn't stop, not even when Con called his Silvers to him. All but four of the largest silver dragons obeyed Con.

"If we want to stop Ulrik, we have to catch the other Silvers," Cain said.

Con turned his large head to him, his purple eyes meeting Cain's.

"I doona think even that will stop Ulrik," Banan said.

"Nay, it willna," Con replied. *"But it's what we have to do."*

Sebastian dove from the sky, his voice filling their heads as he landed. *"More dragons are being killed. I willna lose any more of my clan. I pulled them back, but it wasna enough. The mortals chased them, giving my clan no choice but to defend themselves."*

Con sighed loudly. *"Whatever peace we might have had is gone. There are too many of us to hide. We're meant for the skies, and I'll no' do that to our kind."*

"What are you proposing?" Guy asked.

"We send our dragons to another realm until we can get this sorted out."

No one said anything after Con's statement. Cain wanted to counter, wanted to say something that gave them another option. But there wasn't one. If the humans were now chasing the dragons to kill them, then there was only one choice.

"If there are no more mortals, then we doona have to send our dragons anywhere," Cain said.

Con gave a small nod. *"I've thought of that myself, but it comes back to the vow we made to protect them. That means even from ourselves. They deserve a chance at life, just as we do."*

"At the expense of our families? Our way of life?" Rhys demanded angrily.

Anson shook his head. *"I doona want any part in annihilating a species. It's no' who we are."*

"So, we give up our families? Our freedom?" Darius questioned.

Con looked at each of them before he said, *"We only have two choices. We kill the mortals, which goes against no' only who we are but also the vow we made. Or we send our dragons away until all of this calms down, and they can return."*

"Do you really think they'll return?" Guy asked.

Con nodded. *"I doona want to think about life without my clan, but I must think of what's best for everyone, no' just me."*

Cain bowed his head, his heart breaking in two. *"As I said earlier, no matter what path we took, this was always where we were going to end up. The mortals are too different from us. They fear us and covet the power we have. As much as I want them gone, I doona want to kill any more of them. But I doona want to send my Navies away either. As Con said, we have to think of our clans. Right now, I want to ensure that they live."* He lifted his head and looked at Con. *"I take it we'll remain?"*

"Aye."

"That gives us a chance to set things right for our dragons to return instead of a constant state of battle here," Cain finished.

Noreen sniffed because even though his words had been calm, she could feel he was overcome by heartache. She mouthed his name, mentally wrapping her arms around him to give him strength.

More debate went on for nearly another hour, but ultimately, it was decided that they would open a dragon bridge and send the dragons away. The Kings wasted no time in getting their clans gathered and over the bridge. Cain's was one of the first to leave because he didn't want to put it off.

As soon as the last of the Navies was gone, he turned his attention to helping Con and the others capture the four Silvers. The Silvers were large and extremely powerful, but they didn't stand a chance against the Kings.

Once the four were sleeping and caged within Dreagan mountain, the Kings focused on Ulrik. Noreen's emotions were pulled this way and that as Ulrik was forced to Dreagan. She experienced how deeply Cain felt each word that Ulrik hurled, but it wasn't until Con bound Ulrik's magic that she doubled over from the agony within Cain.

He stood tall, stoic, but inside, he bellowed his grief.

Ulrik's banishment was the final straw. Cain didn't watch his friend walk from Dreagan. Instead, Cain flew to his mountain and paced the caverns, holding in his roars lest the humans hear.

The anguish was too much. Cain knew he had to sleep, or he would follow in Ulrik's footsteps and create even bigger problems for the Kings.

The last thought Cain had as he closed his eyes was flying over his land through a rain shower while a rainbow formed to his right.

CHAPTER EIGHTEEN

Cain took a deep, steadying breath before he opened his eyes. He wasn't sure why he'd closed them in the first place. Maybe because it was easier not to see the emotions—or lack thereof—on Noreen's face.

But as soon as his lids raised, she flung herself at him, wrapping her arms tightly around his neck.

"I had no idea. I'm so, so sorry," she said, her voice catching a few times.

He felt something wet land on his neck, and he realized that she was crying. Actually, she was sobbing. He slowly raised his arms and wound them around her. As odd as it sounded, her embrace actually helped.

All the Dragon Kings had experienced something horrific during that time, and not only sending their dragons away. Why would they sit around and talk about it after? It had been better, as well as easier, to put it as far back from their minds as they could.

Noreen's body trembled with her tears. Cain now regretted letting her see his memories. He would've been able to control his voice and face if he had spoken about what had happened. Instead, she had not only witnessed it through his memories, but she had also felt every heart-breaking and agonizing moment.

He closed his eyes and buried his face in her neck. She smelled so damn good. And holding her was the balm he hadn't realized he so desperately needed.

"How do you bear it?" she whispered.

He shrugged. "What other choice do I have?"

"I thought I understood the Kings before, but my respect for all of you has only increased." She kissed the side of his neck gently. "You have all survived what surely would've killed others."

Cain didn't want to release her, but he made himself loosen his hold and lean back. Otherwise, he might hold onto her for eternity.

And that didn't sound so bad at all.

She blinked at him, her black lashes spiked with tears. He lifted a hand and tenderly wiped the moisture from her face. "We have endured all these millennia because we wanted to be here when our dragons return."

"Will they? Return, I mean?" she asked.

"I doona know. Maybe. Hopefully."

She glanced away. "But not as long as humans inhabit the Earth."

"Aye," he said with a nod.

She inhaled deeply and caressed her hands from his shoulders to his chest. "You didn't know how the mortals came to your realm, but now you do."

"It's another piece to the ever-growing puzzle. Even knowing who Moreann is and why she wants us gone is something we've long needed."

Noreen flashed him a quick smile. "I'll tell you everything. I was going to anyway, but now, I want to give you all the information I have right this second."

Cain chuckled. "We've time."

"I don't want to think that we do. Moreann is viciously vindictive. I can guarantee that whatever she has done with Usaeil is not only not pleasant, but the former queen will also be there for eternity."

At that statement, Cain shook his head. "If you believe that, then you doona know how powerful Usaeil truly is. She hid a lot of it from us, which means, she most likely hid it from everyone else. Including Moreann."

"If you're right, and I think you are, then that means Usaeil betrayed Moreann before I did."

"Aye. Usaeil's plans have been in place for a verra long time."

"And she wanted Con," Noreen said as her eyes grew wide. "Bloody hell. Usaeil wasn't ever going to help us wipe out the Kings. She was going to help you."

"I wouldna go that far," Cain cautioned her. "I think Usaeil wanted Moreann gone, but only so that we could mate with the Fae. Usaeil believed that no humans have been able to bring our children to term because they doona have magic."

Noreen's face scrunched up. "Some of the Kings mated Druids. Not to mention, there is Shara."

"Exactly. Once all of that occurred, Usaeil had no choice but to reevaluate things, but it didna alter the fact that she held firm to the belief that it was the Fae who could give us children."

"With as weak as most Druids on Earth are, she does have a point. Though I hate to admit it."

Cain looked over her head to the grove of trees behind her. "I doona trust Usaeil, but if there is one person who possibly knows Moreann better than you, it's her."

"I understand your worry about Dreagan being attacked, but before you get to planning a war, there are things you need to know."

"You're right, of course," Cain said as his gaze returned to Noreen. "Once you tell me, I'll need to relay it to the others at Dreagan."

She winced, her lips twisting. "Is there an easier way? Maybe a mobile we could use so I can tell you and the others all at once?"

"A mobile wouldna work across realms."

Noreen's red eyes flashed with wickedness. "Well, we are creatures with magic."

"As true as that statement is, it wouldna work."

"What about the connection you have to the other Kings? To talk to them through your mind?"

He hesitated. "It might work."

Despite Cain's attempts, however, he wasn't able to reach anyone at Dreagan. He suspected it might be because of the shield around them.

"It isna working," he finally told her.

She lifted one shoulder in a shrug. "It was worth a shot. You'll just have to remember everything I tell you. As soon as I'm done, return to Dreagan."

"I'm no' leaving you."

Noreen's crimson eyes softened as she smiled at him. "I appreciate that, but we both know I'm doomed. Moreann or one of the Others will find me. You'll have a chance to save all those at Dreagan as well as potentially end the Others once and for all. You have to do that."

"Then come with me. You wanted to fight against the Others."

Instead of agreeing, she shook her head. "The moment I return to Earth, Moreann will know. She'll seek me out, and there will be no time for you or any of the Kings to prepare for battle."

"You think I can no' protect you?" He didn't want to be angry, but he was. He was a Dragon King. He knew he could keep her safe from anyone and anything—even Moreann.

Noreen let her hands fall from him to her sides as she stepped out of his arms. "I know you can. That isn't the issue, and you know it. You brought me to the Fae Realm for a reason. Here, behind this barrier, I'll be safe."

"You doona know that."

"And you don't know that I won't." She smiled sadly. "I won't spend any more time debating this. You need information and fast. I have it, and you need to be ready to listen. Are you?"

Cain wanted to argue, he wanted to make her see his point, but he also realized that there was more at stake here than either of them. "Aye."

"There is a place in Istanbul where we meet occasionally. It's below the Ayasofya in the many tunnels under the city. Only someone with magic can reach it," she explained.

Cain nodded, thinking of the ancient building that had been constructed in 537 AD, first as an Eastern Orthodox Cathedral before it became a Roman Catholic Cathedral, and then an Ottoman Mosque before finally being transformed into a museum. "Why there?"

"Moreann chose it. I don't know why. I never asked."

"How often does the group meet there?"

Noreen's lips flattened. "About once every five years. What the mortal Druids don't realize is that the Fae, Moreann, and the other Druids from her realm meet more frequently. Moreann often made the comment that she couldn't stand waiting for the mortals to make the trek. Never mind the fact that she could've brought them wherever she wanted them."

"She doesna strike me as the kind who helps anyone," Cain said.

"Oh, she's definitely not."

Cain had a hard time keeping his eyes from Noreen's naked body. "Perhaps we should get dressed."

Noreen began to smile. "Something distracting you?"

"Aye," he stated while letting his gaze run slowly down her body. The moment her nipples hardened, a moan rumbled in his chest, and his cock stirred in response.

An instant later, Noreen cleared her throat. "Yeah. Clothes might be good."

Cain chuckled and dressed while Noreen used her magic to put her clothes back on. All the while, she spoke.

"Moreann is used to being in charge and in control. Of course, being an empress for so long has a way of doing that."

Cain could well imagine Moreann and Usaeil butting heads. Both coveted power—and neither shared it well. "The times you saw Usaeil and Moreann together, how were they?"

"Tense. As far back as I can remember, their alliance was tenuous at best. But Moreann needed Usaeil, and at the time, Usaeil needed Moreann." Noreen shrugged. "Things changed for Usaeil."

"But no' Moreann." Cain thought about that for a moment. "I doona think the empress was blind to what Usaeil was doing."

Noreen twisted her lips as she moved her hair away from her face. "Moreann never said anything specific to me, but she was very distrusting of Usaeil, and it had gotten worse these last few years. Not that either of them could do anything."

"The magic binding them," Cain said with a nod. "That kind of bond is extremely powerful, but there are always ways to get out of such a promise."

"Not this one."

"Why do you say that?"

Noreen blew out a breath and looked at the lake. "It had to do with the words used. And before you ask, I don't know what they were. I just remember one night, not long after my parents were killed, that I woke to hear arguing. It was Moreann and Usaeil, and they were talking about the promise that bound them."

"Did one want to break it?"

"I don't know," Noreen said with a frustrated look in his direction. "I can recall the voices because I recognized Usaeil's as well as Moreann's, and I can remember the heated argument regarding the magic used in their promise to each other, but everything else is fuzzy."

Cain raked a hand through his hair and turned in a slow circle to look around him. "Doona worry about it. Everything you're telling me is important."

"What are you looking for?" she asked.

"Whoever formed this shield. It didna make itself."

Noreen threw out her hands before letting them fall to her sides. "You flew over the entire area and saw nothing. There isn't anyone here."

"No' now, but they could return."

"We'll deal with them when and if it happens."

He swiveled his head to her. "And if I'm no' here?"

"Then I'll do whatever I need to do to survive. Now, let's get back to discussing Moreann and the Others."

CHAPTER NINETEEN

Earth

"We can't find her."

Magic sizzled in Moreann's hand at the sound of Brian's voice behind her. "You mean *you* can't find her." She whirled to face him. The moment her gaze landed on him, he took a step back, and his face paled. "How hard did you look? I'm guessing not very."

Confusion filled his features. "That isn't true at all. I looked everywhere."

Off to her left, Orun stood in the long, white robes favored by many on their homeworld. The *drough* had been Moreann's advisor since her second year on the throne. He was also her counterpart on the Others. Orun had despised Brian from the first moment they met.

Then again, Orun hated everyone. She knew he even disliked her. She didn't take it personally. It was just his way. The fact that he was loyal was enough for her.

"I did warn you he wouldn't measure up," Orun stated.

Brian's gaze snapped to him as fury blazed in his silver eyes. "It wouldn't matter if I had found Noreen and brought her here, you'd still find fault with me."

"Yes," Orun replied. "Because you're lacking in all things."

"I'm an Other. That means, I'm something," Brian retorted.

Moreann rolled her eyes and held up a hand, silencing both of them. Her gaze moved behind Brian where the two human Druids stood. The females, while lacking the power flowing in Brian's Fae veins, had more backbone than he. It was too bad they were mortal.

If they had been born on her realm, then they would've been strong. Or they might have been, if the magic stopped draining away. What had begun as just an odd happening had turned into more and more of her people being born without power until she could no longer ignore it.

That's when she had taken matters into her own hands and looked around for another realm for herself and her people. It had taken many, many years before she found the perfect location—Earth. The only problem was that it was occupied by beings stronger than she.

But that hadn't deterred her. Moreann was nothing if not resourceful. She watched the dragons for years, moving from clan to clan to see how each worked and figuring out the hierarchy of things.

That's when her plan formed. The dragons were noble creatures, and she had guessed that they would protect those weaker than they. It was a calculated risk, but one that had to be taken.

When she chose those among her people without magic, she hadn't told them what was going to happen to them. She simply wiped their memories of all but their names and dumped them on Earth. Then she sat back and watched.

There had been a moment where she'd thought the Kings might just eat the humans, but to her amazement, they welcomed her people instead. And with that one move, the Kings sealed their doom.

Though they hadn't yet realized it.

Moreann wasn't just resourceful. She was patient. While the Kings, dragons, and mortals were learning to live alongside one another, she was using the most powerful of those on her realm to her benefit.

She still regretted their deaths, but they sacrificed their lives in the hopes of saving their species—even if they did it unknowingly. She had known exactly what would happen to them. And while the strongest Druids of their realm were kept protected in case they were needed in war, Moreann had ignored the rules put in place eons before that ensured their realm was always guarded.

Because she knew she could protect it if need be. So, she'd made the hard decision and ordered those Druids to channel their magic and combine it. Once they did as she commanded, she used them to see into the future of the dragons and Earth. She learned so very much about the Dragon Kings and how she could bring them down, but unfortunately, she didn't learn everything.

The magic she forced the Druids to use killed each and every one of them before she could see the end to the war. Moreann had been making decisions for the last decade based solely on her gut. She hadn't known that the Kings would find their mates, or that Usaeil would turn on her. And she certainly hadn't seen that Usaeil would fall for Constantine.

"Empress?" Orun called.

Moreann lowered her hand that she hadn't realized

was still raised. For so long, she had known exactly which moves to make because the Druids had shown her. Why couldn't they have lasted long enough to bring her clarity on the final war? Then again, Moreann had believed that everything she'd done would be enough to bring the Kings to their knees.

How wrong she'd been.

And Noreen. That was something that would be dealt with soon. Very soon.

"I've always been able to find you," she told the others in the room. "Do you know why?"

"Because of the strength of your magic," the mortal Druid with dark skin and hair said.

Moreann glanced at her and shook her head. "I marked each of you, just as I've marked every person who has been an Other. I did it so I could find you at any time. I used to tell members of our group that I did it to keep them from betraying me. I knew we were winning against the Kings, and I didn't think any of you going to them would change anything."

It was a lie, but one she kept to herself. To show any kind of weakness was to let defeat in—and she wouldn't do that.

"Do you know where Noreen is then?" Brian asked.

Anger rumbled through her as she turned her attention to the Light Fae. "If I knew where Noreen was, why would I send all of you out looking for her?"

"I-I don't know," he stuttered and took another step back.

As if distance would save him if she lashed out.

It was Orun who asked, "How did Noreen remove her mark?"

"The Dragon King." It was another lie, but it wasn't as

if she would let them know that by Noreen not using her magic, Moreann could no longer find her.

The other human Druid asked, "Could Noreen have left this planet?"

Brian snorted loudly. "And go where? All the Fae doorways are closed."

"But the Dragon King was the one who jumped them all over the world," Orun added.

Moreann turned to her advisor and looked into his narrow-set, hooded eyes. "The King made sure to go to various places multiple times to confuse us."

"Why?" one Druid asked the other. "Noreen should've been the one using her magic."

Brian cut them a dark look. "It was smart, actually, since it's our magic Moreann can track."

The humans' eyes widened as they looked in Moreann's direction. She then slid her gaze to Brian. "Perhaps you aren't as stupid as I thought. How did you know?"

"Because Noreen went out of her way not to use magic these past few weeks. I knew there was a reason, but I couldn't figure it out until you said you marked us. You didn't actually do that, but you do know our magic."

Damn him for being so smart. Moreann didn't respond. She simply returned her attention to Orun.

He ran a hand over his bald head. "Noreen won't use her magic. She'll make sure of that, and by being with a Dragon King, she won't have to."

"But they aren't at Dreagan," a Druid said.

It was the first place Moreann had looked, and she should've realized that it was the last place the King would've taken Noreen. The Dragon King. She gave an inward shake of her head. Moreann hadn't thought much about Cain. He stayed in the background, rarely voicing his thoughts or opinions. She'd didn't believe he would be a problem. Now, she was paying a high price for such idiocy.

"Cain wouldn't have left this realm," Moreann said.

Orun lifted a brow high on his forehead. "But if they did?"

"You know how many realms are out there. We don't have time to search them all."

The advisor shrugged his shoulders. "Maybe we don't have to."

"Noreen has betrayed us. She has no doubt told Cain everything about us."

"So?" Brian said. "Everything is already in play."

Orun sneered at the Light. "Not everything, you fool."

"The important parts are," Brian argued.

Moreann laced her fingers before her and turned to the side so she could see everyone. "Noreen knows everything. It doesn't matter what is in play now. She'll warn the Kings."

"There were only two more instances," the first Druid said. "One has already been removed by Usaeil anyway."

Brian nodded as he looked from the Druid to Moreann. "Exactly. And the other was minor. Everything you put in place centuries ago is what has taken a toll on the Kings. Who cares if they know who we are now? The fact that they've not attacked should tell us a lot."

"It tells us they're waiting for us to make the first move," Orun replied in a dry tone.

Moreann nodded at her advisor and then told Brian, "He's right. However, you also have a point. Let's forget the final five things I was going to throw at the Dragon

Kings and their mates over the next month. We're going to do this another way."

Brian rubbed his hands together. "Now that's what I'm talking about."

"Empress, we need a Dark Fae to complete our group," Orun reminded her.

Moreann thought of Usaeil, who she had locked away. "If I need a Dark's magic, I know where to go."

"Will you have time for such a thing?"

She glared at Orun. "I'm going to make time."

Orun parted his lips as if he were about to reply, but he must have thought better of it because he closed his mouth and stood in silence.

Moreann looked at the Fae and Druids that made up the Others. She had put so much time and energy into her war with the Dragon Kings. No one and nothing would stop her from winning. Her people were counting on her. She wouldn't let them down.

For every day that her people remained on their world, and the magic continued to die, each of them received less and less of it. They needed that power in order to survive, because being without it meant they would be weak and ripe for someone like her to wipe out.

Her people hadn't lived for thousands of millennia building their power and strength for nothing. *She* hadn't sacrificed lives to get close to achieving victory over the Kings only to lose it.

It didn't matter that the Dragon Kings hadn't done anything to her or her people. It was enough that the magic of their realm thrived—even with the Fae, and the poor-excuses for Druids that lived upon it.

Though there *were* a few Druids who had caught her notice. The Skye Druids for one, but also one mated to a Dragon King—Eilish.

Even more concerning was that she felt the power of other Druids, but it was as if they were hidden from her somehow, though she knew they were in Scotland.

It didn't matter. None of it did, because as powerful as those few might be, they weren't her Druids. Which meant, they would all die.

CHAPTER TWENTY

With every word Noreen spoke about Moreann and the Others, the more she found she had to say. She'd known she had a lot of information stored away from all the years she'd spent with them, but she hadn't realized how much.

Then, on top of that, Cain asked questions about things she hadn't thought would mean anything. Though, obviously, given his interest, she'd been wrong.

"Moreann has to have a weakness," Cain said.

Noreen twisted her lips and glanced his way as they walked through more of the forest. He wanted to get a better view of things beneath the canopy of trees, and she found it easier to talk about her time with the Others as she walked. They had trekked for nearly two hours, and while Cain had paused a few times to look at things, they had yet to encounter anyone—or even anything that suggested another person was around.

He grinned at her look. "Everyone has a weakness, lass."

"Even a Dragon King?" she asked, brows raised in question.

Cain gave a single nod. "Even a Dragon King. For the

Fae, it's humans. The Dark doona hide their hunger for their souls."

Noreen's gut twisted at his words, but she knew he was right. "No, the Dark will do whatever they need to in order to feed. It doesn't help that the humans are so willing to give themselves to us."

She felt his gaze, and she knew the question that he wanted to ask—but didn't.

Noreen looked into his deep green eyes. "Ask what you want to know."

"It doesna matter."

"It does, or you wouldn't want to ask it."

After a full minute, Cain sighed. "How many humans have you killed for their souls?"

Noreen walked a few more steps before she said, "Two."

"Thank you for telling me."

But she wasn't finished. "I was supposed to remain in the house Moreann had for us, but she had been gone for a few weeks, and I felt I was old enough to do whatever I wanted. So, I left. I made my way to the city, but it wasn't enough. I wanted to go back to Ireland. Moreann had shown me all kinds of tricks that, combined with the magic I already had, allowed me to master teleportation easier than most Fae do."

"Where did you go in Ireland?"

"Dublin, of course. My mother loved that city. I don't know why exactly, but I remember the smile that would come over her face whenever my father took us."

Cain's hand brushed against hers, and he wrapped his fingers around it. "You felt closer to your mother there."

"I did. I would've gone back to where our home was, but I couldn't remember the location. Dublin, however, was a spot I'd never forget." She laughed, thinking back to that night. "The city is . . . it's mesmerizing. Everything I recalled from my childhood, I saw differently. I walked street after street after street. I saw many Fae, but I chose to remain on my own. When a few appeared to take an interest in me, I quickly made sure to leave the area."

"What went wrong?"

She pressed her lips together briefly. "I don't know why I stopped. There was something about the couple that caught my eye. Maybe it was the way the man held the woman's hand or how he spoke to her, but it reminded me of my parents. The couple held me enthralled for several minutes. I wasn't close enough to see their faces clearly, but their love—and lust—was obvious. I was too focused on them. If I hadn't been, I would've noticed the men who came out of the shadows."

"Drunks?" Cain asked, a hard edge to his voice.

She shook her head. "There was whiskey on their breath, but they weren't drunk. They saw who they believed was a young girl alone at night, and they wanted me."

"You doona need to tell me more."

But she wasn't going to stop now. "The first came up and put his arm around me. He smiled and tried to sweet-talk me, but I wasn't stupid. I knew what he wanted. The other kept his distance so as not to scare me off. I could've teleported or even used magic to knock them away, but I believed because I had magic, I could handle the situation. It never entered my mind that they had been drawn to me because I was Fae. I hadn't hidden my allure, and that's the very thing that had brought them to me.

"I was too confident. But I couldn't see that at the time. I rolled my eyes at the man and knocked his arm away. That didn't please him at all. He grabbed me more forcefully. This time, I gave him a hard push and walked away. Next thing I knew, I was shoved into a dark, narrow alley with both men grabbing at me."

Cain was no longer looking around the area, he stared straight ahead, a muscle in his jaw twitching.

Noreen brought them to a halt and faced Cain to finish her story. "They tore off my shirt. I'll never forget the feeling of their hands on my skin as they fondled my breasts. They were trying to get my jeans off when I noticed that they acted differently. No longer were they hurting me, but their need had tripled. I stopped struggling and just stood there, watching them. There is a distinct rush that courses through a Fae's veins when a human succumbs to us. A mortal might compare it to a drug because that's exactly what it is. It's heady and intoxicating. I knew what was happening, and I didn't want to stop it."

"They were trying to rape you. I wouldna have stopped it either." Fury flashed in Cain's green eyes.

Noreen's insides turned to mush because of it. Then she thought about what had happened next in the story. "The man before me yanked his pants down and held out his cock for me. The one holding me allowed me to have my arm, and while jerking the arsehole off, I drained him of his soul. I watched with a smile on my face as he withered before my very eyes. Then I turned to the other."

"And did the same to him, I hope."

She shook her head. "He would've let me. I saw it in his eyes, even as the desire mixed with fear after seeing what had happened to his friend, but I returned to the house."

Cain's hands moved to grasp her head on either side of her face. He bent down to look her in the eye. "Anyone would've done the same in your shoes."

"I doubt that," she replied. "But thank you for saying so."

He gave her a quick kiss before straightening. Slowly, his hands released her and returned to his sides. "You said you killed two."

"Ah, yes." She drew in a deep breath and turned her head away. "When Moreann returned, my eyes were red, so she knew something had happened. I told her everything. She wasn't pleased that I had disobeyed her, but she was happy that I had made sure not to get raped. I realized then that she wanted me to be a Dark. It wasn't long after that she asked me to go with her when she was set to leave. I agreed because I was so tired of being left behind. She took me to a place I'd never been. The city was so loud, so bright—even at night—that it blinded me. I had no idea why she was in Hong Kong, but I found out quickly enough. She had brought me there to kill again."

Cain's brows drew together. "I would've thought she would want to keep you a Light since she had Usaeil, who obviously wasna going anywhere."

"Maybe since I had already killed once, I took the choice out of her hands."

"From everything you've told me about Moreann, I'm betting she had a plan, and that scheme meant you had to kill."

Thinking about it now, Noreen knew Cain was right. "The deed is done, so it doesn't really matter now."

"Does it no'? You speak of giving my brethren pieces of our incomplete puzzle, perhaps you have one yourself that you need answers to."

It was her turn to frown. "I know everything. Well, aside from why she brought me to Hong Kong that night. I could've asked, but I didn't. I was becoming a part of something, and I needed that."

Cain gave a nod. "What happened that night?"

"I followed Moreann through a maze of streets and

down increasingly narrow alleys until she stopped before a tiny shop. She merely pointed to it and told me I needed to kill who was inside. I asked her what they had done, and she said it didn't matter. She was giving me an order, and she expected me to follow it."

"And you did."

"I walked inside, saw the elderly man sitting on a stool as he was drying herbs for some medicinal purpose. He was an herbalist. The moment I looked into his eyes, he knew why I was there. He didn't cry or beg me not to do it. He simply finished what he was doing and put it in a bag that he then set on the shelves behind him that contained numerous jars. Then he faced me and gave a nod. As I walked toward him, I could see the knowledge he held about herbs and healing. I stopped before him and put my hand atop his. Then I bowed my head and departed."

"Departed?" Cain asked, surprise flickering in his green depths.

"Before I left the shop, I used protection spells on the old man and the store. Then I went to Moreann and told her that I refused to take the man's life. I warned her that he was under my protection and that if she or anyone else touched him, I would come after them."

Cain quirked a black brow. "And she allowed that?"

"I think she wanted to see what I would do. She got her answer. She never asked me to kill for her again."

"But you did kill."

Noreen shrugged, unable to deny the statement. "I did. It was decades later when I was walking the streets of Rome, using glamour to hide my eyes but also my Fae allure. I came upon a prostitute who was being beaten. I stepped in and stopped the man. He laughed and pushed me away, telling me that he'd paid for the woman, and that meant he could do whatever he wanted with her. I can't describe the anger that came over me. I put myself between him and the sex worker and told her to leave. She ran off without another word. The man then raised his fist. I let him hit me. And then I dropped my glamour. In a heartbeat, he was on his knees, panting and begging for me. I ordered him to remove his clothes and lay on his back. As soon as he complied, I took his cock in my hand and killed him."

"Do you feel bad about it?"

"Yes. I could've made sure he never hit another woman again. Instead, I killed him."

Cain gave a nod. "You did what you felt you needed to do. I, too, have killed."

"In battle," she reminded him.

He gave her a dry look. "Do you so easily forget what you saw through my memories? All the mortals?"

She had to look away. "I'd forgotten. But your hair and eyes don't change."

"Maybe no', but taking a life leaves a mark. You may no' be able to see it, but it's there. Trust me."

His fingers touched her hair, and she knew he was looking at how much silver was there. Finally, she slid her gaze back to his.

"You think I've killed more than two because of how much silver is in my hair," she said.

He shook his head and released the strand he held. His fingers softly grazed her cheek before he lowered his arm. "I think the silver that's there appeared because of how much those kills affected you. I used to think the silver indicated how many a Dark had killed. Now, I realize that might account for part of it, but there's much more to it. Did you think I'd look at you differently? Or that I wouldna want to touch you?"

She shrugged. "It crossed my mind. It's easy to forget who someone is sometimes."

"I've known from the beginning who you are, Noreen. It hasna stopped me from wanting you. In fact, your stories have only made me hunger for you more."

She didn't have time to respond as he dragged her against him and covered her mouth with his in a kiss that stole her breath—and set her blood on fire.

CHAPTER TWENTY-ONE

By the stars, he couldn't get enough of her. Cain held Noreen's naked body against him as he entered her with one thrust. As soon as they were joined, there was nowhere else he wanted to be but with her.

He might not have trusted Noreen at first, but that had changed quicker than expected. Now, he couldn't think of a reason why he wouldn't trust her. Their circumstances had put them in a peculiar situation that forced each of them to face things they might not want to.

"You feel so good," Noreen whispered as she rocked her hips with her legs wrapped around him.

His hands cupped her tight ass as he lifted her up and slowly lowered her down. She gasped, her head falling back so that the long strands of her hair brushed his fingers.

She was breathtaking, utterly ravishing. And she was his. There was no denying the chemistry between them, or the way their bodies came together with such raw, unadulterated passion. He'd known lust before. This was something so much more, so much . . . deeper.

He leaned forward and wrapped his lips around her nipple. He ran his tongue back and forth over the tiny nub as her moans turned to cries. All the while, he continued slowly moving her up and down his arousal.

"Cain," she called out as her nails dug into his shoulders.

He wanted to thrust into her hard, to give in to the primal hunger and mark her body as his. But he held himself back. His pleasure could wait. Right now, it was all about Noreen. He wanted her to feel special, he needed her to know that he cared about her more than as a means of getting information.

Cain moved to her other nipple to tease the peak mercilessly. He alternated between sucking and flicking his tongue back and forth over it. Just when it felt as if Noreen couldn't take any more, he stopped moving.

"No," she cried and lifted her head.

Her face was flushed with desire, her crimson eyes half-lidded and filled with need. Her chest rose and fell rapidly. She tried to shift her hips, but he held her still, refusing to allow her any kind of movement while he continued teasing her nipple.

"Please," she begged.

His body ached for release. Even as he tried to control himself, he recalled how he'd liked watching her climax before. Not to mention how good she'd made *him* feel. Once those two things went through his mind, he couldn't hold back any longer.

He shifted them so that her back was against a tree. Cain put a hand there to help protect her from the bark, but she quickly yanked it away. He soon forgot everything else as he began to drive into her hard and fast.

Within moments, her body stiffened as pleasure filled her face. Her lips opened on a silent scream, her body flushing deeply. Cain didn't stop moving. He kept pumping in and out, driving her orgasm further.

When she opened her eyes, he pulled out of her and moved her to her hands and knees. Then he filled her from behind. She gasped in pleasure before following it with a low moan.

He grinned and held her hips as he started to move. Cain couldn't stop touching her beautiful body. He leaned over her, pressing his mouth next to her ear. She shifted her head to the side so their lips brushed.

Their eyes met, and he saw the same fire in hers that he felt in himself. She might have climaxed, but she wasn't finished yet.

That stirred the flames of his desire even higher.

He grasped her hair and straightened, pulling back so she had to raise her head. She called out his name as his tempo ratcheted up a few notches. As much as he liked having a hold of her hair, he wanted to hear her scream in ecstasy again.

Cain released her tresses and reached down to find her clit. The sensitive bud was swollen. As soon as his finger swirled around it, she groaned in response, urging him on. He continued teasing her clit, ruthlessly pushing her toward another orgasm—while trying not to give in to one of his own.

Just when he thought he couldn't hold out any longer, a cry tore from Noreen's throat. He saw her fingers dig into the ground as she pushed back against him.

No matter how much Cain wanted to give her a third one, he couldn't wait any longer. He wanted her too badly.

No one could touch her body like Cain. Noreen accepted that as fact, just as she knew that no one would ever bring her as much pleasure as the Dragon King did.

And she was perfectly fine with that.

Cain was . . . unique, yes, but he was also drop-dead gorgeous, honorable, charming, and sexy as sin.

As her body came down from the high of another mind-altering climax, she put everything about the scene to memory. The way the bark had scraped her back as he filled her. The sound of the leaves as the breeze rustled them. The way the dead leaves felt beneath her knees as he moved them to the ground. The way the soil slid under her fingernails as she dug her fingers into the dirt. The heat of the sun on their sweat-soaked bodies as it filtered through the trees. The carnal, erotic feeling of Cain's balls slapping against her as he filled her again and again.

And the way their bodies and souls became more and more intertwined, entangled. Bonded.

Noreen's body pulsed with contentment from the bliss she'd received at the hands of the Dragon King. It was almost surreal, and yet she knew for a fact that all of this was happening. It wasn't a dream.

She looked back over her shoulder at Cain. His eyes were open and fastened on hers. His fingers dug almost painfully into her hips as he drove into her, but it felt so good.

Their gazes locked, and even when he gave a shout when his orgasm hit, he never looked away. She saw the ecstasy fill not just his face, but his beautiful green eyes, as well.

Finally, he stopped moving. His chest rose and fell rapidly. He slowly pulled out of her. She turned to him, bringing him down to the ground with her arms around him.

"Damn, lass. You're something else," he whispered before kissing her temple.

Noreen beamed as she looked at him. "I can certainly say that you take me to places I've never been."

"And this is just the start," he promised.

She hoped it was, but as she thought of the future, she couldn't see how they could have one. Even if the Kings managed to destroy the Others and Moreann, there was still the fact that she was a Dark. And she had become one all on her own. No one had forced it upon her. No one had made her feel as if she had to.

And while she knew Shara had turned Light, she wasn't so sure she could do it. She liked who she was. Maybe not everything she'd done, but really, who could say that?

If it meant you could be with Cain, would you turn Light?

That was an easy answer—yes. She most definitely would. But it wasn't as if he were asking.

"What has you so deep in thought that you're frowning?" he asked.

She immediately smoothed her brow and shrugged. "Just thinking about everything."

"I hope you're no' worried about Moreann and the Others. I've told you, I'll protect you."

"I know you will," she assured him. "I'm also pretty good at magic myself."

He chuckled and squeezed her tighter. "I doona doubt that in the least. So, tell me what worries you."

"Nothing."

Cain sighed loudly. "Lass, there's no need to lie to me. I hope you realize you can tell me whatever is on your mind."

"It's nothing, really. I overthink things and work myself up on matters that are silly."

"If you're upset, then it isna silly."

Well, when he said it like that, it made perfect sense. Still, she didn't want to blurt out that she was thinking about a future with him when he might only want a fling.

"You're doing the frown again."

She ducked her head into his chest. "Sorry."

"Ease your mind, lass. Tell me what you're thinking."

"Us."

He paused for a moment. "I can certainly see why you would be thinking about us. It's no' common for the Kings to mingle with the Dark."

"And we've been doing much more than just . . . mingling."

Cain chuckled softly. "Aye, we certainly have. And I've no plans to stop anytime soon. No' tomorrow, no' next week, or even next month. I could keep going, but I hope you see what I'm saying."

She thought she did, but she wasn't sure. "Maybe you should spell it out for me."

Cain shifted so that they were looking at each other. "I want you, Noreen. And each time I have you, my desire only increases."

"I want you, too."

"Good. Then we're on the same page."

She nodded because he had let her know that he wanted her for an indefinite amount of time. But did that clear up everything? She searched her mind and still found doubts.

"I see we're no'," he said. But there was no censure in his words.

She put a hand on his chest. "The thing is, I find myself in a unique situation. I like you, a lot. A Dragon King. You're supposed to be my enemy simply because our two cultures have fought. I'm also supposed to hate you because I'm part of the Others."

"You're no longer part of the Others," he corrected.

She suddenly smiled. "That's right, I'm not. But I was. I've been taught to hate the Kings from two different sides."

"And you think there are some who will say something to you?"

Noreen sighed. "I could care less about what others think. I'm just pointing out that I've long believed I wasn't supposed to talk to a King, much less have sex with one."

"Ah, but you have. Repeatedly."

She smiled widely. "And it was amazing."

"Aye, it was," he said as he brought her close for a kiss.

Noreen pulled back and met his gaze. "I like you, Cain. A lot. I think you know that. Maybe it's because I've turned against the Others, or it could be something else I'm not even aware of, but I feel like a fish out of water. I'm clinging to you when I've never clung to anyone in my life."

"I'm the sturdy kind, lass. Cling to me all you want."

Oh, how she wanted to take him up on that proposal. No one had offered her such a thing before. "It's tempting. So tempting."

"Are you afraid I'll let you down?"

"I'm afraid that I'll find I never want to let you go."

He quirked a brow. "Would that be so bad?"

Was he kidding? She shook her head, unable to get any words out.

Cain ran his hand up and down her back. "Is that what you're afraid of?"

"No. The idea appeals to me, but then again, we just met. Everything is always good when people first meet."

"I wouldna say always, but I understand your point. How about we take things one day at a time?"

"Okay. I can do that."

He touched her chin to make her look at him. "And

let's promise to always talk to each other. If you have any doubts or questions, doona hesitate to come to me. And I'll do the same with you."

"I can do that."

He brought her close for a deep kiss. "Och, lass. I do like having you in my arms."

"I like being here very much."

CHAPTER TWENTY-TWO

Noreen wished she could stay in Cain's arms for the rest of the day, but that wasn't possible. She gave him a quick kiss, and he hugged her tightly before both of them got to their feet. She had used magic to remove her clothes, so she used it again to put them back on.

For Cain, she chose jeans and the boots he'd worn earlier as well as a green, v-neck, short-sleeve tee that fit tight over his impressive shoulders. He looked down at himself and grinned.

"Good choice," he told her.

In a blink, Noreen called a gray tee and black pants to herself. Then she finished the outfit off with black boots that laced up the front. She was in the process of pulling her hair up into a messy bun when she noted Cain looking at her footwear.

"Combat boots?" he asked.

She shrugged as she lowered her hands when she finished with her hair. "I suspect we'll be fighting, and I want to be prepared. Unlike Rhi, I don't think I'd be successful meeting an opponent with heeled boots, spikes or no."

Cain chuckled. "You've seen her in those, have you?"

"Oh, yes. Hands down, Rhi is the ultimate badass with amazing style."

"I think you could definitely fight in heels."

Noreen laughed and shook her head. "Don't get me wrong, I love heels, but there is a time and place. Unless you're Rhi, of course."

"Of course." Cain laughed again. "Have you met her?"

"She isn't someone who runs in the same circles as I do. However, I do know Moreann has been obsessed with her."

Cain's smile dropped as his brows drew together. "Because her father was in the Others?"

"Yep. Moreann wanted Rhi to join, but when Usaeil failed to bring her in, Moreann had no choice but to recruit Brian, even though she always planned to replace him with Rhi eventually."

"She was that sure that Rhi would join the group? Even though Rhi is in love with a Dragon King?"

Noreen shrugged and twisted her lips. "That never bothered Moreann. She didn't even have to tell Usaeil to make sure the relationship ended. Usaeil took care of that all on her own."

Cain's face went blank. "What?"

"Usaeil was responsible for ending Rhi's affair with the Dragon King."

"Do you know which King Rhi was with?"

Noreen gave a brief shake of her head. "I asked, but no one would tell me."

Cain pivoted away, raking his hand through his hair. He stopped and turned back to Noreen. "Does Rhi know that Usaeil ruined the relationship?"

"Sadly, yes. Usaeil bragged about it to us. I remember it vividly because we were surprised that she actually showed up for a meeting since she hadn't for the ones before that. Moreann was getting testy about it and had gone to speak to Usaeil herself. Anyway, Usaeil came for that meeting and told us how Rhi had found out and was so upset. Usaeil had thought Rhi would come for her then, but she didn't. I wouldn't have either if I were in Rhi's place. She was too upset. That's never a good way to go into battle. Not that I know a lot about such things since I've never really fought anyone before."

She was rambling because Cain hadn't moved, much less uttered a sound. Noreen pressed her lips together to make sure she didn't keep talking.

"Con needs to know about this," Cain suddenly said.

That surprised Noreen. "Why do you say that?"

"It's difficult to understand exactly, but Rhi has friends among us. She and Rhys are extremely close."

"That doesn't explain why she would go to Con."

"It does when you understand that she and Con agreed to fight Usaeil together. If Rhi knew that Usaeil had instigated the ruination of her affair, then yes, Rhi would tell Con to give them more reason to go after Usaeil—no' that they needed any more."

Noreen frowned as she cocked her head to the side. "I could understand where Con might be upset when he learned that Usaeil had gotten involved in the matters of his Kings, but couldn't it all be fixed by telling the King of Kings what Usaeil had done?"

"It's never that easy when it comes to the affairs of the heart."

"I suppose not." She sighed as Cain took her hand, and they began walking. "Does Rhi know that Usaeil isn't dead?"

"I doona believe so. We've been unable to find her since she thrust her blade into the queen."

"I heard that Rhi and Balladyn were once very close."

Cain gave a nod as he glanced her way. "They were best friends until Usaeil betrayed Balladyn to Taraeth, who was supposed to kill Balladyn."

"Instead, the previous King of the Dark turned him," Noreen finished.

"Aye. I doona believe Taraeth would've done that had he realized how powerful a Fae Balladyn was. Usaeil knew, and while she says she wanted Balladyn gone from the Light because he had fallen in love with Rhi, I also suspect that she knew Balladyn would discover her plans and uncover everything she'd done since he was Captain of the Queen's Guard."

Noreen made a sound in the back of her throat. "Balladyn wasn't king for very long, but he made a big impact. I've no doubt he would've discovered all of Usaeil's misdeeds. But it boggles my mind how jealous she was—or should I say *is*—of Rhi."

"It doesna make any sense to me, but it's what has driven Usaeil for a verra long time. We'd all hoped it was finished."

"Not by a long shot."

"Aye," he muttered in frustration.

Noreen looked at him and waited for his gaze to meet hers. "I'll help you look for her, after Moreann is defeated since the Others are a bigger threat."

His eyes crinkled at the corners as he grinned. "Does that mean you're coming to Dreagan with me?"

"No," she said softly. "It's better for you if I stay here."

"I doona agree with you, but I also willna force you to go where you doona want."

"I want to be with you. I hope you know that."

He nodded. "Aye, lass, I do."

"It's just . . ." She sighed and looked forward as they walked. "I'm not like Rhi. I've never been in battle before, and I don't want anyone to worry about me and take their focus off the fighting."

Cain brought them to a halt and turned her so that she faced him. "I will admit that it takes practice to be a warrior, but I also know that you've got a warrior spirit inside of you."

She rolled her eyes, scoffing at him.

"You do," he insisted. "You came to us, turning against all those you knew. Only the brave would do something like that."

"I intended to tell you and leave for another realm, not stick around and see what happened. I was running, Cain."

He lifted a shoulder in a shrug. "That might have been your plan, but you didna do that."

"You didn't give me much choice."

"Is that so?" he asked with a raised brow.

She lifted her free hand, palm out in a gesture of defeat. "You're right. You gave me all the choices, but you said it in a way that made me believe that I might actually live if I went with you."

"You trusted me."

Noreen nodded slowly. "I did. I *do*."

"That takes courage. It's easy to distrust everyone."

"It's also safer that way."

One side of his lips lifted in a grin. "Aye, you're probably right. But I would say that isna a good life if you're looking at everyone, waiting for them to hurt you."

"That's the way of the Dark. It's why we betray others before they can betray us."

"My point."

She flattened her lips. "I didn't say it was the right way, just the way of the Dark. Balladyn was trying to change that. I honestly think he could've done it. He had a way of getting the attention of the Dark so they actually listened. More than that, they respected him. I can't say any of us ever associated that word with Taraeth."

"Taraeth only cared about himself and the power he could gain. He was ruthless about it when he first came to the throne, but over the years, he became too confident. Ultimately, that was his demise."

"That and believing that Balladyn would always be his lapdog. I think Balladyn intended to take the throne all along but was waiting for the right time. There are rumors that he killed Taraeth after Balladyn found out that Usaeil had left him for dead on the battlefield so Taraeth could kill him."

"That's exactly what happened."

Her eyes widened as she gaped at him. "Really? How do you know that?"

"Rhi," he said. "She and Balladyn became close again over the past few years. He was in love with her, and when he became a Dark, it twisted that love as he hunted her."

"What?" Noreen couldn't believe her ears. "Are you sure about that?"

"Oh, aye. Balladyn caught Rhi and put her in the dungeons at the Dark Palace while putting the Chains of Mordare on her."

Noreen was so shocked all she could say was, "Bloody hell."

"Balladyn believed Rhi was the one who had left at that time. He wanted to turn her Dark as revenge. Except his plan didna work. Rhi was able to break the chains."

"Of Mordare?" Noreen asked in shock.

Cain nodded.

"Those chains are unbreakable."

Cain blew out a breath. "No' for Rhi. She broke them and destroyed a section of the dungeon."

"So that's why the dungeon had to be rebuilt," she said, more to herself than to Cain.

"Balladyn realized then that he still loved Rhi. He set out to woo her after that."

Noreen jerked her head back, giving Cain a skeptical look. "No Light in their right mind would be friends with someone who tried to turn them Dark."

"But Rhi and Balladyn had a past that linked them. Rhi is also one of the most forgiving people I've ever met. She spoke with Balladyn, and he confessed his love. For a time, they were lovers, but that was before he became King of the Dark."

"I could see that happening. But the relationship was doomed from the beginning since Balladyn had his eye on the throne. He wouldn't give up being a Dark, and I can't see Rhi being anything other than a Light."

Cain gave a nod, his lips twisting. "That's pretty much what happened. Balladyn loved her so much that he let Rhi go, but he did back her up when she faced off against Usaeil."

"That he did. It's a tragic love story, especially since he died—and by Usaeil's hand, no less. I wanted more for Balladyn."

"Many of us Kings did, as well. He wasna always a villain, and while he might have been King of the Dark, he was there for Rhi when it mattered. Ulrik was the one who went to him to ask if he would join us, and we found out that Balladyn was already planning on being there with his entire Dark Army."

Noreen shook her head as they continued walking. "I really wish things would've turned out differently for him. Rhi, too, for that matter. It's all so tragic."

"Rhi is strong. She'll survive this, but it might take her some time."

"As much as I'd like to keep talking about this, I think it's time we move on to what Moreann had planned for the Kings next. She won't continue with that, but knowing where her mind is and how it works might help."

"I'm all ears," Cain said with a grin.

CHAPTER TWENTY-THREE

Somewhere on Earth

If she had been furious before, it was nothing compared to how Usaeil felt now. She stood before the house she had built four hundred years earlier. No one knew of it because she'd had her Trackers kill everyone who worked on it, including the architect and designer. By the time her Trackers finished, there wasn't a soul left alive who knew about it.

And that's how she wanted it kept.

The fact that she managed to keep Con from knowing her location was a feat she was proud of. But it wasn't Con who had her attention now. It was Moreann and the rest of the Others.

Usaeil stalked to the house. The Trackers who stood guard dropped their veils upon her approach. Their orders were simple. They were to remain and stand guard while making sure no one got into the house. And the Trackers excelled at their jobs.

She didn't worry about the lone occupant inside, because Xaneth wasn't going anywhere. She had her nephew locked so far inside his mind that he'd never find his way out.

And if he did . . . well, he'd never be the same.

The fact that the thought didn't bring as much joy as it used to was telling. Moreann had managed to snatch Usaeil's body right before the spell Usaeil had put in place eons ago would've begun. Never mind that Rhi had managed to get in a blow that would've killed any other Fae. Usaeil wasn't just any Fae, though—she was a queen.

Moreann had made sure to tell Usaeil that she'd saved her since Rhi had been about to lop off her head.

"Riiiiight," Usaeil mumbled with a roll of her eyes.

Rhi was one of the best warriors the Light Fae had ever seen, but she wasn't that bloodthirsty.

Usaeil came to a halt once she was inside the house as her musings brought up another thought. "Unless the darkness has finally gotten to her."

That made Usaeil laugh. The perfect, incomparable Rhi might not be so infallible now. And it was about damn time. Everyone thought Rhi was so bloody amazing. Maybe now, others would get to see just what kind of person she really was. Usaeil had known what was in Rhi's heart long ago.

She'd seen it despite how blinding the light inside Rhi was. That was partly why Usaeil had done the things she had to Rhi, because she wanted the perfect Light Fae's fall from grace to be so epic, so monumental that no one would ever stop talking about it.

Usaeil smiled happily and pulled in a deep breath before she started toward the stairs. She rushed up them, her long strides eating up the distance to the room where she'd put Xaneth.

When she pushed open the door, her nephew lay upon the bed just as she'd left him. She was curious to know what was going on inside his mind. All she had to do was touch him to get a glimpse of whatever torture he was putting himself through. Then she would be able to push him even harder if she wanted.

However, when she caught her reflection in the mirror on the wall across from the door, she winced. She looked as terrible as she felt, and that simply wouldn't do. It was time she scraped off the grime and dirt that Moreann had inflicted upon her.

Usaeil turned on her heel and found the bedroom she'd shared with Con. Her gaze immediately moved to the bed. He'd been with her for weeks this last time, but they hadn't made love in months.

She could've forced things. She'd wanted him, but she wanted him to come to her of his own free will as he once had. Too much heartache had happened when they were lovers—as well as too many harsh words exchanged. This time, she'd known he was well and truly hers.

Or so she'd been fooled to think.

That blade twisted in her heart, but no matter how angry she was, she couldn't hate Con. She loved him too much.

"Why can't you love me, Con?" she quietly asked the empty room.

She'd done everything. She'd coaxed, teased, demanded, begged, and even tried to seduce him, but the King of Dragon Kings hadn't wanted any part of her once he ended their brief affair.

Usaeil knew that Rhi had something to do with it. After all, Usaeil had ended Rhi's relationship with her Dragon King. It was only fair that Rhi return the favor.

That's why Usaeil had gone to such extremes after she'd kidnapped Con. She'd been so sure that if she could get him away from the influence of the other Dragon Kings and Rhi that she could talk some sense into him. And if that didn't work, she'd planned to use her power.

As much as she'd held out hope that he would see what a catch she was, she'd had no choice but to use magic.

It was too bad she hadn't realized how good of an actor Con was. He'd fooled her better than anyone ever had. She knew she was partly to blame. She'd wanted to believe the lies he fed her so badly that she hadn't seen the truth through the deception until it was too late.

Usaeil shifted her shoulders. She could still feel the agony of the blade piercing her flesh and sinking into her body. And she'd never forget the look of hatred in Rhi's silver eyes as she thrust the weapon hard.

"No," Usaeil said, refusing to think about Rhi winning. "She hasn't won. I'm still alive, and while everyone thinks I'm not around to be queen, they're about to discover how wrong they are."

But first, Usaeil needed to take care of Moreann. The empress wasn't going to be easy to kill. Not because of Moreann's magic, but because of the binding spell in the form of the promise they'd made.

That kind of magic was powerful and irreversible. Or at least Moreann thought. Usaeil knew that nearly every spell had a loophole that allowed at least one member to get free, and she was going to ensure that she found that means of escape.

The problem was that she didn't have a lot of time to do it. And it had nothing to do with Noreen, who Brian wanted her to find. Rather, it was because Usaeil couldn't get to the library at the Light Castle without being seen, and she wasn't quite ready to make that entrance just yet. It would make more of an impact if someone else tried to take the throne, and *then* Usaeil returned.

She smiled just thinking about it. There was something great about grand entrances like that.

Then she recalled that there was someone else who also

had an extensive library—Balladyn. It was a good thing she'd killed him. Otherwise, she wouldn't be able to get to his books. No doubt, there was something in those many tomes that could give her the answers she needed.

She walked to the bathroom. While all she had to do was snap her fingers to remove the dirt, put herself back in order, and have new clothes, she quite liked bathing the human way. She got into the shower to scrub her skin nearly raw before washing her hair three times. Then she got out and ran a hot bath, dropping in a bath bomb once the tub had filled.

While she watched the water turn yellow and then orange, she thought about the book that had been found in the library at the Light Castle. She hadn't been able to get the letters on the page to stop moving, but *someone* obviously could. Whoever had gone to such lengths to make sure that not just anyone could read the book, must be hiding something very important.

Usaeil wanted to know what it was. But she stopped her thoughts there before they could go any further. There was a lot she needed to accomplish, and foes she needed to vanquish before she could think about that book again. If only she'd paid attention to her grandfather when he'd tried to tell her what it was.

She stepped into the tub and lowered herself into the water. Usaeil soaked for over thirty minutes. All the while, she thought about defeating Moreann. For someone who had once been an ally, the empress was turning out to be one hell of an enemy.

But she was just a Druid. A Druid with significant powers, sure, but still a Druid.

Usaeil smiled as she recalled that she had one advantage over Moreann that no one knew about. One that also made Usaeil even stronger—Druids.

While it wasn't as easy to find Druids on Earth as it had once been, there were still many to choose from. However, Usaeil needed to make sure that the next time she took a Druid's power, they were stronger than any of the others she'd used before. Because she needed the power they gave her to last.

Those at Dreagan would do nicely if only she could get to them, but that wasn't an option. There were those at MacLeod Castle, as well, but the moment one of them went missing, all hell would break loose.

She would get to those at MacLeod Castle eventually. But there was another group she could pick from. The Skye Druids thought they were too powerful to be at risk from anyone other than a Dragon King, but they were about to find out how wrong they were.

The Druids at Skye were some of the first humans to gain magic. Like other Druids around the world, the Skye Druids' magic had waned some over the years. Still, it was three times as strong as any other Druid's, except for a select few who happened to be at either Dreagan or MacLeod Castle.

Usaeil needed the Druid magic she took into herself to last for more than one spell, because her battle with Moreann wouldn't be over quickly. Unless she surprised the empress, but that might be wishing for too much.

After some more planning, Usaeil rose from the tub, her magic drying her as she stepped from the water. In two more steps, she called clothing to her.

As she looked into the mirror, she took in the black pants that skimmed her legs perfectly, then her gaze traveled upward to the white shirt that molded to her curves, as well as the black suit jacket that accentuated her waist. The skinny black tie was an added touch that felt like flipping off Con.

She left her black and silver hair loose, showing the pearl studs in her ears. On her feet, she'd placed black Christian Louboutin heels with the unmistakable red soles that matched her eyes.

She hadn't gone out without glamour . . . ever. Did she dare do it now? Not that it mattered. She planned to show everyone who she truly was anyway. Might as well start now.

Usaeil pivoted and walked from the bathroom. She didn't look at the bed as she left the chamber. Once she reached the main floor, she found two Trackers by the front door.

"There are those looking for me. They might get lucky and find this place. It's doubtful, but I'd rather have all of you prepared. Stay veiled, even inside. If anyone does come, I want them to think this place is empty."

The house was as well hidden as it was remote, but that didn't mean one of her many enemies might not get lucky.

The Trackers nodded.

"If," she continued, "someone does come, kill them. Don't let anyone get away. If they do, make sure one of you follows them and takes care of the problem."

Once more, they nodded.

Without another word, she teleported to the place where she had made the doorway to get to Taraeth's throne room. Balladyn had sealed it up, but she was queen. She could get through.

Three hours later, Usaeil finally gave up trying to bust down the seal Balladyn had put up and teleported straight to the Dark Palace. She arrived outside the door. There were few places that she had been inside the palace, and she didn't want to just walk in.

Her gaze moved to the top floor, where Balladyn's quarters had been. No doubt they were warded. Or had been.

He was no longer alive, which meant that there was a good chance the spells were down.

Usaeil tried to teleport in, but found her way blocked. "Damn it," she muttered.

She hurriedly glanced around to make sure no one had seen her. With no other choice, she used glamour to alter her face—but left her red eyes and black and silver hair so no one would recognize her, then she walked to the door of the palace.

The guards looked at her, but they didn't stop her. No one said anything to her as she made her way up the stairs. It took her a moment to realize that the entire vibe of the place was off. When she reached the doors to Balladyn's chamber, there was no one guarding it.

Usaeil walked in and headed straight for the books. Oddly enough, the rooms hadn't been touched. It felt weird to be there, but she shook it off and began to scan the titles of the tomes, looking for any that might hold what she looked for.

CHAPTER TWENTY-FOUR

No matter how long Cain looked on the Fae Realm, he could find no sign of another person. And yet he knew without a doubt that someone had made this section as well as ensured that the shield continued to grow and repair the realm.

It might take thousands of years, but it would happen.

"You don't seem upset about what I told you."

Cain turned his head to Noreen, thinking about the plans that the Others had made against the Kings and mates and their friends. "I'm no' surprised by any of it. Upset? Perhaps a little, but it doesna do any good. I need to focus on other things."

"Like finding whoever did this?" Noreen asked with a knowing grin.

Cain chuckled. "I'm sorry. It's just bothering me, and I can no' figure out why. I am listening to all you're saying, I promise."

"I know. We also both know there's a 99.9% chance Moreann and the group won't continue with the plans since she knows I'll tell you about them."

"It doesna diminish the fact that she intended to

continue hitting at us. Though, I have to admit, these upcoming plans you've told me about doona have the same,"—he paused, trying to come up with the right word—"punch."

Noreen nodded, her lips twisting. "I thought the same thing. For a while, I just assumed that she used all her really good plans at first."

"But?" Cain pushed when she didn't continue.

"I can't place my finger on what's bothering me."

Cain lifted a brow briefly. "Kinda like what's going on with me and this place."

"Exactly." Noreen scratched her earlobe. "This may sound stupid, but I studied all the traps that had been set for the Kings. From taking V's sword to hiding it in Iceland, and then spelling the place so that one of you would have to kill the other just to get it. The planning of it was amazing."

Cain watched her face as her eyes widened, and her speech quickened the more she spoke. It was obvious that she had done a lot of studying regarding what the Others had done to the Kings. And that could come in handy.

"All the bases had been covered," Noreen continued.

He gave a shake of his head. "Most of them. Had everything been covered, then V would've had to kill Roman, but that didna happen."

"Because of Sabina."

"Because of Sabina," he replied. "Same with Dmitri and the bones of the White dragon on Fair Isle. If the Others' plan had come to fruition, the wooden dragon Faith found would've worked, and she would've tried to kill a Dragon King."

"Which we both know wouldn't have happened since you can't die except by another Dragon King."

"Correct. However, I still believe that the Others didna

care who found the wooden dragon—Faith or a Dragon King. Regardless, the effect was for the dragons to attack mankind again and start another war."

Noreen grinned before stepping on a fallen tree and jumping to the other side. "Once more, the Kings thwarted the Others."

"We've done so several times, just scraping by, by the skin of our teeth."

Her smile faltered as she caught his eye. "There is one question that no one would ever answer, not even Moreann. But each time I asked it, she smiled like she knew something I didn't."

"How she intends to kill us?"

"Yes," Noreen replied. "If only a Dragon King can kill another King, then how in the world can the Others do it?"

Cain blew out a breath. "I'm guessing the same way they were able to block V's memories and hold Roman in that prison in Iceland. The same way they've been able to hide from us, not to mention staying one step ahead at all times. The combined magic."

"Are you scared?"

"On our realm, we've been the strongest, the ones with the greatest magic. That has kept us on top from the verra beginning. It's also allowed us to protect our realm. However, the price of that is enemies."

Noreen's nose wrinkled. "You Kings certainly have your share."

"It's something we've accepted. And while we are the strongest, trust me, we've been keenly aware that it was only a matter of time before someone else came that was stronger, faster, more powerful. Someone that could knock us down."

"The Others might have more powerful magic when it's

combined, but even I realized that once the Kings were defeated, Moreann was going to take over. If even one of you could survive, then you could defeat her."

"Do you really think she'd stop? She would continue using the Others to come after us until each and every one of us was dead."

Noreen looked away.

Cain briefly closed his eyes and sighed. "You're saying things that we've already spoken about as a group. Con is nothing if not prepared. He looks at every angle so we can come up with a plan, even if that angle is one in which we're losing."

"Do you think it's possible that all of you can defeat the Others?"

"Aye. Just as I think it's possible that they can defeat us."

There was a long pause before Noreen asked, "You don't still think I'm a ploy to get you to drop your guard, do you?"

"Nay, lass."

"Good." She still didn't look at him. She kept her gaze forward, but her body was tense.

Cain decided to change the topic a bit. "Was it only Moreann who planned everything against us? V's sword and all that?"

"Yes."

"No one else helped?"

Noreen gave a small shrug. "She didn't give them a chance. She came to them and told them what they were going to do, but I don't know how she did it."

"I can see the Druids from Earth bending to her will, and even the Druids from her realm. But the Fae? Especially Usaeil?"

"I thought the same thing," Noreen replied as she glanced his way. "But that's not only what Moreann told me happened. Usaeil also said that's how it happened. Usaeil had some plans too, but Moreann ignored them."

"Probably no' a good idea on the empress's part."

Noreen chuckled softly. "No, I don't think it was."

"So, all of those intricate plans to then attempt to attack our whisky and therefore our money? Does she no' realize that we could shut down Dreagan whisky and still be rich?"

"Like I said, it seemed off. Almost as if Moreann was reaching for anything she could do to hurt you."

"It doesna have the same intelligence or even drive. Are you sure it was Moreann who came up with the plans?"

Noreen shrugged again as she looked his way. "I don't know if she came up with the plans. Like I told you before, she told us what to do, but not where the plans came from."

"Could it be her?"

"Of course. Though she never claimed them as hers, and that's something she usually does."

"What if it wasna her?"

"Who could it be, then?"

It was his turn to shrug. "Someone other than Moreann. Tell me more about her world. You said the Druids there were beginning to be born without magic, and those were the ones she sent to Earth. Since the magic is weakening on her realm, and that is needed to give Druids their power, she went looking for another planet."

"That's right."

"Our Druids are also born with less and less magic. It's because they're mating with mortals who doona have any power."

"But the Fae as well as the Dragon Kings continue to have magic. Not to mention the few powerfully strong Druids who are still here."

He stopped when something out of the corner of his eye caught his attention. "Magic isna endless. Just like everything else on a realm, it has to be tended to. You can no' just take and no' expect some kind of repercussions. Why do you think we built Dreagan where it is? The source of magic for Earth is right there. We wanted to protect it from those who would either destroy it in their ignorance or want it for some profit."

"But the Kings have benefited."

"Just as every magical creature on our realm has. The Kings have no' hoarded the magic. We couldna if we tried. What we do is keep it safe and try to keep it thriving."

Noreen glanced in the direction he was interested in. "If Moreann's realm holds nothing but Druids, and all of them had power at one point, then there's no reason for them to be born *without* magic unless the land was drained."

"Which means, someone took it. Tell me, is it normal for those on Moreann's realm to be immortal?"

Noreen swallowed and gave a small shake of her head. "From what Moreann let slip one night, it's something only the most powerful can harness. She is one of a select few, but the Dragon Kings are immortals. Even the Fae live very long lives."

"Dragons are no' immortal. We Kings are, because that's what happens when the magic chooses us for this role until another comes along who is stronger. The Fae naturally live long lives, though you can be killed. Moreann and her people are no' meant to be immortal. It creates a flux in the order of things."

"You think that's why the magic began drying up?"

"The magic on Earth isna a thing. Nor is it a being. But it does have some intelligence since it looks at every dragon, searching their heart, mind, and soul. It determines if we're powerful enough and have the right heart to lead our clans. Like I said, it chooses who will be Dragon King, no' us."

Noreen's mouth went slack. "So, there's a good chance the magic on Moreann's realm has chosen to stop giving power to the Druids because someone took more than they should have."

"Aye."

"Why hasn't it taken it from her if she's lived this long?"

Cain finally turned his head in the direction of whatever had caught his attention earlier. "I'd like to know that, as well. It seems as if the magic would go after her first, but perhaps it is trying to teach her a lesson, one that she hasna learned yet."

"What is out there?" Noreen asked softly, jerking her chin in the direction he looked.

They held still for several long minutes before a fox darted past them. Still, Cain didn't move. He'd seen something. It had been fleeting, but for just a moment, he'd sworn it was a person. Though he'd caught the movement and glimpse out of the corner of his eye, so he could be mistaken.

Just as he was about to turn away, he saw it again. Something was glowing.

"Noreen, I need you to stay here," he told her in a whisper.

She held his hand tighter. "What is it?"

"I believe it's a who, and if I'm right, then things could be turning in a much better direction."

He gave her a nod as he met her red eyes. When she released him, he headed straight for the spot where he'd seen the glow. As he neared, he kept looking for Rhi's black hair through the thick foliage. When he reached the spot, a smile grew on his face as he expected to greet her.

However, all that was there was an orb the size of a basketball that glowed the same hue as Rhi did.

Cain sighed in frustration. But the more he looked at the orb, the more he began to suspect that the person responsible for the transformation of the Fae Realm was none other than Rhi herself. And he couldn't wait to tell the rest of the Kings.

CHAPTER TWENTY-FIVE

The look of excitement on Cain's face had Noreen rushing to him. Her feet slowed when she saw the large orb. She looked around, expecting to see someone, but there was nothing.

"What is this?" she asked.

Cain's smile was wide. "Do you know that when Rhi becomes angry, she glows?"

"I did see her doing that at the battle with Usaeil."

"It's something she's always fought. If she can no' control it, she could destroy a realm."

Noreen's mouth went slack as his words penetrated her brain. "Are you serious?"

"I am."

"So, why are you smiling?"

Cain's green eyes slid to the orb. "I doona know of another Fae who glows like Rhi, and this orb is glowing just as she does."

Noreen returned her gaze to the sphere. "You think Rhi was here?"

"I do." Cain looked skyward before his gaze moved

around and finally settled on her. "I think Rhi is responsible for all of this."

"I thought you said she could destroy realms."

Cain nodded, his smile fading slowly. "Oh, she can. She's done it before. However, her powers also allow her to create worlds, as well."

"Bloody hell," Noreen murmured. "I didn't think anyone other than a god or goddess could do such a thing."

"As far as I know, no one can. That's what makes Rhi so special."

"Is she a goddess?"

Cain shrugged. "She was born to Light Fae parents, who also had special abilities. Rhi's mother was unable to lie without great pain. She passed that onto Rhi. Unfortunately, Rhi learned to harness the pain so she could tell untruths."

Noreen gave a shake of her head, unable to actually believe that all of this was happening. "If what you say is true, then it could be Rhi's power alone that caused Usaeil's jealousy."

"I've no doubt that played a huge role, but there were other factors, as well."

"If Rhi really does have such potent power, then why have the Dark not heard of it?"

Cain squatted down to study the orb closer. "Because Rhi had no reason to use it."

"To have such power and not use it. I can't fathom the thought."

Green eyes lifted to her, snagging Noreen's gaze. "She *is* using it."

"Now. She could've used it long ago. She could've saved our realm so we didn't have to leave."

Cain studied her for a long moment before he slowly straightened. "If Rhi had saved this realm, the civil war would've continued. And every time the realm was about to be destroyed, she would've had to step in and heal it. Would prolonging the war have helped?"

Noreen looked away, hating that he was right. "No."

"I believe Rhi knew that, as well. She didna want to leave her home any more than any other Fae did. Because of the Fae Wars, she lost her brother, her parents, and Balladyn. And even her Dragon King lover. For centuries, she was on her own with no one but her one friend and queen."

"Usaeil." Noreen took a deep breath and turned her head back to Cain. "Which is why Usaeil's many betrayals cut so deeply for Rhi."

"Aye."

Noreen looked at the glowing globe. "Rhi isn't just a badass warrior, she's also the strongest both mentally and powerfully among the Fae. She could step in and rule the Light. Fek. She could even rule the Dark if she tried hard enough."

"Rhi has never wanted to rule. Her desires have always been simple. She wanted the Light to be safe, and she wanted to be loved by her King."

Noreen knew exactly how Rhi felt. She hadn't exactly been without her fair share of lovers, but Cain was different in all ways. With him, she actually looked to the future. With Cain, she *wanted* a future.

And this was just after being with him for a couple of days. What would it be like months from now? Years? Noreen's stomach churned at the thought.

Would she end up like Rhi, alone? Without her King?

"Lass, what's wrong?" Cain asked as he put a hand on her shoulder.

Noreen shook her head. She couldn't exactly tell him what she was thinking. She would sound . . . daft to be sure. Instead, she shrugged and said, "I'm thinking about everything Rhi lost."

It wasn't a lie. In fact, Noreen found many similarities between her and the infamous Light Fae. Except Noreen didn't have a sibling or a best friend/lover who had turned Dark.

"Despite all of that, Rhi didna succumb to grief. I wonder how she managed it, honestly." Cain lifted one shoulder in a shrug. "None of that matters right now, though. I truly believe this is Rhi's doing. I need to tell the others."

Noreen's heart skipped a beat at the thought of Cain leaving. She'd known it was coming, but she hadn't realized it would be right then. Although, he did have all the information he needed to take to the other Dragon Kings.

She forced a quick smile. The last thing she wanted to be was a hindrance. The Kings had enough to deal with regarding Moreann and Usaeil still missing.

Cain didn't rush off, however. He hesitated and reached for her hand. "Is there nothing I can say that will convince you to return with me?"

"No," she said, though her throat was thick with emotion. "And you know why."

"Because Moreann and the Others will come straight for you."

"Exactly. You and everyone at Dreagan need whatever time you can get to form a plan. Take what I've told you and go with that."

"I didna expect to leave so soon."

"Perhaps it's better that you do." Better for her, because she was already getting attached to him.

He pulled her to him and wrapped his arms around her. Noreen closed her eyes as she nestled against him. She knew that in Cain's arms, she was as close to Heaven as she would ever get.

"I doona want to leave you."

His voice, deep and heavy with emotion, made her smile. "I don't want you to leave either." She pulled back to look at him. "But we don't have a choice."

"We *do* have a choice. You can come with me. We'll protect you. Dreagan is a powerful place. I doona care how much Moreann and the Others think they can defeat us, they can no' get to us on Dreagan."

"I'd rather not tempt Fate." The hardest thing Noreen ever did was pull out of Cain's arms. She stepped back until they were no longer touching each other. "Your brethren are waiting."

"Noreen—" he began.

She quickly cut him off. "Look at this place. It's a wonderland of beauty. We've not seen anyone while we've been here, and you flew me over the entire space where the shield is. I'll be fine."

"What if I missed something? What if someone *is* here?" he asked.

That wasn't something she wanted to think about, but she had to. "I may not be a trained fighter, but I can—and I *will*—protect myself."

"I've no doubt."

She swallowed and smiled then. It felt weak and shaky, but she held it in place. "I'll be fine. Promise."

"Walk back with me," he urged.

The thought of spending more time with him was like grasping for air as she drowned. It was on the tip of her tongue to say "*yes*," but she was barely holding things together now. "You should fly. You'll get to the doorway faster."

"Fly with me, then."

Damn. How could she refuse that? She nodded. In the next instant, Cain had taken her hand, quickly dragging her into a clearing. The moment they arrived, he shifted, shredding his clothes.

Noreen drew in a breath as she gazed at the magnificent dragon before her. When his pale yellow eyes landed on her, she didn't hesitate to rush to him and climb onto his back.

This time, the takeoff wasn't nearly as scary. There was a smile upon her lips as the wind hit her face. Cain dipped one wing and swung them around to head back in the direction where they'd encountered the barrier.

She didn't look at the ground below her. No, her focus was on the Dragon King's back she rode on. She touched his warm scales and caressed a palm over him. In response, a sound rumbled through him that sounded very much like a purr. It made her smile grow. She liked that she could make him feel such things.

But the grin didn't last. All too soon, they came to the edge of the shield. Noreen didn't care that it would take her some time to walk back to the barrier alone, but apparently, Cain did. He dove toward the ground. They didn't even reach it before he shifted, and she found herself in his arms just as his feet hit the earth.

"Wow," she said as she looked into his eyes. "You certainly know how to show a girl a good time."

He gave her a long kiss that instantly ignited the flames of desire within her. Her arms tightened around his neck as she pressed herself against him. He released her legs so they swung downward while he plundered her mouth as if there were no tomorrow.

And for her, there might not be.

When he ended the kiss, he pressed his forehead to hers and sighed. "I willna ask you again to come with me, but if you change your mind, you'll be welcome at Dreagan."

"Thank you."

He lifted his gaze, his hands gently grasping her face on either side of her head. "I'll return for you."

"Good."

His look intensified. "Do you understand what I'm telling you? I'll be back for you. No matter how long it takes, no matter what Hell I have to walk through, I'm returning."

The tears she had kept at bay threatened to fall. She quickly blinked and smiled up at him as she rose to her tiptoes and kissed him.

One tear slipped out, but she hastily swiped it away as she separated herself from him. "I'll be waiting."

"Be safe, lass."

"You, too."

They stared at each other another few heartbeats before he flashed her a smile and pivoted away. Right before he reached the shield, he turned back to her and winked. Noreen lifted her hand and waved. And then he was gone.

She could run after him. She could go back to Earth with him, or at the very least, walk with him to the doorway. But she didn't. As her Dragon King walked away, he took her heart with him.

Even if she somehow managed to elude Moreann and the Others, there was always the battle with them and the Dragon Kings to consider. Noreen wanted to fight alongside the Kings, but she would only get in the way. However, she would wager everything she had that the Kings would win.

At least, she hoped they did.

They were too powerful and too smart for the likes of Moreann. But still, she knew that there was no place for her in Cain's world. Shara was an exception because she had turned Light with Usaeil's help. Noreen wasn't sure that was even an option for her.

If it were, she didn't know if she could do it.

Liar. You'd do anything to be with him. Face it, in a matter of hours, you've fallen in love with a Dragon King.

Noreen ignored her subconscious. It was listening to her heart at the moment. And every time she listened to her heart, she got into all kinds of trouble.

"Farewell, Cain. I hope to see you again, but I don't think I will."

CHAPTER TWENTY-SIX

The moment Cain returned to Earth, all he could think about was getting back to Noreen. He knew inside the barrier on the Fae Realm was probably the safest place for her, but that didn't stop him from wanting her with him.

Or for him to be with her.

He looked around the Fae doorway, fully expecting someone to be there trying to stop him. It was why he'd had his magic at the ready. But no one was there, which put his already frayed senses on even higher alert.

Cain didn't wait around to see if someone would show up. Instead, he touched the silver cuff on his wrist and immediately jumped to Dreagan. He arrived in his own chamber since he hadn't been sure he wouldn't run into someone if he turned up elsewhere in the manor.

Cain threw open his door and rushed out, calling Con's name through their mental link.

"I'm in my office," Con replied.

Cain ran to the stairs and took them up to the third floor. When he reached the top, Con stood outside of his office, waiting for him.

"Tell me you have good news."

Cain nodded as he strode to Con. "Noreen gave me so much information. Should we call the others together?"

"No' yet."

Cain frowned. "What do you mean?"

"I want to hear it first."

Though that sounded odd to Cain, he didn't argue. They walked into Con's office together. For the next hour, Cain told Con everything Noreen had shared with him.

"You're right, something has changed with Moreann and the Others," Con said as he slowly sat back in his chair. "My guess is that someone else planned the earlier attacks on us."

"Right up until the last few years?" Cain asked.

Con's black eyes met his. "What was really done to us over the last decade besides what was already put into place by the Others?"

Cain thought about that for a minute. "Nothing."

"Exactly. Everything we've dealt with in regards to the Others coalesced in the last handful of years, and all of it was put into motion millennia earlier," Con stated.

Cain ran a hand down his face. "Why stop there, then? Why no' keep things going until we were backed into a corner?"

"I can only guess that somewhere along the way, something happened to whoever was helping Moreann."

"Usaeil?"

Con snorted, the only evidence of what he thought about Cain's suggestion.

"All right," Cain said. "If we look at it bit by bit based on what Noreen said, Moreann came to the Others with minute details of how she wanted the plans laid out, down to the second."

Con raised a blond brow. "No one goes from that kind

of planning to grasping at straws, which is what Moreann is doing if she planned to attack our business." Con's gaze narrowed on Cain. "And you trust the Dark?"

"Noreen has everything to lose and nothing to gain from helping us."

"I wouldna say nothing. She's gotten her freedom from the Others."

Cain rose and paced a few feet away. "There is one bit I left out. Noreen said that she was a child when the Fae Wars took place."

"They lasted a verra long time."

"I know." Cain drew in a breath and released it as he faced Con. "She said that a Dragon King killed her parents, burned them alive."

"That tended to happen to Dark Fae, who stood against us in the war."

"They were no' in the army."

There was a slight pause as Con blinked. Then, he sat forward. "There may be many of us, Cain, but I can assure you that no King went out on their own and attacked any Fae, Dark or otherwise."

"That's what I told her. She was there, Con. She said she can still feel the heat of the dragon fire."

Finally, a frown puckered Con's brow. "No one can survive dragon fire but dragons. Maybe she thinks she was closer than she was."

Cain shook his head. "No' by her memories. She didna see which King it was, but she is sure that it was a dragon because she heard the roar as well as felt and saw the fire."

"But she survived?"

"She was unharmed. Moreann came upon her and took her in, raising Noreen as her own."

Con flattened his hands on the desk and pushed to his feet. "After learning all of that, you honestly doona believe that Moreann didna send a pretty Fae to lure you with lies so we'd let our guard down?"

"Nay, I do no'."

"You were with her for two days. A lot can happen in that time."

Cain didn't even think about lying. In fact, he wanted Con to know. "A lot did happen."

"She's Dark."

"So?"

Con nodded, his chest lifting as he drew in a breath. "I trust you."

"And I trust her."

"I wish you would've brought her here. I would've liked to hear her story myself."

"She wouldna come. The moment she returns to this realm, Moreann and the Others will find her. She wanted to give us time to plan."

Con briefly quirked a brow. "Or she wanted time to return to Moreann."

Cain clenched his fists as anger churned through him. "You sent me because you trusted my judgment. If you doona believe me, then I'll take you to her. That way, I can show you the rest of what we found."

"The rest?"

"When Noreen and I reached the Fae Realm, we walked far to get away from the doorway. As we did, I felt something strong enough to make the ground tremble. That's when I found the barrier."

His attention caught, Con asked, "Barrier? What kind?"

"Magical. It's similar to what the MacLeods use to hide their castle from the world."

"And inside the shield?"

Cain smiled. "The Fae Realm is in tatters except for

inside the barrier. Once you pass through it, it's brimming with life—both plants and animals."

"Any Fae? Or other beings?"

"I didna see anyone, and I flew over the entire area, which is twice as large as Dreagan. There was no sign of anyone else."

Con looked away. "Interesting."

"Even more interesting is what I found before I returned here."

Black eyes slid back to Cain. "What was that?"

"A large, glowing orb."

"Glowing?" Con asked in a whisper.

Cain nodded as he grinned. "Just like Rhi."

"You think she was there?"

"I think she created the entire thing."

Con's frown deepened. "If she did, then why was she no' there?"

"I can no' say, but I think she'll return."

"She might no'. Rhi has a . . . peculiar thinking about certain things."

It was on the tip of Cain's tongue to bring up her affair, but he decided against it at the last minute. "It'll take another few centuries, but the Fae Realm is healing bit by bit. The barrier expands, and when it does, it heals the land."

"That sounds exactly like something Rhi would do." Con turned his back to Cain to face the window before crossing his arms over his chest.

Cain waited a few moments before he asked, "What about the Others? Do you still have doubts about Noreen and what she's told us?"

"It's my job to doubt everyone and everything. It's the only thing that's kept us safe all these years. I know it doesna sit well with any of you, but I doona care."

"I know you only have our best interests at heart, but you also need to understand that we want the best for us, as well."

Con dropped his arms and faced him. "Ulrik was going to be betrayed by Nala. Remember?"

"How can I ever forget?" Cain replied testily.

"It was right in front of Ulrik, and he couldna see it."

Cain spread his fingers before fisting them again. "So, you think we're all blind?"

"I think it's easy to dismiss the warning signs you doona want to see."

"Come, then. Let's go see Noreen. I'll let her convince you that what she says is true."

Con glanced at the floor and blew out a breath. "Did it never occur to you that with the magic Moreann has, she could use it on anyone—including Noreen?"

Cain rolled his eyes as he made a sound in the back of his throat. "That's laughable, Con. Do you really think Noreen would go to such lengths, that Moreann and the Others would try and track her, if this was all a setup?"

Con shrugged. "I'm merely putting out a suggestion. I'm verra often wrong, but I like to consider all angles."

"I know." It was one of the things Cain appreciated about Con.

"What do you know of her? Was she happy with Moreann?"

Cain shrugged. "She lost her family and was taken in by someone other than a Fae. I doona think Noreen was unhappy, but neither was she happy. Moreann kept her secluded in a house she had. She would leave for long periods and make Noreen remain inside. One day, after Moreann left, Noreen went to Dublin, which was her mother's favorite city. There, she was attacked and nearly raped by two humans. Noreen used her magic and killed one man. She let the other go."

Con said nothing, merely waited for him to continue.

Cain swallowed. "Moreann returned, and Noreen told her what had happened. She begged the Druid to take her with her, but Moreann still refused until one day she didna. She took Noreen to Hong Kong and ordered her to kill an old man. It would've been Noreen's second murder, but she refused."

"Did Moreann punish her?"

"Nay. Noreen told Moreann that she wouldna kill for her."

Con's lips twisted. "Hmm. Did Noreen tell you how many she's killed?"

"She said two mortals by sex. I didna ask about others."

"I would've expected more with her being an Other. Then again, the Others targeted us, no' humans."

Cain nodded slowly in agreement.

Con sighed loudly. "When you first met Noreen, you said you believed everything you witnessed between her and the Light Fae, Brian. Do you still?"

"Aye. She was terrified, Con. The kind of fear someone has when they know they're being hunted."

"We'll proceed cautiously, but it's time the rest of the Kings and mates know about what you've discovered. Then we'll need to start preparing for war. I want this matter with Moreann and the Others dealt with immediately."

"There's also Usaeil. Noreen says that Moreann imprisoned her somewhere."

Con's lips flattened. "It would've been too easy for Usaeil to actually be dead. One thing at a time, though. First, we'll deal with the Others. Hopefully, along the way, we can find Rhi."

"I doona want to be the one to tell her that Usaeil is alive."

Con dropped his chin to his chest as he leaned his hands on the desk. "I'll tell her."

CHAPTER TWENTY-SEVEN

Death's Realm

"Why haven't you spoken to Con yet? You still think it best we do nothing?"

Erith sighed and turned from the window of her—now her and Cael's—white tower and faced her lover. "You think I want to stand aside and watch?"

"I know you're conflicted," Cael said as he pushed away from the doorway and walked to her. He took her hands and gazed down at her with purple eyes. His long, black hair was free, the top half pulled back and tied with a piece of leather.

"Conflicted?" Erith rolled her eyes and gave a shake of her head. "If only it were that easy."

"It is, my love."

Cael might be more than a Fae or leader of the Reapers now—he held part of the power that made her a goddess— but he was still coming to grips with his new powers and all that his position entailed.

"It's not," she argued.

He raised a black brow. "It is. And don't tell me I can't know what you're thinking. You're still second-guessing yourself about not helping Rhi and the rest against Usaeil, which means, you're questioning everything about the decision of whether to join the Kings against the Others."

Erith smiled up at the man who had stolen her heart so very long ago. She had loved him from afar for thousands of millennia, and she still had a hard time believing he was hers.

"You do know me pretty well," she said.

He bent his head and gave her a long, slow kiss. By the time he pulled back, her mind was blank, and her body was on fire for him.

"Tell me all the reasons you don't think it's a good idea."

Erith blinked as she tried to remember what they had been talking about. After a few moments, Cael's lips turned up at the corners in a satisfied grin. "It's good to know I've got that kind of effect on you. If it helps, you do the same to me."

"That does help," she said with a chuckle. But the smile died as her thoughts returned to the battle that was brewing between the Dragon Kings and the Others.

She faced the window once more and looked out over the domain that had been solely hers for as long as she could remember. Now, however, it also belonged to the Reapers and their women.

"I don't know how long I existed in space before I finally took form. It was even longer before I found a planet and ventured down to it. The concept of time meant nothing to me as I visited realm after realm, searching for anyone who looked like I did. Then I found the Fae. I found you," she said and looked over her shoulder at Cael.

He nodded. "We were at war. I believe the Light and Dark Fae have always been at war."

"Yes. That's all I saw for years," she said and returned her gaze out the window to watch a condor soar across the sky. "It changed me."

His hands came around her upper shoulders as his lips touched her ear. "You don't have to say more. I know this story well."

"Then tell me what I became," she insisted.

There was a long hesitation before he said, "The Mistress of War."

"I killed so many, Cael. So many who deserved it, and even more who didn't." She closed her eyes and tried not to feel the weight of those souls. "I destroyed not just species but planets, as well."

"And you vowed not to do that anymore."

She leaned her head back to rest against his chest. "It was you who changed that. I wanted to be something more, so I put away my armor and sword and changed from Mistress of War to Death. I began the Reapers, taking the strongest Fae warriors who had been betrayed, and giving each of you a second chance at life."

"I'll never be able to repay that."

"You don't need to."

He placed a gentle kiss on her temple. "It's not war that makes you cautious."

How could it after she had battled Bran and his army of Fae? "No. And before you say it, yes, I killed during the battle with Bran."

"You had to. It was either kill or be killed. No one can fault you for that, and while I did almost lose you, I think Bran did you a favor."

Erith jerked and shifted to look at him. "How can you say that? He nearly stole all of my power."

"He forced you to see both sides of yourself. Death and Mistress of War. And look at you now, my love," he said proudly. "You are both—and stronger than you've ever been."

Erith wanted to argue against what Cael said, but she

couldn't. Because he was right. Bran had backed her into a corner. He'd done it because he thought he would win against her, but she had made the decision to embrace the part of her that she'd tried to forget for so long.

"You're right."

"I know," Cael said with a heart-stopping grin. "You should listen to me more often."

She wrapped her arms around his neck and rose up on her tiptoes to hug him. "I do, love."

Her eyes closed as he held her close. Nothing could hurt her when she was in his arms. It was the safest she'd ever felt, the place she sought out every night when they went to bed, and every morning when they woke.

"You still haven't changed your mind, have you?" Cael asked.

She licked her lips as she pulled back to look at him. "I've stood aside for so long."

"So?" he stated with a shrug. "Trust me when I say that every Reaper wants to fight against the Others. Including me."

"You aren't a Reaper anymore," she reminded him.

"I'm also not a Fae, but I still claim to be both. I don't know what I am anymore, and it doesn't matter. I'm with you. That's all I've ever wanted. Call me whatever you want, but understand what I'm saying."

She sighed as she lowered her hands to rest on his chest. "I do. I'm well aware of how the Reapers feel."

"They would never disobey you, you know that. And while they might not truly understand your reasoning, they accept it."

Erith rolled her eyes and gave a bark of laughter. "Begrudgingly."

"Indeed," Cael replied with a smile.

"You feel strongly that we should join the Kings?"

"I do. You told me why you didn't want to join the battle. Tell me why you do."

"That's easy," she said with a shrug. "The Kings have done a valiant job of defending this realm since the beginning of time. Every King has given more than anyone should, especially the current Dragon Kings."

Cael then asked, "You pity them?"

"On the contrary. I've seen their strength."

"So, they can win against the Others."

Erith paused as she considered his words. "I think they have a very good chance, but none of us should underestimate the Others."

"What happens if we don't join the Kings, and the Others defeat them?"

The mere thought of the Others besting the Dragon Kings made Erith not only sick to her stomach, it also made her see red.

"That's what I thought," Cael said. He brought one of her hands to his lips and kissed her knuckles. "Your reaction—all without words, I should remind you—is the response you need to the question you've been unable to answer."

He was right. As he usually was. She shouldn't have second-guessed herself. She let him pull her against him once more as he held her, softly stroking her back.

"No one can know yet," she said. "No one. Not even Eoghan."

"You don't want to tell the Kings?"

She shook her head.

Cael's hands halted. "What about Con?"

"I've not spoken to him."

"Perhaps it's time. You've always known when to go to Con when he needed it. I think now is one of those times. For both of you."

"He's going to ask about Usaeil."

"Tell him the truth."

Erith nodded slowly. "His battle is only beginning. Even if he defeats the Others."

"If anyone can handle it, it's Con. Look at what all he's done."

"Because he set aside his own wants and needs to focus on his brethren. It wasn't healthy. I warned him that he would have to face it all someday. We can only run from our pasts for so long. I know that better than most."

Cael grasped her arms and pulled her back to look into his eyes. "Go to him."

"I love you," she said.

Cael winked at her. "I love you."

With a wave, Erith departed her realm and arrived inside Con's office. She glanced around, but there was no sign of the King of Dragon Kings. She then jumped to his chamber, making sure to face the door in case he was otherwise engaged or naked.

"Quite ballsy, popping into my rooms," he said in his smooth Scots brogue.

He kept his voice even, but she'd known him long enough to know when he was irritated. "I needed to speak with you."

"You always did like showing up out of nowhere, though you usually use different names. I'm glad to know we're past that."

She frowned and quickly glanced behind her to see him holding a bottle of whisky and sitting with his back to her before an empty hearth. Erith faced him as he brought the bottle to his lips and drank deeply.

"How are you?" she asked.

"Couldna be better. You?" he asked without glancing her way.

Her eyes immediately went to the cuffs of his dress shirt where he always wore the first gift she'd given him, the gold dragon head cufflinks. But they weren't there. That gave her pause. She'd never known Con not to wear them. Was he that angry at her that he had set aside her gift?

Hopefully, he hadn't done that with all three of them.

"Before you ask, I don't know where Usaeil is," Erith stated.

"Moreann took her. In case you didna know, she's the leader of the Others. Oh," Con said, sarcasm dripping from his voice, "she's also the one who brought the mortals here. They were the ones born without magic on her realm, and she wanted them gone."

Erith felt as if she'd been kicked in the stomach. How had this information slipped by her? But then she knew. She'd been so wrapped up in deciding whether or not to join the fight that she hadn't done her due diligence and learned all she could. In her fear of making the wrong mistake, she had instead let a friend and ally down.

"I'm sorry."

Con gave a shake of his blond head and stretched his long legs out to cross them at the ankles. "There isna anything for you to apologize for."

"I want to help."

Silence met her words. In a blink, Con was on his feet and facing her. "You want to help? Then find Rhi before she does something no one can save her from."

"You think she's turned Dark?"

"Her eyes flashed red. She's needed by the Fae—both Light and Dark—now that Balladyn is gone."

Erith waited for Con to ask if she knew what had happened to Balladyn's body, but he didn't. She closed her eyes and focused on Rhi. It had always been easy to find the Fae before because Rhi's light shone brighter than any others.

Thankfully, Erith did locate Rhi, but her light was now encircled by red.

Erith opened her eyes to meet Con's black ones. "I can tell you where Rhi is."

"Nay," Con barked. Then he turned his head to the side and drew in a deep breath. In a calmer voice, he said, "Tell someone else the location."

It was on the tip of Erith's tongue to argue, but she thought better of it. She gave Con a quick smile. "I'll see it done. And, in case you were wondering, I'll make sure she's taken care of."

"Good." Con lowered himself back into the chair and brought the whisky to his lips for another long drink.

CHAPTER TWENTY-EIGHT

Noreen didn't know what to do with herself once Cain left. The beautiful area was suddenly strange and eerie. She knew it was simply her imagination, but that didn't help matters.

She wrapped her arms around herself as she turned and stared back in the direction they had flown. It was a long trek back. She was up for it, but why would she return to that spot when she could wait here for him to return instead.

Without a doubt, she knew Cain would be back. His statement had been more than words. A vow had filled his voice, his face, his very essence.

The question was, would she still be here? If she had a choice, Noreen would be, but this was out of her hands. This went far deeper than she could pull herself out of. Her only hope was for the Kings to kill Moreann.

Noreen rubbed her hands up and down her arms, suddenly chilled. She headed to the right where a grove of trees sprung up from the earth and then followed the rise of a hill. She liked the idea of a vantage point. Plus, she would be close by if anyone came through.

That is if someone found the same spot that she and Cain had.

"What are you doing?" she asked herself.

Only a fool would remain, waiting to see if those after her arrived. If she were smart, she'd leave and go to another realm. The more distance she put between herself and the Others, the better.

She glanced over her shoulder to where Cain had gone through the barrier. No matter how tempting it was to leave and save herself, she couldn't. Something held her back, and she knew exactly what it was—Cain.

Why did she have to fall for him? Why did he have to be so amazing? She wasn't supposed to like him, much less find herself thinking of them having a future together.

"I'm a Dark. He's a Dragon King. It won't work."

She shook her head and found herself arguing with . . . herself. "The Kings don't care who their mates are. If they fall in love, that's all there is to it. Rhi and Shara are Fae. Some are Druids. Even more are simply mortals. What does it matter if I'm Dark?"

But she knew the answer. In order to become Dark, she'd had to do evil. In fact, she'd had to kill. It didn't matter how it had happened, she'd done it. There was no denying it. All one had to do was look at her eyes and hair to see the evidence.

"I should leave. Right now. There's no one here to talk me out of it, no one distracting me with kisses or making my body burn." She closed her eyes and swallowed. "It doesn't matter if Cain's here or not. He's already branded on my skin, through to my very soul. No matter how far across the universe I go, I will always hunger to be in his arms."

Which meant, she was royally fekked.

Noreen sighed as she opened her eyes. Her arms

dropped listlessly to her sides as she started toward the grove of trees to start counting the minutes until Cain returned.

She had just gotten settled against a tree when a bright light flashed in the distance. For a heartbeat, she thought it might be lightning, but no thunder followed. Nor did she spot any more flashes.

Intrigued, Noreen jumped to her feet and started in the direction where she'd seen the light. Maybe it was another of the orbs Cain had found. Or maybe it was Rhi herself. She hoped it was the Light Fae. She really wanted to meet Rhi.

Noreen immediately jumped to the location. She stood in the open field, her gaze gradually moving around the area, searching for anything that seemed out of the ordinary. Noreen slowly turned in a circle, but no matter how hard she looked, she could find nothing.

She searched for hours without uncovering anything. The sun was already beginning to near the horizon when she finally stopped.

Discouraged and yearning for Cain, Noreen decided to remain there in hopes that she'd see the flash again. Even though there was a chance that it meant that someone was there, she used her magic again to conjure a bed.

She wasn't a fighter, and she certainly wasn't one who liked sleeping on the ground.

You didn't mind when you were in Cain's arms.

"That was different."

Then she rolled her eyes. She really had to stop arguing with herself. It wasn't a good sign when it came to her mental state.

Noreen yawned and gazed longingly at the large board that hung from several branches. Upon the plank was a thick mattress, silk sheets, and fluffy pillows all calling her name. She sat on the side of the mattress and removed her shoes before she curled up on her side to face the sunset.

She cleared her mind and simply took in the splendor around her. She couldn't begin to count the many colors that lit up the sky as the sun slipped into the horizon. Little by little, the gray sky crept over her until it blanketed everything.

Her eyes were heavy, but she didn't sleep. Instead, she turned onto her back and watched as the stars began lighting up the darkening sky. She had once done this with her parents. She could recall it vividly.

Noreen must have been in the spot between wakefulness and sleep, because suddenly, there was a face hovering over her. She recognized it immediately as her mother's.

"Wake up, sleepyhead," she said with a bright smile as she smoothed Noreen's hair back from her face. "The day awaits us."

There was a smile on Noreen's lips until she realized the eyes she looked into weren't red but silver.

And just like that, the dream or image or whatever it was faded. Noreen gripped the covers tightly in her hands as her chest rose and fell rapidly.

Her mother's eyes hadn't been silver. She was Dark. Just as Noreen was.

But the harder Noreen tried to remember what color her mother's eyes were, the less she could pull from her memories. The odd thing was, she had forgotten her mother's face centuries ago. Yet she had known immediately that's who she looked up at.

The fear of not knowing what was real and what wasn't, made her begin to panic. She knew what it felt like because she used to wake up screaming after her parents had died. Moreann had always been there. While the Druid hadn't exactly been motherly, she had comforted Noreen in her own way.

Noreen knew that if she kept her mind on this path, she would spiral out of control. Her parents were gone. Killed by a Dragon King. There was no bringing them back, nor was there a reason to cry over what had been done.

She focused on a star above her and set about calming her breathing. When she mastered that, she moved on to clearing her mind. Little by little, she gained ground. Right up until she thought about the Dragon King who'd killed her parents.

The fact that she wasn't sure how to feel about that now startled her. She'd hated the Kings for as long as she could remember for taking away her parents. Even though she knew Cain was a King, to her, he was somehow apart from her hatred. She couldn't explain why or how, she only knew that he was.

She remembered him saying that no Kings had strayed from the battlefields, but there were many Kings, and there were ways that one could slip away without being seen.

That brought her back to the story she'd seen from his mind. The Kings she'd witnessed and the actions they had taken had been those of the most noble beings she'd ever encountered. Her mind couldn't reconcile what she'd seen to what she knew had happened to her parents.

"No one survives dragon fire."

She had felt the heat of the fire that day. There were times a flash of it came through in her dreams. It was only ever just for a moment, but when it did, she woke up sweating from the heat of it.

Her mother had been only a few feet from her. If what Cain said was true, then she should've been burnt, as well. Yet, she had no scars. But what about the roar she'd heard? That had been a dragon. She knew that for certain.

She was working off memories that were distorted because she had been a young child, and it was many, many years ago. The few times she'd asked Moreann about it, the empress had told her the same story again and again.

Maybe it was the barrier or the stress she'd put herself under to help the Kings that was causing long-buried memories to fill her mind. At least she hoped that's what it was, because if it was anything else, that meant she needed to be very worried.

Noreen did her best to go back to sleep, but her eyes wouldn't stay closed. She refused to get up because the mattress was so comfortable, so she rolled to her other side and found the half moon hovering over the peak of a distant mountain.

Her mind wandered to thoughts of Cain, of how his deep green eyes crinkled at the corners when he smiled. She thought about how he would reach for her hand when they were walking, or how he liked to make sure she was right up against him when they were lying together.

She didn't fight it when her eyes slid shut. And when sleep called to her, she willingly went.

But it wasn't a peaceful or restful slumber that awaited her. It was filled with screams of the dying, of a woman whose evil laugh made Noreen's skin crawl. She heard chanting and recognized one of the voices, but she couldn't put a face to it.

She knew that whatever was happening was being done to her. She tried to move but was paralyzed. She wanted to open her eyes, to see those around her but she couldn't.

That's when she realized that the screams were coming from her. She tried to move her hands so she could grip her head that felt as if an ax had been embedded in her skull. The pain took her breath away. Every instinct in her body told her to stop it, that she could put an end to the agony.

But she didn't. She let it continue.

Clammy hands gripped her on either side of her head. A voice near her ear said, "It's nearly done."

Noreen jerked because she knew that voice.

It was Moreann.

CHAPTER TWENTY-NINE

He needed to get back. Cain didn't know why the thought kept running through his head, but he knew that it was imperative that he return to Noreen.

The longer he remained at Dreagan, the more he couldn't shake the fear that was settling around him like ice shackles. He tried to concentrate on what was being said as the discussion began about their impending battle with the Others, but he couldn't.

When he spotted Con leave, he started to go after him, but Ulrik stepped in his way.

"You're distracted," the King of Silvers stated.

There was no use denying it. "Aye. I need to get back to Noreen. She's risked her life for us."

"From what you told us, she's safe on the Fae Realm."

"I think she's safe. I'd like to know for sure."

Ulrik gave a nod, his gaze briefly moving away. "Or could it be that you doona like being parted from her?"

"Would that be a problem?" Cain didn't mean to get defensive, but it came out in his voice without a second thought.

A black brow rose as Ulrik stared at him. "She could be anything. The simple fact that she's helping us is good enough for me."

Cain blew out a breath and raked a hand down his face. He felt as if he carried the weight of the world on his shoulders. "Con thinks there's a chance Noreen will betray me."

"Con has to look at every angle. All of us do. Even if it's something that has to do with someone we care about."

"Do you think she'll betray us?"

Ulrik's lips twisted. "To be frank, anything is possible. We know from what little Usaeil told Con and what you've gleaned from Noreen that Moreann is determined to have this realm."

"So, you believe what Noreen told me?"

"You were the only one who was there. You looked into her eyes. You believed it, so aye, I believe it."

"Thank you."

Ulrik snorted. "Doona thank me yet. What I'm telling you is that if we believed Usaeil would do anything to get what she wanted, then I think Moreann would, as well."

"I've spent time with Noreen. She's no' someone who would betray us. I know Con has long believed that there would be another woman who would do as . . ." He trailed off, not wanting to bring up the past.

"Nala did to me," Ulrik finished. "Aye, I know. Con and I have spoken about it at length."

When he didn't elaborate, Cain raised his brows. "And?"

"I agree with him. What happened with Nala wasna accidental. She and I were happy. Was she my mate? Nay, but I didna see that at the time. I wanted a wife, a family, and I cared deeply for her. I thought it was meant to be. The fact that Mikkel could turn her so easily against me was proof enough that I imagined the feelings that I desperately wanted to be there. It wouldna surprise me to find out that Moreann somehow helped my uncle set things in motion. If someone goes to that much trouble for something that caused the mass exodus of dragons, why would they no' do it again?"

Cain frowned at Ulrik as he shook his head. "Look at all the eons that have passed since then with no female betraying us. Look at the most recent years with all the matings. None of them have betrayed their Kings."

"You're right," Ulrik said. "That doesna mean it can no' happen."

"I know what I feel for Noreen."

"And what is that? Do you love her? Is she your mate?"

Aye! It immediately sprang up in Cain's mind, but he didn't say the word. "I gave her my word that I would protect her. She's entrusted her life to me."

"She's a Fae, which means she's no' without skills."

"She isna a fighter."

Ulrik shrugged, his face showing how little that mattered. "She has magic, and if she can get into your mind to see your memories through your eyes, she's bloody powerful, as well. Moreann got lucky in finding her."

Cain clenched his teeth together. He'd hoped that someone would see his side of things when it came to Noreen, but it seemed that Ulrik was just like Con, and only saw the worst.

"By your look, you think I doona like Noreen. That is far from the truth," Ulrik said. "I've never met her. I appreciate what she's doing for us, and I'll gladly welcome her here because of it."

"And if she is my mate?" The words were out before Cain could think better of it.

Ulrik didn't hesitate to respond. "Then you know we will all embrace her and welcome her into our family."

Cain sighed, his body relaxing a bit.

"But if she sets to betray you, and therefore us, you know what we'll do."

They'd kill her, just as they had with Nala.

"She willna betray us," Cain stated in a low, deadly voice.

Ulrik put his hand on Cain's shoulder, a sad smile playing about his lips. "I'm trying to show you what every King here is working through. We believe you. But the Others are no' only after our realm, they also want to wipe us out. I've seen firsthand how dangerous their combined magic is. We're strong, but I doona know how things will go when we face off against them."

"I have that same fear. Why do you think I went to investigate Noreen?"

Ulrik let his arm drop to his side. "I know, my friend. We all have a lot at stake here, and we're all trying to ensure that we've thought of everything. What worries me is how attached you've gotten to her in such a short time."

"She's an amazing Fae. Dark or no', she didna have to help us, but she is."

"That she is."

"I told Con to come with me and talk to her to alleviate his fears, but he left."

Ulrik looked at the doorway Con had walked through earlier, his lips compressing. "Con is doing his best to keep everything going. Let's leave him. I'll go with you."

"You?" Cain asked in shock.

A smile pulled at Ulrik's lips. "Surprised?"

"Aye. I know you and Kellan are helping Con."

"We're all helping each other. This is our home, and some of us have mates, but it isna about that. This is about holding onto what is ours. So, can I meet Noreen or no'?"

Cain smiled easily for the first time since he left Noreen. "Of course. You sure you're all right no' being a part of the battle plans?"

"I'm going to fight. Someone will tell us where we need to go and when. There are enough Kings standing around formulating plans that they willna miss either of us."

Elation rushed through Cain. He would get to return to Noreen quicker than he thought.

"Whether you want to admit it or no', that smile you're wearing says it all," Ulrik pointed out.

Cain laughed, no longer caring what anyone thought. "I can no' wait for you to meet her. You'll see that all your fears are unfounded."

"Then lead the way."

Cain looked down at the cuff on his wrist. "This is yours."

"Aye."

His fingers wrapped around it. While he knew he should return it to Ulrik, the thought of it not being on his wrist so he could return to Noreen at will left him gasping for air.

"I doona need it back now," Ulrik said into the silence.

Cain nodded as he loosened his fingers. "Right."

"You sure the doorway you and Noreen used to the Fae Realm isna guarded?"

"No one was there when we went through, and no one was there when I came back. Noreen was sure the Fae have forgotten about it."

Ulrik's lips twisted. "They probably have. I'm more concerned about the Others."

"I didna see—or sense—anyone."

"Then let's go," Ulrik said as he grasped Cain's forearm.

But Cain hesitated. "Do you need to tell Eilish where you're going?"

"She knows," was all Ulrik said.

Cain shrugged and thought about the Fae doorway as he touched the silver cuff. The moment he and Ulrik arrived at the castle ruins, both looked around, expecting someone to attack them.

"Strangely silent," Ulrik said in a low voice.

"Noreen said it's because of the location of the doorway. No one uses it since it's so isolated."

"That shouldna matter to the Fae."

Cain hated to admit that Ulrik had a point. "As Noreen said, no one goes to the Fae Realm anymore since it's been destroyed. Why would the Fae use it now?"

Ulrik shifted toward him, his face set in lines of worry. "I can understand that part, but the location, no' so much."

"What about it?"

"The field surrounding the ruins is wide open, giving no cover to anyone. I've seen Fae doorways in weird places, but this one seems especially odd."

Cain gave a shake of his head. "I doona care. It got me and Noreen away, and it's going to take me back to her."

Ulrik lifted one shoulder in a shrug. "Well, since we can no' see the doorways, do you remember where it is?"

"I marked it," Cain said with a grin as he made his way into the castle and up the stairs.

Ulrik chuckled when he saw the two small stones set the width of a doorway apart when they entered the chamber. "That was smart."

Cain was smiling when he walked through the door. Ulrik was right on his heels. He paused, giving Ulrik time to take a look at the absolute devastation of the realm.

"This way," Cain said and gripped Ulrik's arm before touching the cuff.

He didn't want to take the time to walk to the barrier when he had the ability to jump to it. Ulrik didn't seem fazed by it at all. Instead, he stared straight ahead at where the barrier was.

"I didna feel it before," Ulrik said. "But I do now."

"Walk through it."

Ulrik lifted a foot and stepped through. Cain quickly did the same. Once on the other side, he began looking for signs of Noreen. She'd said that she'd wait for him, but she could be anywhere within the area of the shield, which was fairly large.

"I'm sure she's around," Ulrik said.

Cain nodded. "I told her it might be a while before I could get back. I thought I'd stay through the battle. If I'd known that I would return so quickly, I would've asked her to remain close."

"There are other ways to find her," Ulrik said. "Shift."

Cain laughed. Of course. That would be the quickest and easiest way to locate Noreen. If she wasn't looking up, she'd hear his roar. "You joining me?"

Ulrik shook his head. "I'll stay on the ground for now and have a look around."

"I'll be back soon with Noreen."

Cain shifted and jumped into the air. As he flew, he kept wishing that Noreen was on his back. She'd been the first person to ride him, and he'd liked it.

He flew fast and low, gliding over the area of the lake where they had made love, and into the forest. He roared as his gaze scanned for any movement, but he didn't give up. It wasn't until he'd made a sweep of the entire area that he grew concerned. Noreen should be there, and she should hear him. Was she hiding? Hurt? Scared?

All kinds of thoughts rushed through his mind as he turned back. As he swung around, he saw a figure step from the trees to the edge of the lake.

Relief filled him at the sight of Noreen. She beamed up at him, waving.

And that's when he knew he loved her.

CHAPTER THIRTY

The excitement that ran through Noreen was so great, she felt dizzy from it. She couldn't believe that Cain was back already.

At first, she'd thought the roar she heard was her imagination. The second time, she knew for sure. That's when she looked up through the dense forest canopy for some sign of him. She was about to jump to the lake when she wondered if it was Cain or another Dragon King.

It didn't help that the erratic dreams from the night before kept playing in her head. So, she ran to the lake instead. The moment she saw his navy scales, she burst from the trees.

Happiness bubbled up inside her as he dove from the sky, rolling into a ball and shifting back into human form right before he landed naked on bent knees, his fingers touching the ground. She didn't even wait for him to stand as she rushed to him.

He straightened in time to grab her as she flung herself at him. It seemed as if a million years had passed since she had tasted his lips, and she couldn't get enough of him.

"By the stars, I've missed you," he said between kisses.

"Shhh," she told him and threaded her fingers into his black hair.

He chuckled, but it soon turned into a moan. She felt his arousal hot and thick between them. Her heart skipped a beat, because even now, she couldn't believe he desired her.

"Wait," Cain said and pulled back to look at her.

She gazed up at him, waiting for him to speak. When he didn't, she leaned in for another kiss, but he held her still.

"You're beautiful."

Noreen smiled at his flattery and let her gaze travel his body. "And you're gorgeous. What are you doing back so quick? Is it all finished?"

"Nay," he said with a shake of his head, his expression filled with regret. "I've shared all you told me with Con and the other Kings. The planning for the battle is being done now."

"Why aren't you there?" she asked. "You should be there."

He gave her a lopsided smile and smoothed a strand of hair from her face. "I wanted to see you. And I've brought someone for you to meet."

She was instantly on guard, though she didn't know why exactly. It wasn't as if Cain didn't believe her and had brought someone to check her story. Then again, it wasn't as if they could check her story anyway.

Her mind flashed back to the dream where she hadn't been able to move or open her eyes and heard Moreann's voice.

"Noreen?"

She blinked and looked at Cain. "Yes?"

"Are you okay, lass? Your face paled for a moment, and you looked a million miles away."

It felt as if she were being pulled from him, which was silly since he was right here, holding onto her. "I'm fine."

"Are you sure? Because if you doona want to meet Ulrik, you doona have to."

"The King of Silvers is here?" she asked, shocked.

Cain continued to study her. "Aye."

"He, too, left the planning for the Others to come here? To meet me?" Yeah, she wasn't buying that at all. "They don't believe what I told you, do they?"

"I believe you, and they trust me."

She shot him a dry look. "You didn't answer my question."

"Doona read too much into this."

"It's hard not to."

He sighed and lowered his gaze to the ground briefly. "You saw the betrayal Mikkel and Nala set up for Ulrik. Con has long believed that another such betrayal will befall one of us."

"And he thinks it's me?" Noreen got so angry, she pulled away from Cain. "I risked *everything* to go to the Kings to tell you what I know. And this is the thanks I get?"

"You have every right to be angry, but please understand where we're coming from, as well. We have to double- and triple-check everything."

She crossed her arms over her chest and raised a brow. "That's the thing. You can't verify anything I've told you. It's my experiences, my memories. You either believe me, or you don't."

"I do."

Noreen knew that he did, but she couldn't control the ire within her. It was silly to believe that the other Dragon Kings would believe her as quickly as Cain had.

She gave a snort and dropped her hands to her sides. "It

doesn't really matter now, does it? Take me at my word, or don't. I've already burned the bridge with the Others."

"I vowed to protect you," Cain said in a low, dangerous voice.

"From where? Dreagan, where you're needed for battle? Because you can't be here. You'd constantly be thinking about your brethren and that you should be fighting alongside them, which, by the way, you need to be."

"Noreen," he began.

She held up a hand to stop him. "You know I'm right. I almost left when you went back to Dreagan. I wish I had."

"You want to leave?" The frown that filled his face was one of disbelief and . . . hurt.

Tears threatened, but she refused to let her emotions get the best of her. "It doesn't matter much what I want anymore. I knew the consequences when I sent that email. For a brief bit of time, I thought I could actually have my life back."

"You can," he insisted.

"No. I gave that up the moment I let Brian see us together. Some will think I'm getting exactly what I deserve as a Dark as well as an Other."

"I doona think that."

She smiled at him, thinking of his kindness and passion. "That's because you're different."

"The feeling I had that said I needed to come back here wasna for naught then," he mumbled.

It was her turn to frown. "What?"

"I had the overwhelming urge to get back to you, felt that you might need help. Now, I see it was simply because I somehow knew you wanted to leave."

"But I didn't."

"How long would you have stayed?" he demanded.

She shrugged, unable and unwilling to answer.

He nodded and looked away as if the very sight of her was too much for him to take.

Movement out of the corner of her eye made her turn her head. She saw a man standing at the edge of the forest, staring at them. His long, black hair was pulled back in a queue at his neck. No doubt, it was Ulrik. How much of the conversation between Cain and she had he heard? Then again, did it really matter?

"I doona think my opinion counts for much, but I'm going to give it anyway," Ulrik said as he started toward them.

When Noreen glanced back at Cain, he had jeans on but no shirt, giving her a view of his dragon tat. Cain was half turned from her, letting them know he wasn't ready to be a part of the conversation.

She looked at Ulrik and waited until he stopped near her. Then she said, "I'm Noreen."

"It's nice to meet you. Since Cain isna up to introductions, I'm Ulrik."

Noreen found herself grinning at the King of Silvers. "I kinda figured that's who you were."

"Well, there are so many about, I didna want to take the chance," he teased. Then he sobered. "I saw Cain land and started here. I didna mean to overhear, but I did."

"You should've walked away," Cain stated.

Ulrik looked briefly at Cain before his gold eyes returned to her. "I am here to meet you and hear some of what you told Cain myself. It's no' because you're Dark or because of anything you've done. I'd be here if you were Light or anything else. As you already know, we've been betrayed in the past, and we doona want to go down that road again."

"I know full well what was done to you. It was reprehensible."

His eyes looked away for a moment. "Cain told us how you were able to get into his mind and see his memories. Tell me about that."

She shrugged. "There isn't much to tell. It's easier if I'm touching the person, and I can only see the memories they're thinking of at the time. I can't go rumbling around in their mind."

"But you see everything?"

"See, hear, and also feel the emotions of the person." She looked at Cain. "I know how torn he was about leaving you to rejoin Con. I also know how it nearly killed him to watch your magic being bound and then seeing you banished from Dreagan."

"So, you saw everything from his perspective."

"Yes."

Ulrik nodded slowly. "Do you use that magic often?"

"Rarely, actually. It not only takes a lot out of me, but dealing with the aftermath of emotions can also take its toll."

"Yet, you asked Cain to see his memories."

"I wanted to know every detail. Every word, emotion, and conversation."

Ulrik raised a brow. "To use against us?"

She should've expected that, she supposed. "How can I use something against you that has already happened?"

"You'd be surprised," was all Ulrik said. "Tell me about the Dragon King attack on your parents."

"No." That was the last thing she wanted to talk about. Even now, just thinking about it made her want to lash out at Ulrik.

In a heartbeat, Cain was beside the King of Silvers. "Leave it," he demanded.

Ulrik stared hard at Cain before his gold gaze slid to her. "I understand that it still affects you, but as Cain also told you, no Dragon King would've strayed from the battle."

"Not even you?" she questioned.

Ulrik's eyes narrowed slightly. "My magic was still bound then. Did I watch some of the battles? Aye, I did. But I didna join in for either side."

"Then how can you be certain that no King went out on his own?"

"Because of Con. He would've known the moment one of the Kings left."

She rolled her eyes. "Constantine might be King of Dragon Kings, but he isn't all-knowing."

Cain snorted but didn't say anything.

Ulrik, however, had a small grin on his lips. "That's the thing others doona realize. Con is the strongest of all Dragon Kings. He has more power, as well. He is the one the magic chose to lead us, and the magic chose wisely. When he makes a decision, it isna what he wants, it's what is best for the Kings. He sacrifices everything for our sake. How many leaders can say that?"

Noreen knew for a fact that Moreann didn't fit into that category. Neither did Usaeil. Balladyn might have, but he would've still had a long way to go.

"Con rules us no' by fear, but with respect," Cain told her.

Ulrik gave a nod as he glanced toward Cain. "And while the Kings fought the Dark during the Fae Wars, none would've broken off to kill any Fae that wasna on the battlefield. Otherwise, I feel certain the magic of this realm would've retaliated in some way."

That wasn't something Noreen had ever considered. Then again, she was learning much about the magic on Earth.

She set that thought aside for the moment as she lifted her chin. "I might have been a small child, but I know the sound of a dragon's roar. I didn't mistake that or the fire."

"But you didna see a dragon," Ulrik pressed.

Slowly, she shook her head. "There wasn't much to see other than flames."

CHAPTER THIRTY-ONE

Cain wanted to stop the interrogation, but he knew it had to be done. He was grateful that Ulrik was handling Noreen gently. However, he couldn't say the same for Noreen's responses. To be fair, though, not many would react nicely to having their word questioned.

Yet, the moment Ulrik asked about her parents' deaths, something in Noreen changed. There was a harshness around her eyes that hadn't been there before, and it concerned Cain.

"It doesn't matter what I say," Noreen stated. "Every King will continue telling me that it couldn't have been a dragon, and I'll continue to believe that it was."

"None of that matters right now," Cain said before Noreen could get any angrier. "Ulrik, you came to talk about Moreann and the Others. Keep to that."

Ulrik's gold eyes met his as he gave a nod. "Verra true. My apologies, Noreen. I can get carried away sometimes," he told her.

"It's fine," she replied tightly.

The open, smiling woman that had thrown herself into

Cain's arms moments ago was nowhere to be found. And he wanted her back. Yet he knew how important it was that everyone be convinced that she wasn't trying to betray them.

They walked into the forest and found a comfortable spot as Noreen began repeating everything to Ulrik. Cain listened, noting the tales weren't verbatim, which meant they weren't lies. They stayed the course, but had subtle differences that liars tended to avoid.

Little by little, she relaxed. Ulrik would ask some questions, and she readily answered them without hostility. It wasn't long before they were conversing like old friends. Then again, Ulrik had that kind of effect on people.

When she finished, Ulrik blew out a breath and looked at Cain. "We're bloody lucky she came to us. There is no way we'd ever have learned any of this information ourselves."

"I know," Cain said with a smile.

Ulrik smiled at Noreen. "Thank you for what you've done. Cain has already promised you protection, but know that extends from all Dragon Kings. Moreann and the Others willna get to you."

"Thank you," Noreen said demurely.

Cain wished they were alone. He wanted to strip her out of her clothes and make love to her for the next few hours.

"What happens now?" Noreen asked.

Cain said, "We get ready for battle, and we keep you from them."

"I understand why you doona wish to return to Earth," Ulrik told her. "And I actually think this may be a good place for you to hide, but we need to come up with an alternative if something happens and you need to leave. Cain needs to be able to find you."

Yes, he certainly did. Cain looked at Noreen. "If you want to be found."

"I do," she told him.

Ulrik climbed to his feet. "That's good. You two figure it out, and Cain can tell the rest of us. I can no' believe someone is healing this realm," he said as he shook his head before looking at Cain. "You really think it's Rhi?"

"Who else could it be?"

Ulrik shrugged. "I doona know. Tell me where you found the orb. I'd like a look at it."

"We can take you to it," Noreen offered.

Before Cain could refuse, Ulrik said, "It's fine. I fancy a look around myself. Besides, you two need some alone time."

"It's there," Cain said and pointed to the east. "Stay on that course, and you'll see the glow, especially once darkness falls."

"Which is on its way." Ulrik gave Noreen a nod and walked away.

Once they were alone, Cain turned his head to Noreen. "I have a question, and I want you to answer honestly."

"I always do."

"I know, but doona think about who I am or that it's me."

She swallowed. "All right. What is it?"

"If you truly believe a Dragon King killed your parents, can you ever forgive us?"

Silence met his question. He should've known it wasn't the right thing to ask, but he had to know. Because if she still held hatred in her heart, then she could never care for him—not like he cared for her.

And if she couldn't care, then she couldn't love.

She waved her hands, and a fire suddenly roared between them. He stared at her over the flames, watching the red-orange color dance across her face. She looked down at her hands clasped in her lap for long minutes.

Finally, she said, "For a long time, I couldn't think about a Dragon King without feeling such hatred that it consumed me. That loathing fed the darkness within me. Between what happened to my parents and what Moreann told me, all I thought about was ways I could take my vengeance out on all of you."

That's pretty much what Cain had expected to hear.

"Years turned to decades, and decades centuries," she continued. "Other things focused my interests, but always in the back of my mind, I maintained the hatred."

"If you felt such . . . abhorrence for us, how did you ever decide to switch sides?"

Her crimson gaze lifted to meet his. "It didn't happen overnight. I know when I originally spoke with you, it might have sounded like that, but it's taken a few centuries. Like I said, it was little things at first that later turned into bigger issues. They overshadowed the pain and anger I felt about what had happened to my parents. Mostly, it was Moreann that caused me so much concern. I knew someone had to do something, and it had to be me. Even if it meant going to the enemy."

"An enemy that you trusted."

"You trusted me," she countered.

He cocked a brow. "You had sex with me."

"Because I wanted you. I still do." She glanced to the side. "The thing is, when I'm with you, I don't think of you as a Dragon King. I don't actually think of you as anyone other than the man who believed me when it was probably wiser not to. A man who vowed to protect me when he didn't have to, and a man who looked past my red eyes and silver hair to the person I am."

Cain rose and walked around the fire. He held out his hand and waited for Noreen to take it before he pulled her to her feet. His mouth covered hers in a frenzied kiss that showed her how deep his desires went, how badly he hungered for her.

She was the one who ended the kiss and put her hand over his heart. She looked deep into his eyes and said, "I would never hurt you. Never. No matter what you may think, please believe that."

"I do."

She rested her cheek against his chest, and he tightened his arms around her. They stayed like that for a long time, each lost in thought. He kept thinking about the moment he'd seen her when he returned earlier. He'd known in that instant that he loved her.

That she was his mate.

There was no denying what he felt. He knew lust, and this was more than that. He knew desire, and this went much deeper than that. He knew yearning, and what he had for her exceeded that.

He hadn't been looking for love or his mate. And yet, somehow, she had found her way to him. He never wanted to let her go, but he knew there was a good chance that he would have to.

Either that or leave Dreagan if Noreen wasn't welcomed.

He heard Ulrik say his name in his mind. Cain opened the link. *"Did you find the orb?"*

"No' yet. I wanted you to know that I understand why you were so adamant about believing Noreen. She's verra convincing."

"Meaning?"

Ulrik chuckled. *"Meaning, I also believe her. I hope she understands this wasna a personal attack on her. We just needed to be sure."*

"I'll make sure she knows."

"Something still bothers you?"

"Aye. The attack on her parents."

"That isna sitting well with me either." Ulrik sighed loudly. *"It happened so long ago, I doona know how we can ever know for sure."*

Cain wasn't going to give up that easily. *"If a King truly did kill her parents, then there has to be a reason why."*

"You are no' going to like this, but I doona think a King had any part in it. I think she was fed a lie."

"I thought of that, as well, but she swears by it. A child who suffered that kind of trauma wouldna let their memories be turned."

"Maybe she didna realize they were. Moreann isna lacking in powers."

Cain's gut clenched. *"If I tell Noreen this, it'll sound like we're attacking Moreann instead of trying to take responsibility."*

"I saw the way you looked at her. She's your mate. If you want a future with her, then all of us need the answer to who killed her parents. I'll keep thinking."

Ulrik severed the link, but Cain knew he was right. He did want a future with Noreen, and that meant they had to know for certain if a King took her parents' lives or not. That was the only way she'd ever be able to truly love him.

The fact that she felt desire was a good step, but it was far from love.

"I'm very glad you're back."

He smiled at her Irish lilt. He loved the sound of it. "Me, too."

"I had horrible dreams last night."

That made him frown. "What kind of dreams?"

"None of them made sense. It was like all kinds of images were jumbled. Almost as if they were puzzle pieces that needed to fit together."

"Has anything like that ever happened before?"

She shook her head. "Never."

He rubbed his hands up and down her back. "Maybe it's the magic here."

"Wouldn't I feel something all the time? It was only when I was alone."

"That doesna make sense."

Noreen gave a half-hearted shrug. "I don't know."

"If you have any more of those dreams, will you try to remember the details? And wake me up to tell me about it when it happens?"

"I will."

He kissed the top of her head. "I still want you to return with me to Dreagan eventually. If you want to, that is."

"I'd love to see it, but more than that, I want to be with you."

"Even though I'm a Dragon King?"

She leaned her head back. "A Dark Fae and a Dragon King. We aren't supposed to match up."

"Says who?"

There was a smile on her face when she chuckled. "The Dark are evil."

"You, lass, are no' evil."

Her face sobered. "Look at my eyes, Cain. Look at my hair. I've done bad things."

"As I told you before, those are simply colors. When I look into your eyes and into your heart, I doona see evil.

I see someone who is trying their best to set things right. An evil person doesna do that."

The smile that pulled at her lips was big and bright. "I'm so glad it was you who found me."

"Me, too, lass. Me, too."

CHAPTER THIRTY-TWO

The moment Erith stepped onto the Fae Realm, she knew something was different. The scene that greeted her was one she knew well—destruction.

She had been on the world when the fighting between the Light and Dark had taken its final toll. While most of the Fae had managed to leave, many hadn't been so fortunate. Most left behind had died on the realm, while a few others managed to find a doorway that took them elsewhere.

Erith wondered why none of the Fae had bothered to ask either Usaeil or Taraeth why they had known there was a place for them on Earth. Perhaps they hadn't cared once they saw the number of humans walking about.

With a sigh, Erith tried to ignore the destruction. Earth was a stunning place, but it hadn't held a candle to the Fae Realm. It had been that beautiful.

Erith didn't understand why Rhi had returned to this place. There was nothing for her here. There was nothing for anyone here. The fact that Usaeil had continued to meet Moreann here was something Erith didn't understand either, because the planet was barely being held together.

She wasn't concerned, because she would survive it. That didn't hold true for Rhi or anyone else who dared to venture there.

Erith's magic reached out, searching for Rhi. Almost immediately, she felt the force of magic so strong it surprised her.

"I've felt that only once before," she murmured to herself as she started off in the direction from where it had come.

She could've teleported, but she wanted to see everything, to make sure she didn't miss a single particle. With sure footsteps, she headed toward the source. And then she encountered it. Not only did Erith feel the waves of magic coming from the wall in front of her, she could see it.

Her lips parted in shock. In all her long years, she had witnessed magic up close like this only one other time. The prismatic colors shifted and constantly changed, moving up from the ground toward the sky. She couldn't stop staring at it, it was so bewitching.

"Cael," she called, knowing her lover would hear her across the cosmos and find his way to her.

In moments, she felt a presence behind her. In his deep Irish voice, he said, "What is that?"

She shouldn't have been surprised that he could see it since he was nearly as powerful as she was now. "Magic."

"That's what magic looks like?"

"That's what this power looks like," she replied.

He came to stand beside her, as enchanted as she by the sight. He raised his hand to the streams of magic and let his palm brush against it. It caused him to smile widely. "Do you know who did this?"

"Yes."

Cael's head swung to her. "Rhi."

She nodded as she met his gaze.

"How?" he asked. "When? And why?"

"I suspect when we find her inside, we can ask her."

His lips twisted as he turned back to the barrier. "Do you think she'll talk to us?"

"We won't know until we try."

"She set up a wall, love. I think that's her way of telling everyone she wants to be left alone."

Erith cocked her head to the side. "I'm not sure it's a wall exactly."

"Then what is it?"

"Only one way to find out," she said and walked through the magic.

The feeling of it passing through her was euphoric. It filled her with such peace and happiness that it was like she was floating. And when she came out the other side, she stared in awe at the scenic vision that met her eyes.

"Bloody hell," Cael murmured a heartbeat later.

Erith looked back at the magic. "It isn't a wall, love. I suspect it's a barrier that surrounds a certain area that has allowed the realm to begin to heal itself."

"You said Rhi could destroy realms *and* create them. You didn't say she could heal them."

Erith shrugged. "Create. Heal. Same difference."

"I'm beginning to understand why you've had an interest in her."

"The question is, is she still the Rhi we've known?" she asked and began walking.

Cael quirked a black brow. "Meaning?"

"Did Rhi begin this before she fought Usaeil? If I had to guess, the answer is yes because it looks as if this has been happening for some time. Look how far the green extends."

"The healing is significant. But you think the darkness has taken her."

It wasn't a question. Erith pressed her lips together. "Con said her eyes flashed red. And when I looked for her, I found her light encircled by red."

"Rhi is strong. She can contain it. She has been for some time."

"It might have convinced her to let it loose to battle Usaeil. Lest you forget, Rhi saw the queen kill Balladyn with a blade in the back."

Cael made an indistinct sound. "Don't remind me," he said angrily. "That would be enough to turn a great many Light Dark, and Rhi and Balladyn were more than just casual acquaintances. They have a very long history."

"Which is why I'm fairly certain the darkness has taken her."

"Would she come here if it did?"

"Even the Dark appreciated the beauty that was the Fae Realm. And I suspect this was Rhi's private haven away from everyone since she knew no one would look for her here."

Cael reached for her hand. Their fingers tangled as they walked deeper and deeper into the territory, each lost in thought. Erith came to a sudden stop when she spotted something large in the sky and turned her head toward it.

"I'll be damned," Cael said as they watched the dragon flying through the air.

Erith recognized him. "That's Cain."

"And that's a Dark Fae on his back."

Erith saw the female the same time Cael did. What was a Dragon King and a Dark doing here? There was no way Con didn't know about this.

"Did Con tell you anything about a King being here?" Cael asked.

She slowly shook her head. Was this Con's way of getting back at her? It might be, and perhaps she deserved it.

Erith turned away from Cain and the female. "We need to find Rhi. We'll talk to Cain later."

"What if Rhi is with them?"

"No one can find her. Con is the one who asked me to locate her. If any King knew she was here, they would've told Con."

Cael glanced at the sky again. "Maybe that's why Cain is here."

"Phelan searched for Rhi. If the half-Warrior, half-Fae couldn't find her, then she doesn't want to be found."

"That could extend to us, you know."

That wasn't something Erith was going to allow. Cael must have seen that on her face because he smiled in return. The trek took them near a vast lake, through open valleys and up increasingly higher hills, and finally into a thick forest.

"She's here," Erith said in a whisper.

Cael's face was set in lines of concentration. A moment later, he said, "I can feel her. She's up ahead to the left."

"I think it might be better if we surround her."

"It's just the two of us," he said, then paused. "Three. There's another King here."

Erith smiled at Cael. He was gaining ground on the many and various powers he now had. "Impressive. You felt the King before I did."

"That's a first," he teased with a wink. Then he walked to the right.

Erith took a deep breath and altered her course to come up on Rhi to the left. She didn't need to walk. She was Death, after all, but she didn't want Rhi to think she had come to claim her soul.

The sound of a waterfall could be heard over the noisy singing of the birds. It became increasingly louder the closer she got to Rhi. When Erith finally came to the waterfall, she could only stare in wonder at the height of it. A rainbow could be seen in the mist as the water tumbled into a myriad of rocks before eventually smoothing out into a small pond.

The perimeter of the body of water was lined with rocks, perfect seats to sit upon and stare at the waterfall. There was something familiar about it, as though Erith had seen it before. While the Fae Realm had once boasted many waterfalls, there hadn't been one like this, of that she was certain.

She tilted back her head and looked at the top of the waterfall. Erith blinked, unsure if the rocks just happened to form what looked like a dragon, or if it had been done on purpose.

Then she realized where she had seen such a waterfall—Dreagan.

Now, she knew with unshakable certainty that Rhi had done all of this. Whether it was on purpose or was a by-product of her sorrow was yet unknown.

Erith knew the Light Fae was here. It took her searching the area twice before her gaze landed on Rhi as the Fae surfaced from the water. Instantly, Rhi's gaze landed on her.

"There's nothing for you here, Death. Leave."

Erith wasn't used to anyone speaking to her in such a way. She raised a brow, ready to reprimand Rhi, when she decided that wasn't the best approach. Instead, she took a deep breath and walked closer to the edge of the pool.

"I'm not here for your soul," Erith replied.

Rhi snorted. "I wouldn't care if you were. Besides, I highly doubt you'd come yourself. You'd have Daire or one of the other Reapers do it."

Erith didn't miss the jab Rhi took at mentioning Daire

since Erith had had him following Rhi for months to keep an eye on her. "Don't you want to know how I found you?"

"Nope."

Out of the corner of her eye, Erith saw Cael move into place as well as the other Dragon King. She was more than a little surprised to see Ulrik, then again, perhaps that was a good sign.

Rhi's black hair was slicked back from the water as she swam to the edge. She paused, treading water as she turned her head, looking straight at Cael. Then, slowly, she slid her gaze to Ulrik. Both men remained half-hidden in the foliage, unmoving.

"You're healing this realm," Erith said.

Rhi didn't respond as she continued swimming. When she got to the edge, she rose from the water, completely nude. Cael and Ulrik averted their eyes as Rhi stared at them, daring them to look.

Con was right to be worried. The Fae Erith watched now wasn't the same Rhi as before. She had been betrayed one too many times, and she had created a protective shell around herself that had nothing to do with the light inside her, and everything to do with the darkness growing within her.

Droplets of water fell from Rhi's lithe form as she moved from rock to rock. She didn't even attempt to clothe herself as she let the bright sun dry her. As she turned to Erith, black leather pants covered her legs, along with a form-fitting black shirt and black boots.

"I'm really tired of finding a sanctuary, only to have others invade it," Rhi said to her. "Did it ever occur to you that I didn't want to be found?"

"Did it ever occur to *you* that people care about you and are looking for you?" Cael retorted.

Erith didn't give Rhi time to answer as she said, "You're needed, Rhi. The Fae need you."

"No one needs me. That was my mistake all along."

Erith watched her walk away, her gaze meeting Cael's.

It was Ulrik who caught Erith's eye. He held up a hand, asking her to wait as he trailed after Rhi.

CHAPTER THIRTY-THREE

"I thought if anyone would get the *fek-off* attitude, it would be you," Rhi said when she realized that Ulrik followed her. "But I'll say it instead. Fek off."

He chuckled as his long legs caught up with her. "The attitude change isna that different, you know."

She rolled her eyes. How she'd loved her solitude. She hadn't even cared when Cain had shown up, because he hadn't been able to find her. She knew he wouldn't stay long, and he hadn't. But then he'd returned with not just Ulrik, but Erith and Cael, as well.

A regular party.

Just what she needed. She finished that thought with an epic eye roll.

"Your nail polish is chipped."

She halted and turned to glare into Ulrik's gold eyes. "So sweet of you to notice. Now, leave."

"You've always loved having your nails done. It's not like you to let that go."

"Why should I care about my damn nails? Why should I care about anything?" she demanded, moving closer to him with every word as anger roiled within her.

*Show him your power. It will only take once to prove
your might.*

Rhi ignored the voice of the darkness. She hadn't been
able to silence it since she gave into it before the battle with
Usaeil. Then again, she'd known what she was doing. She
had accepted it.

Then.

And now.

"I'm not the same person I was."

Ulrik drew in a long breath and then slowly released it,
sadness on his face. "None of us are. Every soul on every
realm has a path to walk. The entire point of living is to
learn, to grow. To change."

"Some don't move forward, Ulrik. Some move backward."

"Aye," he said with a solemn nod. "I went backward for
many, many centuries. I can never undo the things I did,
and a great lot of them were no' good. But I do my best to
make up for it now."

"Because you want to."

He stared at her a moment. "Aye."

"Well, that's the thing. I don't want to change. I like who
I am." It was a lie, but no one needed to know that.

A frown furrowed his brow. He swung his arms wide.
"Look at this place. Look what you've done. No Fae could
ever accomplish something like this. Your people will
eventually be able to return here."

"No, they won't. I plan to destroy it for good once it's
healed."

Ulrik took a step back as if slapped. "You can't be serious."

"I am. I've lost everything. I have nothing anymore, and
I realize that's no one's fault but mine. I failed Balladyn. I
failed my brother. I failed . . . everyone. But the one thing

I did was kill Usaeil. Now, the Light have a chance to start over."

Ulrik's gaze couldn't hold hers. He looked away the moment she said Usaeil's name. Her gut clenched in dread, but then she remembered the feeling of sinking her blade into that traitorous bitch's body.

"There's something you need to know," Ulrik finally said. "Usaeil made sure she couldna die. Though, I suspect had you taken her head, the spell wouldna have worked."

"Death took her," Rhi said, her gaze narrowed. "Right?"

"No," Erith replied from behind her.

Rhi closed her eyes. This couldn't be happening. The only reason she had been able to get through each day was knowing that Usaeil was gone.

"I'm sorry, but the Others took Usaeil," Death continued. "I wouldn't have intervened."

Rhi whirled around. She could feel herself glowing as the fury swept through her hot as lava. Tears of rage burned her eyes. "Did you take Balladyn? Or do the Others have him, as well?"

"We took Balladyn," Cael said.

Rhi kept her eyes on Erith. "You're fekking Death. You had your chance to take Usaeil's soul many times, but you didn't. You told me to do it, and when I tried, the Others stepped in. How powerful are you?" she bellowed. She sent a scorching look at Erith. "You're supposed to be a bloody goddess, and you've stood by and did nothing. *Nothing*!"

"There are things she—" Cael began.

Rhi cut her eyes to him, stopping his words with just a look. "Don't. Don't you dare make excuses for her. All of this could've been averted."

"I told you long ago that Usaeil was yours to deal with," Erith said.

Ulrik cautiously took a step toward her. "Rhi. I'd really like to get back to Eilish. Could you bring the glowing down?"

"Leave. All of you," she ordered. "Including Cain and the Dark with him. If any of you return, I'll kill you on sight."

Rhi spun around and stormed off. And to her disgust, tears fell down her cheeks. All this time, she'd thought she had won over Usaeil. Turned out, Usaeil had triumphed again. And Ubitch was still out there somewhere.

She didn't know how far she walked before her tears were coming so fast, she couldn't see. She paused next to a tree and leaned against it, all the while, pretending that it was a person who wrapped his arms around her and told her that everything would be all right, that he would stand beside her and help her deal with all of it.

Suddenly, she straightened and angrily swiped at the tears. "But I am alone. I've always been alone. And I will always be alone. I deal with things myself."

You have me. You've always had me. Together, we can do anything.

Rhi kept walking until she reached the edge of the barrier. She had remained on the Fae Realm, telling herself all kinds of lies because it was easier than facing the truth. She had listened to the darkness for so long, she wasn't sure what the truth was anymore.

You don't want to know the truth. If you did, you would seek it out.

The darkness was right. She didn't want to know, because then she'd have to make a decision about whether to help her friends or continue doing her own thing. She'd spent so much of her life helping others, and what had it gotten her?

Nothing. Absolutely nothing.

She'd given her friendship to Usaeil, only to be betrayed again and again and again by the queen. She'd fought for the Light, but they were just as quick to shun her. She'd given her friendship to so many, treating them as she wanted to be treated, and yet some took advantage.

She had given her heart to the only man worthy of it, and he'd tossed it aside as if it meant nothing.

You don't need the Dragon King. You have me.

The tears threatened to come again, but she refused to give in. She did need her King. She'd tried to find love with someone else.

The darkness began to laugh. *Try? You can't lie to me. I can see into your heart, Rhi. You can continue trying to love someone else, but the truth is, you don't want to. You want to keep loving the Dragon King, even though he doesn't love you. You like how it feels to be abandoned, discarded.*

"Stop!" she yelled, her hands on either side of her head.

The light had never spoken to her, only the darkness. She wished the light would speak up, but no matter how bad it got, it never tried to sway her.

When the darkness didn't speak again, she lowered her hands and sniffed. "I've not loved again because I can't. My heart is his, even if he doesn't want it. It's why I broke it off with Balladyn. He deserved more. So much more than I could give him."

"I would've taken you any way I could've had you."

She stilled at the voice behind her, a voice she knew well. Her heart thudded in her chest. Rhi spun around and looked into Balladyn's face as he stood five feet from her. A tear slipped down her cheek. Then he held out his arms.

It was all the invitation she needed. She ran to him, throwing herself in his arms as she sobbed. He held her tightly and let her cry. She didn't know how he was there, and it didn't matter. All she cared about was that he was alive.

"I did this to you," he finally said as he stroked her back. "When I captured you and chained you in the dungeons of the Dark Palace, I knew the darkness would be too seductive for even you to resist."

She shook her head, unable to find the words.

"I'm sorry, Rhi. So very sorry. You were my friend. I had no right to blame you for what happened to me, and I certainly shouldn't have tried to punish you for it."

She lifted her head and blinked through her tears until his face came into view. "You didn't do it."

"I did. I hope one day you can forgive me, but right now, I need you to listen."

Rhi sniffed and touched his face. "Are you real?"

"Yes," he said with a grin. "I'm real. Death called me here for you."

"You're a Reaper, aren't you?"

A slow smile spread over his face. "We'll discuss that later. Right now, you're more important."

She shook her head, but he gave her a little shake.

"Rhi, I mean it. The proverbial shite is about to hit the fan. Things are spinning out of control everywhere. There's infighting between the Dark and Light as many try to claim the thrones."

"So," she said with a shrug.

"The Others are getting ready to deal the final blow to the Dragon Kings."

She looked away. "The Kings never needed me. I was always there to help, but . . . well, you know why I did it."

He gave her a sad smile. "Because you love him."

"I'm pathetic."

"You're the kindest, most honorable, most beautiful, and strongest person I know. You killed Usaeil. Who cares that she was able to bring herself back? You took her out once, and you can do it again."

Rhi frowned as she shook her head. "Who says I want to do it again?"

"You can make sure she stays dead this time."

Rhi shook her head, not saying anything.

"As for the Others, Moreann is interested in you."

Rhi's gaze met his. "You know why, don't you?"

"I do now," he said with a nod of his head. "You need to tell the Kings, Druids, Warriors . . . everyone. You can't be faulted for what your father did. The simple fact that the Others want you means something. You could be the key that brings them all down."

She pulled out of his arms and paced a few steps away. "First, Death had me followed, and now the Others. Why?"

"Why not ask Erith yourself?"

Rhi halted and glared at him. "Don't you think I've done that?"

"Perhaps now is the time she'll tell you."

That made her think it might actually be possible. She wasn't special. Sure, she knew how to fight, and she glowed when she was mad, and then there was the healing of the realm thing, but it wasn't as if she flaunted those things. Few knew she even possessed those abilities.

"Usaeil befriended you because you draw people in without meaning to," Balladyn told her. "Your light, even now with the darkness around you, shines brighter than any other Light Fae's. You only want the simple pleasures in life, and Usaeil couldn't stand that. She began to hate you because no matter how much power she attained, she could never be as happy as you."

Rhi had to look away before she started to cry again.

"There are two more things I have to tell you before I go."

Her head swung back to him. "Go? No. I need you to stay."

"I'll always be close. That I can promise you. Now, listen. First, the Light need you. You can put things in order once more."

She rolled her eyes. "I was banished, remember? Besides, I'm pretty sure there's someone else acting as Captain of the Queen's Guard."

"I was referring to you becoming the queen."

Rhi gaped at him in horrified shock. "Have you lost your mind?"

"Far from it. Now, this last part is the most important. Are you listening?"

"Yes," she said with an exaggerated sigh.

Balladyn walked to her and touched her face with the tips of his fingers before his arm dropped to his side. "Your Dragon King still loves you."

"Wh—?" Rhi began, but Balladyn was already gone.

She looked around, her head turning this way and that, but she knew her friend was nowhere to be found. However, he had left her a lot to think about.

CHAPTER THIRTY-FOUR

Noreen's body hummed with lethargy and contentment after her and Cain's frenzied lovemaking. He held her to his chest, his hands softly caressing her back as he rested against a tree.

"Can we stay like this forever?" she asked with a grin.

There was a smile in his voice when he said, "Sounds good to me; lass."

She sighed, her eyes growing tired. "When do you think Ulrik will return?"

"I doona know. He's been gone much longer than I expected."

Though she wanted to ignore the worry inside her about falling asleep and what she might find in her dreams, she couldn't. Noreen sat up and looked into green eyes she was coming to seek out.

"What's wrong?" Cain asked, a frown on his face.

She smiled and shook her head. "I'm just wondering if we should look for Ulrik. And thinking that we might want to put on some clothes."

Laughter rumbled in Cain's body. "Clothes, perhaps."

Noreen used her magic to redress them without either of them moving. "He might have found Rhi."

"Are you trying to tell me you'd like to go see what Ulrik is up to?" Cain asked, a brow raised in question.

"Maybe," she replied with a shrug.

He let out a long, forlorn sigh. "You'd rather leave the comfort of my arms and talk to Rhi than stay with me."

"Oh, I'm definitely going to be taking advantage of your arms later, but," she said as she wrinkled her nose, "I do want to meet Rhi."

"Then let's go see what we can find."

Noreen couldn't contain her smile as she got to her feet. "What are you doing?" she asked when Cain didn't move.

He held up a finger, his gaze in the distance. Another few moments passed before he stood and said, "I was asking Ulrik where he was."

"And? Did he find Rhi?"

"That he did."

"Are you serious?" she asked, barely able to contain her excitement. "I'm really going to get to meet her?"

Cain laughed and took her hand. "That you are."

She saw him reaching for his cuff. In the next blink, he had jumped them across the vast lake and into the forest. Noreen turned around at the sound of the waterfall and walked toward it when she saw it.

"We flew over this," she said.

Cain came up behind her and put his hands on her shoulders. "Aye."

There was something curious in his voice. Noreen looked over her shoulder to ask him what was wrong when she spotted Ulrik standing about twenty feet from them. And he wasn't alone.

The instant she looked at the petite woman with her

long, blue-black hair and lavender eyes, she grew anxious. Perhaps it was the black leather and chainmail outfit she wore, which resembled that of a warrior.

No matter what Noreen told herself, the need to run was great. She didn't want to be near the woman.

"Lass?" Cain asked in a worried tone.

She turned her head away and tried to control her rapid breathing. Her hands were clammy, her blood like ice in her veins. *Run!!!!*

Noreen tried to move, but Cain's hands clamped down on her, preventing her from going anywhere.

"Tell me what it is?" he insisted.

She shook her head and closed her eyes, willing herself to teleport away, but for some odd reason, nothing happened. Which didn't make sense. She felt her magic within her. She knew it was there. So, what was stopping her? It certainly wasn't Cain.

Then she knew. The woman.

"Maybe this wasna a good idea," Cain said.

Noreen didn't know who he spoke with, and she didn't care.

"I wanted to meet her," said a female voice. "Especially after all Ulrik told us."

Us? Had the woman just said *us*? Noreen knew without a doubt that she had to leave that very instant. She attempted to jerk free of Cain's hold, but his grip didn't so much as loosen. She tried to teleport away but wasn't able to do that either. It was like something was holding her there, and she feared it was the woman.

"Open your eyes."

The command came from the woman who now stood in front of her. Noreen wanted to refuse, she wished she could do anything other than open her eyes, but that's exactly what she did.

Her gaze locked with lavender orbs. The woman's face gave nothing away, but Noreen had the distinct impression that she was searching through her mind. Whoever the woman was, she wasn't Fae, nor was she a Druid. But she was incredibly commanding and beautiful.

"Who are you?" Noreen asked.

The woman tilted her head slightly. "No one of import."

"I'd disagree."

"Why do you say that?"

Noreen leaned back to get closer to Cain. "Because you're powerful."

"The Dragon Kings are powerful," she retorted.

"That they are, but your magic is . . . different."

The woman smiled slightly. "You've made some very good allies among the Kings."

"I didn't intend to befriend them. I merely wanted to help them."

"Interesting, that," came a male voice. A moment later, the man walked into view. He was tall with coal black hair, a face to make angels weep, and purple eyes. Despite the color of his irises, Noreen knew he was a Light Fae.

Or had been.

He was something else entirely now. Similar to that of the woman.

It was Ulrik who said, "Cain was sent to find out if Noreen's story was true. He said he trusted her, and we trust him."

"Yet you're here," the man stated.

Ulrik shrugged. "As you know, we've been betrayed before. My presence was only to satisfy that."

"And are you satisfied?" the woman asked.

Ulrik's gold eyes briefly lit upon Noreen before they moved to Cain. "Aye."

"Hmm," the man said.

"I didna bring Noreen for an interrogation," Cain said. "She only wanted to meet Rhi."

The woman's face changed, showing a heartbeat of worry that was quickly covered. "Rhi is in a bad place. Now isn't the time for Noreen to meet her."

Without looking, Noreen knew that Cain and Ulrik were staring at each other, no doubt having a private conversation via their mental link. She wished she could do the same with Cain, because she'd tell him that she'd changed her mind and wanted to leave. Immediately.

"Do you fear the Kings?" the woman suddenly asked her.

Noreen hesitated at the question. "I know they could kill me."

"So could the Others, but that didn't stop you from going to the Kings," the man stated.

Noreen shrugged. "I knew what I had to do. As I told both Cain and Ulrik, something has changed with Moreann. She isn't the same. Then . . . well, I learned the truth about what happened between the Kings and the mortals."

The woman cocked a brow. "Meaning Moreann told you something different?"

"Yes."

The man and woman exchanged a glance, but they didn't say more on the subject. Instead, the man asked, "Did you expect the Kings to protect you from the Others?"

At this, Noreen laughed. "I expected to get as far from Earth as I could. I knew that was my only chance. And no, I didn't presume to think the Kings would believe me, much less offer me protection."

A rustle in the foliage stopped everyone from speaking further. All heads turned to the right as Rhi pushed aside a large leaf from a plant and came to a halt. Her eyes scanned the man and woman, Ulrik, Cain, and then finally landed on Noreen.

She didn't say anything to Noreen. Instead, Rhi looked at the woman. "Thank you."

"I thought that might help you. And you're welcome."

"I . . ." Rhi paused and looked away. That's when Noreen saw the spiked lashes and realized that the Fae had been crying. "I hadn't dared to hope."

The man said, "You could've asked. We would've told you."

Rhi nodded her head of long, black hair and tucked the strands behind her ears. She sniffed and looked between Cain and Noreen. "I didn't expect this."

With four words, Cain's entire attitude changed. He kissed the top of Noreen's head. "Neither did I."

To Noreen's surprise, Rhi came toward her. While Noreen had wanted to get as far from the woman as possible, with Rhi, she wanted to get close and learn all she could.

Rhi held out her hand. "It's nice to meet you, Noreen. I'm Rhi."

"I've waited a long time for this opportunity," Noreen said. "There isn't a Fae alive—Dark or Light—who doesn't know who you are. You're a legend."

Rhi shook her head. "You're very kind, but I think you may be exaggerating a bit."

Noreen realized that she hadn't yet shaken Rhi's hand. She immediately reached for it. The moment she did, something flashed in her mind, going off like a bomb.

And just like that, everything fell away—including the spell she hadn't known was there. Noreen stared into Rhi's silver eyes and remembered that Rhi had been her target all along, because that was who Moreann wanted Noreen to bring in.

The email to the Kings, the talk of switching sides, all of it had been nothing more than a spell that Moreann had put in place after Noreen came up with the plan. It was a way for them to get at the Kings from the inside, as well as finally getting a hold of Rhi.

"Is everything all right?" Rhi asked.

"Lass?"

The sound of Cain's voice snapped Noreen out of her thoughts. She dropped Rhi's hand and forced a smile, all the while shaken to her very core.

When Noreen glanced to the side, she noticed that the woman with the lavender eyes was staring at her—as if she had seen exactly what was in Noreen's mind.

CHAPTER THIRTY-FIVE

Cain felt the shiver go through Noreen the instant she touched Rhi. The way Noreen's body went taut set off alarm bells in his head. He glanced at Rhi, but she didn't seem to notice anything.

The only one who had an inkling that something had been exchanged was Erith, simply by the way she was staring at Noreen. And with Noreen being Fae, Death could take her soul right then and there.

He shifted so that he put Noreen behind him, breaking her hold on Rhi. Erith's lavender eyes slid to him.

Cael was the one to say, "That wouldn't stop us."

"Everyone take a deep breath," Ulrik said as he walked to stand beside Rhi.

Rhi looked at everyone with confusion. "What's going on?"

"Nothing," Cain replied. He glanced at Noreen to see her gaze on the ground, and he could still feel her shaking. Something had upset her greatly, and he wanted to know what it was.

"Hello?" Rhi said louder, a frown puckering her brow. Erith didn't say a word. She kept her gaze on Cain before she teleported away with Cael following instantly in her wake.

Rhi cleared her throat, her arms crossed over her chest. "One of you nimrods better tell me what's going on right now."

Cain looked to Ulrik. *"I doona know what's wrong with Noreen, but something has transpired."*

"You better figure it out quick. Erith and the Reapers are our allies."

"I wasna going to let them harm Noreen."

Ulrik gave a slight nod. *"Because she's your mate."*

"Aye."

"Have you told her?"

"No' yet."

"Perhaps now would be a good time."

Cain looked at Noreen. *"I need answers, and I doona believe she'll give them to me with you and Rhi here."*

"Then we'll leave."

"Nay. We will."

Rhi was glaring daggers by this point. "Seriously? Someone talk. Now."

"I'm sorry," Cain told Rhi as he touched the cuff on his wrist and took himself and Noreen back to their previous location.

Even when they were alone, Noreen wouldn't look at him. She didn't pull away, though. Which was a starting point.

"Talk to me," he urged her. "What happened?"

She turned away from him.

He could sense her distancing herself from him both mentally and physically. She was hiding something, of that he was positive.

"I know you, lass. There isna anything you could say that would change my mind about you."

She drew in a deep breath. "I disagree."

"Then tell me."

Finally, she looked at him. "Do you know what I see when I look at you?"

He shrugged, his mind searching for something to say. "I doona know."

"I see a man who is fierce and lethal to anyone who would harm those he cares about. I see a man who would do anything for those he loves. I see a dragon. A King. Someone who has suffered untold pain and deserves nothing but happiness for the rest of his days."

"You speak of Utopia. There is no such place," he said, as his concern grew with every word. It sounded as if she were trying to tell him good-bye.

She smiled sadly, her gaze briefly dropping to the ground. "I think there was once such a place. It was on Earth long before any mortals or Fae ever arrived."

"We are like any species, lass. There are good times and bad."

"Not like us," she said and swiped at something on her cheek that he suspected was a tear. "Not like the mortals. The Dragon Kings are what we should all aspire to be. Noble. Honorable. Selfless. I'm none of those things."

Now he knew something was wrong. His gut clenched in trepidation. "That isna true. Look at what you've done for us."

She laughed and turned away so he could no longer see her face. "You should get far away from me. And forget everything I've told you."

"I can no'."

"Whatever obligation you feel toward me, I release you from it. Now go, Cain."

He took a step toward her and reached out a hand but

dropped it before he touched her. "I can no'. And I willna. Because you're my mate."

She swung around so fast that she nearly tripped on her own feet. He steadied her, but she quickly jerked out of his arms.

"Is this some joke?" she demanded angrily. "You think to woo me to remain by your side with that?"

He sighed and made his arms drop to his sides. "If you've no' noticed, we dragons are no' much of a jesting lot. And we never joke about things like that. A dragon mates for life. We know our mates."

"Ulrik was wrong."

"Nay. He initially thought Nala was his mate, but he's known for some time that he wanted so badly to find love, that what he thought was love really wasna."

She motioned between them. "That's what you're doing here."

"If it was, I wouldna have put myself between you and Erith."

Noreen rolled her eyes. "That was the woman's name? Who is she?"

"No' someone you want to mess with."

"Yeah, I got that," Noreen replied testily. "You still haven't told me who she is. And I don't guess you will."

He shook his head. "There's a reason for that."

"It doesn't matter. Please leave."

"Nay."

"Then I will."

He grabbed her when she tried to walk away. "What has come over you? You were fine until you and Rhi shook hands. All you've wanted was to meet her. Was she no' what you thought?"

"This has nothing to do with Rhi."

It felt like a punch to Cain's gut. "You're lying."

Noreen's crimson gaze met his. "Don't ask for the truth. I can't give it to you."

"Then tell me what changed."

"Me. That's what changed."

He threw up his hands in agitation. "You're no' making sense, lass."

"Don't call me that."

Cain was taken aback by the fury in her words. "You've never minded it before."

"I do now."

The more he looked at her, the more he noticed subtle differences. Her arms were crossed over her chest as if she were closing herself off. She wouldn't maintain eye contact, and her voice had a hard edge to it.

Some might see all of that as her being combative. Cain saw it as someone who was trying to protect themselves.

"Have you done something you believe Rhi knows about? She's a good person. She would never harm you, and even if she tried, I wouldna let her."

"For fek's sake, stop!" Noreen yelled. "Just stop. Why do you have to be so nice?"

He hesitated as her words sank in. "Because I care about you."

"That was your mistake."

He could've sworn he heard her say, *"And my mistake was caring for you."* But he didn't call her on it.

Noreen's face was a mask of indifference. "I'm not worth your time, and if you were smart, you'd forget about me."

"I can no'. You're my mate. I'll stand by you through whatever it is you're going through."

She stared aghast at him. "Bloody hell. You really mean that, don't you?"

"You say that as if you're surprised. You shouldna be. We've shared a lot in the short time we've been together."

"And you trust too easily."

There was something in her words that made his gut clench. "Why do you say that?"

"Because," she said with a shaky voice. She swallowed and looked away. "I'm not who you think I am. I'm . . . all of this, it was my idea. Moreann cast a spell so I wouldn't remember anything, and you'd believe me." She gave him a beseeching look. "I wasn't after you. I never intended to have sex with you or fall for you or anything."

"What were you after?" he asked stonily.

She swallowed again. "Rhi. Those bad dreams I told you about? I think it was the spell breaking down, which shouldn't have happened." Noreen glanced up and around them. "I think it's the magic of this place that interfered with Moreann's. And then touching Rhi. It wiped everything."

Rage. Betrayal. It all swirled within him like a violent storm waiting to unleash itself on the one responsible. Cain managed to keep it all in check.

For now.

"The things you told us about the Others? About Moreann?"

A tear dropped down her cheek. "All true."

"And you expect me to believe that?"

Noreen shook her head. "No, but it is. You can have Tristan check my memories, if you'd like."

It shouldn't surprise him that she and the Others knew of Tristan's ability.

"I don't know what to do," she said and leaned back against the tree they had made love against not so long ago. "Everything is all mixed up in my head. I know what I once felt for the Kings, and my loyalty to the Others, but now . . ." She looked at Cain. "Everything is different."

He couldn't believe Con had been right all along. And to know that he was the one who had been betrayed hurt worse than he ever thought possible.

"Erith," he said. "I need you."

In an instant, Death was at his side. She looked at him for a long moment before she turned to Noreen.

Noreen pushed away from the tree. "What's going on?"

"I'm giving you to someone who will make sure you can do no more harm to us," Cain told her.

Noreen shook her head as she glanced at Erith. "You put yourself between me and her. You said you'd stand by me."

"That was before you confessed to betraying me. What have you told the Others?" he demanded.

"Nothing! I've been with you." She took another step back, unaware that Cael was there, waiting for her. "My target was Rhi. I told you that. Moreann wants her more than anything."

Cain turned his attention to Erith. "It's asking a lot, I know."

"No, it isn't," she told him. "I knew something was odd about her, and I was able to see the spell fail when she touched Rhi. I suspected she would need to be . . . kept . . . for a while."

Cain turned his back to Noreen and leaned close to Erith before he whispered, "No' her soul."

Erith frowned up at him. "She's Fae. It's my job as judge and jury to decide when it's time to reap her."

"No' her soul," Cain repeated.

A long moment passed before Death gave a nod of her head. Then she looked at Cael. Cain kept his back to

Noreen. He didn't turn around when Cael grabbed her. He didn't turn around even when Noreen screamed his name or when the shout was cut short as they teleported away.

The silence that followed was even harder to bear. Cain wanted to bellow, he wanted to scream. He wanted to hurt something as badly as he was hurting.

He threw back his head and let out a cry that turned into a roar as he shifted. Then he took to the skies and broke through the barrier. He smashed through what was left of the buildings, rained dragon fire down on already burnt forests, and wreaked havoc on everything else.

But nothing soothed his battered heart.

CHAPTER THIRTY-SIX

There was no denying that she was in a prison. Though it might be pretty. Noreen stood within the concrete walls, floor, and ceiling painted with various murals in so many colors, she couldn't begin to count them all. The light, while not blinding, came from everywhere. She wished there was a window, but if there were, that might tell her where she was.

She had stopped fighting, stopped screaming when Cain hadn't helped her. Though what had she expected? And she had told him to get away from her. Yet, she hadn't lied when she said that everything was mixed up inside her.

Noreen rubbed her chest where her heart used to be. It felt as if it had been ripped from her, leaving a gaping hole behind. Emotion tightened her throat, but she wouldn't shed any more tears. She had done this to herself. No one was at fault but her.

It was why she hadn't wanted to tell Cain. She knew what his reaction would be. She'd known because she would've done the same thing.

You're my mate.

His words rang through her head, making the ache

within her even worse. Cain had looked beyond her past, beyond the coloring that signaled her as a Dark, beyond any of her deeds.

He had seen *her*. All of her.

And what had she done? She'd thrown it back at him in the worst possible way.

Noreen walked to the nearest corner of the large room and leaned against it before she slid to the ground and stretched her legs out before her. She remembered when she had come up with the idea for how to get to Rhi—through a Dragon King.

The Light Fae was Noreen's main target, but she also thought it would be quite fun to betray a Dragon King. After all, a King had taken away her parents. Didn't they deserve that and more?

She closed her eyes in remorse because she had thought that way once. She had also believed everything Moreann told her. Now, she knew most of it had been lies. She would've never learned that had she not carried through with her plan.

Noreen leaned her head back and opened her eyes. One thing she did well was plan meticulously. She'd known that in order for everything to work, she had to be believable. That meant she couldn't remember any of her life before—and neither could anyone else in the Others, except for Moreann.

The empress was the one who had put the spell in place, and she was the one who would ensure that everyone in their group truly believed that Noreen had betrayed them.

The fact that everything had worked perfectly should've made Noreen proud, but she couldn't seem to dig past the shame of her actions.

She blinked. Actually, not everything had gone to plan, because if it had, she wouldn't be feeling this . . .

remorse, this soul-destroying guilt. She'd be celebrating because she wouldn't have told Cain anything or acted any differently when she met Rhi. In fact, she would've taken Rhi to Moreann right then, effectively ending any hint of someone wiping out the Others.

Noreen had so many conflicting emotions within her that she didn't know if she was coming or going. Her head began to ache, and she wished Cain was there to help her sort through it all.

Cain. Just the thought of him made her heart heavy. She'd found something unique and extraordinary with him. She had known it the moment she met him, and especially when he kissed her.

His kisses had been amazing. No one had ever embraced her so completely, so thoroughly, perfectly. He had intoxicated her, invading every part of her until he was everywhere—and she craved him with a need that had left her breathless.

That was all before he had claimed her body, and she his. Now that she knew what it was like to be in his arms, to have him deep inside her, there would never be anyone else who could pleasure her but him.

"You're my mate."

If she'd never touched Rhi, she could've had a good life with Cain. They would've mated, seen countless dawns, enjoyed untold nights of pleasure, and loved.

Love.

Noreen thought back over her years. Nothing she had told Cain had been a lie. There were parts she hadn't remembered and so didn't tell him, but at the time, she hadn't lied. Now she knew that she had enjoyed her power over mortal men and made use of it.

And they weren't the only ones. Male Dark had been just as susceptible. Many had claimed to love her, but she had scoffed at their words. She hadn't believed such an emotion was real, nor had she found anyone who made her actually consider making a binding union with. Because she didn't trust anyone.

Trust. Love.

She had found both in a Dragon King, who had every reason to ignore her, but believed her and made sure she was safe.

There was no way she could ever make it up to him. Not that she'd get the chance. No doubt she would be in this prison until someone came to sentence her for her crimes. That someone would be a Dragon King.

Would it be Cain? No, he wouldn't want to speak to her. It might be Ulrik, but in her gut, Noreen knew that it would be Constantine. After all, it had been Con who decided that Nala would die.

Noreen couldn't stop thinking about her time with Cain. Despite years of living under Moreann's rule, and then as part of the Others, that world seemed like it belonged to another person, not her.

She hadn't lived until Moreann placed the spell on her. That was when Noreen got to experience what life could be like, what she might have gotten had her parents not been killed.

By a Dragon King.

Everything always came back to the Kings. She wished it didn't, but there was no way around it. She was connected to the Kings whether she liked it or not. It was too bad it wasn't the link she wanted now—that of a mate.

"I'm sorry, Cain," she whispered and dropped her chin to her chest.

The words would never reach him, and even if they did, he wouldn't believe her. *She* wouldn't believe her, not after everything she'd done.

"You expect me to believe you're sorry?"

Her head snapped up at the deep voice and she found herself staring into purple eyes. The man looked like he could cheerfully kill her at any moment.

"I don't care what you think," she told him.

He gave a snort. "That's why you said the words aloud? Because you didn't want us to hear?"

"I said the words aloud because I won't ever get to say them to Cain."

"As if he'd believe you. Not after what you've done."

She looked away, the words cutting deeper than she'd thought. "I'm aware of that. You don't need to rub it in."

He was silent for a moment. "You've not asked me who I am."

"You wouldn't tell me anyway. I know you're Fae, but not like a normal Fae. I'm guessing you were a Light, and one with position."

His eyes narrowed. "Why would you say I had position?"

"It's in your bearing."

"And you? What about you?"

She shrugged. "Why do you care about me? I betrayed the Kings, and that means death."

"That's right. You saw Nala's death through Cain's eyes," the man said.

There was nothing for her to say, so she didn't respond.

The man clasped his hands behind his back and regarded her. "What was the plan?"

"To get Rhi." She didn't even pretend not to know what he was referring to. "And before you ask, Moreann has long sought out Rhi."

"Rhi isn't hard to find."

Noreen shrugged one shoulder and glanced at the man. "Apparently, she is to Moreann."

"What about the Light in your group? Or you? Usaeil had her."

"I know," Noreen replied with a roll of her eyes. "That was one of the things Moreann and Usaeil fought about. The queen hated that Moreann wanted Rhi so badly, so Usaeil refused to bring her."

The man nodded slowly and crossed his arms over his chest. "And the Light in the Others?"

"Brian is a buffoon."

Was that a hint of a smile on the man's lips? It must have been her imagination.

"You?"

Noreen blew out a breath. "I'm Dark. I kept to the Dark, as we do."

"So, after you met Rhi, what were you to do?"

"Get to know her, get close to her as only someone who is friends with the Kings can do. Then, once the spell broke, I was to take Rhi to Moreann."

The man released a long breath. "That's quite a plan. Did you have Cain chosen?"

"Of course not. I had no idea which King they'd send, but I knew they would send someone. The kind of information I had was something no one could pass up. I was counting on that. I just didn't expect Cain."

"Meaning?"

Damn, did he ever relent? But she knew the answer. Why fight it? She was a prisoner, after all. "I'm good at planning such things. I thought of every scenario except for Cain. I didn't count on . . ." Did she have to say it? She would rather keep it to herself, but she knew he would keep digging until she finally told him. Why go through all of that? It was better to save everyone time.

"I didn't count on Cain being so kind or . . . the attraction between us," she said in a soft voice.

A black brow quirked. "You assume I believe you."

"I know you don't. You asked, and I'm telling. I lied to hurt both Rhi and the Kings, so everyone will believe what I say now to be nothing more than half-truths and additional lies."

"That's right," he said with a hard glare.

Noreen looked to the side.

"This could also be part of Moreann's magic."

She gave a shake of her head, wishing she was alone with her thoughts so she could return to the time she and Cain had been together. "My hope was that the King who found me would offer sanctuary. I thought it might be at Dreagan, but I was also thinking it could be somewhere else. The Fae Realm was an option, but it was low on the list. I found an old doorway just in case and had Moreann include that in my memories. I didn't know about Rhi forming the barrier and healing the planet."

Noreen paused as she recalled the feeling of passing through Rhi's shield. It had felt as if the magic had gone right through her. "I think the destruction of Moreann's spell began the moment I passed through the shield Rhi put in place there. It didn't begin immediately, but soon after, I started having horrible dreams about Moreann doing something to me."

"The spell?" he offered.

She met his gaze, nodding. "I think. It was extremely painful. There was more. Like what I felt wasn't lining up to my memories." Noreen flattened her lips. "It's hard to explain. I just knew something wasn't quite right. Then Cain returned, and I knew he could help."

"How?"

"I-I don't know how to explain it. It's just something I knew. That if I had a problem, he would be there to help me work it out."

The man's gaze held a wealth of disregard. "Then what happened?"

"I got angry when Ulrik came because I knew the Kings didn't believe me. I couldn't figure out why I was so mad. They had every right to question me again. Now I know my feelings were because the spell was breaking down, allowing my old thoughts through."

"Then there was Rhi."

Noreen wrinkled her nose. "The moment I touched her, she was able to break through Moreann's spell. No one has ever been able to do that. I was left with my new feelings and thoughts, trying to be shoved aside by my old."

"And you didn't know what to do?"

"No," she admitted in a small voice. "Because I knew I'd done the one thing the new me had never thought to do."

"Betray a Dragon King."

She looked into his purple eyes filled with disgust. "It's worse than that. Cain told me I'm his mate."

CHAPTER THIRTY-SEVEN

"Don't," Rhi said as she walked up beside Ulrik outside the barrier as they watched Cain's destruction.

Ulrik looked at her askance. "He needs to calm down."

"He needs to get it all out. Holding it in isn't wise. Ever." She looked pointedly at Ulrik. "You know that."

It took a second before he nodded. "No, holding it in isna good. But if he doesna get control soon, he might never again."

Rhi looked back at the navy dragon. "Give Cain a little more time. He's hurting, and he has to let some of it loose."

"This has turned into a complete clusterfuck," Ulrik mumbled as he looked down at the ground.

"Want to tell me what's going on?"

Ulrik scrubbed a hand down his face. "Actually, I'd prefer no' to, but if I doona, you're likely to go to Dreagan for answers, and that wouldna be good right now."

"Well." She turned to face him. "Then you better spit it out. All of it."

Gold eyes met hers. After a long sigh, Ulrik began the tale of how Cain and Noreen met and why. By the time he finished, Rhi was in a state of shock.

"It's going to kill Con to realize that he was right all along," Ulrik said.

She turned to the side, numb. "At least Cain discovered things before it was too late."

"Only because something about touching you brought the spell down. Noreen told Cain all of it."

"You believe her?"

"I doona know," Ulrik replied with a shake of his head. "It's no use asking Cain. He's too torn up at the moment to think straight either way."

Rhi drew in a long breath. "I think it's best if we not discuss Noreen in front of him for a while. Return to Dreagan and fill Con in. I'll stay with Cain."

"That's no' happening. You willna be able to control him."

"Control?" She let out a bark of laughter. "Sweet cheeks, I'm not controlling anything. I'm watching him to make sure he doesn't go anywhere."

Ulrik held up his silver cuff. "Good thing I swiped this before Cain realized it. Otherwise, he might try and leave this realm."

Rhi didn't even want to think about what Cain could do if he got out. Thanks to Ulrik, that wasn't going to happen.

"Seriously. Go to Dreagan," Ulrik told her.

She cut him a hard look. "I've been by myself for a reason. I've no interest in going to Dreagan."

"Rhi," Ulrik began.

She faced him, giving him a look that dared him to finish that sentence.

He threw up his hands in defeat. "Fine. I'll go."

"Cain won't leave here. I can promise you that," she said.

Ulrik pointed a finger at her. "You're going to have to go to Earth sooner or later."

"I know. I've got Usaeil to find—and kill. Again. Not to mention, I'll be fighting the Others. No way this Moreann person is getting near me."

Ulrik put his hands on his hips and shook his head as he looked at the ground. "Fuck me. I actually thought Noreen was speaking the truth."

"She was. At least, she was until the spell broke."

His head snapped to her. "You think all she told us was the truth?"

"I do. Otherwise, how would she convince you? It had to be the truth. No doubt once she set out on her mission, whatever plans the Others had changed."

"If they want you badly enough to go through all these motions, then you have to be really important."

She waved away his words. "We'll talk about that later. Right now, you need to get to Con."

Ulrik hesitated a moment longer before he gave a nod and touched the cuff. Once he was gone, Rhi jumped to where Cain was. She hollered up at him, trying to get his attention. When that didn't work, she teleported atop him.

"Hey, you big oaf!" she bellowed and pounded him on the back. "I'm trying to get your attention."

Cain halted mid-bellow and dipped his wing so severely—and unexpectedly—that she fell off. Rhi managed to use her magic to jump to a mountain peak near her so she didn't plummet to her death. Unfortunately, she didn't land on her feet.

She winced aloud when she found herself with her knees bent to the side and her face in the dirt. She blew out a breath, causing a lock of her hair to move out of her face as she pushed up on her hands.

"At least I didn't die," she said to herself.

"That was bloody stupid. You could've been killed."

Rhi looked up to find Cain standing before her, naked.

She briefly let her eyes run down his body, and while he was impressive, he wasn't her King.

She climbed to her feet and dusted herself off. "I had to do something to get your attention."

"I'd like to be left alone."

"Yeah, I get that. I've been feeling that for some time now, but people keep intruding on me. It's only fair I do the same to you."

His green eyes moved away, his hands fisted at his sides. "What do you want?"

"Noreen and Moreann went to a lot of trouble to find me. I think we need to find out why."

"Be my guest," he replied and turned away, shifting as he did.

Rhi knew she had this one chance to stop him, to get Cain to move his anger aside and consider another possibility. "Noreen didn't lie to you."

He paused, his wings outstretched. His large dragon head turned to her, pinning her with pale yellow eyes.

"Think about it. While the spell was in place, Noreen was truthful. She had to be in order for you to trust her. And once the spell was broken, she could've gone on lying, could've completed her mission. But she didn't. She told you what was going on."

Cain folded his wings and looked away.

Rhi moved closer to him. "I know it hurts. She set out to betray a Dragon King. Not you specifically. I don't know what transpired between the two of you, but I saw you put yourself between her and Death. You'd only do that if she was your mate."

A growl rumbled from Cain, telling her she was treading on dangerous ground.

She threw up her hands. "You don't want to hear that,

and I won't mention it again. But you know I'm right. I think if there was more to say, she'd tell you."

In a heartbeat, Cain was facing her, his nostrils flaring as he stood over her, looking down at her as if he wanted to envelop her in dragon fire.

No doubt he did, but she knew he wouldn't. She was telling him things he'd already thought to himself but wasn't quite ready to face. She was making him face it, though.

"Why did she tell you about the spell?" Rhi asked. "She told you because she feels something for you."

Or it could be another part of the plan. Rhi wasn't sure, and honestly, it didn't matter. Either way, they could use it to their advantage.

The old Rhi would've never dared to even consider this, but the new Rhi didn't really give a shite about hurting anyone's feelings. The truth needed to be discovered—and the sooner, the better.

"You asked Erith not to take her soul," Rhi continued. "You love Noreen. If you think she has any feelings for you, then use that to get answers. You may not want to consider it, but use her as you were used."

Cain shifted back into a man, his face a mask of torment and anguish. "I doona think I can look at her again."

"Remember, this wasn't against you. She would've gotten close to whatever King was sent to her, but something developed between the two of you."

Cain snorted, his eyes cutting away. "She probably would've slept with any King who helped her."

"Maybe. But they wouldn't have found their mate like you did. And you wouldn't have told her about being your mate if you didn't believe she felt something for you."

"It was a lie."

"Maybe. Maybe not. We won't know until we talk to her."

His head swung back to her. "How can we believe anything she says?"

Rhi smiled then. "Sometimes, you Kings can be so thick. Have you forgotten you have an ace up your sleeve?"

There was a pause before Cain said, "Tristan."

She nodded, smiling. "Ding ding ding ding. We have a winner, folks."

"I'm no' sure I can do this," he said in a low voice.

Rhi walked to Cain and took his hand, keeping her eyes on his face. "Yes, you can, because it has to be you. She'll be so focused on you that she won't know what we're doing. Besides, she's with Erith. Death can do whatever she wants."

"Then she can create me. I doona have to be there."

Frustrated, Rhi released a long sigh. "There's no getting out of this. Hold in your hurt until it's all over. There's a chance you'll discover the real Noreen is the one who has been with you."

It was a lie. A huge, fat lie, but Rhi didn't care. She'd say whatever she had to in order to get the information she needed—regardless of who she hurt.

That's my girl.

She inwardly flipped the darkness off. Her battle with it was just beginning, and she wasn't sure she was up to the challenge. After all, she also had Usaeil and Moreann to deal with.

There was only so much Rhi could handle, and she knew she was at the end of her rope. But she had enough left to at least take care of Usaeil.

"You're right," Cain said as he lifted his head. "I'm a Dragon King."

"Yes, you are."

He nodded. "I'll do it."

"Awesome. Now, put some clothes on, stud."

In a blink, jeans, a shirt, and boots covered him. Then he said, "Erith."

They didn't wait long before Death appeared. She looked from Cain to Rhi. "What's going on?"

Cain was the one who said, "I want to talk to Noreen."

Erith's lavender eyes swung to him. "I don't think that's a good idea. You're too close to this."

"She has information," Cain insisted.

"And I'll get it."

Rhi decided it was time to step in. "Cain needs to know what is fact and what is fiction. While he's talking to her, keeping her occupied, we thought Tristan could delve into her mind to see what he can learn."

Erith said nothing for a long, silent moment. "Is this what you want, Cain?"

"Aye," he stated.

"All right."

No sooner had the words been spoken than Cain was gone, leaving Rhi with Death. She wasn't afraid, though. In fact, Rhi didn't expect to live much longer.

"And what is it you plan to learn?" Erith demanded. "I know the state Cain is in, and he didn't come up with this plan."

Rhi shrugged. "So? We need information."

"You mean *you* need information."

"Again, so?"

Erith gave her a hard look. "We're better when we all fight together. It isn't good for any of us to go out on his or her own."

Rhi gave a bark of laughter. "Funny since you were the one who kept telling me Usaeil was mine to take out. Odd how we weren't all a *team* then."

"Careful."

"Or what? You'll take my soul?"

Erith gave her a derisive look. "No. This."

Rhi gaped as she was left alone on the Fae Realm.

CHAPTER THIRTY-EIGHT

Despite her hope that the purple-eyed Fae would leave her, Noreen found her answers only intrigued him more.

"You're Cain's mate?"

She wanted to roll her eyes but held back. It wouldn't do her any good to show such disrespect. She might not know who this man was, but the strength of his magic was evident even to her. Just as the woman's was.

Thinking about the pair of them caused a chill to race down Noreen's spine. The couple wasn't anyone she wanted to piss off. Unfortunately, it looked like she'd done just that. But who were they? And why didn't Moreann know about them?

"I wouldn't suggest silence as an answer."

She was startled out of her own thoughts. "I was thinking. Sorry." Noreen licked her lips and wished to be talking about Moreann and the Others, not Cain. Because when she spoke about Cain, she thought of his arms, of how he'd looked at her with such yearning, such . . . care in his deep green eyes.

And she'd royally fekked that up.

"It's what he told me," she finally replied. She shrugged.

"I knew he liked me. People don't have the kind of sex we shared if there isn't a very strong attraction."

Purple eyes bored right into her. Noreen almost asked if it'd be helpful if they could dive inside her head and get all the answers without putting her through this. The interrogation, the feeling of being trapped, was all part of the process. For all she knew, torture might be in her future.

And she deserved every minute of whatever they doled out to her.

"What do you think of Cain?" the man asked.

Her eyes dropped to her feet. "I already told you."

"No, you didn't."

Maybe she hadn't. Perhaps she'd just been telling herself. It was getting harder and harder to remember what had happened and what hadn't.

She gave a little shake of her head to try and clear it. "I counted on the Kings' willingness to help those in need when I set up my plan."

"You put a lot on the fact they'd help not only a Dark, but also someone part of the Others."

"I did. It was a long shot, and if it didn't work, we weren't out much. But if it did . . ." She let her words trail off. There was no need to elaborate. Noreen cleared her throat. "The Others have studied the Dragon Kings for a long period. Or, I should say, *Moreann* has. She's documented nearly all of it, and it was always available to any of us who wanted to study it."

The man immediately asked, "Did you?"

Noreen nodded.

"Any particular King?"

She knew what the man was asking. "No, I didn't target Cain. As I said, I had no idea who they would send to me. Everything I knew about the Dragon Kings was wiped away with the spell."

The man dropped his arms to his sides. "But you knew of Cain."

"Yes." She lifted her gaze to his. "Moreann has a list of all the Kings and their colors. She didn't always know their names, but she kept a detailed list."

"Who was she most interested in?"

Noreen made a face. "That's a silly question. It was Constantine, of course. He's the leader, the strongest of them. She knew that to defeat him would be the first step in clearing the way for the removal of all Dragon Kings."

"Did she think she could kill him?"

"She planned on Ulrik doing it." Just saying the words made Noreen's stomach turn viciously. She drew in several calming breaths not to get sick. "She. . . ." Noreen had to stop and try again. "Everything that happened to Ulrik began with Moreann speaking to Mikkel. If she hadn't interfered, there's a good chance none of that horrible business would've transpired."

The man squatted before her and trapped her gaze with his purple orbs. "And when that plan was foiled?"

Noreen swallowed, her throat and mouth dry. "She knew that with the right magic combination, there was a chance the Others could kill a Dragon King."

"Really?"

If she thought the man's eyes had been filled with fury before, she'd been wrong. They burned with a wrath so great that it appeared as if the purple irises were lit from within.

Noreen nodded woodenly, wondering if it would be the Dragon Kings who killed her or if it would be this Fae. "Moreann never actually said it, but I think that's why she wanted Rhi so badly."

"To use with you? Or with Usaeil?"

"I have no idea," Noreen replied with a shrug. "Usaeil's much stronger than I am."

His gaze raked over her. "Obviously, you have some benefit. Otherwise, you wouldn't be a part of the Others."

"Moreann trained me from the day she found me after my parents' deaths."

The man made a sound in the back of his throat as he straightened. "You seem very sure about how your parents died."

This again. She should've known. "Yes."

"Stand up."

Was it time, then? Was she about to die? She pulled up an image of Cain's face in her mind as she got to her feet. It would be the last thing she saw before her life ended, and if she were lucky, she'd get to take it into whatever afterlife she was granted.

The Fae walked around her slowly. She held still—barely—wondering if she'd feel it when he took her life. But he came back around, and she was still breathing.

"You think I'd be the one to take your life?" he asked, a brow raised. He issued a loud snort. "You obviously have a lot to learn about the Dragon Kings."

She didn't deny that. The things she knew, or *thought* she knew, had come from Moreann. They had been colored by her thoughts of the Kings, and not many of them had been actual accountings. Then again, Moreann would say what Noreen had seen through Cain's memories was colored by what he'd experienced.

The problem was, both were right. She had been able to witness both sides, and she knew without a doubt that the Kings had been dealt a very unfair hand. They hadn't always done right, but for the most part, they had.

And they weren't trying to destroy a species just to have their planet.

It sickened Noreen to realize that she had been such an integral part of the Others. Going to such extremes that she had not only been the one to come up with the plan, but had also implemented it.

"You've told me quite a lot," the man said.

She realized he'd been watching her, but she didn't care anymore. Let them see whatever they wanted. It wasn't as if they'd believe anything she said. "And you're wondering how much of it is true."

"I know how much is the truth."

His statement took her aback. She frowned and found herself studying him. "How?"

He shrugged. "Let's just say that I have friends with special . . . gifts."

"Then ask me anything you want so I can give you whatever answers you need."

"The thing is, we're not sure if the spell is gone."

"It is."

He gave her a flat look. "Is it? Before you touched Rhi, you didn't have a clue it was even in place. Now, you want me to believe that it's all gone?"

"Yes."

"Are you a hundred percent certain?"

Noreen hesitated, thinking about how painful it had been for the spell to be put in place. She recalled the dream where Moreann's hands had held her head as she said the spell.

She hadn't asked Moreann what the spell was. She had trusted the empress, but that didn't mean Moreann trusted *her*. There was a chance Moreann had added something to the spell.

"You need to kill me. Or send for Con or whoever, but I need to die," she pleaded with the man.

He calmly stared at her. "Why?"

"In case Moreann added something to the spell. It's exactly something she'd do. I've already hurt enough people. I don't want to be a part of this anymore."

"Perhaps that's what she added in," the man stated. "To make us feel sorry for you and not kill you."

Noreen shook her head, her gut churning with the possibility that she could do even more damage. "I can't remember, and I don't want to take the chance. The look in Cain's eyes when I told him . . ." She shook her head, but no matter what she did, she'd never forget that. "I can't do that to anyone else."

"You think that now. You might not tomorrow."

"It's the now I'm most concerned with," she said, her voice growing louder. Noreen took a deep breath and tried to calm herself. "I know what I was. I still have those memories, still feel some of the anger and resentment I lived with all these centuries. But I also continue to feel the things that happened after the spell. This"—she waved her hands at herself—"new me is the one concerned about my situation. I know what I've done. I know the people I've hurt. I know what's planned, and I'm begging you. Please, end my life."

There was a flash of sadness in his eyes before he looked away. "That isn't my decision to make."

"If it were?" she prodded.

Hard eyes looked at her. "I'd have killed you the moment you revealed your betrayal."

"It might not carry much weight, and I know I have no right to ask, but could you tell Cain that I'm sorry?"

The Fae stared at her a long time. Then he said, "No."

She shouldn't have expected anything more. He'd shown a smidgen of sympathy, or what she believed was compassion. But she'd been wrong.

There was no fight left in her to lash out or say anything

to attempt to get the upper hand. For one, because there was nothing for her to gain. This Fae, whoever he was, had her in a tight spot.

He turned his back to her and took a step before he stopped. With his head turned to the side he said, "You said Moreann is powerful enough to have remained alive for untold centuries."

"Yes."

"You believe she has the magic to put a spell such as the one she put on you to remove your memories temporarily and replace them with something else so that everything reverted back as it should have?"

Noreen nodded. "Without a doubt."

"You've seen her do this spell?"

"No, but I've seen her do things that others couldn't. During her long life, she's acquired a tremendous amount of knowledge and power."

The man let her words fade. "So, how then did the spell malfunction? How is it you have your old self mixed with this new one?"

"I don't know. I've been trying to figure that out."

"Do you want this new you removed?"

Noreen shook her head before she had time to even think about it, because the idea of her memories of Cain and their time together gone was too much to bear.

The man turned his head away. "Of course, you'd say that. You may claim to want to die, but inside, you're fighting to stay alive."

CHAPTER THIRTY-NINE

Cain couldn't watch anymore. He pulled his hand from Noreen's body and turned away, but Con stood in his way. The King of Kings didn't say a word, but then again, he didn't have to.

"She feels no pain," Erith told Cain as she came to stand beside Con.

Cain glanced behind him at Noreen lying still upon a concrete slab. They were in an abandoned human fort on an isle off the coast of Scotland near Edinburgh, which was once a Reaper base. It had been shrouded in both Reaper and Death's magic for months now. The Dragon Kings had added theirs, making it impossible for anyone to get through it or detect that Noreen was there.

"Cael put her under the moment he took her from the Fae Realm," Erith continued. "She has no idea any of us are here or what is happening to her."

That didn't help Cain much. "I know exactly what she's feeling and seeing since I was touching her."

"I never said this would be easy," Erith replied.

Actually, she hadn't said shite, but Cain didn't point that out. All she'd done when she took him from the Fae

Realm was bring him here and tell him to lay his hands upon Noreen. Cael and Tristan were already touching her, their eyes closed. Tristan had the ability to get into someone's mind, and Cael was there simply to interrogate her so Tristan could determine what was truth and what wasn't.

The moment Cain came into contact with her, he was able to see the entire scene. The concrete box she was in, which was similar to the room she lay in except every surface had a painting upon it.

What struck him the most was how sad she looked. She hated herself for what she'd done. That was obvious. And he wanted to believe it. With all his heart, he wanted to think that she hadn't meant any of it, but he couldn't.

She had fooled him so perfectly, and he wasn't going to allow her to do it again.

Cain had listened to her speak to Cael for several moments. Then, out of the blue, Tristan put one of his hands on Cain. In a blink, Cain was able to see what Tristan saw. Cain was then able to tell that the words Noreen spoke were truthful.

But, as Cael had pointed out, were they the entire truth, or only what was left of the spell that had somehow gone wrong?

That's what Cain couldn't handle. He wanted to believe Noreen, he wanted to protect her and fight for her. She was, after all, his mate.

But he couldn't.

His heart hurt too much.

Erith walked to stand beside him. She briefly put her hand on his arm and met his gaze before she moved past him to join Cael and Tristan.

Cain then met Con's black gaze. He was surprised that Con hadn't demanded Noreen's death already. Cain wasn't sure what he would do when that came about, because he knew it would. Eventually. When everyone had extracted all the information they could from Noreen and when she was no longer of use, she would die.

The thought made Cain want to lash out at someone, anyone—himself included. He had, under the most incredible circumstances, found his mate. His mate! She was his match in every possible way.

At least this version of Noreen was. The old Noreen, the original one, wanted him dead.

Con motioned with his head for Cain to follow him. They walked out of the room and down the concrete corridor until they came to a door. Con walked outside so they faced the North Sea. The water was calm, in complete discord with Cain's own emotions.

"You knew," Cain said.

Con blew out a breath. "I didna know it would be Noreen, but I've long suspected that a woman would betray us once more. It left too deep a scar on us for it no' to happen again. I'm sorry it was you."

"Nala wasna Ulrik's mate."

"But Noreen is yours." Con's chin dipped to his chest for a moment. Then he lifted his head. "There is nothing I can say that will make any of this better."

Cain shrugged and put his fingers into the front pockets of his jeans. "I'm no' asking you to."

"Are you no'?" Con demanded as he looked his way.

It took a moment before Cain could look his King in the eye. "If there was something I could do to change the outcome of this, I would. But there isna. So, I sit and watch, soaking up what time I have left with her. But you willna send me away as you did Ulrik."

"It would be for the best."

Cain shook his head and shifted to face Con. "I'll be the one to do it. It's the least I can do for her."

"The fact you're losing your mate will tip you into dangerous territory. If you take her life, we'll lose you."

"Now that I've found her, I'm nothing without her. You know that better than any of us."

Con's gaze slid away. "You think to take a jab at me with such a reminder. It willna work."

"The hell it willna. I know it hits home. I know it now more than ever because I'm going to lose my mate. The thing is, you could change things for yourself."

"I can no'."

Cain shoved at Con's shoulder. "You selfish bastard! You had what I'm going to lose!"

With utter calm, Con met his gaze. "And I let it go."

"Why? I want the real reason, no' the shite you've told us before."

The mask Con always wore slipped, letting Cain see the heartache, the agony, the fury that he always held so close to his chest. "The real reason? I'll give you the real reason. There was a spell upon us no' to feel anything toward humans. We'd been at war with the Fae for decades. And I found my mate. How could I continue to be so happy when none of you were so fortunate? How could I bring her to Dreagan, take her as my mate, and live among all of you when it would only be a matter of time before jealousy and hatred festered in each of your hearts because you didna have what I did?"

By the time Con finished, his voice was raised, his nostrils flared, and his fists were clenched at his sides. Every King suspected that Con had given up his mate for them, but Con hadn't actually confirmed it until that instant.

Without backing down, Con glared at Cain. "Do I know

how you feel? The sting of no' having her, of knowing she'll never be in your arms again? The ache of never hearing her whisper your name, of no' sharing the pleasure of your bodies? Oh, aye, Cain. I know exactly what you're going through."

With that, Con turned on his heel and walked away.

Cain put his hands on the railing of the wall and looked out at the blue waters. The sun was rising slowly. The rest of the realm was going about their day, unaware of the upheaval the Kings and Reapers dealt with.

If the pain he felt right now was just the beginning, Cain wasn't sure how Con had survived all these millennia without his mate. Cain had always respected Con, but now, he had even more admiration for the King of Kings.

"If I could spare you this, I would."

Cain was shocked to hear Con's voice behind him. He hadn't thought Con would return after their exchange. "I know."

"All the times we've been to war, it was to save the humans. Never have we done battle to save our very existence."

Cain pushed away from the railing and turned to Con. "That's the reason I went to see Noreen to begin with. I knew how imperative it was to get an advantage on the Others. If I'd known—"

"You couldna have," Con said, waving away his words. "None of us could. No matter what path we took, we were meant to travel down this road."

The words made Cain pause. "Ulrik once said that while he hated what happened to him, the banishment and binding of his magic forced him to face things he never would have before. He said that he's a better Dragon King because of all of it."

"Aye," Con said in a low voice as he put his hands into

his pants' pockets. "He wouldna have found Eilish had he been married to Nala."

Cain's brows drew together as he turned his head to Con. "You know, you could say that about all of us. Look at each King and how they found their mates. None of it would've happened had we no' fought with the mortals."

"I've no' thought too much about that, but you have a point."

"Which means, I needed to walk this path." Cain pursed his lips. "I just wish I knew why."

"You trusted a Dark when few of us would have," Con pointed out.

Cain looked toward the fort, thinking of Noreen within its walls. "I need to talk to her."

"Do you think that's wise? I know what Rhi said, but we're getting information without you."

With a nod, Cain turned his head to him. "I do. Regardless of what's happened, I fell in love with her. I know she feels something for me, as well. That wasna part of the spell. That manifested on its own."

"I didna consider that. You think you can look through your resentment over the betrayal to see past any lies?"

"Tristan will be there to help me. Besides, I owe no' only Noreen this, but myself, as well. If there's a chance I can help our cause, then I'll do it."

Con put his hand on Cain's arm, stopping him. "I know you'll do whatever it takes, but I want you to know, I'd rather have you to fight with us than the information."

"You can have both."

"Can I?" Con asked, a blond brow raised in question.

Cain couldn't reply because he wasn't sure of the answer himself.

Con released him and gave a single nod. "Be careful, my friend."

"I willna let you down."

Cain turned and went back inside, his strides lengthening as he hurried to the chamber where Noreen lay. He didn't stop until he was beside her. Then he touched her and was yanked back into her mind.

This time, Cain appeared beside Cael. The Reaper was in mid-sentence when he spotted Cain. Without a word, he bowed his head and vanished. Then Cain turned his focus on Noreen. Her face said it all. If the surprise were any indication, she hadn't thought to see him.

"I'm sorry," she said. "I know you don't believe me, and I understand that, but this might be the only time I get to say it, so I want you to know. I'm so, so sorry."

"Is this you talking? Or the spell?" Cain asked. Tristan had touched him once again, so he was able to see if she were lying or not.

Noreen shrugged. "I don't know. I feel both of me inside, but the old me wouldn't have been apologetic. The new me, the one you know, that's who is torn up over all of this."

Cain didn't need Tristan's magic to know that Noreen spoke the truth. He could tell it on his own. "How long is this new Noreen going to be around?"

"If I could destroy the old me, I would. I don't like the person I was, regardless of why or how I became her."

He kept his distance from her, but it was hard, so very hard. "You say that because you feel remorse."

"The old me felt it, as well, but I told myself that whatever I had done to whoever it was had it coming." She sniffed and tucked a strand of black and silver hair behind her ear. "It made it easier to deal with things. Now, I can't do that."

"There is much you've told us, and more I'm hoping

you'll share. But there is one thing we have to delve into before anything else."

She nodded emphatically. "Sure. Whatever it is."

"Your parents' deaths."

She stilled, the refusal on her lips. Instead, she swallowed and said, "Okay."

CHAPTER FORTY

Of course, they'd want to know about her parents. Noreen should've been prepared for that since she kept telling them she didn't want to talk about it. Maybe it was for the best, though. Now, the Dragon Kings could learn which of them had killed her family.

Please don't let it be Cain.

Noreen wouldn't be able to handle it if it were Cain. He was the only reason she was holding on, with all her might, to her current feelings. It was all because he'd shown her another way of life that she didn't want to let go of.

It would be easy to slip back into the old Noreen, the one who hated everything and everyone. That life was there, waiting for her to return.

But she didn't want it. She didn't want any part of it or the horrible person she'd been. It didn't matter that she had done things because she didn't think there was another way. All the responsibility for her actions lay squarely on her shoulders alone because she could've fought for her freedom.

She knew that wasn't true. Moreann didn't easily let go of anyone. The only way that anyone got to leave the group was by death. And Moreann's hold on Noreen had been . . . suffocating. The empress had dictated every move in Noreen's life. It was all she'd ever known.

Her thoughts ground to a halt as she came to a sudden— and shocking—realization. What if her plan hadn't been about getting Rhi for Moreann? What if her scheme had been her way out of the Others all along?

The revelation was so unsettling that her stomach roiled viciously, causing her to bend over, her hands on her knees as she took in deep breaths.

"Noreen?"

Cain's voice called to her, his concern making her want to reach for him. Instead, she nodded and held up a hand. "Give me just a moment."

"You're verra pale."

"I'm not feeling well."

Thankfully, he didn't say more, allowing her time to get herself back under control. Slowly, she straightened to look into green eyes that had gazed at her with such passion and love before. Now, they were filled with doubt and suspicion.

"If you want to know about my parents, then I'll tell you all I know. Again," she told him.

Cain's nostrils flared as he drew in a breath. "You said yourself that you were but a small child. A child's memories can no' be trusted since they doona always understand what they see or hear."

She couldn't refute that. "I know what Moreann told me. It went hand-in-hand with my memories."

"She saw the dragon?"

Noreen hesitated before she nodded.

Cain's eyes bored into her. "What color did she say it was?"

"I—" Noreen began, but she couldn't finish, because

she didn't know the answer. "I know she told me. She had to have told me because she was meticulous about logging information about each of you."

Cain didn't seem disappointed at all in her statement. In fact, it appeared as if he'd expected just that. "Can you go back to that day? Will you bring me with you, telling every detail you can remember?"

It was the last thing she wanted to do, but for Cain, she'd endure Hell itself. Because she loved him. Her heart missed a beat as the words fought to get past her lips, but she held them back. He wouldn't believe her. So, she'd hold the sentiment in her heart.

For now.

Noreen closed her eyes and let herself drift back to that long-ago day when her parents had died. Many of the memories had faded over time because she hadn't held onto them. But to her surprise, it all came back in vivid color now.

Her knees threatened to buckle when she looked around the cottage. It hadn't been large, but it had been comfortable. She was playing with her favorite doll on a huge, ornate rug in the living area.

The furniture was well used but in good condition. Sunlight poured in from the many windows that were open to let in the fresh air. She heard whistling from outside. Noreen smiled as she remembered the tune her father had always sung.

The door opened, and in stepped a man. He was tall with a head full of long, black hair that was pulled back in a queue. His silver eyes landed on her, and a huge smile broke out over his face.

"There's my beautiful girl," he said and walked to her, sweeping her up in his arms.

Emotion choked Noreen as her little arms wrapped

around his neck as he twirled her around the room. As her father settled her on his shoulders, Noreen saw a woman standing in the kitchen, arranging a bouquet of flowers in dazzling colors.

"You spoil her," the woman said and turned to set the vase on the kitchen table.

Noreen's lungs seized when she gazed at her mother. Her black hair hung over one shoulder in a thick plait that fell well past her breast. Silver eyes grinned at Noreen before they moved to the man.

"Of course, I spoil her," Noreen's father said. "Just as I spoil you, my love."

Her mother walked to them and grabbed Noreen's small hands before she rose up and placed a kiss on her father's lips. "I'm so fortunate to have the both of you."

"Pretty sure I'm the lucky one," her father replied and wrapped an arm around her mother.

Noreen wanted the memories to stop right there. She didn't want to see any more. She knew she wasn't telling Cain any of it, but she couldn't. The words were lodged in her throat—along with her heart.

There was a knock at the door that caused both of her parents to frown. They looked at each other, concern in their eyes.

"It can't be," her mother said.

Her father glanced at the door. "We know what we have to do."

Her mother nodded and flashed a smile up at Noreen before she faced the door while her father set her on the floor with her doll.

"Noreen, my sweet, you need to listen carefully," he said as he squatted beside her, holding her gaze. "No matter what you hear outside, don't move from this spot. We'll be back to get you. Do you understand?"

She nodded, trying to hold onto his hand to get him to stay. Even at that young age, she knew something bad was about to happen, and she wanted to stop it. She called out for her father, but he simply gave her a kiss on her forehead.

"I love you, my sweet. I'll be right back," he said and got to his feet.

She wanted to follow, but she knew better than to disobey her parents. So, Noreen remained on the rug, holding her doll as she watched her father leave the house. Once the door shut behind him, she continued staring at it, waiting for her parents to return.

It felt like an eternity passed. She didn't hear any words, didn't see anyone else. But she knew something was going on outside.

Suddenly, there was a loud roar that startled Noreen so badly she screamed. The roar sounded again. She put her hands over her ears and squeezed her eyes shut, wanting the sound to stop.

She heard her name. Her eyes flew open as she saw her mother rush into the house with her father right behind her. Something bright illuminated the area behind him. He shouted her mother's name, but his eyes were on Noreen.

Noreen stretched out her arms, reaching for them both when the first of the flames burst into the house. They seemed to grow right before her eyes, swallowing her father first. Noreen screamed for her mother as tears coursed down her face. Her mother's fingers touched hers, but it was too late. The flames devoured her, as well.

Noreen felt her fingertips burning, but she didn't care. Nor did she turn away from the flames. But they didn't come for her. In fact, they stopped and retreated instantly.

Leaving nothing behind but the charred remains of what was left of the house and the ashes of her parents.

Noreen ignored the still-burning rug and reached through the flames to touch what was left of her mother.

She was so focused on her mom that Noreen never saw the woman enter. She was just suddenly there. She wore a long, burgundy robe-like outfit with her light brown hair pulled away from her face. Her green eyes stared at Noreen for a long moment.

"This is the last place you need to be, little one," the woman said. "It's a good thing I came along when I did. Shall we go?"

Noreen shook her head and ignored the woman's hand. She wasn't going anywhere.

"You don't really have a choice. You're just a child."

Noreen looked at the woman, noticing for the first time that her voice wasn't the same as her parents'.

The woman blew out a breath. "I'm here to save you, Noreen. I can help you get revenge on those responsible for taking your parents. You want that, don't you?"

She did. More than anything.

"Good," the woman said and held out both her hands. "Come now. Your future awaits."

Noreen let the woman lift her into her arms and settle her, a little awkwardly at first, on her hip. Noreen looked over the woman's shoulder at her parents because she knew she might never see the place again.

Once outside, she gazed at what was left of the cottage while the rest smoldered, and tiny flames struggled to remain alive. Then, in a blink, the beautiful green countryside was gone, replaced by a cold, dark room that would become her home for the next several years.

Noreen's eyes flew open as the memory faded. At least she tried to open her eyes, but she couldn't. And her memories weren't done with her yet.

They took her to a time in the not too distant past where

she stood at a table looking down at a book with her name on it. It was by sheer chance that she had stumbled upon it. Her hands trembled as she opened it, looking over her shoulder as she did in case Moreann appeared.

But the empress had been otherwise engaged of late, thanks to Usaeil. That gave Noreen the time she needed to do some searching. As she read through the first few pages that described finding a child with just the qualities Moreann had been searching for, she came to realize that the empress had approached her parents, offering to buy Noreen. Of course, her parents had refused.

Over the next few pages, Moreann went into detail about how she'd gone to the cottage on that early Wednesday morning and tried for a final time to buy Noreen. Moreann knew, one way or another, she was leaving with the child.

And when Noreen's parents refused again, Moreann attacked—with fire.

The roars had been for Noreen's benefit to make her *think* it was a Dragon King so Moreann could instill instant hatred in Noreen for them. And it had worked.

With every page Noreen read, she realized that everything Moreann had told her was a lie.

For the second time, she was coming to realize the truth of her life. Except this time, Noreen no longer had to hide it.

Fury swept through her. She let out a scream of rage. And when she opened her eyes, Cain stood over her, his hands on either side of her face.

But they weren't alone.

CHAPTER FORTY-ONE

"Noreen! Look at me," Cain called through her screams.

Through Tristan's link to her mind, Cain had seen everything, felt every emotion that ran through her as if it had been his own. And it left him rocked to his very core.

He glanced up at Tristan to find his face taut, as well. Delving into someone's mind was a tricky thing, and Tristan could usually guard himself against such an intrusion of emotions. But not this time.

Not with Noreen.

Cain had a feeling it had something to do with Noreen's gift.

"Bloody hell," Cael murmured from the right side of Cain.

Cain looked at the Reaper to find his hands flat on the stone table, his head hanging down, and his eyes squeezed shut. It appeared as if everyone in the room had experienced Noreen's memories.

She kept screaming, the anger and resentment coursing through her as vividly as it had the first time she'd learned she had been betrayed. Her back arched, and her fingers curved as if she wanted to wrap them around Moreann's neck.

"I didna know clearing her memories would do this," Tristan said over her.

Cain gave a shake of his head. It needed to be done, and now he had to wake her. He'd known from the beginning that there were things regarding her parents' deaths that had nothing to do with the Dragon Kings. Now, he had his answers.

He just wished they hadn't come at such a high price for Noreen.

With a little shake of her shoulders, he said her name again. This time, she stopped mid-scream, her eyes snapping open.

"Noreen?" he asked softly.

A tear leaked from the outer corner of her eye and fell into her hair. "She lied to me."

"She's lied about a lot of things."

Her gaze left his and looked around the room. "Where am I? What happened to the other place?"

"You were always here," Cael told her as he lifted his head. "We put you to sleep and spoke in your mind."

Her voice was low when she said, "Oh."

Cain wanted to wipe the tear track from her face, to gather her in his arms and hold her. But he did neither. He forced himself to loosen his hold on her arms and release her. Despite what he'd seen in her memories, she had still betrayed him.

He wanted to believe everything he'd seen. And while that memory of her parents' murders had been true, he didn't know what else to believe. Tristan could determine if the memories had been tainted by magic and tampered with. And while that helped, Cain still couldn't forgive her.

Her eyes met his when he released her and dropped his arms to his sides as he straightened.

"Easy," Tristan told her as she looked wildly around.

Her fingers gripped the sides of the table while her chest rose and fell rapidly. She was anything but calm, not that Cain could blame her. He didn't know how she remained so still. He would've sat up, at least, but Noreen didn't move.

She licked her lips as her gaze moved to Cael. "If I'm still alive, it's because you need information."

"You want to talk about that instead of what your memories revealed?" Cael asked.

Cain clenched his teeth together to keep from telling Cael to back the fuck off. When Cain lifted his gaze, it was to find Tristan's dark brown eyes on him.

"If anyone can get through to her, it's you," Tristan said through their link.

"I can no'."

Tristan gave him a flat look. *"She's your mate. Fight for her. Fight for the truth!"*

Cain knew he was right, but it didn't make it any easier. He caught Cael's attention and gave a slight shake of his head, telling the Reaper to stand down. Then Cain held out a hand to Noreen. She observed him for a few minutes before she slid her palm against his.

He helped her to sit up, then released her. "Tristan used his power to get into your mind."

Tristan came around to stand beside Cain and looked at Noreen. "You can only see the memory that the person is looking at, right?"

"Yes," she answered.

"I can see anything I want."

Noreen swallowed loudly. "Anything?"

Tristan bowed his head in a nod. "It takes some time

to search through everything, which is why Cain directed you to the memories we wanted you to look at."

"To prove it wasn't a Dragon King," she stated as she looked away.

Cain had known she would think that. "We wanted to know if one of our own was responsible, because we would've gotten to the bottom of it. If it wasna a King, then we needed to know that, as well. As did you."

She glanced at him but quickly looked away without replying.

Tristan said, "We know you didna have to tell Cain about the spell or betraying him. We're trying to get to the bottom of things the easiest and fastest way we can."

"Because you can't believe anything I say," she replied.

Cael snorted. "No. We can't. Neither would you in our place."

Cain swiped a hand through the air and looked pointedly at Cael before he softened his expression and turned back to Noreen. "Why did you tell me about the spell?"

"Why do you think?" she asked testily. "I regretted it, and I wanted it all to go away."

"But it didna. I doona know what's real. I doona know if everything we talked about was truth or just part of the plan."

She rolled her eyes and shook her head. "Put me back under. I'd rather suffer through memories than see the look of contempt on your face."

"You betrayed us!" The anger rose up unexpectedly. Cain thought he could control it, but he couldn't.

All those years ago, he'd thought he understood how Ulrik felt, but he hadn't. No one had. But Cain did now.

There were tears in Noreen's eyes when she looked at Tristan. "Can you put me back to sleep?"

"I can," Cael told her.

Tristan held out a hand to stop Cael. Then he turned his head to Noreen. "You doona have to be asleep for this."

"Whatever," she said and lay back down.

Tristan put his finger on her head and touched Cain with his other hand. Cael moved back, seemingly no longer interested in being a part of Noreen's memories.

"Is there anything you want to know?" Tristan asked her.

That surprised Cain. He didn't ask what Tristan was about, though. Instead, he let the King of Ambers continue on the path he'd taken.

Noreen gave a single nod. "I want to know what happened after I learned the truth about my parents."

"Close your eyes and think about the last thing you remember," Tristan guided her.

In an instant, Cain found himself seeing through Noreen's eyes as she closed the book about herself. She carefully stashed it away where she'd found it, then returned to her bedroom where she paced for hours as her mind churned through everything she'd learned.

She alternated between anger and tears, flipping from one emotion to the other like someone tossing a coin. He was shocked to discover that Noreen had wanted away from Moreann for a very long time, but the empress always found a way to tie Noreen to her.

That was the night Noreen knew she had to find a way to get away from Moreann once and for all. And there was only one way to do that—she needed to go to Moreann's enemy.

Noreen considered Usaeil, but she knew the queen would never believe her. Then Noreen came up with a daring plan, one that was the perfect out—betraying the Dragon Kings.

It took her a month to sort through the various situations and outcomes of approaching Moreann with her idea.

When she did, Noreen used Rhi as the hook to get the empress on board. Noreen made sure to word things just so, so Moreann believed it was *her* idea to put the spell on Noreen.

Another two months went by as she and Moreann worked out more details, including how the Others would think Noreen had double-crossed them, how she would get back to Moreann, and the spell that would be used.

Then it came time for the spell. Noreen was blindfolded as Moreann transported her to the Druid Realm where several other Druids joined them. They held Noreen down as Moreann began the spell. It was a long, uncomfortable process. The first slice of pain that zoomed through Noreen's head had Cain reaching for her hand. She had it fisted, but at his touch, they threaded fingers.

Sweat beaded his forehead as Moreann's spell intensified. Noreen screamed—both in her memories and in real life—from the agony. The Druids holding her kept her pinned to the table until she passed out from the pain.

Before she did, she had one thought—Moreann had added something to the spell.

Cain had to agree with her. There had been something tacked on at the end that Moreann hadn't spoken to Noreen about.

Noreen's next memory was of being near Dreagan and not doing any magic so none of the Others could find her. For days, she'd considered going to Dreagan before she finally decided on sending the email, hoping that would work so she could get away and live her life.

The memories continued through the internet café where she sent the message, and then Brian finding her on the street. She had been terrified then, but she'd played it off well. And when Cain had found her, she'd wanted to run, but hadn't been able to. There had been something about him that had stopped her.

When he felt her instant attraction to him, he pulled away from Tristan. But that didn't stop him from seeing her memories. They fast-forwarded to the Fae Realm where they stood together right before he kissed her.

"Stop," Cain told her.

And just like that, he was disconnected from her mind.

"I think I know why Moreann wanted you so badly," Tristan told Noreen.

Her eyes opened to look up at him. "Why?"

"Cain pulled away from me, but he could still see your memories because you projected them into his head."

She shook her head. "That's not possible. I've never done that. I just . . . I wanted him to know that what I felt wasn't a lie."

"You did." Tristan looked at Cain before he walked from the room, leaving the two of them alone.

Cain found his gaze locked on their hands. "I'm sorry Moreann killed your family."

"I'm sorry I used you to get away from her." Noreen sat up and swung her legs over the side so she faced him. "My memories are clear now. Tristan can vouch for me. Should we bring him back?"

Cain shook his head. "Tell me."

"Moreann all but shackled me to her. She didn't like me being with the Fae. I've long tried to get away from her, and I saw the Kings and Rhi as an out. I never intended to go back to her."

"That's no' what she planned. She added something else to the spell."

Noreen's lips twisted. "I know. But I don't know what it is."

"There's something else you might have overlooked."

She frowned. "What?"

"Your parents were Light Fae."

Her gaze went distant as she returned to her memories. "No wonder I could never find our house," she murmured. "Moreann didn't want me as a Light. That was for Rhi. She wanted me as a Dark."

"Why, when she had Usaeil?" Cain asked.

Noreen shrugged. "I don't know, but we can find out."

"How?"

"I go back to her as a spy for you."

"No," Cain stated adamantly. "Absolutely not."

CHAPTER FORTY-TWO

It was the perfect plan. Noreen knew it, but in order to pull it off, she had to convince Cain and the other Dragon Kings. As well as whoever the purple-eyed Fae was.

"I know you think I'm going back to her to betray you again, but I'm not," she told Cain. "Have Tristan stay linked to my mind so he'll know."

Tristan's brow was furrowed as he glanced at Cain. "It's more than that. Any number of things could go wrong. For one, even if I could maintain the link over such a distance, it would only allow us to know if you've betrayed us again, not what will happen."

Her gaze moved from Tristan to Cain. "I can do this. I want to do this. I *need* to do this," she implored. She held out her hand to Tristan while keeping her gaze on Cain. "Touch me, Tristan. Let everyone know I'm speaking the truth."

"There's no need," came a deep voice from behind Cain.

There was a heartbeat of hesitation before Cain shifted to the side to reveal a tall man in a dark suit. The jacket was buttoned, but he didn't wear a tie. His blond hair was wavy, his eyes black and bottomless. Noreen swallowed as she realized she was looking at Constantine, King of Dragon Kings.

Con raised a brow. "You know me?"

"Yes," she said with a nod. "You're Constantine."

He and the purple-eyed Fae nodded to each other as Con walked forward to stand beside Cain. Con eyed her for a long moment. "You've put us in a predicament I'd hoped never to be in again, but one I knew would happen."

"I did what I had to do," she replied.

Con put his hands in his pants' pockets. "As we have on many occasions. Thanks to Tristan's magic, we know you're telling the truth."

There was something in the way he said the words that got her attention. "You mean, you think I'm telling the truth that I believe *now*. You think magic still has a hold of me."

"Maybe," Con said with a shrug.

Tristan crossed his arms over his chest as he looked at her. "There is an abundance of magic within her, but the feel of Moreann's magic is vastly different from Noreen's."

"Could she put a spell on herself?" Con asked Tristan.

It was the Fae who said, "It's a possibility."

"And I wouldna know it," Tristan answered.

Noreen found it difficult to sit as they talked about her as if she weren't there. She looked at Cain, who stared at the floor. He'd touched her, spoken to her, but she didn't dare believe that he had forgiven her. There was a good chance that he would never forgive her, regardless of if she was his mate or not.

"She killed my parents," Noreen said, barely keeping back the rage that was bubbling inside her like a volcano ready to erupt. When Cain looked into her eyes, she focused on him lest she explode. "She lied to me about . . .

everything. She convinced me to hate the Dragon Kings and to kill. I can't prove it, but I know she had a hand in me turning Dark. I found all of this out and then came up with the plan to contact the Kings. You saw my memories, you know this."

"Aye," Cain whispered.

"I did it to get away from Moreann. Yes, it meant betraying the Dragon Kings, but my only thought was to get away from her and give you a way to defeat her and the Others. I didn't set out to hurt you simply because it was fun. If you believe nothing else, believe that."

Cain was silent, his face showing nothing. Then he said, "I do."

Relief rushed through her so swiftly that her shoulders slumped. "Good."

"And that's where we find ourselves," Con stated. "In a verra difficult position."

The Fae then said, "Perhaps not."

Cain looked at him. "What do you mean?"

Purple eyes met Noreen's. "Why don't we ask Rhi what she thinks?"

"Why?" Noreen asked, confused.

Tristan's arms dropped to his sides. "You can no' really think Rhi would willingly be taken to Moreann?"

Noreen immediately shook her head. "That can't happen. Moreann wants Rhi badly. I don't know why bu—"

"Then we find out why," a woman said with an Irish accent.

Con's nostrils flared as he slowly turned. That's when Noreen spotted Rhi in an all-black outfit—complete with black stiletto boots that had silver skulls and spikes on them—standing behind him with her arms crossed and her face filled with irritation.

"How long have you been there?" Cain asked.

Rhi shrugged without taking her eyes from Con. "Does it matter?"

"I gather you've been there long enough to get the gist of what's going on?" the Fae said.

Rhi pushed away from the wall and dropped her arms without answering. She walked between Con and the Fae and came to a stop before Noreen. It was all Noreen could do not to fidget as Rhi's silver eyes bored into hers.

"I know what it is to be lied to," Rhi told her. "I know what it is to realize the life you had was nothing more than a lie. I know what it is to be betrayed by those closest to you."

Noreen frowned, unsure what was happening.

Rhi blew out a breath. "I might not have seen your memories, but I saw Tristan's, Cain's, and Cael's faces."

Noreen made a mental note that the purple-eyed Fae's name was Cael.

"They believed you," Rhi finished. She held silent for an extended period of time before she turned her head and looked at Con as she said, "And I want to know why Moreann wants me."

"Doona do it," Con implored.

Rhi ignored him as she turned her attention back to Noreen. "What do we need to do?"

"I was to get close to you and get you away from the Kings then bring you to Moreann," Noreen explained.

Rhi shrugged. "Sounds good to me."

The men in the room all spoke at once, each listing their reasons why Rhi shouldn't go. Noreen saw firsthand how much Rhi was loved, but she wondered if the Light Fae knew it.

Rhi held up a hand to silence everyone. She looked at

each of the men, starting with Cael and ending with Con. "It's my life. That means it's my decision."

"It's more than just your life," Cael stated.

Rhi's shoulders lifted as she pulled in a deep breath. "Usaeil got away. I plan to right that wrong, and one way of doing it is by going to the Others. That will infuriate Ubitch."

"She's trapped," Noreen put in. "Moreann made it clear that she's holding Usaeil captive."

Rhi gave a derisive snort. "Sweetie, it's just a matter of time before Usaeil escapes. Well?" she asked Noreen. "Do you really want to do this or not?"

Noreen looked at Cain, who gave a slight shake of his head, telling her he was against the plan.

"I can no' believe I'm saying this, but this could work," Tristan said.

Cain's head snapped to him as he glared at Tristan. "And if it were Sammi sitting here saying this?"

"I didna say it would be easy," Tristan replied. "I said it might work."

Cael sighed loudly. "Tristan's right. This could work, but it's going to take careful planning as well as the Kings and Reapers."

Noreen nearly fell off the slab of concrete. Had he just said *Reapers*? She put a hand to her stomach as she wondered who the lavender-eyed woman was. Then she decided it was better that she didn't know.

"Nay," Con said.

Rhi quirked a brow and saucily said, "Oh?"

Constantine looked Noreen's way. "Because if we've discovered anything about Moreann, it's that the empress is careful. She'll go to extremes to ensure that Noreen hasna aligned with us."

"He's right," Noreen said.

Unfazed, Rhi shrugged. "That's what planning is for."

"Moreann will expect that we flipped Noreen to our side," Cain said.

Cael nodded slowly. "I know if I sent one of my people on such a mission, I'd take steps to make sure they weren't turned."

Tristan's lips twisted. "Noreen, how do we go about preparing you for Moreann's interrogation?"

This was the part Noreen hadn't been looking forward to. She couldn't hold Cain's gaze as she said, "Moreann is going to want details about all of you. Who I spoke with, what we talked about, and what all I told you about her."

"Are you a good liar?" Rhi asked.

Noreen made a face. "I'm decent, but Moreann won't just ask. She'll use magic."

"Can we help you with that?" Tristan asked.

"No," Noreen quickly said. "I don't know if she can detect dragon magic, but I'd rather not test it."

Cain flattened his lips before he said, "I agree. However, I doona like you going in unprepared."

"She won't be," Rhi replied. "I'll be with her. And if all of you have forgotten, I'm Fae. Moreann might be able to detect Fae magic, but I doubt she can determine what's Noreen's and what's mine."

Cael brightened. "That could work. I could also help out."

"Are you sure?" Con asked, a silent question passing between them.

Noreen wished she knew what the secret was they didn't want her to know. She was pretty sure she wasn't supposed to know about the Reapers, so she kept her mouth shut about that. The fact was, Moreann had no idea about the Reapers or their alliance with the Dragon Kings. And it was definitely something Noreen didn't want to pass on to her.

"I don't know what will happen when we get there," Noreen told them.

Rhi shrugged. "It doesn't matter."

Noreen realized the others were staring at them. She kept her eyes on Rhi. "It does to me. I didn't lie to Cain when I said I've always wanted to meet you. The Dark talk about you as if you're untouchable. You've made your mark, Rhi, and there is too much going on for anything to happen to you."

"When it's my time to die, then it's my time." Rhi shrugged, her lips turning up at the corners. "No one can stop Death."

"The Others are already powerful enough. If Moreann gets you, then . . ." She trailed off, not wanting to finish.

Rhi put her hand atop Noreen's. "It doesn't matter what that woman says to me. There is nothing that will make me join her."

"And Usaeil?" Con asked.

Rhi's eyes closed briefly before she turned her head to look at Con. "I will kill her, and make sure she's dead this time."

"She might fight with you against Moreann," Cain said.

Noreen watched as Rhi looked away. When she did, Noreen caught a flash of red in the Light's eyes. Noreen jerked her gaze to Cain to see if he'd seen it, too, but he only shrugged at her.

"What happens if Rhi were to join the Others?" Cael asked.

Noreen swung her legs back and forth. "It would mean that Brian is no longer needed. Moreann would most likely kill him."

"And if Usaeil returns to the fold?" Cain asked.

Her legs stilled as the truth settled around her. "Moreann would kill me."

"She may kill you anyway," Con said. "Especially if she doesna know if she can trust you or no'."

Noreen pushed off the table and landed on her feet. "It's a chance I'm willing to take. I have to, because the Others must be stopped. Moreann must be stopped."

CHAPTER FORTY-THREE

Somewhere on the north coast of Scotland

Time was running out. Melisse didn't know how she knew it, only that she did. She fought the need to return to Dreagan—not because of the Dragon Kings, but because she wanted to see Henry.

It was foolish. Utterly idiotic. But she liked him. She didn't want to. In fact, it had been a complete surprise to find that she wanted to be around him. It didn't help her situation, however.

She gave a snort as she stood looking out over the water. The cliff fell below her hundreds of feet, but that didn't stop her from standing right on the edge. Falling didn't frighten her.

In fact, few things scared her.

But there was one who did.

Melisse knew she would have to face her fear soon enough, but not yet. First, there was the matter of the Dragon Kings. She still wasn't sure yet what she was going to do. If it weren't for the imminent war brewing between the Kings and the Others, Melisse might be worried that Constantine was doing nothing.

But his attention was diverted.

Or was it?

Her gaze narrowed with the thought. Perhaps his attention was on her, and he was leading her to believe otherwise. The more she thought about it, the more the King of Dragon Kings could be doing that very thing.

But . . . why? It didn't make any sense.

Her thoughts turned back to Henry. His kind hazel eyes, his wide lips, his thick hair. He was . . . beautiful.

"Stop," she told herself as she closed her eyes.

She had to get her head on straight, or all of this would have been for naught. Despite telling herself that, she nearly said Henry's name, wondering if it would bring him to her again. And if it did? What then? What would she tell him?

"What can I tell him?" She shook her head. "Nothing."

Are you sure?

Henry wasn't a Dragon King. Maybe she could—her thoughts halted. No. She could never do such a thing. It would be the wrong thing, and it would put Henry in the middle.

Besides, just because she was attracted to him and thought the feeling might be mutual didn't mean he would take her side.

Melisse rolled her eyes. Take her side. Right. He would never do that. He was friends with the Dragon Kings, which meant he would listen to them—and believe them. No, she was better off remembering to keep things to herself until she decided what to do.

Henry stared at the map, but he didn't see the various pins stuck in the many locations. No, his thoughts were on Melisse as they had been for days. Seeing her near Dreagan had been exciting, and he still wasn't sure why she had left so suddenly.

His gaze kept returning to the north coast of Scotland, but he didn't know why. There were no pins there, nothing that would garner his attention.

Then he felt something strange inside him. He'd felt something similar when he was in Madrid right before he found the Druid's house. His magic—or whatever it was inside him—was still so new that he hadn't yet figured out how to use it or even what it all entailed.

He was the JusticeBringer, which meant he doled out justice to the Druids. His sister, Esther, the TruthSeeker, had discovered as much. He wasn't supposed to find Druids. Was he?

How many had told him that he was still learning his powers? That it would take time for him to determine everything he could do, especially since there was no one around to explain exactly what a JusticeBringer or a TruthSeeker did?

Henry pulled his gaze away to another part of the map. He was no longer looking for Usaeil. Initially, because the queen was supposed to be dead, but now he'd learned that the leader of the Others had taken Usaeil and was holding her captive. If Henry hadn't been able to find Usaeil before, he certainly wouldn't now.

He raked a hand through his hair and turned away from the map. He couldn't help with Usaeil, couldn't help with the Others, but he'd been determined to find the stolen weapon. Unfortunately, even that had been a bust.

Con told him he was here for a reason. Henry wasn't so sure of that anymore. Maybe being the JusticeBringer didn't mean anything. Perhaps he just kept thinking he had some sort of magic or powers because everyone told him he did. It could be that he didn't have a bloody thing.

He slapped his hand on his thigh and took a deep breath

before he turned back to the map. And just like before, his gaze went to the north coast of Scotland.

"Something's there," he murmured.

He didn't know what it was, but he wanted to find out. Henry walked closer to the map and pinpointed exactly where his gaze was—Cape Wrath.

Henry spun around and strode from the cavern, moving down the tunnel and then out through the conservatory. He didn't talk to anyone as he made his way to the garage where the cars were kept. Con had told him that he could use the vehicles whenever he needed, and he was going to take Con up on that offer.

No sooner had he entered the garage and reached for a set of keys than he heard his name. He paused at his sister's voice, but Henry knew he couldn't leave without telling her.

"What's the rush?" she asked as she walked up.

"I need to go for a drive."

She narrowed eyes the color of nutmeg at him and cocked her head to the side. "What aren't you telling me? And don't say 'nothing,' because I know you, Henry North."

He blew out a breath, realizing the futility of trying to lie to his sister. "I've got a feeling something is up north. I want to check it out."

"Something as in a Druid?" she asked.

"Maybe," he said with a shrug. "Or it could be the weapon. It's just a feeling I have, and I need to check it out."

"I'll come with you."

Henry was already shaking his head, getting ready to come up with some excuse as to why she should stay, when Nikolai said Esther's name.

She turned to her mate, a smile on her face. "I'm glad you're here. Help me talk some sense into my brother."

Henry looked into Nikolai's baby blue eyes and was shocked to find that the Dragon King was on his side.

"Actually," Nikolai told Esther, "I think Henry should go on his own."

Esther's mouth dropped open. "You can't be serious. Henry and I are a team. We're supposed to work together."

"He's just going to check things out. You went out on your own, remember?" Nikolai reminded her.

Henry hid his smile. He gave Nikolai a nod of thanks and got into the black Mercedes G-Class SUV. When he started the engine, Esther was still trying to convince Nikolai that she should be with Henry. When Henry started backing out of the parking spot, his sister shouted his name, but he didn't stop. He drove away from Dreagan, pointing the SUV north toward Cape Wrath.

It wasn't long before his mobile phone rang. As expected, it was his sister. Instead of answering, Henry turned off the ringer.

The drive took a little over two hours, but it was two hours too long. When Henry pulled into the quaint town of Cape Wrath, he wasn't sure what he'd expected to find. It certainly wasn't the stunning beauty of the blue waters and majestic cliffs.

He might have a location of where he wanted to go, but he didn't know exactly where once he was in the village. So, he drove around, taking roads this way and that until he found himself headed toward the Clo Mor Cliffs.

His stomach churned with excitement and trepidation— as it did every time he went skydiving—as he parked the SUV. He looked at the walk to the cliffs, his gaze searching for . . . anything. Finally, he turned off the vehicle and climbed out.

He made his way to the rockface. His attention was caught by the turbulent waters while kittiwakes, puffins, and fulmars drifted along the currents and stood upon the impressive natural rock formations.

The wind swept over him, taking his breath while at the same time offering him new life. It made no sense, and yet that's exactly what it was. He could've looked at the astonishing magnificence all day. How could something so exquisite be so near and he hadn't known? Now that he'd seen this place, he wasn't sure he could leave.

Something out of the corner of his eye caught his attention. He glanced to the side and saw a woman with long, silver hair with black ends. Almost instantly, his gaze jerked back to her because he knew it was Melisse.

And she was staring at him.

He'd heard his name the other day and knew it had been her. Had she called for him again? And how was he able to keep finding her?

They stared at each other for a long time before he took a step toward her. Once he moved, she did, as well. They slowly met in the middle.

"What are you doing here?" she asked in a bewildered tone.

He grinned. "It's good to see you, too."

"I'm sorry," she said with a shake of her head. "I am glad to see you, but . . . what are you doing here?"

Henry shrugged, his hands wanting nothing more than to reach out and touch her face. He couldn't explain the draw he felt toward her, but he liked it. "I really don't know. Something called me to come here. Was it you?"

Her lips parted to answer, but she looked away instead.

"It can't be a coincidence that we continue running into each other," he said. "I want to be your friend, Melisse. You can trust me."

She looked at him and smiled sadly. "I'd like you to be my friend, but I don't think you'll be able to."

"Why would you say that?"

Melisse released a sigh. "It's too difficult to explain."

"Something is drawing me to you. If it isn't you, then what is it? You can deny it all you want, but I get the feeling we're supposed to be together."

He meant as friends, but his tone made it sound like something more. He'd be just fine with that. Hell, if he were honest, that's exactly what he wanted. He couldn't stop thinking about Melisse. Asleep or awake, she was on his mind more than anything else.

She swallowed and turned to the water. "I love this place."

"It's beautiful. Just as you are."

Melisse ducked her head, a pleased smile on her face. "Thank you."

"I think you want to be my friend. What's holding you back?"

"This place makes me feel as if everything is insignificant," she said, ignoring his question. "I've always felt as if the breeze blows away my cares and worries. Here, I can forget what troubles me and simply soak up the grandeur."

He didn't take his eyes from her. "Do you come here often?"

"It's been a very, very long time since I've been here. I don't know why I've put it off so long."

"I once worked for MI5. I still have connections there. Sooner or later, I'm going to find out who you are," he told her.

She laughed softly and glanced his way with her unusual whitish-silver eyes. "In some ways, it would be easier if you already knew."

"Then tell me."

"I . . . no."

He moved closer. "Why? What are you afraid of? Is it the people I live with?"

"No."

It was just one word, a simple one at that, but it said everything. And with that utterance, Henry knew she understood what Dreagan was, and just who lived there.

"Are you a Druid?"

Melisse shook her head.

"A Fae?"

She briefly closed her eyes and shook her head again. "I should go."

"Don't," he pleaded and moved to stand in her way. "I'll just find you again. And again. And again. And I'll find out who you are. Maybe then you'll trust me enough to tell me whatever it is you're hiding."

She turned away from him without another word and began walking away.

Henry's mind worked to find something, anything to make her stay. He didn't know what caused him to latch on to it, or why he even thought to say it, but the minute his mind landed on the words, he knew it was right.

"I know what you are. And I know why you're hiding from those at Dreagan."

Melisse suddenly halted. Slowly, she turned to face him, her eyes wide and her face pale. "You're guessing."

"Am I?" he asked and walked to her. "Are you sure of that?"

She couldn't hold his gaze and looked away. "Return to your friends, Henry. You should forget all about me. It was wrong of me to approach you in Madrid."

"Forget you? Not going to happen."

Melisse licked her lips as she briefly met his gaze. "Please, leave."

"I've had a feeling for a while now that something particular brought me to Dreagan. My sister and the others think it's because I'm the JusticeBringer, but that isn't it at all."

"Henry, please," she begged and took a step back. "Whatever you're thinking of saying, don't. Once you speak it, it can't be taken back."

"Con told me I was destined to find the weapon. I just never thought it would be a person."

She shook her head in shock. "No."

"Yes," he said. How had he not seen it before?

"Con really told you that you'd find me? I wondered why he didn't come for me."

That made Henry frown. "What do you mean?"

"Every King of Dragon Kings is able to locate me at any time."

"If he wanted me to do it, then he had his reasons," Henry said. Although it was going to be the first thing he asked Con about the next time he saw him.

Melisse held up a hand to stop him when he moved closer. "Henry, you don't know what you're doing."

"I know I keep being drawn to you. That's something. I think it's better for both of us if we can determine why that is."

"Con wants me dead."

Henry halted as if struck. "If Con wanted you dead, he would've come for you himself. You know that as well as I do."

She wanted to run. Henry could see it, see the struggle in her face. Seconds turned to minutes as she fought the battle inside her.

Finally, she sighed. "Fine. You win."

"Good. Let's go to Dreagan."

She didn't budge. "That isn't going to happen."

"Don't you want answers?"

"Yes," she said with a nod.

He fought frustration. "We'll get that by talking to Con."

Melisse closed the distance between them and put her hand on his face. "You have a good heart. Don't ever let anyone change that."

He opened his mouth to answer her, but no words came out. He was unable to move, unable to speak as she turned and walked away. It wasn't until she had driven off that he was able to move again.

Anger churned within him now. He wanted answers, and Con was going to give them to him.

CHAPTER FORTY-FOUR

Cain felt as if he were being pulled in a million different directions. He knew the best way to get to Moreann was to use Rhi, but he didn't like that idea. He knew that to end the Others, infiltrating them was a splendid idea, but he couldn't fathom Noreen doing it.

And he knew doing nothing was akin to sealing their doom.

Yet, he couldn't say any of that. All he could do was look at the woman who had stolen his heart as easily as she smiled. The thought of not having her in his life left him gasping for breath, as if someone was squeezing the life out of him.

"Don't," was all he managed to get past his lips.

Con put a hand on his shoulder and then left the room. A moment later, Cael and Tristan followed, leaving only Rhi.

The Light Fae looked at him and gave him a sad smile. Rhi appeared to begin to say something, then opted not to. She nodded at Noreen and then walked away, her heels clicking on the concrete floor.

Finally, he was alone with his mate.

"I have to do this," she said.

"No, you doona."

She looked down and blew out a breath. "You know I do. No one else can. It has to be me."

"We'll find Usaeil. Maybe we can talk her into doing it."

Noreen shook her head and raised her gaze to his. "I betrayed you. I betrayed all the Kings. The only reason you're speaking to me now is because Tristan was able to show you the truth of my memories. In any other case, you'd never be able to believe anything I said."

"But this isna any other case."

Her lips twisted as she lifted one shoulder. "The truth of the matter is that you'll always wonder if I'm lying."

"I willna."

"Now who's lying?" she asked with a wry smile. "I care about you. In fact. . . ." She paused, her lips trembling.

He knew she was trying to tell him that she loved him. He could see it in her eyes, but the words wouldn't come. Cain took her hands in his. "You are my mate, Noreen. Now that I've found you, I doona want to lose you."

"That isn't for you to decide."

"It is if we perform the mating ceremony."

Her brows drew together as she gave him a shocked look. "You can't be serious."

"I am. You'll be protected as my mate. Moreann willna be able to kill you."

"Don't," Noreen said as she pulled her hands from his and took a step back. "You want this now because your emotions are all over the place."

He sliced a hand through the air. "I want this now because it's the sensible thing to do. We can be together once it's all over."

"You have that much faith that I'll succeed?"

"I do," he stated with a nod of his head.

Still, she kept her distance. "And what about a year from now? Five years? Hell, fifty? Will you still think this was a smart decision when you can't stand to look at my red eyes or the silver in my hair. Or what about me? How do you think I'll feel when you question everything I say, or bring Tristan to search my mind?"

Cain blinked, shaking his head in confusion. "That willna happen."

"You can honestly stand there and tell me that you don't care that I betrayed you?" she asked, her arms crossed over her chest.

"Of course, I care, but I understand now."

"Because of Tristan's power."

Cain threw up his hands in frustration. "Why does that matter? We know the truth. All of us. Especially you. *That's* what matters. You're my mate. I love you."

"Our time was . . . wonderful. But that's all it was. A slice of time that's now gone."

This couldn't be happening. Every King who found his mate went through a lot, but never had a mate refused a King. Was he doing something wrong?

Or was there just something wrong with him?

"Doona do this," he begged her. "I know how you feel about me."

She shrugged. "It's already done."

"You can change your mind."

"I'm a Dark as well as an Other. You're a Dragon King. We were never meant to be together."

His hands gently grasped either side of her face as he stared into her crimson eyes. "Fuck everyone. I know what I feel. I know what you feel. That's what matters."

"It's what should matter, but it doesn't. You and I both

know that. No one trusted me to begin with because I'm an Other and a Dark. You should've kept your distance."

He was losing her. He was holding onto her, but she was slipping away from him like sands through an hourglass. "Lass. Please."

Noreen reached up and wrapped her fingers around his wrists before she tugged his hands away. "Don't beg. You're a Dragon King."

He closed his eyes as she walked around him and out of the room. He didn't go after her. It would be pointless. Nothing he could say would change her mind. She was stubborn that way. If only she had let them do the mating ceremony, then the worry eating at him would leave because he'd know she'd come home to him.

"Cain."

His eyes opened at the sound of Con's voice. "Now isna the time."

"I thought you might want to be in on the plan."

Cain put his hands on the table where Noreen had lain not so long ago. "I think it's better if I'm no'."

The silence stretched so long that Cain thought Con had left. Then the King of Kings said, "Noreen is your mate."

"Is this where you tell me now isna the time to do anything about that?"

Con blew out a breath. "I'm going to tell you to fight for her."

Cain straightened and slowly turned to face Con. "Even though she's a Dark as well as an Other? Even though she betrayed us?"

"Yes, to all questions. I knew Nala wasna Ulrik's because she didna love him. I can no' say the same about Noreen."

"I know she cares about me," Cain said.

Con reached for the dragon head cufflinks he'd always

worn but Usaeil had destroyed. When his fingers met a button instead, he dropped his arms to his sides. "I know what it is to live without my mate. It's the worst kind of hell you can imagine. So, I tell you again, fight for Noreen."

"She willna let me."

"She doesna need to know," Con said, one side of his lips turning up in a smile.

Cain grinned then, finally understanding what Con was telling him. "I think I will."

"Good. Let's go." Con turned and walked from the room.

Cain was right beside him. "Are Cael and Erith going to help?"

"Cael wouldna say," Con said, a note of irritation in his voice.

"Did you ask Erith?"

"She's no' here."

Cain's brows drew up on his forehead. "You'd think she'd want to at least hear what all has transpired."

"She must have other business," Con replied. "No doubt Cael will relay everything to her."

Cain put out a hand and stopped Con before they reached the others. "Do you think Noreen and Rhi can pull this off?"

"I wish I could tell you what you want to hear, but I can no'. There is too much against us. But what I do know is that Noreen is right. This is the only way to get to Moreann without an all-out war that brings in the humans, and Noreen is the only one who can do it."

Cain's chest tightened. "I can no' lose her."

"You need to face the fact that there's a good chance you might."

"If I could talk her into the ceremony bef—"

Con interrupted him with a, "Nay."

"But you said you knew she was my mate."

"If Noreen doesna want to do the ceremony, then it can no' be done. You know this. And talking her into it is no' the same as her wanting to do it."

Cain didn't want to admit the truth, but he had to. "I can no' stop the feeling that I'm going to lose her."

"She willna be going in alone. She'll have Rhi."

And that was the only thing stopping Cain from going stark-raving mad.

CHAPTER FORTY-FIVE

She was really going to do this. It was a stupid, crazy plan. But it was the only one Noreen had.

"It's going to be okay," Rhi whispered when they were finally alone.

Noreen glanced at the Fae. "You know she might kill us both on sight."

"She might." Rhi's lips twisted. "If that's my way to go, then that's my way to go."

"What about your Dragon King?"

Rhi's silver gaze slid away for a heartbeat before she met Noreen's eyes. "I loved him before I knew him. I'd always known he was out there, waiting for me. And when I found him, I'd never known such happiness, such . . . bliss. Then I lost him. But I've never stopped loving him. I'll continue loving him from this life into the next and the next and the next."

"Even though he hurt you?"

"The kind of love we have isn't one that can be ignored."

Noreen made a face, not understanding. "If you two love each other, then you should be together."

"Yes, you and Cain should absolutely be together."

"This isn't about me and Cain."

Rhi raised a brow. "Isn't it? You're his mate, and all anyone has to do is watch your face when you look at him. Your love for him is there for all to see. So, why didn't you tell him?"

"Because . . . because it's too hard."

Rhi nodded slightly. "I can't be with my King because he's made it so. But you can be with yours. I have to say, you're an idiot for not being with Cain."

Noreen wanted it more than anything. When he spoke about the mating ceremony, she'd immediately wanted to say yes. Not because it would make her immortal, but because she would be his in every way.

But that wasn't why he wanted to do it. He wanted to ensure that she lived, which was nice and all, but what about their future? He could be bound to someone he discovered he couldn't get past lying to him.

"I betrayed him and all the Kings. If there's a chance for me and Cain, it'll be because I helped end Moreann and the Others," Noreen told Rhi.

"Cain doesn't care about that."

"You didn't see his face when I told him what I'd done." Noreen tried to erase it from her memories, but it was burned in her mind. "He was so hurt. It's a wound that might never heal."

Rhi smiled as she looked down at her hands. "That's the funny and wonderful thing about love. It's very forgiving."

"Have you forgiven your King?" Noreen desperately wanted to ask who it was, but if Rhi wasn't going to freely give that information, then she wasn't going to probe.

"I wouldn't go that far." She looked up then, her eyes filled with tears. "But I miss him so much."

Before Noreen could respond, Rhi turned away just as

Cain, Tristan, Cael, and Con walked into the room. Noreen found herself staring at Cain, unable to look away from his deep green eyes.

"There's still time to change your mind," Tristan said.

Rhi snorted loudly. "It's time this bitch's reign ends. If she wants a place for her people, then she should look at fixing her own realm instead of taking what isn't hers."

Cael raised a brow. "This isn't ours either."

"I know that, but we were allowed to stay," Rhi retorted.

Noreen noted that Con didn't say a word during the entire exchange. To help with her nerves, she fisted her hands. It did little to calm her. She, better than anyone, knew what she and Rhi would be walking into.

She had told Rhi how volatile Moreann could be, as well as how deceptively calm the empress could get. Rhi laughed, saying Moreann sounded like Usaeil. In fact, both women were eerily similar. Perhaps that's why their alliance had never truly come together.

It was a good thing, too. Because if it had, the Dragon Kings might not have stood a chance at all, regardless of their power and might.

That was the most terrifying thing. Moreann had been smart enough to figure out she needed Usaeil to fight the Kings. Fortunately, both women's need to lead kept them at odds constantly. Then, Usaeil had fallen for Constantine. That was the straw that broke the camel's back.

"Let's get this rolling," Rhi said into the silence. "I've never been good at being patient."

It was on the tip of Noreen's tongue to call the whole thing off because she couldn't stand the thought that she might not make it back to Cain. Then she remembered all the horrible things she'd done throughout her years. It didn't matter that Moreann had brainwashed her. The sins lay at Noreen's feet, and hers alone.

"Ready?" Rhi asked her.

Noreen nodded and slid her gaze to Cain. Her breathing became difficult as fear took hold of her. She wanted his arms around her one more time, to feel his lips on hers. To hear him call her "lass" once more.

He gave her a smile and mouthed, "I love you."

In her head, she was shouting *I love you, too*, but she didn't let the words out. Then Rhi grabbed her arm, and they were gone.

When they arrived in the back room of a store, Noreen bent over, bracing her hands on her knees as her gut twisted with regret, and tears filled her eyes.

"We'll get back," Rhi told her, rubbing her back. "Keep telling yourself that. You'll be amazed at what that will do for you. Trust me. It's gotten me out of many hairy situations."

Noreen sniffed and straightened as she wiped at the tears on her face. "I should've told him how I felt."

"You should have," Rhi stated. Then she shrugged. "But it gives you a reason to return to him. Right?"

"It does."

Rhi gave her a once-over. "Good. Now, we need to get you in the right frame of mind to meet with Moreann, because if she saw you now, we would certainly die."

Noreen drew in a deep breath and pursed her lips as she slowly blew it out. "You're right. Give me a few minutes."

"You're a Dark," Rhi told her. "Remember that."

"What's that supposed to mean?"

Rhi rolled her eyes. "You seriously need me to tell you? Fine. Why do you think Light turn Dark?"

"Because they do evil."

"That's partly true, but it's because the darkness calls to them and offers them more power. You would've no doubt been a formidable Light, but as a Dark, you've got even more magic and power. You need to use that."

Noreen shook her head. "I don't know if I can."

"You're going to have to. You don't have a choice. Moreann will make sure of that. Be on guard. Don't underestimate her and expect her to double-cross you."

Noreen took Rhi's words to heart. "Moreann has never feared me. Never."

"Oh, I bet she has, she just hasn't shown you. Just as I know she's feared Usaeil. Moreann might be strong, but she doesn't compare to Fae magic. She's lied to you for years, forming you into what she wanted you to be. Why do you think that is?"

Noreen searched her mind but came up empty. "I don't know."

"It's time you found out. Don't hold back. No matter what she does to me. You get back to Cain."

"This is so odd."

Rhi gave her a quizzical look. "What is?"

"I've always wanted to fight beside you. I can't believe it's actually happening."

"Well, it is. And, frankly, I'm glad to have you on my side."

"You don't think I'll deceive you?"

Rhi shrugged, her lips twisting. "You might, but it's a chance I'm willing to take to get close to Moreann. And if you need help remembering that she's your enemy, think about your parents."

Cold fury filled Noreen. She could never forget what Moreann had done to her parents, as well as to her. No longer would Noreen be Moreann's puppet.

"Now, you're ready," Rhi said with a smile.

Noreen met the Light's silver eyes and touched Rhi's shoulder. "Prepare yourself."

In a blink, they were in a field with vibrant green craggy mountains rising up all around them. Noreen didn't move as she dropped her hand. Neither she nor Rhi said a word.

Then Noreen whispered, "Now."

Rhi looked around before turning to her in anger. "This isn't the nail place you told me about. What is this?"

Noreen looked at her and lifted her chin, ready to play her part. "This is what it's all been about."

"What are you talking about?"

"The email to Dreagan, meeting the Dragon Kings, and convincing them I was turning on the Others. It was all to get close to you. To bring you here."

Just saying the words made her want to vomit, but Noreen knew it wasn't just her life on the line. It was Rhi's, as well as the Dragon Kings', and every mortal on the planet.

The area behind Rhi moved as if rippling, and then Moreann stepped out. Her light brown hair was pulled back in a ponytail. She might have made herself immortal, but she couldn't outrun aging. Moreann wore her usual long robes, this time in a beige and gold combination.

"You always do come through, Noreen," the empress stated as her green eyes landed on Rhi.

Rhi spun around and gave Moreann a once-over. "And you are?"

"Someone who has waited a very long time to meet you."

Rhi shifted so she could see both Moreann and Noreen. "Well, I've no desire to meet you, so I'm going to go."

"No, you won't," Moreann said with a smile.

Rhi cocked a brow. "Actually, I will."

"Not if you want to know about your father."

Noreen inwardly winced. She should've known that Moreann would use Rhi's family against her. It seemed to be something the empress excelled at.

Rhi glared at Moreann for a few seconds. "I know my father."

Moreann laughed and glanced at Noreen. "No child knows their parent. That's not how it's supposed to be. But I can give you insight into yours."

"As you knew him," Rhi retorted.

Moreann gave her a hard look. "I know you were in the mountain in Iceland. I sincerely doubt you didn't read the stone wall there since it was in the Fae language. That means you saw your father's name as one of us."

"Us?" Rhi said the word as if it were poison. "You mean an Other?"

"That's right. Just as Noreen is."

Noreen wanted to deny it, but she couldn't. At least, not now. In her eyes, she hadn't been an Other in some time. She was pretending for Moreann's benefit now. But soon, that would come to an end.

"My father was a good man," Rhi said.

Moreann shrugged. "He knew the Dragon Kings held too much power on this realm. He wanted to take it from them."

Rhi let out a bark of laughter. "Now, I know you're lying. He was grateful we had a place to go and that the Kings allowed us to stay."

"That might have been what he told everyone else, but that's not what he told me when he joined our ranks. Should I tell you all he did to fight the Kings?"

Rhi crossed her arms over her chest. "Actually, you can go to Hell. I'm done."

"In point of fact, you aren't going anywhere."

"You think you can hold me?" Rhi asked in a cold voice.

Moreann merely smiled. "I want you with us. I've waited a long time to talk to you. Your father left you a letter."

"Give it to me."

"You have to come with me," Moreann replied.

Noreen looked at Rhi. It was a trap. They all knew it. A part of Noreen wanted Rhi to get away while she still could, but that wasn't going to happen. And the minute Rhi moved toward Moreann, Noreen knew that the game had truly begun.

CHAPTER FORTY-SIX

There had never been another time in Cain's long life when he wanted to go to war more than in that moment. It was all he could do to stand there while his woman, his *mate* went into battle.

"I doona like this," Cain said for the third time since Noreen and Rhi had departed.

Con stood a little in front of him and Tristan. "Patience."

"It's running out," Cain replied through clenched teeth.

Suddenly, Cael appeared before them and nodded at Cain before he looked at Con. "All went well."

"They didna see you?" Tristan asked.

Cael gave him a flat look. "I'm a Reaper."

"You're more than that," Erith replied as she materialized beside him. "You're a god."

The two exchanged a smile, but Cain didn't appreciate the discussion.

"No, they didn't see him," Erith told Tristan. "All is well."

Cain clenched his hands into fists. "We assume so. We

shouldna underestimate Moreann. She might have known you were there and didna say anything."

Cael shook his head. "She's powerful—for a Druid. But she can't compare to a Fae, much less a Reaper."

"Or what Cael is now," Erith added.

Con turned his head to look at Cain. "Our plans move forward, then. We each have our roles. Ulrik has already gotten everyone at Dreagan ready in case the battle moves there."

"It's about fucking time," Cain mumbled.

Erith's gaze caught his. "I know this is difficult for you, but Noreen is a strong Fae. She can do this."

Cain looked at her for a long moment. "I doona doubt her."

"You doubt me?" Death asked, a black brow raised.

Before he could answer, Con said, "What Cain is saying—badly—is that he's worried about everything else. There are a lot of strings moving in this plan."

"A plan I wasn't here for." Erith nodded. "Valid reasons."

No one asked her where she'd been, but Cain thought about it. Then he decided to let it go. They needed the Reapers, Death, and whatever Cael now was. As much as it grated on him, Cain knew Erith's caution to him had been founded. He needed to calm himself.

But Noreen was alone with Moreann and the rest of the Others. How could he be composed in such a situation? He kept telling himself that Rhi was with Noreen, but that didn't help. The fact that no one knew why Moreann wanted Rhi bothered Cain. The unknown factor could swing things against Noreen and the Kings in a blink.

It felt as if all the nerves within Cain's body were on

fire. He needed to move, to shift, to fly, to *do something* instead of waiting. He wasn't good at that. He was action and violence and fire.

A hand came to rest on his shoulder. Cain turned his head to find Con next to him. Everyone else was gone. Had he been so lost in his thoughts that he hadn't realized the others had departed? It certainly appeared so.

"Can you do this?" Con asked.

Cain looked hard at him. "Without a doubt. I just need to get to Noreen."

"That might no' be possible. You know that."

"I doona do well standing around when my mate is—" He halted his words, knowing full well that if anyone understood his dilemma, it was his King.

Con's hand dropped away. "There was never a time I doubted us winning in any war. No' even when all of you sided with Ulrik against the mortals. I knew we'd win."

"But?" Cain asked when Con stopped talking.

Con's black gaze slid away. "With everything the Others have done to us, I know this will be our greatest battle to-date. Everything hinges on this. Nothing else matters right now. No' Usaeil, no' the Fae. No' even the missing weapon."

"That I doona believe. The weapon can destroy us. For all we know, Moreann has it."

Con shook his head as he looked at Cain. "Despite what the Others know of us, that isna something they discovered."

"How can you be sure?"

"Because they would've gotten it long ago if that was the case."

Cain studied Con for a long moment. "You doona seem worried about the weapon as you once did. Why?"

"We've bigger problems."

"Bigger than a weapon that could end us?" Cain gave a shake of his head. "That I doona believe. What are you no' telling us?"

"A great deal, actually. Focus on your mate and the up-coming battle. Let me worry about the weapon."

Cain wanted to argue, but he knew Con was right. He had to focus all of his attention on what was going down in a very short time. That is if everything went according to plan.

"The Others willna see us coming," Con assured him.

Cain, however, wasn't so sure.

So far, so good. Noreen wasn't sure if that was a good thing or not, however. Moreann hadn't paid much attention to her. Instead, the empress's focus was centered on Rhi.

Now that they were in the manor that Moreann had hidden from anyone else, Noreen saw Brian standing off to the side, his gaze narrowed on Rhi. Brian might not have been Noreen's first choice to join them, but he wasn't the complete idiot that Moreann made him out to be. He was deducing what was going on right before his eyes, but he was wise enough not to draw attention to himself.

Noreen, Brian, and Orun all stood as silent observers as Moreann gave Rhi the letter from her father. The mortal Druids were conspicuously absent, but then again, Moreann rarely included them in things—something the humans didn't realize. If they did, they might not be so willing to join the Others. Maybe someone should tell them.

"What? Are you going to stand over my shoulder and watch me read this?" Rhi asked Moreann with a healthy dose of side-eye that would make anyone step back.

Noreen bit her tongue to keep from smiling when Moreann gave Rhi space. There was silence in the round ballroom as Rhi waited until Moreann had moved away before she started reading.

Just a few seconds in, Rhi speared Moreann with a deadly look. "Did you read this?"

"Of course," Moreann said with a smile.

Rhi returned the smile, but it was anything but nice. "Was it yours to read?"

"No, but I'm the leader."

"Funny thing about thinking such thoughts. Usaeil's mind went on a similar path. I would've ended her had you not stepped in."

Moreann stiffened, her smile fading. "You weren't supposed to know about that yet."

Yet. That word hung in the air like a live wire. Noreen's gaze moved between the two women, watching and waiting for what would happen next.

"Apparently, Noreen was supposed to befriend me in any way possible," Rhi replied. "She said the one thing that would draw me in and get me to you. A mistake I won't make again."

Some of the tension left Noreen, but it was only a reprieve. Things were just getting started. She looked at Orun, who couldn't take his eyes off Rhi. Noreen couldn't decide if he liked the Fae or not. Rhi was turned mostly away from him, and Noreen sincerely hoped Rhi didn't forget everything Noreen had told her about the Druid.

Noreen then glanced over at Brian. She did a double-take when she realized that he was gone. She didn't know when he'd left, only that he had. There was no telling where he'd disappeared to, but she wasn't worried. Brian was no doubt running for his life, which was a wise decision.

Rhi went back to reading the letter. Whatever was in it had a profound effect on the Light Fae. Despite Rhi doing her best to keep her facial features even, it was obvious the words her father left weren't anything she'd expected.

Noreen wished she could talk to Rhi. She couldn't help but worry that whatever was in the letter might change the plans that had been made. It was, after all, from Rhi's father. Family had a way of muddying the waters in such situations.

Rhi slowly folded the paper and slid it beneath the collar of her shirt to put in her bra. Then she looked at Moreann. "You expect me to believe that really came from my father?"

"Yes," the empress replied, her hands linked before her.

Rhi gave a little snort. "He could've left that behind so I'd find it. Why leave it with you?"

"Because he knew how important the mission of the Others was. He also knew you were . . . dirtied . . . by a Dragon King. If he'd tried to tell you before he died, you wouldn't have listened. He also knew that it would take you a while before you were in the right frame of mind to hear him."

"Wow. You really knew my father." Rhi rolled her eyes. "In case you were wondering, that was sarcasm."

Moreann blew out a breath. "I'd hoped you would be more accommodating than this."

"I disappoint people." Rhi shrugged. "It's a thing."

Noreen bit back another smile. Rhi truly was something to watch in such situations.

Rhi walked slowly around the room, her gaze on Moreann. "If you believed that I'd come here, read that letter, and fall in line with you, you were sorely mistaken."

"Oh, I knew it would take more than that."

Moreann's smile sent a chill down Noreen's spine. Her mind raced with the possibilities of what Moreann could have up her sleeve, but she didn't know Rhi well enough to know what would work and what wouldn't.

"I see I've got your attention," Moreann said with a smirk as Rhi came to a halt. "You've no idea how long I've waited for this moment."

"Get on with it," Rhi ordered.

Moreann laughed. "I want this planet. It will be mine. I've made sure of that. Noreen thinks she knows everything, but there is much I've kept from her, and, well, the rest of the group, as well," the empress said off-handedly.

Noreen's heart raced, and her palms grew clammy. This couldn't be true. Could it? There was no way to get word to Cain, no way to prepare any of them.

It was Moreann's turn to walk to Rhi. She stopped a few feet from her. "I've got your brother."

"You're lying," Rhi said. But there was no heat in her words.

Moreann's brows raised. "Am I?"

"Rolmir is dead."

Moreann's lips turned up in a smile.

Noreen's chest constricted. This couldn't be happening. But it was.

"You think that will make me join you?" Rhi asked icily.

Moreann laughed and shook her head. "I took your brother when your father disagreed with one of my plans. It was done to keep him in line. I think it'll work well to do the same for you."

"Rolmir is dead," Rhi repeated.

Moreann shrugged. "I don't really need your brother,

but I thought he would be a bonus to you. He's not really dead. Or is he?"

"Fek off," Rhi said in a low, deadly tone.

"Such language," Moreann said with a tsk. "I don't need him, dear Rhi, because the final piece to this game I've been playing with the Dragon Kings is . . . *you*."

CHAPTER FORTY-SEVEN

They were fucked. Noreen knew it, and there was nothing she could do about it.

While Rhi still reeled from Moreann's statement, the empress looked to Noreen. Her evil smile was cold and calculating. "Did you really think you could outsmart me? *Me?!* I left that book for you to find so you'd know what I did to your parents."

Rage filled Noreen, turning everything red as she longed to lash out and destroy Moreann.

"Look at you," the empress said with derision. She gave a shake of her head. "You were supposed to be some kind of savior for the Light. You and Rhi were supposed to join together and fight Usaeil, becoming close friends and setting up a council of Dark and Light to rule the Fae together. It was foretold that the two of you would bring peace to the Fae as well as a tight alliance with the Kings. I couldn't let that happen."

Noreen felt her magic run through her with such speed that it burned her veins. She wanted to lash out at Moreann, but she managed to control herself long enough to hold back. There was more to be learned. Then she'd kill Moreann herself.

The empress didn't seem to know or care how close Noreen was to giving in to the darkness that called to her.

"What you and Rhi were foreseen to do together would ruin everything I was planning. So, I changed it."

Noreen glanced at Rhi to find the Light staring at her. Neither moved as they looked back at Moreann in unison.

"How did you know about our future?" Rhi demanded.

Moreann gave a little shrug, a secret smile on her face as she eyed both of them as if they were mud beneath her shoe. "I'm empress. I learned to live forever. I could easily find a way to see whatever future I wanted. I saw yours first," she told Rhi. "But only because of your affair with the Dragon King."

The empress made a face as if just saying it was distasteful. "I tried to stop it, but a love like yours can't be held back. I realized that almost too late, but then I used the one thing I could. Usaeil. She was the perfect puppet to do what I wanted. She was so confident that she was more powerful, that she didn't even suspect me. It only took a few words to make her jealous, and then Usaeil did the rest on her own to break up your little affair."

"I'll kill you for that," Rhi stated in a calm voice.

Moreann continued as if she didn't hear. "Neither of you realize how much power you have. If you did, you would've used it long ago. In Rhi's case, she was so desperate for her lover that she had blinders on to anything else. A few times, you came close to thwarting me for good, but it always came back to your King." The empress laughed and then looked at Noreen. "As for you, well, I thought I could convince your parents to give you to me, and figured then I'd kill you. They didn't believe anything I told them, so I took them out of the equation."

Noreen had never loathed anyone as much as she hated Moreann. The darkness showed her all the ways she could kill the empress to deliver the most pain and prolong the Druid's death. It would be so easy to give in, to unleash the dark magic within her and lash out at Moreann.

An image of Cain's face filled her mind. She pictured him smiling down at her, and just like that, she was able to get control of herself again.

"But you didn't die," Moreann said. "You stopped the fire from touching you, and you nearly prevented it from taking your mother, as well. But I made sure that didn't happen. Had you been a little older or more aware of your magic, you might have been able to save them."

Noreen's throat tightened with emotion. Hearing those words drowned her in despair once again. So, she searched her mind for Cain since he was the only thing that could keep her from falling into the darkness forever.

Moreann laughed as she looked at Noreen. "I knew your future. I thought killing you would be the way to go, but then I had the idea of turning you Dark and keeping you under my thumb, doing as I wanted. Once I had you, I conjured your future again and saw exactly what needed to happen to bring about . . . this," she said and lifted her arms as she looked between Noreen and Rhi. Moreann's limbs lowered as she sneered. "You think it was your idea to betray the Dragon Kings and bring Rhi to me? Afraid not. I set that up. Just as I left the book out for you to find with my written account of the day your parents died."

"I'm going to kill you," Noreen said as she gathered her magic.

Moreann threw back her head and laughed. "Oh, it is great when a plan comes together."

"You're fekking insane," Rhi said into the silence that followed.

The empress drew in a breath and released it. "Whatever the future had in store for both of you is changed. The power I spoke of, neither of you have tapped into it or even grasped the fact that you have it. You can't win. I've seen all of this. I know how it ends."

"With your death," Noreen replied.

Moreann pressed her lips together and shook her head, her face a false mask of regret. "No, dear. In fact, you'll be dead in just a few minutes. Rhi will be glowing and past the point of help. The Kings will arrive, thinking they're coming to kill me, but they will have a choice to make. Take Rhi—and it'll take all of them to do it—away from this realm so she doesn't explode and take the planet with her. Or let her stay and kill everyone."

Rhi tapped her finger on her leg. "You honestly think the Kings will leave this realm? You're going to leave that up to chance?"

"Chance? No," Moreann replied. "Your King is going to make sure you get to safety. I'm counting on that. They'll believe Noreen died while fighting me, and you helped her, which is why you're glowing. The Dragon Kings, in their stupidity, will think they can return to this realm when, in fact, it'll be mine."

Noreen's stomach dropped to her feet. There was no time to warn Cain, no time to get away. And she hadn't yet told him that she loved him. Why had she been so stupid? Why hadn't she said the words?

Because she hadn't believed herself worthy. And now she was going to die without telling him what was in her heart.

"You've thought of everything, then," Rhi said.

Moreann's smile widened. "I always think of everything."

"Really? I doubt that," Noreen said.

Moreann looked between the two of them. "If you're trying to outwit me, it isn't going to happen. I've foiled many attempts on my life with others much more powerful than either of you."

Rhi suddenly smiled and looked at Noreen. "She really is full of herself."

Noreen had no idea what Rhi was talking about, but she went along with everything. "Absolutely."

"I don't have time for this," the empress said in a bored tone. "Orun."

With a flick of her hand, Rhi had the *drough* up against the wall. He let out a strangled cry, his eyes beseeching Moreann for help.

"You'll make time," Noreen announced.

Moreann shrugged, her lips turning down slightly. "Kill him. There are many more on my realm who can take his place."

His eyes widened in shock and then outrage, but Rhi continued holding him.

Rhi gave a shake of her head. "Your mistake is thinking you're smarter and more powerful than everyone else."

"I am," Moreann declared.

Rhi rolled her eyes with a dramatic sigh. "Far from it, actually. You missed three things in your all-seeing plan."

"Oh, really?" Moreann asked with a quirk of a brow. She crossed her arms over her chest. "Enlighten me."

Noreen glanced behind her. Were the Reapers here? Cael had assured her that she and Rhi wouldn't be alone, but so far, no one had made an appearance, and it was nearly time for someone to show themselves.

Rhi grinned. "My pleasure. First, you didn't count on Noreen falling in love with Cain. You, of all people, should know what a bond between a Dragon King and his mate is."

Moreann's eyes narrowed. "There wasn't time enough for them to fall in love."

"Really?" Rhi asked sarcastically.

Noreen then said, "It's true. Cain told me I'm his mate. And I love him."

There was a second of uncertainty on Moreann's face that she quickly hid. "So what? The Kings can't find us."

"Second," Rhi said, "you didn't count on me attacking Orun."

"I've already told you, I don't care about him."

Rhi chuckled. "My point exactly."

Moreann shrugged in confusion. "What point?"

But Rhi continued without explanation. "Third, you didn't keep a close enough eye on your Light Fae, Brian."

"Brian?" Moreann glanced around for him. "What about him?"

Noreen then realized why Brian had been acting so strangely when they all showed up. It wasn't just because he knew he was going to be replaced. It was because he had a secret. "Brian found Usaeil."

Moreann sighed loudly and swung her head to Noreen. "So? He can't get her out."

"Are you sure?" Rhi asked. "Where is he?"

The empress threw up her hands. "I don't know or care."

"You should," Noreen added, wondering for herself if Brian really had freed Usaeil.

Moreann gave a pointed look to Rhi. "Those are your three things? I don't see how any of that is going to stop my plans."

"Did I say three?" Rhi asked Noreen.

Noreen nodded. "Yep. You said three, but you meant four."

Rhi looked back at Moreann. "I did mean four. You see,

the fourth is a rather large piece of this so-called plan you have. You totally missed it."

"What might that be?" Moreann asked in a bored tone.

Rhi gave a nod to Noreen, who said, "Death and the Reapers."

This time, there was no denying the look of dread on Moreann's face. "You're both lying."

"No, we're not," Rhi said.

At that moment, six Reapers and Cael appeared out of nowhere as the sounds of dragons roared outside the building.

"You hear that?" Noreen told Moreann. "That's your plan falling apart."

Rhi snapped her fingers. "Damn. I'm really messing things up today because there was a fifth item. When all of the previous four things come together."

The moment she finished speaking, she released Orun, who immediately turned on Moreann. The empress was quick, though, and erected a shield around herself. It kept out Orun, but the Reapers' magic was stronger. Her shield weakened quickly with the onslaught of the orbs of magic thrown by the Reapers.

There was a tearing sound above her. Noreen looked up to see the ceiling jerked away as Cael's navy scales came into view, and he landed in the room, causing the entire manor to shake. A gold dragon landed beside him, while an amber dragon flew above.

Noreen smiled as Moreann was surrounded by Dragon Kings, Reapers, and Orun. Her shield was weakening, and just at the right time. Cain reared back his head and released not fire, but a cone of hot sand, directed right at Moreann.

The heat of the sand was so close, Noreen had to raise

her hand to shield her face. She looked over at Rhi to find the Fae screaming something, her face contorted with rage as she released magic orb after orb in Moreann's direction.

Noreen followed the trajectory of the orbs and saw that they weren't directed at Moreann but at Usaeil—who was protecting the empress.

CHAPTER FORTY-NINE

Magic and power surged through Cain in a volatile storm of fury and retribution that he unleashed upon Moreann. And it felt fucking great.

When the moment came for him, Con, and Tristan to attack Moreann's stronghold on Earth, Cain had only one thought—get to Noreen. The band around his chest hadn't loosened its hold until he'd torn off the roof and spotted her unharmed.

Dimly, he heard someone shout his name. He recognized Noreen's voice and slid his gaze toward her without moving his cone of hot sand away from Moreann.

"Stop!" Noreen shouted.

Cain hesitated and looked at Con to see him roar with fury. Cain ended his attack and found himself staring at none other than Usaeil. Where had she come from? How had she gotten there? And how in the hell had she managed to protect herself and Moreann from his power?

Time seemed to stand still as everyone stared in outrage at the queen. But she only had eyes for one person—Moreann.

"NOOOOOOO!" Rhi bellowed and leapt into the air,

her sword appearing in her hand as she swung it down toward Usaeil.

At the same instant, Cain, Noreen, Con, the Reapers, and Cael all let loose a volley of magic toward Usaeil and Moreann. But it did no good.

The pair was gone.

Rhi landed, her chest heaving as she stared in horrified dismay at where her two nemeses had been.

"Don't move," Noreen ordered.

Cain swung his head to find a bald man glaring at Noreen, who she now held with magic. They might not have Moreann, but they had another member of the Others.

Noreen smiled, but it held no humor. "You aren't going anywhere, Orun."

"Do what you want with me," he told her as he raised his chin. "Moreann has already let me know what my loyalty and service to her has gotten me."

Con shifted, making sure to clothe himself in a suit at the same time. He walked to Rhi and looked at her, but she didn't turn her head to him. After a few seconds, Con made his way toward Orun, where Cael joined him.

Tristan remained in the air, flying higher to keep a lookout on the area. Two Reapers stayed in the room, while the other four went to search the residence. As for Cain, he remained in dragon form, waiting.

"Where is she?" Noreen asked Orun.

The Druid's beady eyes glittered with hatred. "Why should I tell you?"

"Because we can make life easy for you. Or we can make it difficult," Con replied.

Cael looked the Druid up and down. "You attacked Moreann. Do you think she'll let that go?"

"She was going to let Rhi kill me," Orun said, anger causing his voice to rise.

Noreen twisted her hand, making her magic tighten around Orun. The Druid winced in pain. "You've seen what she's capable of. Did you really think you were immune to her disregard?"

"Yes," Orun squeaked out.

"Then you're a bigger fool than I was," Noreen told him before she loosened her hold.

The Druid drew in a deep breath and rubbed at his throat. "You should kill me now. I won't tell you anything."

"Oh, I think you will," Cael said.

In a blink, Rhi stood before Orun, her sword at his throat. "Where did Usaeil take Moreann?"

"As if I know," the Druid replied with a sneer.

Noreen made a sound in the back of her throat. "You know Moreann better than any of us. You know something."

Cain watched as Rhi pushed the tip of her blade against Orun's throat, and a bead of blood welled before rolling down his neck.

"As Con said, we can make your death easy or hard," Rhi said. "I prefer the hard way. If you keep silent, I'll get my wish."

No one moved to stop Rhi. Cain wasn't sure if it was because they believed she was bluffing, or if it was because they knew she wasn't.

Noreen lifted her other hand. Orun cried out in pain as he fell to his knees. He kept his chin raised since Rhi had yet to move her sword.

"I suggest you talk," Con said in a calm voice.

Orun scowled first at Rhi and then at Noreen before he said, "Moreann hated Usaeil. She wanted the queen dead, but she had to get Rhi to join us first."

"Why?" Cael demanded.

Orun's beady eyes came to rest on Rhi. "Apparently, Usaeil is afraid of Rhi."

Rhi lowered her blade and took a step back. "You're lying. Everything you say is a lie."

"It isn't," Orun insisted. "Remember what Moreann said about you and Noreen? Before she altered both of your futures, it was the two of you together who took out Usaeil."

Cain's gut twisted. This wasn't something he knew, and he was sure there was more to it.

Orun suddenly laughed. "None of that will happen now. Moreann made sure of it."

Cain took a step toward the Druid and leaned his head down to look at Orun. Then Cain growled long and low, letting his top lip lift to show razor-sharp teeth. The Druid looked up at him with fear in his eyes as his body began to shake.

"Orun is right," Noreen said. "Moreann did change me."

Rhi moved her blade just a little, leaving a nick on the Druid's neck before she lowered the weapon and looked at Noreen. "She might have changed our lives as well as some of who we are. But she didn't change all of us."

Noreen and Rhi shared a smile.

"Is that all you have to tell us?" Con asked the Druid.

Orun remained silent.

Cael dropped his arms to his sides. "I suppose Cain can eat you now."

Instantly, Orun's face paled. Sweat beaded his brow and top lip. "P-p-please."

"Please, what?" Cael asked. "Make it quick? Trust me. It won't be."

Orun shook his head, never taking his eyes from Cain. "I-I can help you."

"You doona seem too forthcoming," Con replied.

Orun glanced at Con. "I can tell you who the Druids on this realm are."

"So can Noreen," Rhi stated.

The Druid held up his hands as if that would stop Cain. "Usaeil thought she c-could hide from Moreann, but the empress t-trapped one of Usaeil's Trackers and spelled it. I-I-It told Moreann all of Usaeil's hiding places."

That was certainly information they could use. Cain wasn't sure if Orun was lying in a desperate attempt to stay alive or if it was the truth. If it was a lie, they'd find out quick enough and end his life, so Cain was thinking the Druid might just be telling the truth.

Cael looked at Con. "That could be useful information. Then we could plan our attack."

Rhi gave them a black look. "No."

"No?" Cael asked with a frown.

Con said nothing as his gaze swung to Rhi.

"That's what I said," Rhi told them. "I waited too long to go after Usaeil as I wanted, and then when it finally happened, it was on her terms. Not this time."

Tension ran through the room as everyone looked at Rhi. Cain watched Orun, who stared at the Light Fae as if he weren't sure what to do with her.

"And Moreann?" Con asked.

Rhi shrugged. "I'll take care of her, as well."

Cael's frown deepened. "Alone?"

"I'll be with her," Noreen said.

Rhi shook her head. "I'll deal with Moreann also."

"Rhi," Cael began, but she pinned him with an angry look.

Cain saw Noreen move closer to him. He looked her way to see her jerk her chin to Rhi. Things were getting out of hand, but he didn't see a way to stop it.

"Moreann claimed to have Rhi's brother," Noreen suddenly said. She turned her head to Orun. "Is that true?"

When Orun didn't immediately answer, Cain slowly parted his lips and let a growl rumble through him.

The Druid closed his eyes and nodded. "She has Rolmir."

"He's . . . dead," Cael said.

Rhi slid her eyes to Cael. "Exactly. Moreann holds his body and soul."

Cael shook his head, confusion filling his face. "That's not possible."

"Perhaps you should find out," Con told him.

Cael looked at one of the Reapers, who gave a nod and vanished. Then Cael met Rhi's gaze. "I'll get you answers."

"Sure," Rhi said with a look that said she thought anything but.

Noreen got everyone's attention. "What happens to Orun?"

"We know just the place for him for the time being," Con answered.

Cael smiled and called for two Reapers, who instantly appeared and took hold of Orun. In a blink, they were gone.

Cain returned to human form. The moment he did, he called a pair of jeans to him so he could cover up, but Rhi wasn't looking in his direction.

There was so much he wanted to say to her, but now wasn't the time. Soon, though.

"Rhi," Noreen called.

But Rhi didn't look at her. "I know what you're going to say."

"No, you don't. The way you feel about Usaeil? I feel that a hundred-fold toward Moreann. She killed my parents, pushed me into becoming Dark, and altered my life so you and I wouldn't be friends. Moreann is mine."

Cael opened his mouth as if to respond, and Cain shook his head, telling the Reaper to remain silent. If anyone could talk to Rhi, it might be Noreen. It was a long shot, but right now, that's all they had.

Rhi turned to face Noreen. "After all her lies, the last thing you should do is believe anything Moreann told us."

"Does it matter if it was truth or lies? Moreann went to great extremes to keep me from being Light and knowing you."

It killed Cain not to know all the details of what the empress had told the women, but he could wait to hear it all from Noreen later.

Rhi's gaze slid away, looking at a distant wall.

Cain gave Noreen a nod of encouragement when she glanced at him.

She took a step toward Rhi. "My parents deserve justice."

"So does every dragon and Dragon King," Rhi replied as she met Noreen's gaze. "I'm doing this alone."

Cain was grasping at straws when he asked Rhi, "What if you're doing exactly what Moreann wants you to do?"

The words were out of his mouth before he really had time to think them through, but the look on Rhi's face said he'd hit the mark dead center.

"He's right," Noreen said. "Moreann never said how things would go down so that your King would save you, only that he would. And that it would take all the Kings, which would leave this realm vulnerable."

Shock went through Cain. He glanced at Cael to see the Reaper nod that Moreann had, indeed, said those words.

"Rhi," Cain said, "if we want to change what Moreann

has seen, then we need to do it together. All of us. Kings, Reapers, and Fae."

Cael nodded. "Together."

Rhi looked at each of them in the room, stopping at Con. "No," she said right before she vanished.

CHAPTER FORTY-NINE

What did she do now? Noreen could only stare in shock at the space Rhi had occupied. "She left."

"We should've expected that," replied one of the Reapers.

Noreen ignored him. She might know of the Reapers now, but that didn't mean she was entirely comfortable with them. Especially given all the stories she'd heard about them through the Fae. While most young Fae learned of the Reapers through their parents, Noreen didn't find out about them until she was much older. Which made them even scarier to her.

Cain stood near her. Noreen wanted to reach out to him, grab hold because she feared he was the only thing that would keep her upright after all of this.

"There's nothing for us here," Cael said. "The Reapers have been over every inch. Though I suspect the Kings will want a look themselves."

She saw Con nod once out of the corner of her eye. In the next moment, Con, Cael, and the others, including Tristan, were gone.

Noreen looked around at the room she knew. "Do you know how many meetings we had here? All the times we discussed how, with each year, we were coming closer and closer to ending the Kings?"

"That was before you learned the truth of who Moreann was."

"Everything I've known, everything I learned and thought, it's all been one huge lie," she said as she finally looked at him.

His deep green eyes were locked on her face. A lock of black hair hung over his forehead and into his eyelashes. "It's over now. You get to live as you want."

"Over?" She gave a loud snort and shook her head. "Moreann is still alive. We were supposed to have killed her today."

"She might no' be dead, but the Others are finished."

He did have a point. Noreen blew out a breath. "I'd hoped for some closure, but I don't think that will be enough now that I know all of it."

"I might no' have heard what she told you, but like Rhi said, how can you believe Moreann?"

Noreen paused as she considered his question. "Because it all makes sense. She saw my and Rhi's futures. From what Moreann saw, Rhi and I teamed up and took out Us-aeil. We then formed a council with both the Light and the Dark to rule all Fae. Moreann said that Rhi and I had power we didn't even know about."

"I believe that," he said with a slight grin. "We saw what Rhi is capable of, and I think that's just the beginning. The way you can get into someone's mind and see their memories? I think that's just the tip of what you can do. Moreann wanted you and Rhi out of the way because she fears what you can do on your own. Imagine if you and Rhi teamed up?"

She wasn't convinced. "I can see Rhi as someone powerful. But me? No, I don't agree."

Cain lifted a brow and gave her a penetrating look. "You can't be serious."

"Maybe if I'd stayed Light, but I'm Dark."

"You keep seeing that as a bad thing."

She gawked at him. "Because it is! I'm evil."

"I've seen evil, lass. I've been up close and personal with it, and I can tell you with all the certainty in the universe, you are no' evil. Have you done wrong? Aye. We all have. Who knows what kind of Fae you'd have become as a Light. What I do know is that Moreann made a dreadful mistake the moment she pushed you toward the darkness."

Noreen frowned as she shrugged. "How did you come to that conclusion?"

He smiled and moved a lock of her hair behind her ear. "Because, by becoming Dark, you tapped into great magic. That's why most Light turn Dark is it no'? They want to increase their power."

"Bloody hell," Noreen murmured. She'd been so caught up in the truth and lies that she hadn't seen what was right in front of her until Cain pointed it out.

His smile widened. "Exactly."

"Moreann thought she controlled me, which she did. That's why she wasn't afraid of me."

"That was her mistake. You know she killed your parents, and you know she molded you into the Fae that she needed. It's time you become the woman you are. Forget the past. Doona consider the future. Be in the now, because that's all we have."

She wanted to touch him, but so much had passed between them that she wasn't sure if she should. Then she recalled his words. The past needed to be forgotten, and while she'd never truly forget it, she could make the choice to go forward without letting what she had done—and what had been done to her—define her actions.

"I thought I was going to die today," she told him.

A muscle ticked in his jaw as his gaze darted away for a heartbeat. "I might have been a little worried that something like that would happen."

"I stood in this room and could only think of one thing."

"Oh?" he asked, hope flaring in his eyes. "What was that?"

She swallowed past the emotion filling her. "You. And I realized I had one regret."

He moved closer. "What was it?"

"That there was something I didn't get a chance to tell you."

"I'm here now."

She licked her lips and inched forward so that they were nearly touching. "I love you."

The words were barely out of her mouth before his lips were on hers, kissing her as he held her tightly against him. She wound her arms around him and sank against his hard form.

Her body came alive in his arms, her heart bursting with joy . . . and love so deep, so profound that she knew that even time would lie still for it. The kind of love that transcended everything while holding the two of them together.

Cain tore his mouth from hers as he hugged her, his arms holding her securely, tenderly. "I love you so much it hurts, lass."

She knew the feeling exactly. They held onto each other as their hearts and souls united. Noreen couldn't help but feel that she and Cain had been destined since before time itself. That everything that had occurred had been meant to be.

Noreen closed her eyes and moved her face into the crook of his neck. "I wish all of this were over, but it isn't."

"We'll face whatever happens together. I'll always be by your side," he promised.

Tears welled in her eyes and slipped down her cheeks to fall against his skin. "I don't deserve you. I don't deserve to be happy, not after everything I've done."

Cain leaned back and caught her gaze. "Remember what I told you? Stop thinking about the past."

"I'm trying, but it's hard."

"Then I'll simply have to distract your mind with other, more pleasurable things," he replied with a grin.

She laughed, sniffing as she wiped at her tears. But the smile died. "I'm scared. Really scared. Moreann and Usaeil together is a dangerous combination. I thought they hated each other, but it might have all been a lie like everything else."

"Rhi willna go into battle alone. She might think she is, but that willna happen."

"Good. I wasn't lying when I said I wanted revenge."

"We all want a piece of that. But be careful with thoughts of vengeance."

She flattened her palms on his chest. "I will, but I also know that you'll help me if I stray too far."

"Aye, lass. I certainly will," he said in a deep whisper before he gave her a gentle kiss. "I want nothing more than to take you back to Dreagan and make love to you for days, weeks."

"But we can't," she said with a nod. "I understand better than most. The Others might be finished, but the battle with Moreann and Usaeil isn't."

Cain sighed, his lips compressing into a tight line. "There is much we need to prepare for at Dreagan. I fear it will take up quite a bit of time."

"Okay," she said, wondering what he was getting at. "I gathered that would happen."

He grinned at her. "That means I—*we*—need to be at Dreagan."

Noreen chuckled and slid her arms around his neck. "Is this your way of asking if I'm all right going to Dreagan? Because the answer is yes. I'll go anywhere with you."

"Perfect answer," he replied before he pressed his lips to hers. "I can no' wait to show you everything there."

"Then what are we waiting for?"

He let the silence grow between them as he searched her face. "I meant it when I said we should do the mating ceremony. Part of it was because I wanted to make sure you wouldna die, but it's also because I want you."

"I'm yours. I've always been yours. I just didn't know it until you found me."

"Aye, lass. I've always been yours, as well. I want to make it official, though."

She swallowed and looked down at his throat. "Everything between us has moved very fast. I think we should give everyone time to adjust and get to know me."

"Fuck everyone else," he stated.

Her gaze jerked to his. "You don't mean that."

He gave a firm nod. "I do. This is about us."

"I know it is, but we'll be living at Dreagan. I don't want to be somewhere I'm not wanted."

"That willna happen."

"You can't guarantee that."

He started to reply, then decided not to.

"I'm yours, Cain. I will always be yours whether we do the ceremony or not. I'm Fae, so I don't die quite as easily as a mortal."

"But you can still die," he interjected. "And we're going to war."

"Give me a little time?" she asked. "It's not that I don't want to be mated to you, but you see, in my heart, we already are."

He smiled as he released a breath. "I see your point. I just doona want to lose you now that I've found you."

"Are all the women at Dreagan mated to their Kings?"

"Nay," he replied reluctantly.

She kissed the side of his neck. "Then, we willna be alone."

"Just as long as we're together, then," he said before he took her lips in another searing kiss.

It was some time before they broke apart, each panting heavily, their bodies burning with need.

"I doona wish to linger in this place," he told her.

She shook her head. "Me either."

"Dreagan, then," he said with a smile.

Noreen returned it and thought of the home of the Dragon Kings as she threaded her fingers with his. "Dreagan."

In the next second, they stood atop one of the mountains on the vast sixty-thousand-acre estate. Noreen looked around at the wild beauty before her and was awestruck.

"Come," Cain told her. "I'll show you my mountain."

When she looked at him, he was in dragon form, waiting for her to climb up onto him. She wasted no time in doing just that. There was a smile on her face as he leapt from the mountain and dove straight down before he spread his wings and caught a current that took them straight up into the sky.

Noreen drank in the stunning sight below her, but she didn't get to enjoy it long. Cain soon altered his course and headed for an opening in the side of a mountain. Once inside, she slid off him and tried to get a glimpse of the cavern, but he took her hand and led her deeper into the mountain to a smaller chamber where a bed awaited them.

Their gazes met as they shared a smile. Noreen removed their clothes with just a thought. A laugh escaped her when he lifted her in his arms before tossing her onto the bed.

"It's the first day of our new lives together," he told her as he moved over her.

She reached for him, threading her fingers into his hair. "The first of many. Now, come here so I can kiss every inch of you."

Their lips met, and words ceased as desire took hold, their love wrapping around them.

CHAPTER FIFTY

Ulrik stood with Vaughn as they looked at the celebration before them. Three more Dragon Kings were now mated.

"When do you think your time will come?" Ulrik asked.

Vaughn gave him a dark look. "I've no interest in a mate."

"You're no' the only King who's made such a boast. Need I remind you of Keltan?" he asked, motioning to the King of Citrines, who was dancing with his mate, Bernadette.

Vaughn drank down the last of his whisky. "That wasna a boast. It was fact. Besides, Keltan and Bernadette are perfect for each other. I'd still like to know how in the world the women find the dresses to match each King so perfectly."

Ulrik shook his head. "I asked Eilish that same question earlier when she came in talking about the gowns. She likes all of them, but her favorite was Gemma's. Something about the sequins," he said with a shrug.

"I'm just happy that with the disbandment of the Others that Bernadette finally agreed to the ceremony with Keltan."

Ulrik searched the area for the three newly mated couples. Keltan and Bernadette in her satin citrine ballgown with its spaghetti straps were smiling up at each other. Her short, black hair was pulled away from her face to show off the large oval citrine that hung from the gold chain at her throat—a gift from Con.

Next, he spotted Roman and Sabina off in a corner, talking as their hands rubbed all over each other. Sabina's dress was a pale blue. Eilish had called it an A-line, whatever that was, but the sleeveless front dipped into a deep V that showed off her breasts. A floral appliqué ran from the narrow straps at her shoulders to various lengths past her hips. Ulrik spotted Con's gift to Sabina—dangling teardrop aquamarine earrings.

It took some time before Ulrik spotted Gemma and Cinàed. They were swaying together slowly, despite the fast tempo of the song. Gemma's dress hugged her body with thin straps at her shoulders. The gown was covered in iridescent sequins. Her long, ginger hair was pulled up, showing off her long neck. It wasn't until Cinàed lifted her hand to kiss her knuckles that Ulrik spotted Con's gift. The bracelet was a silver cuff with Celtic knotwork. The cuff was narrow but widened at each end to hold the moonstone gems.

"How does Con find the jewels? And how does he know what to get each woman?" Vaughn asked with a frown.

Ulrik shrugged. "I've no idea. I asked him once, but he never answered."

"It's his way of telling you it isna our concern."

Ulrik snorted. "Aye. The bastard."

They shared a laugh. Ulrik looked around for Con, but as the minutes ticked by without any sign of him, Ulrik became worried.

"When was the last time you saw Con?" he asked.

Vaughn lifted one shoulder in a shrug. "After the ceremony. He briefly spoke to all three couples."

"He's no' here."

Vaughn's gaze scanned the room. "That isna like him."

"No. It isna. Then again, he hasna been the same since they returned from confronting Moreann."

"Nothing really happened there."

Ulrik sighed as his mind quickly went over what had been recounted to the rest of them. "That we know of."

"Now isna the time to go asking around. This is a celebration," Vaughn cautioned him.

Ulrik scanned the faces until he found Eilish. It took her but a heartbeat to look his way. He motioned to the door with his head, letting her know he was leaving for a bit. She smiled and winked in reply.

"I'm going to find Con," Ulrik told Vaughn.

"That's a hornet's nest you probably doona want to mess with."

"The last thing he needs is to be alone."

Vaughn nodded slowly in agreement. "Want me to come with you?"

"I think it's better if I go alone."

"He's no' going to want to talk."

"Then he can listen," Ulrik stated with a grin.

Vaughn barked in laughter. "Good luck with that."

Ulrik's smile didn't last once he left the room. He stood in the middle of the manor and thought about where Con would go, and he realized there was only one place where no one would dare to bother him.

Which was why it was exactly where Ulrik was headed.

Ulrik took the stairs three at a time until he reached the top floor. His steps didn't slow as he walked to Con's chambers. Ulrik paused at the door. He knocked and turned the knob. No surprise, it was locked, but it took nothing to open it. He walked in and stood in shock at the disarray before him.

Con's chambers were always in order, nothing ever out of place. It looked as if a tornado had ripped through the room, shredding books and toppling furniture.

"Get the fuck out."

Ulrik's head turned toward the doorway that led into another room. He walked toward the sound of Con's voice, stepping over broken furniture and other debris. Once at the door, Ulrik looked inside to see a fire roaring in the hearth. He could just make out the red books being devoured by the flames.

Con sat on the floor with his legs stretched out in front of him as he leaned back against a toppled bookshelf. More books, these in brown leather, were strewn over the floor. Ulrik couldn't see Con's face given the angle of their positions.

"You doona listen well," Con said as he tossed another red book into the flames.

"No' when a friend is drunk and hurting."

Con issued a loud snort. "I'm no' drunk. No' yet, at least. But I'm getting there."

Ulrik walked into the room and saw the many empty bottles of whisky lying about. "Want to talk about it?"

"I think my 'get the fuck out' answers that quite well."

In all their years, Ulrik had never seen Con in such a state. It concerned him. He might not have been around when Con's relationship ended, but he'd heard from the Kings that Con had simply refused to talk about it. He had holed himself up in his chamber for days. When he came out, it was like nothing had ever happened.

"You're missing a hell of a party."

Ulrik righted a chair and sat. He got his first good look

at Con. His hair was in disarray, his shirt was ripped and stained, and he wasn't wearing any shoes.

Con's head rolled toward him. "It's better that I be alone. I'm fine. So, leave."

"No' going to happen."

Black eyes narrowed dangerously. "I could command it. I am your King."

"You're my friend first and foremost. Besides, you're sotted. You couldna make me do anything."

"Leave!" Con bellowed.

Ulrik leaned back in the chair and set his ankle atop his opposite knee. "I think I'll stay."

"I'm no' going to talk."

"I didna ask you to."

Silence stretched. Another five minutes passed before Con reached beside him. Ulrik spotted the pile of red books. Con's fingers fumbled when he grabbed for one. He ended up taking two, but he couldn't hold onto the second. It fell from his grasp when he tossed them toward the fire. Sparks flew and the logs hissed when the book landed in the flames.

The second journal, however, landed on its spine and fell open. Ulrik saw the entry. His heart clutched when he read, *"I miss you more every day. The pain is unbearable. Without you, I'm noth—"*

Con snapped the notebook shut without looking at Ulrik. He then tossed it into the fire.

"Burning them won't make the words go away," Ulrik said.

Con tilted back a bottle of whisky and drank deeply before he said, "It's worth a try."

"You could—"

Con's head snapped to him. "If you call yourself my friend, you willna finish those words."

"Because you can no' hear them? Or you doona want to?" Ulrik asked angrily.

"Does it matter?"

Ulrik lowered his foot to the floor and leaned forward. "I've no' been back long, but even a blind person can see you're hurting. You hide it well. Most doona even know it. But I know you. I can see past the barriers you attempt to put up. If you doona rectify this . . . situation . . . it'll kill you."

"Maybe that's exactly what I deserve."

"Con. Nay," Ulrik said with a frown, concern tightening his stomach.

"The past can no' be changed, Ulrik. I can no' undo the things I've said or done. I made that decision long ago."

"It was a stupid one."

Con smiled sadly and returned his gaze to the fire. "It wasna, and you know it."

"Things are different now."

"But I lost her long, long ago."

Ulrik raked a hand through his hair. "You have no'. Doona be a fool a second time. Go to her. Talk to her, beg her, but for all our sakes', do something."

"I am," he said and threw another journal on the fire. "I'm doing my best to forget her."

"No King is supposed to live without their mate once they find them. The fact you've survived this long is a blasted miracle. I think it was your stubbornness that has kept you going, but that's no' going to last much longer."

Con took another drink of whisky. "It'll last long enough for me to see Moreann and Usaeil defeated. That's all I need. Then you'll take my place."

Ulrik was so surprised at Con's words that he couldn't fathom a response other than, "Nay."

"You can tell me that all you want, but I get the last say," Con said as he flashed a smile at Ulrik.

"We need you."

Con's lips tilted. "None of you ever needed me. You're fucking Dragon Kings. I know I made a mistake allowing the mortals to remain here."

"We all agreed."

"But had I no' said it, it wouldna have happened."

Ulrik shook his head. "You can no' know that."

"Everything that's happened since can be laid at my feet."

"Including all of us finding our mates. That wouldna have happened if the mortals hadna come."

Con waved his hand as if wiping away those words. "Our dragons are gone. V is too afraid to find out what's happened to them, so he willna look. And I doona blame him. I doona wish to look either. They could be dead for all I know. They could've suffered horribly, and none of us were there to protect them."

"Or they could be thriving. We doona know."

"I know they are no' here where they belong," Con said as he met Ulrik's gaze. "It was my decision to send them away because I honestly thought they could return. The size of my ego astounds me sometimes."

Ulrik snatched the bottle from Con's hand as it was on the way to his mouth and took a sip. "I left you no choice but to send the dragons away. It was the best decision before more were killed."

Con leaned over and found another bottle. It took him two tries before he righted himself. He removed the cap but didn't drink. "I'm tired. I'm so tired. We were no' meant to be in these positions this long."

"No, but we are."

"It's no' much longer for me."

Ulrik threw his bottle into the fire, causing the flames to roar. "Stop talking such nonsense and get your ass together."

Con said nothing, just threw another journal into the flames.

Ulrik stood and strode out. After he calmly shut the door behind him, he knew that drastic measures needed to be taken if they didn't want to lose Con.

EPILOGUE

"I suppose you want a thank you."

Usaeil laughed as she stared at Moreann. The empress had nearly been defeated, but she wasn't letting that cower her. "Save your breath."

Moreann raised a brow. "Well. Isn't that a surprise?"

"I'm full of them."

The empress lifted her chin. "How did you get free?"

"Not all of your group is as loyal to you as you believe."

"Brian," Moreann said with a roll of her eyes.

Usaeil grinned. "He knows I'm his true queen."

"You'd be dead by Rhi's hand if I hadn't taken your body."

Usaeil ignored the words. Things had progressed quickly with Moreann and the Dragon Kings, which hadn't left Usaeil time to get to as many Druids as she'd wanted. She'd taken the lives of three, which was why she had been able to get Moreann out of the manor.

But she was depleted now. Luckily for her, there were more Druids waiting to die so she could face off against Moreann.

"We should be planning our revenge against Noreen, Rhi, and the Kings," Moreann said.

Usaeil hid her smile. "Don't forget about the Reapers."

"Oh, yes. Those as well," she said with a roll of her eyes.

Usaeil continued to stare at Moreann.

"Am I missing something?" the empress asked testily. "Since you got me out of there, I assume you have a plan."

"Oh, I have a plan, all right," Usaeil said as she turned and left the room.

She closed the door behind her with magic. The moment she heard Moreann trying to get out of the room, she let her smile free.

Northern Ireland
The Light Castle

Rhi walked through the white halls of the castle. Those about ceased their conversations the minute they spotted her. As she walked, silence followed.

She didn't stop until she reached the throne room. No Queen's Guard members stood there. In fact, she hadn't seen any guards anywhere. It was a good thing the Dark were also in disarray. Otherwise, they could've come in and wiped out the Light with little effort.

A smile pulled at her lips as she imagined the look on Balladyn's face had he been there. But he wasn't. At least, he was alive. That was something.

Rhi didn't need to look behind her to know that the Fae were pressed together, watching to see what she would do. The last thing she wanted was to be queen. She cared nothing about power, but someone needed to take control. She could do that for the time being. Bringing order to the Light so that a proper king or queen could be found.

She took a deep breath and threw open the doors of

the throne room. The last thing Rhi wanted was to talk to anyone, but she didn't have a choice. She needed to bring some stability to her people, but she also wanted to lure Usaeil out. Rhi wouldn't have come up with the idea had Balladyn not told her to be queen.

So, she drew in a deep breath and turned to face the crowd. "We're Light Fae. A powerful people. Usaeil betrayed each and every one of us for years. Her reign is finished. It's time to look to the future, to what we can achieve. As of this moment, I want the Queen's Guard to report and take their posts."

"Are you our new queen?" someone asked.

It was on the tip of Rhi's tongue to say yes, but she couldn't do it. "I'm going to make sure the castle remains running, and the Light are protected while the candidates are looked over to figure out who will rule us."

In the back of her mind, Rhi couldn't help but think of what Moreann had told her regarding the council of Dark and Light Fae that ruled over both sides.

Not that it mattered. She doubted she'd live long enough to see that come to fruition.

"Queen Rhi!" a voice shouted from the back.

Within moments, the rest of the Fae were shouting it, as well. Rhi had this one moment to stop them, to tell them she didn't want to be queen.

Then she thought of Usaeil and the revenge she so desperately wanted against her former queen. And Rhi remained silent.

ACKNOWLEDGMENTS

A special shout out to everyone at St. Martin's Press for getting this book ready, including the amazing art department for such a stunning cover that matches the character to perfection. Much thanks and appreciation go to my exceptional editor, Monique Patterson.

To my amazing agent, Natanya Wheeler, who is on this dragon train with me.

A special thanks to my children, Gillian and Connor, as well as my family for the never-ending support. I also can't be remiss in forgetting to thank Charity and J. S. for all the incredible support, graphics, ideas, and laughter.

Last, but not least, G.

Hats off to my incredible readers and those in the DG Groupies Facebook group for keeping the love of the Dragon Kings alive. Words can't say how much I adore y'all.